Also by Jennine Capó Crucet

My Time Among the Whites: Notes from an Unfinished Education
Make Your Home Among Strangers
How to Leave Hialeah

SAY HELLO TO MY LITTLE FRIEND

a novel

JENNINE CAPÓ CRUCET

SIMON & SCHUSTER
New York   London   Toronto   Sydney   New Delhi

100 YEARS
SIMON &
SCHUSTER

1230 Avenue of the Americas
New York, NY 10020

First Simon & Schuster hardcover edition March 2024

SIMON & SCHUSTER and colophon are registered trademarks of Simon & Schuster, LLC

Simon & Schuster: Celebrating 100 Years of Publishing in 2024

For information about special discounts for bulk purchases, please contact Simon & Schuster Special Sales at 1-866-506-1949 or business@simonandschuster.com.

The Simon & Schuster Speakers Bureau can bring authors to your live event. For more information or to book an event, contact the Simon & Schuster Speakers Bureau at 1-866-248-3049 or visit our website at www.simonspeakers.com.

Interior design by Carly Loman

Manufactured in the United States of America

10 9 8 7 6 5 4 3 2 1

Library of Congress Cataloging-in-Publication Data has been applied for.

ISBN 978-1-6680-2332-7
ISBN 978-1-6680-2334-1 (ebook)

CONTENTS

Contents

I always tell the truth, even when I lie.

—TONY MONTANA, *SCARFACE*

SAY HELLO TO MY LITTLE FRIEND

ETYMOLOGY

They were already on the water—twenty or so experienced sailors and divers and one biologist. They'd set out before sunrise in two speedboats loaded with explosives, along with a pilot and a scout in a seaplane overhead, which would prove crucial. These people were on a mission, and this story is as Miami as it gets, but like so many Miami stories—and there are so, so many worth telling—it really starts somewhere else and a long while back. This one begins on the gray waves of Penn Cove, all the way over in Washington State of all places, on August 8, 1970.

The goal that day was to capture several orca, preferably females, preferably juveniles, though it's likely those would be the only kind for which this crew could even try, seeing as how all orca, but especially adult males, are enormous. This kind of capture had been done before, but not by these sailors or this biologist. It was the kind of work that had a high turnover rate, as people could not, after doing it once, be induced by money or anything else to do what they'd done again. Which was partly why this time, with this contract, they were hoping for a larger haul: six or seven whales, if possible, and they were aiming for the lucky number.

That morning was cold despite the summer day—not a surprise, as the water there is freezing compared to what you get in Miami. There was fog; there was rain, but as the day went on it tapered, felt more like mist, then disappeared. The pod they were tracking and eventually chasing at some point split in two, and while the orca fooled the boats and the sailors—the family sent the children one way, with their mothers, while the rest led the boats in the opposite direction—they didn't fool the pilot for very long, and when the scout, binoculars pressed over eye sockets, saw what the orca had done—that they'd *devised a plan* to protect their young—he almost refused to radio down to the boats and give them their new location.

1

In the end, the sailors got seven, one being the wished-for juvenile female. The biologist with them estimated that this whale was between two and four years old. But *estimate* is just another word for *guess*: the truth is, no one outside of this orca's own family knows for sure how old she really is.

Ask the biologist: At what age is it safe to remove an orca from its mother? The biologist will shake her head and say, Whatever age it would be okay for you to lose yours.

Decades later, this whale remembers that morning well, still sometimes startles out of her half-sleep from the sound of the explosives used to divide them, or worse, from the piercing sensation of her mother's call—a memory but a sensation still—echoing over her from the other side of the sudden nets, from outside the floating pen in which she was trapped. She did not know how to get out. Her mother and aunts did not know how to get her and her cousins out. Those outside the pen stayed close and waited and panicked and blocked the boats and the ropes, the attempts to lasso them. They swam directly into the nets on purpose, hoping to tear them. They roughed up the water and spewed out every form of protest but in the end, their children were taken from them. She was the last of those captured to be lifted out of the ocean in a stretcher, the last one dragged onto land and into a vessel for transfer—a tank no bigger than her own body.

Five of their family died that day—drowned by the nets—their bodies sliced open and stuffed with rocks, anchors tied around their tails, lost, for a time, to the bottom of the sea. The others captured along with her all died within five years of that morning. What else could you call her survival but a miracle? What other word could you possibly use to describe it?

These aren't rhetorical questions.

One answer: you could just call it a fact. Or maybe, if you're trying to be funny: a fluke. Or maybe, in this case: the beginning of a legend.

Of her own beginnings—her first years in the ocean and not yet in a tank—she remembers everything, only some of those memories distorted by captivity: how she learned the sounds of her family, how she could speak with them before ever leaving her mother's body thanks to the other miracle of water. Of knowing too—without the help of sound and again thanks to water—where each of them was and what they were sensing, regardless of proximity. She knew their voices before their faces, felt their bodies within her own: facts that work like promises, sensations she still touches in her mind, the last reverberations of home that she absorbed as she was lifted out of the Salish Sea.

Here's another fact: the tiny tank situation didn't improve upon her forced relocation to Miami. She was given the name Lolita—whoever came up with it never read Nabokov and so didn't intend the allusion; they just thought the name sounded fittingly *tropical*—and has since lived in the smallest tank in the world.

And at first, she wasn't in there alone. Lolita—*so courageous and yet so gentle,* the veterinarian who chose her for the Miami Seaquarium said of her during the evaluation that preceded their offer to purchase her—joined the tank's current occupant, her adopted boyfriend-brother: a male orca known as Hugo, a whale not much older than her, captured three years earlier, who would, in time, devote an entire afternoon to bashing his own head against the concrete walls of their tank in order to kill himself. That day's attempt—not his first—proved successful.

Lolita remembers that day too, and how she'd thought, at the sight of all that new blood in the water, at how this time, he no longer rose up for air: No, no, Hugo, *no.* But also: *Finally.* And also, to her terrified surprise, because she knew her kind were meant to live in families and did not know what this verdict meant for her own sanity: *Good riddance.*

Good riddance to the sound of his teeth gnawing against the edge of the tank. Good riddance to his bites, his swipes, his lunges at her and at their trainers. Good riddance to his circling and circling; to ten years of him taking up space in a tank too small for even just one of them; to his existence serving as a constant reminder of all she'd lost and of where she was not.

But that was years and years ago now.

She is still in that Miami tank, swims each day through the scene of his death. Hugo has been gone for close to four decades, replaced by dolphins in a misguided attempt to keep her company. She's grown used to their noise and can block out the nonsense of their language, learning to notice only the silence before they rake her with their teeth. But now there is this new noise, this rumble from the depths of this doomed city. Not another whale—no, definitely not—but a man, new to her. She hears something inside him, a precursor to his manhood, something that feels familiar, frighteningly—almost impossibly—like herself. When the tide is high and the water seeps into the city, as it does more and more each day, she thinks she can sometimes hear a call from the base of his brain, long-range and full of mourning and somehow still a child's, his cries—in a language she knows he's losing, the phrases indecipherable to her but their meaning known—hovering undetected in the hallways of his own memory.

The Lummi phrase for her kind means *our relations under the waves.* The Latin phrase means *of or belonging to the realm of the dead.*

Yes, inside him, there it is, the meaning almost a song: something he's forever letting go of, something he doesn't realize he's killed.

¡DALE!

A BOSOM FRIEND

His name is Ismael Reyes, but almost everyone calls him Izzy. He considers the day he got the cease and desist letter from Pitbull's legal team the worst day of his life, the reason being that his short-lived role as the number-one unauthorized Pitbull impersonator in the Greater Miami Area had actually been his best attempt at a life plan yet—or at least, the plan most likely to earn him enough easy extra money to move out of the townhouse he shared with his Tía Tere: his mother's sister, though he never thought of her that way, as he'd barely known his mother. Technically, despite by Miami standards maybe being a little old for the role, Teresa had played the part of Izzy's only parent since he was seven. And technically, it could be said that Izzy already lived on his own: in his Tía Tere's garage-turned-efficiency, with its own separate side entrance and his own key and everything; his only reasons for going into her part of the townhouse were if he had to use the kitchen or the bathroom or if he wanted to watch something on cable. The conversion of the garage into an almost-apartment was his high school graduation present, the mostly legal though definitely unpermitted construction project a gift from his Tía Tere, who'd recently begun praying that he'd move out soon so she could rent out the room to recoup its cost, hence her tacit endorsement of Izzy's cash-only Pitbull impersonator business plan. But that letter, written in some very official-sounding language, made it perfectly clear that Izzy's weekly photo ops at Dolphin Mall, his appearances at the Two-for-Tuesday happy hours at the Ale House down in Kendall, his standing near—but technically never in!—the entrances of several fading South Beach clubs: basically everything about his side hustle that had given him any recent hope about life after high school—and not being forever limited by the little he made working part-time at Don Shula's Hotel & Golf Club in Miami Lakes—had been deemed illegal.

Copyright infringement, punishable with fines so large that the price tag of just an initial infraction was more than what he guessed his mother would've made in her entire life in Cuba, had she never tried to leave.

He was disappointed. Although not *Born and raised in the county of Dade* (only the latter being true), he'd committed to the daily shaving of his head to evoke the dull sheen of the real Pitbull's dome. He'd practiced the snarky giggle littering his lyrics, memorized all the words that rhymed with *culo*, invested in a well-tailored white blazer. On his drives to and from Don Shula's, he'd even made himself listen to Pitbull's latest album, the just-released *Climate Change*—the record didn't have a single hit on it despite having more featured artists than it did actual tracks—because he figured that was the record the real Pitbull would be trying to promote-slash-salvage after its disappointing mid-March debut, peaking at number 29 on the *Billboard* 200, pobrecito Pitbull. Point is: Izzy really thought he made a good Pitbull. And he *did*, if he kept on his sunglasses—Izzy's eyes are brown, not blue. There was also the issue of his age and his height, as the real Pitbull is pushing forty and had maxed out at an angry five-seven, whereas Izzy has just turned the big Two-Oh and is blessed to have made it to five-eleven-and-a-half: great for Izzy's life in general but not-so-great for the Pitbull business. He'd charged less than he wanted and crouched down in photos for exactly those reasons—he was a reasonable guy! He imagined Pitbull to be one as well despite all the sonic evidence suggesting otherwise.

If only Izzy could just talk to him, cut through all the lawyers and shit, make his case man to man: that having a younger, better-looking version of yourself showing up in the Miami neighborhoods you list in almost every song would only elevate your quote-unquote brand; that Tía Tere lives for your remixes and is your biggest fan (not true at all, she thinks Pitbull is a hack and a clown, changes the station like a reflex whenever she hears his voice, but she did appreciate that Izzy had, prior to getting that letter, something relatively safe to do on weekends, something she wrote off as a strange but undeniable calling that also happened to earn him some cash); that imitation is the sincerest form of flattery or whatever; why do you even care, you're already rich as fuck; et cetera, et cetera. Izzy was sure he could change Pitbull's mind, maybe even end up in the background of a music video or something.

Alas, he understood from the letter that discussing the terms with the man himself was not an option, so the time had come for him to fully commit to his original life plan—the plan of his heart—to the idea that he'd dismissed as a fantasy a couple years earlier, as high school graduation loomed and as late-night movies on cable flooded over him from the one ancient and decidedly not-smart television in his Tía Tere's townhouse, a plan he'd reasoned away as probably too far-fetched and crazy-sounding, even by Miami standards (or at least, his experience of them; he can—and should!—thank his Tía Tere for the limits on *that* kind of knowing). He'd told himself his original plan was barely a plan at all, that it was more inherently dangerous and too ambitious, and why even go that route when he had in Pitbull an innocuous enough Mr. 305 turned Mr. Worldwide, a quote-unquote rapper who was really just a barely bilingual auto-tuned business-man ticking off the Latino box on the commercial music industry's checklist for crap with a resounding *Dah-leh?* But with Pitbull himself having weighed in on Izzy's future, he could see the ways he'd under-estimated himself, how he'd denied himself the pleasure of taking his cues from his *real* hero. He could no longer follow that easier path, as he had—right in front of him—his message from Pitbull-slash-the Universe-slash-the black-and-white image scowling at him from the movie poster on the wall across from his bed. The time had come for him to accept his destiny, to believe that the world really could be his, to embrace his Cuban birth and his huge balls; he would re-make himself into Tony Montana for the new millennium, Miami's modern-day Scarface.

What this meant immediately: he could let his hair grow back, which was a huge relief, as no twenty-year-old should play at being bald when nature hasn't forced it on him. It meant he needed his very own Manolo, a guy to follow him around and hopefully do most of the boring but necessary stuff largely behind the scenes. It meant—if he really wanted to be authentic here—that he would need to quit his crappy job at Don Shula's in order to get a crappier job as a dishwasher in a Little Havana restaurant, a job that he and his Manolo would eventually quit once shadier shit was in the works. It meant he needed to practice saying *hello to his little friend* and ramping up his usage of the word *fuck*. He needed a pet tiger and a Michelle Pfeiffer, but really, if he wanted to avoid falling short this time, he needed to start out aiming higher: he needed something better than a tiger or a Pfeiffer—a more dangerous pet and/or lady. He needed *Super* Manolo. Because Izzy's mistake with the Pitbull route was that he'd tried to *become* that man rather than *surpass* him. This time, with this plan, he would have to surpass even what he could not yet imagine.

He needed to watch the movie again, probably.

So no, despite what Izzy thinks, the day that brought the letter killing his first American Dream was not the worst day of his life, not by a long shot. Technically, *that* day is both already behind him and also hanging ahead of him, the memory and possibility of it already sensed—somehow—by Izzy's Better-Than-a-Tiger: Miami's favorite and only captive orca, known here as Lolita, this sinking city's whale, simmering in the too-warm water of her tank, ever-circling the concrete, hoping and waiting for him.

LOOMINGS

What else does Lolita know? It might feel impossible to imagine, but why not try: she knows she's in Miami, Florida, but that she's not from here, that such a thing is impossible. She knows roughly the location of her still-living family members—and so, of her mother—though this is less known than felt, which is the case for much of what you'd call *knowing*. She knows *Lolita* is just a stage name, a character, not the name she was born into but it's the one to which she's long answered. She knows, roughly, her age, that she has been in this tank for several decades, that her rituals around each sunrise have helped her keep track of the passage of long time—and so she knows the year is 2017, though she doesn't use that number to mark it: you can't know what number she holds in her mind—how could you?—only that it's much larger, maybe a different shape. She knows her show times. She knows that people like the water even though for her it's too warm—and so she does her best to drench the crowd every day, twice a day. Why not? It seems to her that it takes very little to make people happy, and when people feel happy, she knows it: she can, at times, sense that joy directly in the minds of those still too young to have achieved coherent speech (a phenomenon likely attributed to the paralimbic region of her brain; in the ocean, this structure would've allowed her to communicate with members of her pod without any sound at all—the best word for that, given the limits of this language, being *telepathy*). She knows she is the Most Important Thing at the Seaquarium, and she knows—somehow—that *Seaquarium* is not a real word. She knows—no, be accurate: knows *of*—LeBron James and him taking his talents to South Beach, though he and his talents were actually in Downtown Miami, across from her tank on Virginia Key, meaning: not South Beach at all. She knows South Beach is, for now, three or so feet above sea level. She knows something is wrong with the warming water and with the ground, and that it feels like a sinking—but no, it's the water rising from the limestone below to meet her; she thinks maybe this is part of some greater plan to get her out of that tank, but of this she can't be sure. She knows only that something is rippling that was not rippling before, not at this rate or at this amplitude, that the sound of it comes and goes with the tides, and so every day she listens for as far as she can listen, swaying her fat-filled jawbone in and out of the water when her trainers believe her to be resting. And it's in this listening that she hears Izzy, halfway across the city, wondering while he showers where the fuck he's going to find a Manolo and a Pfeiffer and, eventually, something like her.

THE HUNT BEGINS

Izzy decides to start with interviews. He knows he needs to watch the movie again—he knows, he knows—but for now he thinks he can move forward on the Manolo front without a refresher. Granted, Tony Montana already knew the real Manolo from their lives in Cuba; in the movie, Tony didn't need to go searching for his Manolo, but Izzy figures that when you're crafting yourself into Scarface, the only way to dive in is to accept where you're at, then move the right pieces into place so that the money, then the power—and after that the women, according to the film's stated logic—can eventually flow your way. He pulls down his high school yearbook from the bookshelf where there isn't a single other book and turns to the back, to where people signed it. Most of the signers were women, but there were three guys—he counts them; two are named Rudy—and it is these three fellow Hialeah Lakes High grads who have, the way he figures it, an automatic berth into the Manolo Interview Round.

He looks up each guy on Instagram—but doesn't follow them, as that would make him seem like a try-hard—and shows their pictures to his Tía Tere, asking her what she knows and claiming he's looking to reach out and make friends, something she half-heartedly reminds him to do *in real life* whenever she sees him looking at his phone. His Tía Tere knows people, is basically the central spoke in her network of cubanas metidas, their headquarters being the Sedano's Supermarket on Palm Avenue where they buy their lottery tickets. Every area-Cuban of a certain generation knows Teresa and her story, which is also Izzy's story: how she took in her nephew after his mother drowned trying to cross over, how she'd raised him as her own—even though she'd never wanted kids herself, she liked to remind people. If his Tía Tere didn't know someone directly, she knew their mother or their tía or their madrina, so within half an hour Izzy has a workplace and a cell number for each guy. He considers texting them but decides to show up at their jobs instead; he wants to see them in action, *in real life*, but more importantly, he figures catching them by surprise is what Tony Montana would do, and given that hunting for a Manolo already strays from—or perhaps predates—the literal *Scarface* plot, Izzy wants to do whatever he can to start this shit off right.

The first one, the one not named Rudy, works at Pembroke Lakes Mall all the way up in Broward, at the T-Mobile stand right near the food court. It would be a better sign if he worked for Verizon or AT&T, but whatever, dude's got to start somewhere, right? Irregardless of any cease and desist letter, you can't just start off as Mr. Worldwide, not without first spending some time as Mr. 305.

Not-a-Rudy (his name is Geovany) looks exactly the same as he does in his yearbook photo. Same shitty block of a beard hiding a weak chin, same fade, same too-big-to-be-real diamond studs in his earlobes. He's even wearing a tie like in the picture, though this one is T-Mobile pink instead of the standard-issue black ones they sling around your neck when you sit for your senior year portraits. The only thing maybe different about him is his neck, which is for sure thicker, Izzy thinks. Or maybe just stronger.

—Wassup, chico, Izzy says, the endearment a holdover from his Pitbull act. He slaps forearms with the guy across the stand's counter and adds, It's been a minute.

—Ernie! the guy says. What happened to your *hair*, dog? Coño, look at you, you're fucking diesel.

—It's Izzy, bro. Ismael.

Izzy definitely lifts but doesn't consider himself *diesel* by any means. He barely thinks of himself as *ripped*, maybe on his way to *jacked*, which is, as far as he understands, still a couple levels shy of *diesel*. Is it Izzy who doesn't see himself accurately, or is this guy bad at sizing people up? If it's the latter, shouldn't that disqualify this guy from being a potential Manolo, given that sizing people up is probably an integral part of the job? Plus, the guy misremembered Izzy's name: not exactly good signs, not that he thinks he's looking for any.

Then by way of apology the guy says *Coño, fuck me, my bad* like three times, so Izzy considers him back in the running: he already has the vocabulary. He's got a break coming up, so they make plans to meet at the Sbarro in four, maybe five minutes.

Izzy sits with his back to the heat-lamped pizza glistening behind the sneeze guard to keep from buying all the slices. Thinking about rubbing his still-bald head with the garlicked grease pooling in each cheesy pizza crater also sort of works to keep him from wanting it. He wants to think that his days of consuming cheap mall garbage are as of right then literally behind him. Already he feels on his way to being too powerful to waste time thinking about something as basic as food. He can't remember if the movie ever shows Tony Montana actually eating anything other than cocaine.

Six or seven minutes later, the guy sits down across from him, a Diet Coke in his fist. He spreads his knees so far apart they knock away the empty seats on either side of him and says, Are you fucking 'roiding, bro? They say that shit shrinks your nuts but only if you do it like, *a lot* a lot.

—Nah, bro. I don't mess with that shit.

—You sure? You interested though? No pressure, whatever, how you been?

—Good, good. Busy. I'm trying to be like the next Scarface.

—Like the rapper? *My mind is playin' tricks on me!* I didn't know you could rap!

—No, like *Scarface* Scarface. Like the original. Tony Montana, like *her womb is so polluted.*

The guy leans back and says, Sorry to tell you and not for nothing, but you aren't Scarface material, bro. Like *at all*, if you're asking me. Which you basically are and I say you can't pull that shit off.

—Coño, bro. I'm *not* asking you. I'm looking for a Manolo.

—You know you sorta look like Pitbull with your head shaved like that? Except for the eyes, the guy says, smoothing down his tie. Fucking brown eyes wrecks it.

The guy spins his phone on the table between them.

—Oh cuz you're such big shit, working at T-Mobile. Can't even get a job at a real place like Verizon.

—Fuck you, bro, the fuck *you* even doing with your life?

—I just told you. I need a Manolo.

—*What?* I ain't no fucking Manolo! The guy grabs his phone and shoves it in his front pocket, then points at Izzy with sideways gun fingers. You'd be *my* fucking Manolo if anything, freaking ESL motherfucker. Remember back in middle school, you still had that ref accent in math saying *pa-ra-BO-la* instead of *pa-RA-bo-la?* Straight up Manolo shit right there, he says with a good tug on his crotch.

Izzy stands up and says, Oh you think so? Whatever, I did better than *you* in that class, so fuck that. He flexes his pecs, feels his traps engage along the ridge of his shoulders and the sides of his neck, making himself as big as he can. Fucking weak-ass motherfucker. Do you even lift, bro?

The guy doesn't stand up. He just sits there and laughs, rolling his Diet Coke can between the palms of his hands. Izzy tosses a crumpled-up napkin on the floor and stomps away.

—The fuck is your problem? the guy says to the chairs Izzy's shoved out of his way. Coño, bro, you always seemed a little sad back in the day but you know what? Get as ripped as you want, doesn't matter, your fucking head's still *off.*

The guy points his gun-fingers to his own skull, but Izzy doesn't see it. He's cutting across the food court, trying to tune the guy out, but he can't help it: he hears the guy yell, Good luck, Manolo!

Izzy drives to the gym straight from the mall, deciding he needs to lift for a while before finding the next guy, the first Rudy. He has never taken steroids, but as he watches his arms and chest flex in the mirror wall, he wonders if the dough of his high school fat somehow absorbed steroids through the sweat of the guys around him. Maybe he hasn't been wiping off the machines so well. He thinks of garlic knots and imagines himself swallowing them whole but not digesting them: instead, each greasy lump magically migrates to his biceps, bolstering the muscles from underneath, the crusts pushing up his skin like some kind of bread-based implants. He benches ten pounds more than he's ever done, thinking not of the danger of carbs, but of what else they could come to mean: forbidden blasts of energy, quick and undeniable power.

KING TIDE

It doesn't rain while Izzy is inside the gym, and as he leaves, there isn't a cloud in the sky; the clouds don't roll in from the Everglades until later in the day, the heat and humidity and pressure summoning them from the west each afternoon, the storms they bring controlling the rhythms of Miami life with more force than any clock or rush-hour traffic pattern. And yet a puddle of what is definitely water surrounds his car as if it had poured for the last hour. The water was there when he arrived but he didn't notice it as he got down from the car, the puddle small and oily enough earlier that he'd just parked over it, assuming it had leaked out of some other car's engine. Now he has to lunge across what looks like a custom-made moat, straddling a couple feet of water and leaping into his front seat to keep his sneakers dry.

All around the city this is happening more and more, water seeping up from the ground: sunny day flooding. Izzy doesn't call it that, or know that others call it that, or know the terrifying science/magic behind it, how—because it's connected to the tides—even the moon is involved. This city is, for him, just kind of wet all the time, and yeah, maybe it's worse than it used to be. Every time he has to cross over a sudden puddle like this, he figures a storm just passed, a quick one he just must've missed or didn't notice—what else could it be? He doesn't want to think about it. Besides, he's been doing splits over puddles since his first days in Miami. So many memories of his Tía Tere taking him to school and driving super slow so as not to make a wake, her Corolla floating over floods bumper-high after even the quickest and slimmest of rain showers: the water in the ground even back then was already so high it couldn't take on a drop more.

It's this water that is coming for him, for his Tía Tere's townhouse, for almost everyone's homes, starting with the septic tanks, many of which are failing. It's an inevitability: every septic tank in this city will

fail. Because they are slowly being submerged. And there's no way
to (legally) put those houses on the public sewer system if they ar-
en't already: already, to dig down in those neighborhoods is to hit
water before you get deep enough to lay new pipes. It's why the city
of Miami Beach raised the roads by a few feet, buying themselves another decade or two of tourism. It's why the first dozen floors of every
new building downtown—buildings with owners who live in other
countries, all taking out huge insurance policies waiting to be cashed
in with the next big hurricane—are dedicated to parking. It's why
there are roaches everywhere in this city, inside every home no matter how often you clean it or have it cleaned, no matter how much
pesticide you ring those homes in—those *fucking cockroaches* that
Scarface curses by name are just trying to stay above that rising water
line. The roaches, the ants, the palmetto bugs, the garter snakes, the
green and brown anoles, the geckos, the toads, the salamanders, the
various kinds of termites, even the opossums sometimes: they have
no other choice but to come inside to stay dry. More and more, and
for now—and depending on the moon and the time of day, month,
year—inside your house is the safest place, because yes, they can float,
maybe even tread water for a while, but unlike other creatures in this
city, they aren't designed to swim forever. They're coming inside because they want to survive: they are all, like Lolita in her tank (though
given what the floods could theoretically mean for her, she shares
little of their trepidation), listening to the water coming up from the
ground, to the future glimpsed when it's at its highest. To the promise of what it will reclaim.

THE HUNT CONTINUES, ENDS

The interview with the second guy—the First Rudy—occurs a couple days later at Westland Mall in Hialeah, which is much closer to Izzy's house and a far cry from the last mall in Pembroke Pines. What to say about the differences between these spaces, what they each imply about the communities they serve, about the people who enter them? For now it's enough to say that Westland Mall is, no matter how many seating areas they cram between those kiosks, a dump. It is at a kiosk for cell phone cases—not even cell *phones* or their various service providers; it is that bad—that the First Rudy works.

The First Rudy is perhaps a bit forgettable but was always good to Izzy during the one year they knew each other, having refrained from calling him Dough Boy or Pillsbury or Vaca Frita, this last nickname clinging to Izzy since elementary thanks to his stint in ESL. To be clear: Izzy was never fat, exactly—at least, not in a way that he could own, like various rappers of an earlier era (Big Pun, the Notorious B.I.G.; both now dead, though only one from health issues that could be attributed to morbid obesity). But he'd been chubby in a way that made girls think he would make a great Best Guy Friend and not much else. All through middle and most of high school, he kept his shirt on at the beach. In the shower, staring down, he sometimes worried because he was growing breasts big enough that the line of cleavage he could engineer when he pushed them together almost gave him a boner. Then, without trying very hard at all really, it melted away—late puberty, who knows—and graduation brought a search for a job, and his part-time at Don Shula's came with a free gym membership, and now people like Not-Rudy thought he was *fucking diesel.* Whether that term is accurate or not, his shirts did finally fit him well, the sleeves of everything tight around his arms and shoulders in ways that made people look at him, ways that had let

19

him pretend to be a stronger-looking Pitbull. His body had changed enough since graduation that the First Rudy, upon seeing Izzy, did not even recognize him.

The First Rudy spends the opening minutes of his unknown re-union with Izzy trying to sell him a phone case that will protect his device in up to thirty feet of water. The case is meant for divers, but this is not the angle he uses; he instead argues that this is the case you want if you are like, around a lot of pools. Or have a pool yourself. Or if you go to the beach a lot. Or maybe the Everglades. Or if you have a friend with a boat, or a friend with a cousin who has a boat.

Izzy doesn't fit any of these categories yet, but he likes the case, how sturdy it feels, the way it makes his phone feel huge in his hands. When Izzy agrees to buy it, he asks if there's a discount for old high school friends, and it's then that the First Rudy realizes who it is he's talking to. Izzy pays for the case—ten percent off—and leaves without mentioning his need for a Manolo, because despite Manolo's sidekick status, he still needs to have some kind of balls—for christ's sake, he goes on to marry Tony's sister behind his back, or something like that; it doesn't matter to Izzy, because as far as he knows he's an only child and so has jettisoned this plot aspect—and the First Rudy's wrinkled Dockers and the deep sweat patches under his arms and dabbing his lower back—which Izzy glimpsed when the guy bent down to look in the bowels of his kiosk for a case in silver, the color Izzy requested—rightfully showed Izzy that this First Rudy, as nice as he'd been in high school, could not even be Manolo's Manolo.

And so that leaves Izzy with the third man, the Second and Final Rudy, who does not work at any mall. No: he works at La Carreta on Bird Road—not as a server, as his Tía Tere had assumed, but as a dishwasher, and when the hostess corrects him about it, Izzy is as close to overjoyed as someone trying to reinvent himself can come. Be-cause the real Manolo's first job in the U.S. was as a dishwasher; Tony washed dishes too, alongside Manolo; it's a sign!—a literal sign, taped to the wall by the hostess stand that reads DISHWASHERS NEEDED. He makes note of it and then circles around the back of the restaurant, jogging between a dumpster and a stack of pallets, trying to keep his excitement in check: he wants to believe in fate but Tony Montana would probably say that fate is just going hard after whatever it is you want, that you make your own fate in this country, et cetera.

When Izzy spots him through a window in the restaurant's back door, the Second Rudy is washing dishes while wearing a hairnet like in that part of the movie where Manolo washes dishes while wearing a hairnet. Sweat coats Rudy's face, and he looks miserable and angry as his dark brows interrupt the shiny film of his skin. He raises a forearm to his head and tucks his skull into it, and as he drags it across and over his head, he sees Izzy—who has decided to wave, sort of. Rudy waves back, saying, Hold up, I know that dude, his words landing in the steel trough brimming with dishes and hot water and a soap-and-mildew smell Rudy can no longer stomach. He pulls his apron over his head and, after wiping his face and neck and arms with it, goes outside to see his high school friend.

Izzy cannot tell from the hug if Rudy remembers him fondly. It's the kind of hug where one man blocks full torso contact via the buffer of a cocked elbow; a hug with a built-in pushback. A two-handed hug, or the type where one hand rests—only for a second—on the back of the hug-receiver's head before dropping down to the less intimate spot of a shoulder, would've indicated that Rudy not only remembered Izzy but that he was glad to see him here, at his workplace. But no, it's a guarded hug despite the backslapping and the Oh my god, bro, how are you that accompanies it. And so Izzy proceeds with some caution.

It isn't necessary: Izzy and Rudy are, in many ways, the same man—both young, both treading the water rising around them, both as yet unaware of how lost they are in the version of Miami that leaves them longing for little more than a life prominently featuring nightclub bottle service and a girlfriend with an impressive set of augmented breasts. Even before he hears it, Rudy is as ready for Izzy's plan as Izzy is. They are so primed for this adventure that, had that arm not been folded between them, they might've, on impact, merged into one man.

They sit behind the restaurant on the hood of Rudy's Nissan Altima as Izzy lays out his idea, knowing full well that he isn't sure what it really entails, saying over and over again that Tony Montana didn't know either, that that's actually sort of the point. It was time to take some big risks, to take advantage of this city, to let what it had to offer find them. They just had to put themselves out there in a big way. Rudy rubs the stubble along his jaw with his whole hand, leaning forward every time Izzy hops off the car to face him. Izzy's rant is full of vagaries, but neither Izzy nor Rudy can tell because Izzy relays it with a force Rudy can't help but respect, even admire. All Tony Montana had at the start—aside from his word and his balls—was ambition and a massive sense that he deserved better, that he was destined for something bigger, something huge, something borderline unconquerable—and didn't they have that too, deep down? Before Izzy can make his mouth ask the next question, Rudy asks one himself: Do you need a Manolo?

—I do, I do, Izzy says. Do you remember the part where they both work at washing dishes and Tony gets fed up and they quit? It's after they kill that Communist guy in the camp in exchange for green cards.

Rudy laughs and says, I think my parents have the DVD but honestly, I haven't seen that movie in forever. I just don't wanna wear a fucking hairnet anymore.

He rubs his hands together as if washing them or trying to start a fire. The night is so hot and muggy, but neither man feels it; neither man has ever been any place where the air is any different.

—I don't actually know if that really happens, Izzy says. But I think it does. At the beginning.

Then he ventures: We should probably watch the movie again.

And Rudy takes it up: We should, we should.

FIRST NIGHT-WATCH

Scarface was released in 1983, and it is set in 1980—seventeen years before Izzy is born but not so long ago that he doesn't understand the backdrop of the Mariel boatlift. The boatlift could've brought over his mother, but it didn't: she'd just turned fourteen, and *her* mother—Ocila, the parent she and his Tía Tere shared—had raised her to trust the Revolution, to fight rather than flee, to regard her half sister as a traitor. Ocila had even named her Alina, after Castro's daughter. His Tía Tere—who had a very different dad with very different politics—came to the U.S. with her father (may he rest in peace) on one of the last Freedom Flights in 1973, meaning: on a plane, a trip over two years in the making that lasted barely an hour.

Ninety miles might not seem like a long distance, but you know these are no ordinary ninety miles: the miles are years, and the years are faces you never see again and voices you might hear once or twice, assuming whoever you left behind can forgive you for long enough to accept your call from Miami or New York. The miles are fights and betrayals and rewrites of familial history that paint someone as a bad guy: *Say good night to the bad guy.* The miles for some are a silence; for Alina and countless others, the miles are a grave.

In the end, Izzy came on a boat, like Tony Montana. But Tony's mother and sister were waiting for him in the U.S.; with Alina gone, all Izzy had was an aunt he'd never met, and he'd heard Alina curse her name enough times to have feared how she'd treat him—felt terrified at the news that this traitor-aunt had agreed to sponsor him after a case worker called her from Krome Detention Center with the surprise news of his arrival and his legal status as an unaccompanied minor—but Teresa, from then on his Tía Tere, turned out to be just a regular woman who wanted to do right by her sister's memory, to give him a chance at the life her sister had lost in the attempt to bring him to the United States, suspicious as that attempt may have seemed to her. She'd spent those first weeks wanting to pelt him with questions about Alina and whatever had compelled her to get on that raft after years of not just refusing to do so but of wishing a literal watery death to any Cuban who'd attempted to leave that way, but everything she'd binge-read in her first weeks as a parent to un niño traumatizado told her to be gentle, to let him come to her. And anyway the truth now was he remembered next to nothing—about Alina or the voyage. It's also true that his Tía Tere knew very little about him prior to his arrival—only his birthday, which Alina had mentioned in a letter Teresa has long since torn apart and buried in an effort to give that pain back to the earth. The year he arrived, he'd already turned seven.

In *Scarface*, Al Pacino plays Tony with an accent Izzy can't place. It is like nothing he's heard in Miami, like nothing that comes out of his own mouth or out of the mouth of anyone he interacts with. Is it supposed to be Spanish, the accent? Does Izzy have an accent? His guess is no, and in Miami, he doesn't. His accent would only be discernible away from here, where it would be obvious and possibly even as comical as Tony Montana's, depending on the listener. But in Miami, his English sounds like most everyone else's English, or he just speaks Spanish, which quickly turned clunky in his mouth, littered with almost as many English words as his English is.

In *Scarface*, the character of Manolo is played by an actor named Steven Bauer. Steven Bauer was born in Cuba and named Esteban Echevarría but he changed it somewhere between his stint as a teenager named Joe Peña on the PBS bilingual sitcom *¿Qué Pasa, U.S.A.?* (where he's listed in the credits as *Rocky* Echevarría) and his being cast as Manolo in *Scarface*. Whatever he wanted to be called, he was and is one of maybe two actual Cubans cast in a movie that purports to be about Cubans. His Cuban-ness is what reportedly got him the role over his non-Cuban competition: John Travolta.

Even though the name Steven Bauer sounds more Anglo, his Spanish accent as Manolo is much heavier than when he was on PBS and still going by Echevarría. You can imagine some director type telling him to lay it on thick, but neither Izzy nor Rudy understand why he hams it up in the movie when his new name clearly indicated he was heading—or hoping to head—in a different direction, as evidenced not only by the name change but by his somewhat disastrous marriage, from 1981 to 1989, to Melanie Griffith, una americana who would go on to also marry *Miami Vice*'s own Don Johnson (twice, as in once in 1976 and then again in 1989, like right after divorcing el pobre Steven), as well as America's favorite Spaniard, Antonio Banderas, who plays a Cuban musician in *The Mambo Kings*—a movie Izzy and Rudy have never seen, based on a Pulitzer Prize–winning novel they've never read, written by a New York–born Cuban guy they've never heard of—and, of course, the cat in all the *Shrek*s (Izzy and Rudy love the *Shrek*s). Steven Bauer's more recent credits include a cigar-smoking boss in the music video for the song Secret Admirer (by Pitbull), and the kidnapper in the music video for the song Hold On, We're Going Home (by Drake), in which he only has one line (he has zero lines in the Pitbull video), and he says it nice and slow and with a white guy accent—he doesn't sound Cuban at all. Izzy doesn't even recognize the old guy from the Drake video as the same guy who plays Manolo. But admittedly it's been like four years since that song came out, and Izzy watched the video maybe once and not even all the way through.

Izzy and Rudy briefly discuss the accents—or more accurately, the *performance* of accents—days after first meeting up as they pass the worn case for the special edition *Scarface* DVD between them while sitting on Izzy's-but-really-Tía-Tere's couch.

—We don't have to do that, right? Talk like that? Rudy says.

—Of course not. We're not acting, this is gonna be real life.

—But if we're trying to be like these guys –

—This is more a spirit of the law, letter of the law thing.

—Meaning?

—What we want – what we *need* is to move up in the world in an aggressive way. That's all we're trying to do. Anything that doesn't directly relate to that, no big deal.

Rudy pauses the DVD, asks: What about the drugs?

Izzy shrugs. Says, I wouldn't say the drugs are like, mandatory.

—Bro, are you serious? This whole movie is about drugs.

Rudy flips away from the film to the cable setting, scrolling through the channels, looking for the Marlins game. He says, I don't want to mess with that shit. Doing is one thing, selling is another. My parents would fucking *kill* me.

He finds the game and curses the Marlins for being down by two runs in the ninth inning; it's only the second game of the season, but the Marlins lost the first, so despite the length of the season, Rudy's ready to give up. He falls back on the couch with a gust of air and says, Fucking Marlins, bro. Breaking my heart since like forever.

—I'm not saying it won't be shady, just doesn't have to be drugs.

—Plus I don't want to end up dead, Rudy says.

—We definitely will deviate from that part, for real. Izzy leans back on the couch too, points to the game. They got two outs and no one on base, he says.

Rudy rubs the top of his head with his whole hand, like he's about to pick himself up. I know, he says. But I can't *not* watch it. It's like, a sickness. How shady you thinking?

—I have no idea, maybe not even that shady. Maybe gambling? Or betting?

—Those are the same thing.

Izzy reaches for the remote but Rudy tosses it to his other hand in time to keep control of it. Izzy sucks his teeth and says, Change it back to the movie already. We got shit to figure out.

—The game's almost over, bro. Let me see my Marlins lose and then we can get back to work, okay?

And Izzy—because he's your Tony and Rudy is just your Manolo; and because held deep in him is a memory he can't fully conjure of being pulled by both arms into a speedboat by a man speaking muddied Spanish, a spotlight behind this stranger blinding Izzy just before he collapses, his body spilling onto the deck; and because Izzy also is a true Marlins fan (they do exist), having fallen in love with the team immediately after seeing a billboard for season tickets within minutes of his first glimpses of Miami from his Tía Tere's car—Izzy is the one who stumbles on the beginnings of a plan, on their version of the commodity that made Tony Montana so rich. He smacks Rudy on the shoulder maybe five times in a row.

—Baseball players, he says. We can like, get them here. For like money.

On the screen, the umpire calls a second strike.

—You mean be like scouts? Rudy says, a tried-and-true Manolo. We aren't trained to do scouting. That takes like *years*.

—No no, like helping players get here from Cuba. Like defecting.

—Is that a job? I mean, I know you can *get* smuggled but can you *do* the smuggling?

—Yeah, there's ways and stuff. There's people. We could be the people. Or help the people. I mean, Scarface started small and then ends up on top of the whole game.

—But how do you get into that? We don't even have a boat.

—Probably we start by learning the system for how they do this with rafts for regular people, get into that system, figure out how it's done. Then we work our way up to helping athletes or whatever.

—So we *don't* need a boat?

He hits Rudy again.

—Not yet, Izzy says. I might know people – or I guess my tía might know people, a guy who knows a guy. From like, when I came over. When I was little.

—For real? Rudy says.

He wants Izzy to say more, but because Rudy's parents have raised him right, he knows better than to ask certain questions, doesn't want to offend anyone by making certain assumptions. Rudy, born a United States citizen—though still Manolo despite what should be an obvious disqualification—knows almost as much about the circumstances of Izzy's crossing as Izzy does, meaning: not much at all. What Rudy does know—not by direct experience but by a kind of cultural osmosis, it's sometimes that thick in Miami's air—is that asking the wrong person the wrong question can get you in a lot of trouble. Better to let people talk, is what his father always said, what a lot of guys' fathers said.

—Yeah, she's gotta know someone who knows about this shit. The bringing people over part, not the athlete part.

Rudy nods slowly and says, I know people like that too. A guy who knows a guy, like you said.

In Miami, it's hard *not* to know a guy who knows a guy: another truth hanging in this city's air. Rudy rubs his head again, deciding how much to say.

—Mine's is the uncle of this guy that works with my dad, he finally says over a commercial. He goes out on his boat once, maybe twice a year and picks up balseros in the middle of the night, drops them off closer to shore. He's never gotten caught. Says if anybody asks he tells them he was just out fishing, but you know what that means.

Izzy doesn't, not exactly, but he keeps this to himself, not because he had a father who'd taught him to let others talk (he's not even sure he ever met the man), but because he doesn't want to admit how little he actually remembers from his own crossing.

The game ends—another loss for the Marlins, making it two in a row to start the season—and Rudy adds, I know some groups say they do it for free, like anti-Castro people, but they aren't the only guys in the game. This guy I'm talking about? He charges ten grand a person, unless they're a relative. Then it's just five grand.

Izzy whistles, says, That's a start, right? We can talk to him and to my people too, compare notes, find out about the system. There's always a system.

He has never thought for long about the price of his own passage, of who ultimately paid it. All it cost him was his mother, a woman he sometimes worried he should miss more; the only feeling he could regularly conjure for her now was a soggy kind of gratitude for getting him on that raft. Whatever hole her death had left in him, his Tía Tere had initially filled it, and eventually the hole filled up with Miami itself, with the urgency to fit into his new American life. The person Izzy was when he grabbed the arms of the man on that speedboat had, as far as he was concerned, drowned along with his mother. He'd arrived unassisted, totally legit, no question about it, that was the story. That was the only way through it: to pretend it had happened to someone else. Becoming a modern-day Tony Montana would be easy compared to that earlier transformation.

He takes out his phone, admires the case and its waterproof qualities, thinking maybe it was a smart and even necessary investment after all. He's grateful to the First Rudy, sweaty as he was, for the discount. Outside, a passing thunderstorm pummels the townhouse—the downpour flooding their street in minutes—but at the game on TV, everything is dry thanks to the closed roof over Marlins Park. They switch back to the DVD and finish watching the movie, Izzy taking notes on his phone.

He types, LESSON 1: DONT UNDERESTIMATE THE OTHER GUYS GREED

He types, LESSON 2: DONT GET HIGH ON UR OWN SUPPLY (N/A 4 US?)

He types, EVENTUALLY GET SKINNY AF GF (MAYBE NOT SKINNY?? HAS TO BE WHITE GIRL THO??)

He types other things and then abandons his note-taking after the scene where Scarface goes to some old lady's house and it turns out she's his mother, who apparently hates him—a scene he doesn't at all remember despite the many times growing up when he'd watched this movie on cable. Maybe it always got cut for time, along with all the *fucks* and whatnot. He doesn't remember if the mother is even important to the plot. He hopes not. He doesn't want to think about it and so he tosses his phone on the couch and closes his eyes for a second, imagining instead his Michelle Pfeiffer—or more accurately, what he hopes will be his Michelle Pfeiffer's gigantic butt.

As the storm dumps the last of its rain on Hialeah, no one but Lolita hears the water lapping its way up Izzy's driveway. She understands; she shares and knows his bone-deep loneliness even as he pushes away the sensation with thoughts of big booties. Of course he wants to seek out the woman first, not knowing as she does that he should let the woman find *him*, and definitely not knowing that she—Lolita—might be the catalyst for all he is truly after. She rises for a breath. There is so much she could tell him.

HARK!

The storm passes quickly enough but as usual these days, the water everywhere lingers. For that you can thank the king tide and the extra nudge of a full moon, along with the well-established theory that humidity, given its overbearing tendencies, is inherently omniscient. Add to all that the fact that Lolita's tank, unlike the Marlins' ballpark, sits uncovered and therefore completely exposed to the same rains flooding Izzy's street, the storm water joining the treated salt water surrounding her. And remember that she's stuck right there by the bay, trapped at the edge of the ocean, on land barely above sea level, all of it getting drenched, meaning: eventually everything flows her way. In this super-saturated instant, as above so below, it's more than enough.

She hovers just beneath the surface, where the rain is still mingling in a greater concentration with her tank water, and she hears Izzy say, Instead of a tiger, what if we get like, a dolphin?

—You can't buy a dolphin. An alligator we could get no problem.

—That's why a gator's not enough. A dolphin – *that* says power. The Dolphins got one, right?

—They do? I thought that was just in that old movie. Where Jim Carrey wears a tutu.

—I think that's where I saw it.

—I don't know if that's real, bro. How you even gonna keep it alive?

—Obviously this comes after we already have money for a tank. And like a warehouse.

—Maybe we should like, research that? If it's even possible? Like, go to the Seaquarium, talk to trainers?

—Shamu is there too, Izzy says. And the muscles surrounding Lolita's eyes contract and she sinks down because she hates when she senses this, because she is not Shamu. There is no Shamu anymore but they are all Shamu. Shamu has become the token orca, the one-and-only Killer Whale (though this term is out of fashion and should not be used, even though it's used still, like so many other offensive terms). She has never met this whale and yet this name makes the rounds of her stadium whenever she performs, only sometimes corrected. She is learning—still learning—that it does not matter what anyone calls her. It should've never mattered.

What does she know of Izzy's time as Pitbull? Not much: it's not that she doesn't have the capacity, it's that she only just started sensing him through the water as a distinct presence. All she knows of his Pitbull phase is that it's over, a lifting of noise that lets her now sense even what he's buried and forgotten. Before, she registered Izzy only as an occasional queasy feeling, something she could ignore or that she blamed on the rotting fish sometimes mixed in with the rest of her food—sensations she felt all the time, possibly for others just like him, and ignored. When Izzy was playing at Pitbull, he didn't have to think hard about how to do it or what it meant, his thoughts during his gigs a kind of soothing static. Much like the real Pitbull, Izzy's act boiled down to yelling a few standard phrases and putting his arms around people's shoulders. He looked women and girls up and down and licked his lips, told them to get naked for him and dance, then let out a gurgled laugh that was supposed to mean, *Nah, Mami, I'm just playing but no seriously take off your clothes.* Sometimes he saw, in his periphery as he posed for a photo with some girl who thought he was the real deal, a large or largish man standing by, shaking his head. *I went to high school with Pitbull,* these men would say. *You are not Pitbull.* He'd worried about a confrontation and wondered if he needed to enlist some help, since probably the real Pitbull roamed Miami's malls flanked by bodyguards. Lolita senses only the echo of this dread, registering it in her body as a kind of acid reflux easily relieved by vomiting.

So fine, he's coming to talk to the trainers. He's interested in the dolphins who too-eagerly perform alongside her, but once he sees her, he will think: *Whoa.* At the show's end, he will push his way to the front of the crowd, wanting badly to press his hands and face against the glass surrounding her tank. Izzy will crouch in a puddle and look into her eye through the distortion of the glass's thickness and he will feel something break in his mind and that will be her, in there for good.

She rises for a breath, hears him say: We need better clothes.

Izzy still has his Pitbull suit, but when he wears it, he of course gets mistaken for Pitbull, and he's fairly certain that's illegal now. Aside from the Pitbull suit, he has the black suit his Tía Tere bought him for graduation, which doesn't totally fit him anymore because he's lost the weight around his waist and gained mass in his shoulders. Still, he's worn it when he's been required to look sharp for events at Don Shula's and it's worked fine. Rudy also has his suit from graduation, which also still mostly fits. So at best they have two-and-a-half suits between them, and while they agree that they don't need full-fledged three-pieces, they do both feel strongly that some well-tailored jackets might be necessary. This will, at the very least, result in people probably taking them more seriously as they move around the city. They also agree that neither of them has the kind of cash flow at the moment to actually buy these bespoke jackets, so the plan for now is to wear their graduation ones to the Seaquarium and see how that goes.

Izzy has a vision of himself standing on a foot-tall platform surrounded by mirrors, getting fitted for the perfect suit—no, *suits*—each with a matching vest. He is standing in a room full of bolts of fabric, touching each of them—purples, dark greens, pin stripes in electric blue—and saying, *This one, this one, this one.* Rudy is standing behind him, arms folded across his chest, nodding and eyeing other bolts of fabric—good ones, but not as vibrant in color as the ones Izzy finds himself choosing. Rudy just gravitates toward the sorts of colors that say *Manolo*, and neither guy feels bad about this at all.

A revision, then, to their plot: first you get the money, *then you get some jackets*, then you get the power.

Anything, Lolita thinks as she sinks to her tank's shallow bottom, is possible.

THE OCEAN AND ITS DEPTHS

That Friday, Izzy and Rudy sit in the front row of the Killer Whale and Dolphin Stadium at the Miami Seaquarium. Izzy feels surprised at how close they are to the bay—the ocean is right there, just beyond the Manatee Exhibit and Salty's Pirate Playground, basically a straight shot down an access road leading to some scraggly trees that line (and mostly block) the view of an abandoned-seeming concrete boat slip near the park's filtration systems. Next to the slip, park water spills out in a froth from who knows where back into Biscayne Bay.

Despite the proximity of the ocean, Izzy and Rudy are sweating through their graduation suit jackets as they watch Lolita's show. Chilled tank water burps over the edge of her enclosure with her every move, splashing onto the baking concrete at Izzy's feet. You'd think he'd be mad at the potential ruin of his shoes but no: he laughs like a little kid at his soaked sneakers.

Sunlight Zone

During her wave-to-the-crowd tail splash—this behavior signaling the merciful end to the afternoon performance—something in Lolita's jaw sizzles in a new way as she rolls onto her side and underwater, her tail fin slapping and slapping and slapping and slapping and slapping and slapping and—wait, she holds her flukes still against the water's surface for a second longer to make sure it's really this close, yes, it is: the sound from across town laughing, here now, in the crowd—and slapping and slapping before a trainer, who has no idea that they've been one choice away from death every single moment of every single day they've come in to work, can even get the whistle to their mouth to call off the behavior. In that pause between slaps, Lolita can't see what's coming exactly, only that it's him—Izzy, the one she sometimes hears from across the bay—only his love. This love: she can already sense from his voice, which buzzes through the fat in her jaw as she comes up to breathe, that he doesn't yet know to call it that.

Twilight Zone

(Can a whale and a man fall in love? Of course! There's a whole other book about exactly that—a crazy, obsessive kind of love, more or less—another big book Izzy's never read, but why would he? It's super long and besides, he was never that book's intended audience. That book might have a lot going for it to some, but it never imagined a guy like Izzy reading it. The proof: look at that title. Like Izzy would ever in this lifetime risk walking down a Miami high school hallway holding some fat book about dick.)

Sunlight Zone

After the show, Izzy does something typically only attempted by children in attendance: he runs up to the tank to get close. Rudy stays in his seat, posting a photo of his wet shoes and performing a mild rage via various face-water-spilling emojis, a rage that is entirely false but that will get many likes and comments such as ROTFLMAO and WHERE U AT BRO? His sister will comment, You took the car for THIS?!?, and when he deletes it, she'll post, STOP DELETING ME!!!!!!

Izzy insisted they wear their grad suit jackets and black jeans in order to look sharp despite his Tía Tere's warnings that the sun that day would show no mercy. Under the jacket he wears a slim-fitting T-shirt, same bright white as his sneakers, its tightness being Izzy's strategy to distract from the fact that the jacket is a little big on him. He's hoping the jacket will make him stand out as someone important and serious to the trainers after the show. The sneakers only slightly undermine this intention, and only in the eyes of transplants and tourists. This is Miami after all, where guys like Izzy have been trained since infancy to prize a set of Jordans over almost everything. Even his Tía Tere hadn't said anything about his choice of footwear.

It's been only a couple days since Izzy's first fade in months, and so Izzy looks very handsome, meaning: less like Pitbull. He pulls his sunglasses from his face as he approaches the tank's glass wall.

For some reason, he wants Lolita to see he has brown eyes.

Midnight Zone

He's been in this stadium in front of this whale before but he doesn't remember this. He was seven, just barely off a raft and officially a first grader again—this time in English, a school year lost to the ocean. He was on a field trip customary to many Miami-Dade County students: *Come on out / for a day of fun / at the / Mi-a-mi / Seaquarium!*, the commercial's jingle demanded. He doesn't remember, but he walked around the park all day wishing for a sister. He thought he maybe already had one but that she'd been left behind in Cuba. It could be true, this seven-year-old reasoned. Another mother, same father— something like this: already at seven he knew how fractured a family could be. A sister would mean he had a father back there too—some-one he'd never known on or off the island. And of course, maybe a new mother, though he already thought of his Tía Tere as this. There was no other option.

Ismael, some chaperone finally yells, and he's back, his face sticky with his sweat's salt and the sea's—this is the closest he's been to the ocean since being pulled from it months earlier. He is standing by a shallow pool brimming with sting rays all circling in the same di-rection. Signs he can't yet read encourage him to touch gently. The other children are arms in up to their elbows, but he'd taken one look in the pool and thought, *Pancakes*, then, *No thanks*. Words he never thought he'd know.

Go stick your hand in the pool, Ismael, this same chaperone yells.

He is still much better at Spanish than English and so misunder-stands her. He steps to the pool's edge to do as he thinks he's been told, not wanting to get in trouble, his head just above its rim, then leans over the foot-thick wall, wiggling across it on his belly, obedi-ently dipping in his head.

The chaperone of course stops this (how many Miami kids would be dead if not for some classmate's overtaxed parent during some field trip slapping your hand away from a baby gator's mouth or prying your fingers from a parrot's beak?) but not before the very tips of Izzy's hair soak through with ray water.

He'd thought, *My sister's down there,* as a way to make himself do it. Somehow it felt more possible, less devastating—thinking *sister* instead of *mother.* And now that he's been stopped, he feels the loss of both—one imagined, one real—as something itching in his bones. The backs of his knees feel cold as his legs bend and unbend: he is flailing, screaming, the chaperone's arms around his waist, pulling him away and away as she thinks, *What the fuck is wrong with this kid?*

His mother's name: Alina, though he'd never known her as that until she was gone. What is this imagined sister's name? If he could remember for her a name, that would convince him she was real. What was her name? What was her name?

He heard someone near him scream it: *Lolita!*

No, that wasn't it.

But again, insisting: *Lolita! Lolita!*

A girl to his left with a streak of snot snailing across her forearm has that forearm extended out, the hand at the end of it pointing. One of the smarter girls, she's in the advanced reading group and everything. A girl who can be trusted, whose report card states she has leadership skills, meaning: maybe Lolita was it, if this girl says so. At school, snot or no snot, she tended to be right about things.

With the pointing, she indicates a whole looming structure: Lolita's Stadium, home to the Killer Whale and Dolphin Show, the tank in which they keep their orca. The first graders, even the smart girl, aren't aware that the adults responsible for them have been herding them in this direction all morning. The plan is to catch the early afternoon Lolita show and then unpack the bag lunches once a chaperone retrieves them from the bus (this poor chaperone missing Lolita's grand finale splash to head out to the parking lot). Lolita is a sister only to a few in a pod of whales thousands of miles away, but this classmate saying Lolita's name as an answer to Izzy's unspoken question lodges the name in his mind—a literal spot in his brain that remained dark and unbothered until just over a decade later, when he peels off his sunglasses and the sun's glare flashes off Lolita's body and stuns him and lights it back up.

Twilight Zone

Lolita senses Izzy's new remembering and thrills at it—a sensation she hasn't felt since her ocean childhood—and she rushes straight at him from the other side of her tank, toward the black-and-white smear of him distorted through the glass. She knows it's distorted and she also knows exactly the wall's height and that if she were to spyhop to get an accurate picture of him via air, she wouldn't see the whole of him: the tank wall comes up to his chest. Of course she knows that he couldn't possibly be one of her kind, but through the water's murk and the thick glass—and with noise pinging as always in her jaw but at that instant more intense thanks to a bad angle she typically remembers to avoid, thus heightening her usual delirium—she imagines the possibility, and so wants him with her, submerged, wants him to know her misery as the thought flashes that the black-and-white of his clothing is an insult, like the wetsuits her trainers wear in a sad attempt to be matchy-matchy with her own markings, but she's at her tank's edge now, and the mini tidal wave she's directing over him, lasting just over a second and filled with the energy of her own rage, tells her everything about his literal and metaphysical posture: from the water as it rushes toward him she knows that insulting her wasn't his intention, no, not at all, and so she tells him through the water to stay, to let the wave crash over and soak him, directs him to deny the instinct, the reflex to raise his hands for protection from what cannot be protected against—coming water. He does as she says and he can't explain why, thinks it's his own idea—she knows this instantly through the water even though he does not.

What comes back to her in the milliseconds before the water falls away from him: his awe; his need; the magnitude and confusion of all that he's lost; how the loss maps itself over her own memory of being stolen from the sea, the sensation here as sudden and painful as a strike to her side from a dolphin.

She halts and hovers in the water—still lapping and drenching, more faint now in what it tells her—turning her head slightly to the right to stare at what he is with her left eye. She knows from the dumb opening of his mouth-hole as he laughs that he cannot believe they are finally, finally together.

She wants so badly to plug the hole with herring.

Sunlight Zone

Izzy has, up until this moment, mistakenly thought orca eyes were the whole of the white part. But now he sees her real eye, a baseball-sized, flesh-surrounded orb at the front of the white patch. He is almost disappointed by its smallness until he looks closer and recognizes something; he does not know what to call it and can't right away admit what he suddenly feels: that she is much, much smarter than him.

Twilight Zone

Izzy's interrogation of the trainer on duty during a tank-side trainer Q&A session:

—What does she eat?

—In the wild they eat salmon, but here at the Miami Seaquarium, well, we feed her herring because it's healthier.

No it isn't.

—Herring has more nutrients in it than the fish she would eat in the wild.

They have trained me to eat it.
What other lies will she feed you.

—I saw this one video online though? They were eating like, seals and dolphins, like hunting and shit.

Some of us do this.
Sometimes we kill just for sport. Just like you.

—Please watch your language, sir. And, well, orca are gentle and loving animals. Lolita here, some of her best friends are dolphins.

—I don't know about that, lady. I don't know about the herring either. I mean, how long can that last? What choice does she even have? How'd she even get here?

—Killer whales are found in all the world's oceans. Lolita here, she's been with us here at the Miami Seaquarium almost her whole life.

Almost. Just like you.

—Was she like, rescued or something?

Ask the hard questions as they come.

—She came to us from the Pacific Northwest.

—So she's a long way from home then, huh?

—No, no – she's right at home here, aren't you, big gal?

home home home home home home home

—Whoa, she okay?

—Ha ha ha ha. Quite a splash there, huh, big girl? All in a day's work here at the Miami Seaquarium! Anyone else have a question? Anyone else?

Anyone.

Anyone?

The Abyss

(And Lolita is here now too: anyone, anyone? She's become just as much a part of this city and this narrative as anyone born here, hasn't she? She's been trapped in Miami over fifty years, knows all too well its sunrises and sunsets and storms and dirty seawater. At what point would you say her perspective counts as a local one?)

Rudy and Izzy, their feet squishing in their sneakers as they leave Lolita's stadium once it's clear the trainer won't answer any more of their questions:

—There's no way a pet dolphin is gonna work, Rudy says.

Remember he is your sidekick.

—I know that, Izzy says. You think I'm stupid? You think Tony Montana could really keep a tiger in his backyard?

—*That* actually could happen in real life, I think. Same with an alligator. But a dolphin? A freaking *killer whale*? That thing shouldn't even be in there in the first place. That thing is smarter than me and you put together.

He is a fine choice. He has enough sense.

—How do they keep the water cold enough? Izzy asks.

—Electricity bill must be fucking crazy, Rudy says.

A cost to consider, one among many.

—Damn, it's like being trapped in a bathtub, Izzy says to the air.

—Let me call this guy I know, used to live near my house, used to talk to my sister a while back but now we're friends. I bet he can get us an alligator if we say we're interested.

—What if she's a metaphor?

—She *who*? My sister?

                                    A metaphor is also a living thing.

—No, hear me out. What if Lolita's a metaphor?

—What's a metaphor? What's it for?

                                    That is a good question.

—That's a good question, Rudy. A good question indeed.

The Trenches

Of course she's a metaphor. Of course she is. There's no escaping that, just as there is no escaping that tank. *What's it for*, Rudy asks. And in his question, a truth: metaphors have utility, a purpose. What is she? Allow the suggestion of some context-specific possibilities, if only to convey that the danger's been considered and in fact embraced whole-heartedly (there's no other way through this): she is el exilio; she is Cuba under the embargo; she is a generation of Cubans born in the United States, enacting—with every prayer and purchase—a version of the cubanidad regurgitated by your parents like so many force-fed herring; she is most obviously anyone/everyone trapped and expected to perform; she is an artist-turned-mascot, given an arena to circle ad nauseum where she can perform only what she's been taught without room for much more; she is greatness trapped in the shittiest of circumstances; she is Spanglish, and she is the resistance to Spanglish; she is Fidel Castro and Fidel Castro's ghost and Raúl Castro and Raúl Castro's mesh trucker hat; she is America's approach to climate change; she is America and she is the climate itself—a catastrophe; she is this nation's broken immigration system; she is the refugee in limbo, in a detention center, in a cage; she is Izzy's childhood; she is Ishmael and she is Melville's clear authorial voice; she is Ahab and she is Tony; she is Miami—beautiful, improbable, doomed; she is, like every single one of you, an accident of history.

But she is also herself, still alive and swimming in circles. And later that evening, back at his Tía Tere's house, sitting on the same couch where he and Rudy rewatched *Scarface* for the first time in years, Izzy cannot shake her. It's not only his fault: she will not leave him alone. She has been screaming in his direction since the park closed, aiming her long-range distress calls toward him in Hialeah and not toward the general northwest for the first time ever since she landed in Miami. She is attempting, with varying degrees of success depending on the hour and the moon's pull on the earth's waters, to reach the part of him newly opened to her and to so much more, that part of consciousness most of those on land have evolved away from using, newly awoken in him: a physical location in his brain. He cannot understand that this is what's happening. He doesn't know that there are entire societies built on the steady and subtle communication—a deep knowing—between orca and their relations on land. That in their case, with orca still in the wild, the connection is magnanimous, reciprocal, and real.

And there are people who have no claim to those cultures but who are close to the water who believe that orca communicate with them, people who believe a thought to be something else: a missive from the sea, loaded with information about health and location and needs and even wishes, even sympathy. These people call in to researchers, reporting a feeling—*I think Granny's in trouble*, they'll say of the oldest known orca, who is almost or just over a hundred years old and supposedly still out there swimming. They describe the feeling as rare and strange and like a kind of quiet knowing.

With a wild-born orca driven daily to the brink of insanity by captivity, the nature and stability of this potential connection is anyone's guess. It's anyone's guess how it might be used or abused, with what frequency or intensity. It's anyone's guess how captivity might pervert the sensation itself, how the physical body of its recipient might manifest the occasional lighting up of their brain's once-dark corner. With Izzy, his guess is he's getting a migraine. He has never had one before, but an ex-girlfriend of his suffered them like clockwork, timed along with her period, and he never believed in her claim of an aura until now. He wonders if he still has, in a drawer somewhere, the Tiger Balm he'd rub into her right temple. He decides maybe he should eat something, drink some water. He's shocked by his sudden thirst.

Sunlight Zone

Later that night, Izzy stands in front of the microwave in the kitchen he shares with his Tía Tere, reheating the previous evening's dinner of picadillo and rice, when another burst of pain swarms the right side of his brain. He folds at the waist and puts his head on the counter, rolling his forehead against it. The pressure helps but not enough.

From the dining table, his Tía Tere asks, ¿Qué te pasa?

Then in that way women like her have, she answers for him: Probably too much sun at the Seaquarium. That's what it is.

She goes back to the crossword puzzle on the last page of *People en Español.*

She fills in some squares with her pen and adds, That's what you get for wearing a jacket in this heat.

—I told you, the jacket was for authority, he moans into the Formica.

The microwave beeps and he pulls out a tub of now-too-hot food.

When he sits at the table across from his Tía Tere, she asks, How much *authority* did you have as you sweated through your shirt?

His fork hits the sides of the Tupperware. It sounds like he's digging in a plastic bucket.

He waits to know the answer, and there it is.

He blows her a squeaky kiss, because he loves her.

—Enough, he says, smiling.

AN INHERITANCE

Teresa, landing somewhere between an abuela and a mom from this city's perspective: religiously devoted to Walter Mercado and to *Sábado Gigante* before it went off the air, yet throughout Izzy's schooling active enough in the PTA to keep him classified as one of the good kids in the minds of his school's administrators. Teresa, who raised Izzy on walks around the neighborhood and taught him to greet and engage his vecinos so as to get the choicest neighborhood gossip while also signing his school field trip forms and sometimes chaperoning said field trips—even in spite of the other guardians, all mothers a decade or two younger than her, mothers whose mere presence and affect made her feel older than she was, less entitled to her nephew than she was. She didn't actually give a shit what they thought of her—age comes for everyone, and also: she knew all she and Izzy had gone through to become what they'd become to each other; she knew how much paperwork, the cost of the lawyers, the fees and court dates and hearings it had taken to get Izzy's citizenship and her legal guardian status. All these things—along with the literal time spent caring for him—more than qualified her to sit on a school bus and accompany Izzy's class to Zoo Miami (formerly Metro Zoo) or Jungle Island (formerly Parrot Jungle Island) or later, in middle school, Kennedy Space Center (probably always called that). But that proof didn't make it any less lonely, sitting on those buses, a whole bench near the front to herself because of course Izzy wasn't going to sit with her—but neither did any of the other mothers, as if her age were contagious, or as if she'd drowned Izzy's biological mother herself, or worse (though admittedly improbable): as if these other mothers somehow knew about her sister's devotion to Castro's Revolution and viewed Teresa as contaminated. Ultimately, whatever the reason, this shunning was a blessing, because space limits meant *someone* had to take the seat next to her, and inevitably, whatever long-suffering public school teacher assigned to Izzy that year would collapse onto the bench, claiming the aisle seat left empty by the mothers who'd headed to the back of the bus, as if they were still the students and not the grown women who'd volunteered for this. Teresa was old enough to know to just let this poor woman—Izzy's teachers had always been women, all of them Haitian or Cuban or Dominican or some combination thereof—have five fucking minutes of quiet time to herself.

Though the bus was anything but quiet, what with the other chaperones refusing to do their jobs in favor of ingratiating themselves to their child's friends. But that noise was at least blessedly, literally behind them, her and this teacher. And another blessing: both content to smile in greeting and nothing more; Teresa sits there, looking out the window, watching the palm tree trunks whizz by, her purse on her lap, hands folded over it, a posture that reminds this teacher of a younger version of her own mother. And as the relief of having successfully corralled every one of her forty or so students safely onto that bus and en route to Zoo Miami/Metro Zoo sinks in, the teacher—whoever she is—starts to relax enough that her mind can wander, and she gets curious about this quiet mother next to her, can't remember which child is hers. Feels a little sorry for her that she's not sitting with the other mothers, then a little impressed by this same fact. She wonders about this and—even at the sacrifice of the faux-quiet she'd relished moments before—asks this woman some version of the question: *Remind me whose mom you are again?*

Teresa recognizes this moment every time, when she gets to use their story to make Izzy stand out where previously he was just another Cuban boy, another boy to monitor and keep under control, another potential troublemaker, so she says, like it's an apology: I'm Ismael's aunt.

And the surprise on this teacher's face is a door Teresa has walked through time and again, giving over to a stranger all Izzy has lost in the hopes that the telling casts a spell of protection and care over him and this teacher for the rest of the school year. A spell that meant a little more patience when patience made a difference, one where the teacher could and would see herself as the mother figure they didn't think he had, where the teacher would conflate his story with that of Elián González—the whole city still suffering from the hangover of that ordeal, Izzy's arrival coming almost four years after Elián's but with the opposite result—and so this teacher would extend some kindness, some extra vigilance: a call to Teresa rather than to the principal, for instance. *Let them feel sorry for him*, Teresa would tell herself as she revealed as plainly as she could that Ismael came from Cuba on a raft at seven, that his mother, her sister, had died in the crossing. She knew this truth: pity meant protection.

This is the only thing Teresa will give her sister credit for: that the way Alina chose to die at least gave Teresa a version of a story she could give away—quietly and privately and with a practiced sense of reluctance—to some teacher, school year after school year. Which is how Izzy has avoided the worst of what boys his age and with his background face growing up male in Miami: fights, gangs, detention, expulsion, arrest, drug use, drug charges, assault charges, time in juvie, death. Her sister had given Teresa a compelling way to protect him, a way to make him stand out against the forty other students in a teacher's classroom. One that didn't depend on his own excellence—something she'd sensed early on he didn't have in him. Not a deficiency, really—not if he'd been born white and elsewhere, which was all the more reason to protect him from becoming the kind of man this city churned out. All the more reason for Teresa, for as long as he'd been her responsibility, to protect Izzy from himself.

LUNCH

Izzy shows up at Rudy's workplace the day after their Seaquarium visit with a new black-and-white marbled notebook wedged under his armpit. He has, since the previous day's meal of leftovers, made several lists in it, some of them his, some of them Lolita's, though he doesn't know the difference. He feels compelled to do this old-school, to write everything out longhand rather than type it into his phone: holding his phone makes his hand ache with tiny vibrations; holding it close to his face sometimes makes his head pound. Sometimes when he holds it with both hands he registers a faint yet disturbing whizzing sound, like a wasp's drunkish hover near his ear. He thinks he can hear the phone's internal mechanisms whirring, working quietly; that's what he thinks the new noise is.

The next step on the notebook's very first and most important list is to get hired as a dishwasher alongside Rudy so they can then both quit (at Izzy's urging, of course) in a blaze of Scarface-like dirty-apron-throwing glory. Izzy actually has this step—getting hired—written down as Step Three, because Steps One and Two were finding a Manolo and taking his grad suit to get dry-cleaned because the jacket reeked of grajo and dirty water thanks to the Seaquarium trip. The Seaquarium trip he decides to leave off the list entirely; maybe they shouldn't have jumped ahead that far without more capital; they don't even have money for better suits yet. Acquiring a badass intimidating and totally illogical pet would require a list all its own. He wants to be precise, methodical. Quitting the dishwashing job doesn't even come until Step Six.

Here is the first page of his list as of that day:

1. Find a Manolo.*
2. Get grad suit dry-cleaned.†
3. Get hired as dishwasher.
4. Get hooked up with shady dudes who hire us for job of some sort.
5. Do job and <u>EXCEL</u>.
6. Quit dishwasher job the minute we feel tried by boss – walk out in a show.
7. Get paid by shady dudes/get hooked up with another (<u>BIGGER</u>) job.
8. Do that job and <u>EXCEL</u>.
9. Meet future wifey (aka, Michelle Pfeiffer – should hate me at first but not really).

The list stops there because Izzy wrote it in block letters and in permanent marker, and so his words are as big as his ambitions. He is completely aware that Step Four depends on chance, on luck. This bothers him immensely and also diminishes his respect for the film. In the film, Tony and Manolo are owed for a revenge murder they committed while being held in a refugee camp erected underneath an expressway; they killed a guy who, back in Cuba, had worked under Castro but who'd come to the U.S. on the Mariel boatlift and was stuck in the same camp, awaiting processing just like them. They'd been hired by some anti-Castro somebody who was now powerful in Miami—and whose brother was tortured by the now-dead Communist. A little later in the movie, Tony's new boss is thanking him for executing *that Communist son of a bitch*, and Tony tells him not to mention it, that killing that guy was fun. Or something like that—it came early on in the movie and Izzy didn't understand that the shadowy

---

* He wrote down this task and immediately drew a line through it, complete.
† Ibid. (Though technically he'd outsourced this one that morning to his Tía Tere.)

connections and loyalty stuff would end up being important, especially in Miami.

So now, ensconced in a booth at La Carreta on Bird Road, he
wonders how the hell he's going to orchestrate all this shit. That's
exactly the question he's come to the restaurant to investigate. That,
and Rudy had asked him to come by at the end of Rudy's lunch shift,
saying he had something to show him.

The Bird Road La Carreta is arguably the epicenter of Spanish-
speaking Westchester social activity, but Izzy is a stranger to Westchester: this version of Miami is a good twelve miles south of his own
experience of Miami-Dade County and one of its oldest communities;
home to Tropical Park and thus home each holiday season to Santa's
Enchanted Forest, the nation's most spectacular, most magical, most
visible-from-the-Palmetto-Expressway Christmas-themed entertainment park; defined in large part by Bird Road itself, the most traf-
ficked roadway in all of Florida outside of the expressways. The road
is home to both Bird Bowl—the place of employment at one time
or another (and for various weekly durations) of almost every teen
boy within a five-mile radius—and the business formerly known as
Ultrazone, an excellent laser tag facility whose longtime manager was
a pedophile (though his pedophilia was not the cause of Ultrazone's
end; for that we can predictably blame the economy; the building is
now home to an expansive and thriving sex shop). Izzy knows none of
this. He just thinks this La Carreta is louder and dingier than the one
he frequents up north. This one, to his eye, is too dim; the lighting
yellows the faces of the almost exclusively Cuban patrons. Everyone's
skin looks like various kinds of melted wax. The tables are too close
together, as if the restaurant hadn't anticipated the hub it would become. It smells deliciously of grease and bread and rice and other
starch-forward food items and disgustingly of bleach and old water. It
smells of raw and fried garlic. The patrons are essentially screaming
at each other but don't think of it that way; their voices soar over the
clang and clatter of active cutlery. Every table has too many plates
on it, as all elements of an entree come on separate vessels. People
swing their hips around and behind chairs, a sort of matador-dodge
on their way to and from their tables.

All the barking, the slapping, the nudging and pushing. The smell of eating. The place would remind Lolita of a seal pullout were she to see it for herself. Izzy opens a menu and imagines her there, her bulk filling the whole restaurant, her flukes smashing the tables behind her, her dorsal fin slicing through the ceiling. He decides to order fish because it's the only entree on the menu he feels compelled to eat—even though he's never tried their bacalao before.

The waitress comes over, hair pulled back so tight it's an automatic facelift. She is about the age his mother would be and she calls him mi amor and querido but she doesn't mean it, isn't even trying to sell it, saying it more to the pages she's flipping in her notepad, trying to find the next blank one. When he orders bacalao she looks up, her pen over the page, and says, Hoy no es viernes. She purses her lips, and Izzy goes back to the laminated sheets between his fists, sees the box on the menu with the days listed in it, how the specials coordinate with the weekday, and he's ordered Friday's dish on a Saturday. Izzy is not even that hungry, so he says forget it and asks for a plate of mariquitas. She takes in his fade and the notebook and how his phone is on the table (in an overblown case) rather than in his pocket where it belongs and she is angry that the puta of a hostess seated yet another too-young-to-tip deadbeat type in her section. Officially convinced that that puta is trying to destroy her, she decides she'll take it out on this boy's mariquitas, skimping on the oil and garlic and not waiting for a fresh-fried batch before bringing him the dregs of the bin just behind the kitchen's swinging double doors. Why even bother with asking what he wants to drink? It's water. These kids always want water. She's taken a full step away from his table when he says, Oh and a mamey shake! Un batido de mamey, por favor.

She doesn't know why this addition to the order takes her by surprise, why he suddenly looks like a little boy to her—the way his face opens at the thought of a beverage that really should count as dessert, like he was overjoyed that he could just order it and have it show up, but also like he was asking her for permission to have one, as if it were her job not only to bring it to him but to approve of him drinking it. And her heart breaks for him, at how the order comes in both languages, as if both sides of his brain finally kicked on at the thought of so much sugar and ice and fruit and milk. His mouth open, he waits with a whale-wide grin for her to acknowledge she's heard him. The silver filling his molars winks at her, and she imagines each one is a sweet tooth. She doesn't bother to write it down; she'll make the shake herself. She nods, tucks her chin to hide her smile, and takes the route she's perfected from that booth to the kitchen. She pushes the kitchen door right into Rudy.

He'd spotted Izzy's Nissan Altima, parked next to his own (technically borrowed, for now) Altima, in the lot when he'd taken out the trash, was about to do a lap through the dining room for dishes—not because he needed to, but because he wanted to see if Izzy was really there; he has a surprise for Izzy, some encouragement. Rudy sees from the waitress's face as he crashes into her that Magda's beef with the hostess must've flared up: Izzy must be seated in her section. Rudy puts his hands up surrender-style, lets her pass, then grabs an empty brown tub and a rag from the murky bucket by the door and heads out on the premise of dirty dishes.

He pretends to wipe down Izzy's table as they say hello. He scans the rest of that part of the dining room. His surprise—or more accurately, the guy who promised to hook him up with the surprise (the same guy who's hooked him up with the loaner Altima)—isn't there yet. He isn't sure the guy would come inside, now that he's thinking about it. He wants to check his phone but the hostess is watching, and he agrees with Magda that she's heinous and a metida and a snitch.

—You fill out an application yet, he asks Izzy.

—Not yet.

—Don't slack, they just hired another guy part-time. What's that?

He chins at the notebook the way Lolita would at a bucket of fish.

—Why don't you guys have bacalao every day?

—Do I look like the manager?

Rudy throws the dish rag into the brown tub and reaches for the notebook, flips through the pages, settles on the first one.

—What about the part where we talk to those guys we know? You left that out.

Rudy means the boat guys, the guys in the *system*. Something Izzy hadn't left off his list on purpose but still. He leans back in the booth, drags both his hands down his face.

—Shit, Izzy says, and he pulls the notebook from Rudy and draws a big *X* across page one.

—Bro, you could've, you know, added it in on the side?

—No, I want it to look perfect.

He rips out the page and starts rewriting the first two items on the next blank one deeper into the notebook. He again draws a line through each of them right after he places them on the page because they are, still, done. This perfectionist tendency is a new one, one he's borrowing, only recently spilling into his personality. It's the same one that causes Lolita to lunge at her trainers when she executes a behavior to the best of her abilities but it's still considered wrong and so she gets nothing—*nothing* for all the work and effort that goes into deciphering what more those holding all the food could possibly want from her. (This was before the advent of the neutral response signal, which cut down significantly on the aforementioned lunging. There is no such equivalent signal to calm guys like Izzy.) He writes, again in permanent marker, *Talk to the dudes who smuggle in Cubans on boats – figure out system – get involved in system* all as one item as the new number four, bumping down to number five the more arbitrary *Get hooked up with shady dudes who hire us for a job of some sort*. He looks at this new version of their list—now a whole step longer!—and is pleased with how much more agency they have in it; he doesn't know to call it that (to him *agency* means FBI, CIA, INS, et cetera), but he does feel a sense of control over his own destiny that the first version lacked in this step, meaning: he feels just a bit more like Tony Montana.

Near the end of Izzy's meal—the shake is fantastic and not too sweet; the mariquitas are too thick and lacking in garlic and mostly they're just shards of plantain rather than the long, translucent strips he'd been craving—Rudy sends over that afternoon's manager to interview Izzy despite him not yet having filled out an application. When the manager learns that he and his Tía Tere's families come from the same neighborhood in Havana, Izzy is hired without any further discussion. The guy doesn't even ask for references; he doesn't need them, says he believes in loyalty and trusts fate. He makes the incorrect though common assumption that he already knows this young man, that he was—no, *is* this young man; that this young man couldn't possibly be lazy or a thief or some kind of delinquent if they share that geography, that history. They've got a connection. They have to watch out for each other. This is what el exilio is all about. *This*, this right here, the guy says as he taps the table between them with a beefy pointer finger. Izzy nods and crosses his arms to keep from saying anything else about himself, intuiting just how far he'll be able to push this new boss or maybe anyone he'll come to work for or with—because he can intuit much more than he ever could prior to his visit to the Seaquarium—and, after signing some papers and being handed his apron, he begins envisioning his revised Step Seven: the spectacular glory of his exit.

Back at the Seaquarium, an entertainment staff member is reading a report filed the day before by the trainer who hosted the meet-and-greet after Lolita's Friday early afternoon show summarizing the audience's questions. He notes that one eager fan asked many of the session's questions. *Pushy kid*, he thinks. He determines the questions, though many, are no cause for alarm, and he rates the interaction highly in the scoring system.

The Miami Seaquarium changed ownership three years ago, in 2014, and so belongs to the Spanish-owned corporate entity Parques Reunidos. Which means Lolita also belongs to them. Everyone has been very worried about their jobs, about the future of the park in general. About Lolita. Will the park sell her? Give in to pressure to rehome her in some sea pen near Puget Sound? Like the park's previous owners, these new ones have chosen not to comply with the federal order that her tank be enlarged. The monthly fine for being in violation of the ordinance is like a kind of rent on the small tank, is the thinking. Much cheaper than renovating. Though nothing has changed much besides where the money comes from and where the money goes, the entertainment division has given every single Lolita show the highest possible evaluation since just the rumor of the sale surfaced. Just to be safe. To communicate the show's importance to the park. But Lolita knows she's gotten less precise in her movements over the last few decades, mostly in ways her trainers and doctors can ascribe to aging. She understands that the job means fish or no fish. She understands who's in charge when it comes to the fish—and only the fish, because she also knows that she can stop working for that reward at any time, refuse to perform, thus negating even the fish's power. But she knows such a protest would be met with investigations; they will assume she's sick, prod and inject her with antibiotics and narcotics, lace her food with supplements tasting bitter or of sand. She remembers Hugo, his protest, his suicide. She knows that she has to stay alive and loved in order to maintain any hope that she'll see her home again, her mother again. It's enough to keep her splashing. It's a choice she makes daily, hourly. According to what she senses during the trainer meet-and-greets, she is apparently a lucky girl. A lucky, lucky girl.

And luck is why Rudy is worried about how Izzy can't wait to quit a job he's had for barely ten minutes, why Rudy is reluctant for them both to eventually walk away from their paychecks; jobs can be hard to come by in this city. Don't forget this all started with Izzy losing one.

Don't forget this either: Tony Montana was never afraid of hard work, of getting his hands dirty, of making sure his particular brand of justice was served. There is a scene in *Scarface* where Tony watches someone murder his coworker by carving them into pieces with a chainsaw. Naturally, they are in a bathroom when this happens. The actor playing the victim is tied up in the shower, arms raised and slung over the curtain rod, mouth gagged, standing in the tub. He looks less scared than straight up shocked that he's about to be pruned down to a torso while still alive. Like a this-would've-been-my-last-guess kind of face. Tony mostly hides behind a shower curtain—and good thing too, because he is definitely in the splash zone. (And where is Manolo? Slow pan from the bathroom window to him out in the getaway convertible, distracted by a white woman in a bikini, a woman whose presence keeps Manolo from doing the one job he has, which is to come upstairs in five minutes, or presumably if he hears someone fire up a fucking chainsaw.) It's a tight shot—the only way to sidestep the artifice of the whole ordeal—and the director holds it, holds it. Can you imagine the person whose job it was to squirt that thick red liquid on Al Pacino's face with the kind of flourish (a whip of the wrist) that evokes death-by-chainsaw? Can you imagine the hilarity—instead of the horror—were the camera to zoom out just enough to capture the whole spectacle?

And seconds later, the wide shot of Tony in the street, gun pointed at the forehead of the man who'd wielded the chainsaw. It's the middle of the afternoon. No fewer than twenty white folks—the old kind who used to haunt Ocean Drive, long before it was the South Beach to which LeBron took his talents—watch in horror as one of these new Cubans shoots another spic at point-blank range, his body propelled backward by the bullet. They have no clue about the carnage they've missed, don't even notice that both men are already covered in blood.

The condominium where the chainsaw scene was filmed sold in 2009 for seven million dollars. How many layers of paint, do you think, did it take to cover that mess? What kind of person wants to walk into their bathroom each morning and think, *Ah yes, this is where the magic happened*? Even if you remodel it—turn that tub into a walk-in shower—in an effort to completely erase what happened there, the first time you cut yourself shaving and you see that trickle of blood: there's just no way the images don't come flooding back.

The least believable thing about this scene, what you might comment on as extras scramble away from Tony and his gun, isn't that it occurs in broad daylight in the middle of the street with no less than twenty witnesses, but that Manolo was able to so quickly and so easily, on Ocean fucking Drive no less, find a parking spot so close to their place of work.

Good employee parking: maybe the only thing that Izzy—now an employee of La Carreta—will miss about his time working at Don Shula's. That and the gym access. He definitely won't miss his manager, who's always taking time off to get her face sandblasted by her friend on the spa side of the resort and who always thinks Izzy is flirting with her when he is definitely not doing that. He texts her HEADS UP I QUIT, and she writes back LOL HEADS UP YOURSELF MACHO. He blocks her number, then deletes the whole thread.

Right there in the booth he slips the apron around his neck, grateful for its new and temporary weight.

THE CASTAWAY

As per the movie and as per being a human in Miami, getting a new job—and therefore the fact that their plan is indeed in motion—requires a celebration. Rudy figured this would happen and has thought ahead, much like any good Manolo would do: his surprise for Izzy shows up in an Escalade in the form of Danny, a guy four years older than Rudy who grew up in the same neighborhood but who'd moved to Gables by the Sea at sixteen, when his father's contracting business blew up—a year after his mother's death and months after his father's remarriage to the woman who'd been helping him run the business. And so Danny found himself the son of rich people he very much didn't like or trust who'd insisted on enrolling him in an all-boys Catholic private school he absolutely hated. He used the windfall to finance the adventures of his friends from the old neighborhood in an effort to resist becoming the kind of Miami person he'd despised, the kind mostly populating his new high school. Years earlier, when his father and stepmother bought him a Mercedes for his eighteenth birthday—a company employee delivered it, as they were vacationing on Marco Island—he'd let his aspiring street artist friends tag it up, covering it with spray-painted emblems they were still working to perfect. He'd filmed the whole thing and set it to house music produced by another friend and called it his first music video. He'd since turned his body into a similar canvas: when Rudy introduces him to Izzy in La Carreta's parking lot, Danny is shirtless but wearing a too-short floral vest, and so his haphazard collection of tattoos—a striped stylized eyeball, the wobbly face of a pit bull, various hearts and initials that Izzy can't decipher, a reptile slinking across his waist that Izzy guesses is an iguana but maybe is a dolphin—is on its usual display, shifting in and out of clear view thanks to the vest.

Danny deserves a novel all his own—which might be true of almost everyone born and raised here—and this one will in time return to him, as his seemingly unlimited resources, his fearlessness, his family's business connections coupled with his basically good heart, and his likely access to a speedboat may prove vital to Izzy. But this afternoon, he is just there as a favor to Rudy, whom Danny always remembers as a little brother type: an annoying but sweet kid with a mouth full of braces, a kid with a cute but maybe-too-young-to-mess-with baby sister, a kid too innocent-seeming to fall in with the more dangerous aspects of the neighborhood crew. Back in those days, Danny had always ignored him a little, hoping it would hurt him enough to make him keep his distance and feel himself left out and listen instead to his parents.

The White Diamond paint job of Danny's Escalade is coated from the doors down in layers of Everglades mud. Izzy thinks to look at the license plate but it is unreadable, caked over in a way that seems very intentional. They all slap backs and forearms in greeting and Danny asks, You ready?

Rudy rubs his hands together and holds them to his face. Show him, he says.

Danny presses a button and the Escalade's liftgate hisses open.

Except it keeps hissing even after it's all the way up. Inside, where the two rows of seats normally perch, are five or six alligators of varying sizes and in various states of frustration. They all have duct tape around their mouths but the two smallest ones—each just a couple feet long—seem to have snapped their jaws loose of it.

—I was already running low on tape when I caught those last minute, Danny says to the hissing. Fuck, they look *pissed!* Don't be mad, my babies!

He moves to the trunk and begins whisper-talking to them and making kissy noises. The untaped gators stand together at the trunk's edge, pink mouths open, the others piled behind them, more resigned to whatever fate awaits.

Rudy puts his arm around Izzy's shoulders and says, What do you think?

Danny reaches in and spins the smallest gator around by the tail and grabs him by the torso. He clamps his fist around its mouth and kisses its face. I love you, he says.

—These are – for me? Izzy says.

—Not exactly, Rudy says. I just want you to see what's possible. I texted Danny this morning that I might need a gator.

Rudy tugs his phone from his front pocket, finds the conversation, and shows it to Izzy.

Izzy reads: LOL DRIVIN BACK RT NOW WIT 6 IN MY TRUCK BRO WERE U AT

And while Izzy is impressed, he is also disappointed: anyone in this city can get a gator, delivered to their workplace, within six hours of asking for one. He knew this to be true even if he'd never seen it happen firsthand. Miami is a miracle: a dude who was once your neighbor could fill his Escalade with alligators; Izzy could get hired into the job that would launch his dreams just because of where he'd been born; a TV star had just become the president. (None of these men voted in the prior year's election, for different reasons—though if they had, they would've all voted for the crazy TV star not because they agreed with anything he said but just to see what would happen, thinking that whatever came to pass would never reach them down in Miami anyway. What did it matter to Izzy who was president? What Izzy thinks about the daily flooding, the fact that it's clearly getting worse: that's what happens when you live so close to the ocean; he knows to drive slowly through the bumper-high puddles that come and go with the tide. What Izzy thinks about the uptick in hurricanes, their increased size and strength: could be worse, he could've still been in Cuba when those fuckers hit; plus the storms always turn, more or less, and it's annoying how his Tía Tere keeps making him put up the shutters and then take them down for nothing but a lot of rain. What Izzy thinks of the embargo: who cares? What Izzy thinks of the travel ban the new president has enacted: nothing, he doesn't pay attention to the news; he's already here; he has a lot going on. What Izzy thinks of the fact that he can't easily return to his country of birth to see if anyone knew his mother, knows his father: nothing, he doesn't let himself think about that, not ever, and even when it threatens to come through, perhaps after a bad night's sleep or a nightmare, he would never think to connect it to something as far away and impossible as a president. He is twenty years old and has a car payment and an insurance payment and wants to move out of his Tía Tere's townhouse. What would a president have to say about any of that?)

—What are you gonna do with these, Izzy asks Danny.

—These are already sold to these people up in Southwest Ranches.

All three know this means extremely rich people, only some of whom make their money via methods that are currently legal, and so Izzy knows, for now, to leave it alone.

—They make pretty good pets, Danny says. For a little while. They like pools.

He takes the little gator and twists its body back and forth and sings *swim swim swim swim* while floating him through the air. And if they get to be too much, he says, you just call me up and I free them in a canal. I charge for that part too.

Izzy is doubting his choice of Manolo, something Tony Montana doesn't do until near the end of the movie. Not that this guy Danny could be it—this guy is in a league all by himself, already has his own schemes going and seems kind of touched in a way Izzy can't read and is mildly afraid of. But he's wondering now if Rudy's imagination is maybe too weak for this: can he really think bigger than your typical Miami ridiculousness?

Whatever you need, Danny seems to be saying, the gator back in the truck with the other captives. But is it Danny's voice he's hearing or is it a version of his own, pulsing too loud in his head? You know where to find me.

Are these men ultimately too entrenched in the imagined ethos of this city to see that ethos for what it is: a falsity they themselves might be perpetuating with their every move? How to find some way out, some way to whatever—whomever—might now be home? How to transcend all this, how to escape it. How to escape.

Whose thoughts are these, Izzy wonders.

ANTHROPO-SCENES

They have this in common: they are fascinated by screens. Lolita has just one but it is massive, hovering overhead. She watches and watches and watches and watches it, showcased behind the trainer's stage bisecting her tank. Seaquarium staff have sometimes, when tropical storm or hurricane warnings close down the park, even shown her whole films—documentaries, musicals, whatever DVDs a trainer had in a box marked DONATE languishing in their car's trunk. Her favorite though: she loves to watch the images of herself doing the performances, the edited footage of her routine playing on a loop between shows, and she spends that time talking to herself up on the screen, cheering herself on. She loves watching the footage so much that it works as a better behavioral reward than food, than physical touch.

Yes, she knows about Tilikum and the murder, the one that happened in a tank north of her. Of course she does. Every orca in a tank knows about it. They knew about it before it happened, could sense the idea floating around him and spreading for some time. Many of them, herself included, had even tried to discourage him from killing again—the woman was his third—in the only way they knew how, thinking and thinking and only the ones born in the wild like her and like Tilikum could still do this but thinking and thinking and thinking: Don't, don't.

He heard them but kept silent.

He'd done it before and none of them had suffered any more than usual for it, had they? Whatever came next would be worth it. Over and over again, their barely formed families, broken. His children—most of them he never knew—taken from their mothers.

He'd been captive long enough to absorb the sensation of—the need for—revenge.

And so he went for her hair, that fibrous mass they'd left behind long ago because what would it serve them, in the water? Nothing.

Nothing but drag.

The joy of her ponytail in his mouth—its tickle the last sensation he greeted as he took his final breath before joining her again in death.

Lolita had done what she could from down south but it wasn't enough and now no one is ever in the water with her, and her life is worse and better for it. She knows that trainer died—and that Tilikum also is now dead, his body hauled from the water instead of left to rest there—and she knows about the documentary and can hear on some weekends the chanting, that there are still enough people outside the park to fill wide swaths of the audience but no, they stay outside with their signs, trying to help her. So far, no one hears them either.

Like others in her situation, she has learned over time how to imitate the sounds her trainers make when they think they are imitating *her*. They think, *This is progress*. She laughs at them and they take it as her being in good spirits and she guesses that's true enough.

Between performances, her trainers occasionally switch out her footage with videos of wild orca, playing sounds she recognizes, sounds she knows as her family. And other times the sounds are familiar but what they say is incomprehensible to her, nonsense—the tones off, a language she doesn't speak though she wishes she did.

She faces it anyway and tries to understand.

Gibberish shoots in and out of her head.

Like Izzy, she is subjected daily to dance music, to bass. The singers of the songs that play during her performances have changed over time but not their backbones—not the beat, the *oonzt oonzt oonzt* the train-ers step and clap with, used to mark time in her shows. Lolita knows that at their core, all the songs are the same. Izzy, for all his exposure, has yet to realize this.

And then there's language. Both she and Izzy are losing the ones of their heart—neither of them by choice—the sounds they heard in the womb.

Hers she acquired before birth, as all sound reached her undis-torted and undiminished thanks to the medium of water. She was born already knowing which voice belonged to which relative, already knowing the story of herself and of her family and how those were the same thing. She emerged already knowing all the language she would need in that world.

Izzy's language came later, learned over time and by listening through the medium of air and breath. And before that tongue could be fully mastered, a new world demanded a new language, one nec-essary for survival, one that came at the expense of the other—the urgency of acquiring it something else Izzy shares with her.

But only one of them knows the silence that lingers in the loss. Only one of them knows to fear it.

A leashed tiger in a backyard, pouncing down the rock-face of its en-closure: the image from *Scarface* passes quickly as Tony and Michelle Pfeiffer, fresh from saying *I do*—he's still in his tux and she's in her wedding gown, bouquet in the hand not holding Tony's—run down to watch the animal. *She's a tiger*, Tony thought when he first met his now-bride, so the implication is it's a wedding gift. From whom to whom? Tony to Michelle Pfeiffer? When did Tony buy the tiger? When did he have that enclosure built?

The tiger stuff goes by so fast—without a shred of dialogue to explain what the fuck a tiger is doing in the newlyweds' backyard—because you're not meant to question it, to wonder at the logistics. It's meant to impress you, make you feel something—maybe worry, or a vague unease—but you're not supposed to think about it too hard, or at all. Your questions about how it got there are beside the point.

Pan away from the happy couple to the captive tiger headed their way; cut to a speedboat chopping across the ocean.

Izzy doesn't yet know this, but you can buy whales too. Every whale not born in a park was sold to a park at some point. Michael Jackson once tried to buy Keiko, the whale who played Willy in *Free Willy*, after the movie inspired people around the planet to demand Keiko's release; audiences did not like learning that Keiko was in fact still trapped in the same shitty tank that the fictional whale managed to escape. His offer was declined, but not because it wasn't generous.

What's the going rate for an orca? How much was Lolita? When Izzy finds out, he is surprised—after having seen Lolita with his own eyes—at how relatively inexpensive she originally was, even for 1970. A few thousand dollars. Now she's worth millions. She's worth thousands of tigers.

Izzy is at the library, flipping through a book. He learns that an orca moves her head from side to side to orient herself to whatever sound she wants to key into. That they can taste but they have no sense of smell. He doesn't check the book out—he doesn't have a library card and doesn't want to sign up for one. What's the point? He takes pictures with his phone of the pages he thinks will help him do . . . he doesn't even know what. Books are dumb and outdated and basically going extinct and not of any use to him outside of the information they contain, information he'd rather get through YouTube if he could. But most of the stuff he'd seen on YouTube about orca was really fucked up and involved some angry people and some sappy music designed to make him donate money. He isn't trying to be political here. He just feels compelled to understand, as best he can, how Lolita experiences the world. She of course works to keep him away from those videos, sending a kind of static his way, which he registers as the onset and then the sudden dispersal of a headache, something he attributes to the sappy music. She doesn't want him seeing those videos—like the one where those north of her tortured a pelican dumb enough to land in the tank, or the worse ones that eventually always get taken down like the trainers in the tanks. She doesn't want him to feel afraid. She doesn't yet want him to see what her kind are capable of doing. She allows nothing that could in any way keep him from coming to her.

And besides, there's so much that she's done that hasn't been caught on video—and even if it were, the footage could never capture the whole story.

A duck and her nine ducklings land one morning on the surface of the water across from her in her tank, and despite her enclosure being no deeper than she is long, she skims the concrete bottom until she is directly beneath them.

She knows from the instant they splash down that the ducklings are disoriented, lost. She knows that they are hungry, that their only recourse is to follow their mother anywhere. She knows the mother landed here for a reason.

Without making a single ripple, and starting with the duckling farthest from its mother in the line evolution and instinct have taught them to form, she rises so her rostrum is precisely under each one's webbed feet, and sucks each duckling into her mouth without even breaking the surface.

She's done this before, done this so many times, with so many different, suffering kinds of distant kin. She loves each of them, loves them all so much, even the mother, to whom she shows the same mercy.

She appreciates, with a kind of reverence, the flapping of their wings as they scratch against her tongue and teeth before she swallows.

Izzy wants to go back to the Seaquarium more than feels healthy. But Lolita isn't mentioned anywhere on the list in his notebook; she's nowhere exact in his plan. Where could she even go? Where could he possibly just squeeze her in? No, she would have to be the entire list. She'd be the whole notebook.

A new question floats into his dreams: is she asking him to rescue her?

Could she really be asking this of him? How? How could that even happen?

Ask yourself: How does Ahab track down Moby Dick in the vast, endless ocean given the limited technology available to him—why believe *that*? That incredible coincidence. How does Melville make it feel inevitable?

Here is how: by denying the reckoning for as long as he can. For pages and pages and pages.

CLIMATE CHANGE

HER MARK

An orca's response to an impoverished environment is essentially the same as a human's response to an impoverished environment on the level of brain chemistry and structure. The amygdala, the hippocampus, the hypothalamus: all are—in their attempts to process and cope with the stress of confinement and/or isolation and/or improper socialization and/or the general fucked-up-ness of their mind-numbing and overwhelmingly unnatural surroundings—atrophying and degrading in response. The science is perfectly clear, according to Lori Marino, the almost-perfectly named whale researcher cited in book after book about orca in captivity and in the wild. There are MRIs, cross-sections of orca brains and human brains. They have the same architecture—the same structures in the same places in relatively the same proportions. The only noticeable difference is a horrifying one, given the nature of captivity: in orca, all these structures are more complex, more highly evolved, than they are in humans. It is not absurd, by any stretch of the imagination, to conclude that they feel all sensations and memories more intensely than humans do, both joy and anguish. Imagine the smartest human being you know. Imagine the most sensitive human being in your life. Put them together and drop them in the ocean and you're maybe almost there.

So much of the human brain is devoted to language. How limiting, how pathetic even, to have evolved toward speaking rather than sensing. An evolutionary wrong turn: the limits of talking, the circling and circling in a tank too small—in a tank at all.

The day they took her: the details find her, carried in the memory of the water surrounding her; her mother and her mother's mother telling her which direction to go, sending her signals, but she didn't know what the sailors called the Labyrinth the way her mothers did.

How could she? Two years old that morning, maybe as old as four or six. It's been decades since she swam with those who would know her true age.

At the behest of her trainer, she rises up and into air—this way of looking she does for this trainer when asked, most times—and she feels the stands, full. She senses all the two- and three-year-olds in the crowd, as well as all the even younger ones. The very small ones can still hear her. This means something. But they are clearly too slow still: they laugh when she breathes, the simplest reason to rise. She feels herself become their first memory, the same way she could feel the trainers' heartbeats and respirations back when they were allowed to swim with her.

Gravity returns her fully under the water, into the memory of herself at two: her departure from who she was meant to be and into this other life. She feels the wrongness of her circumstances as a frequent throb near the front of her head. She feels it with every attempt to find something—anything—new in this circle of water, all of the ocean just beyond its sides. She senses the sea's proximity, tastes it now on the hands of those feeding her after the asked-for surfacing. The true ocean is on them—again the urge to drag each of them down, to spread the ocean somehow. The desire sings above her skull—just in front of it—as loudly as the absence.

Anger is desire accompanied by pain for retaliation against an unjustified act directed either against yourself or against those near to you. Would she not be justified, then, to consume this trainer whole? To consume them all? To consume only the soft, vital parts and leave the rest for birds to break down? There are some of her kind who eat only the tongues of their prey, doing this after drowning them. She contains the strength and know-how to drown whales five times her size. The water vibrates with this reality.

Sometimes there are shots and pills and she suspects it is poison but she welcomes it. Some of it makes the pain dissipate, the boredom relax its grip. Her keepers call the front of her head her *melon*. Her melon. She works each day to forget this for fear that the knowledge of it will make her bite down on those who pat her tongue in reverence after feeding her—bite down down down.

*   *   *

And where's Izzy? He's at home, his notebook in front of him, cross-ing out Step Seven on his list.* He's doing this in advance: barely a week has passed since he was hired to wash dishes alongside Rudy and already it's the day he's chosen as the one when they'll quit; the gas alone is costing Izzy more than the job pays; plus, having his hands under running water all day is making him feel crazy and over-whelmed. They're quitting during the Thursday dinner shift, and Izzy has a vague script for the blowout that mostly centers around the concepts of being a man and deserving respect. Although the shady dudes noted in Step Five of his revised list have not yet to his knowl-edge materialized, he figures it's okay to skip ahead because Rudy has made progress on Step Four and tracked down—thanks to the help of his much more organized and college-enrolled younger sister—a university-certified expert on the kinds of people who smuggle Cu-bans into the United States after arranging to intercept them at sea. Or something like that: they'll know more after the meeting tomor-row, which is why they plan on quitting that night; that, and they have lined up better temporary jobs working with Danny. Izzy has not yet realized that Danny counts as a shady dude—Danny's youth and kind-ness go against *Scarface*'s portrayal of shadiness—and that becoming part of Danny's fledgling iguana hunting business, which he is doing without a permit and so is illegal despite the city's dire need to deal with the invasive species, counts as the shady job from Step Five in which they can <u>EXCEL</u>. Izzy doesn't realize that in fact, and for now, everything is going as planned. His last day as a dishwasher is actually exactly on schedule, which means he should be meeting his Michelle Pfeiffer any minute now.

He wastes the rest of his early afternoon eating shit and scrolling through Instagram, looking at the profiles of people he went to high school with who all seem to be doing more with their lives. One of them is working a version of his old job at Don Shula's (he won't

---

*   Step Seven of the revised list: Quit dishwasher job the minute we feel tried by boss – walk out in a show.

last a month); another is having her first baby. He spends too long looking at the posts of this one guy, Alex Palacios, who has recently started his own business where he helps people start their own businesses. Somehow a church is involved; in his bio, the guy calls himself a *Godtrepreneur.* Izzy keeps scrolling through this guy's posts because he can't figure out how he makes money, or why the church looks so much like a club—is the church *in* a club? Is he a pastor but for businesses? He keeps looking, then feels a migraine's singe suddenly at his temple. It only subsides once he leaves the guy's profile and returns to his endless feed. Lulled back into a trance by the many images he thumbs past, he stops scrolling to watch a live video of a car haphazardly blocking a lane of traffic as smoke pours out from under its hood. Just after pressing the heart and typing five laugh-crying faces in response, he hears a *boom* sound in the video a couple seconds after he hears it in real life, and he realizes this car situation is happening a block or so away from him, right down the street. He has plenty of time before he has to meet up with Rudy to quit, so he slips on some sneakers—no socks because his Tía Tere isn't home to remind him it's gross—and walks to the corner, his own phone filming just in time to catch a girl emerge shoeless from the driver's seat.

ALL ASTIR

He wasn't supposed to meet her this way. He was supposed to meet her in the cavernous and high-ceilinged living room of a three-story mansion as she descends inside a completely superfluous glass elevator after being summoned by a soon-to-be-ex-boyfriend for a night out in Miami. He would notice her from his spot on a white leather couch, where he was presumably in deep conversation with one of the aforementioned shady dudes he had yet to actually meet. The shady dude's voice would fade out—he would not even notice that Izzy's attention was elsewhere, zooming in on the love of his life, a woman way too skinny for a guy like Izzy, being flaca pero like sick flaca, like cocaine flaca, which later you learn is not mean but accurate. Izzy imagined the rest of the scene: they'd head from the mansion to a club with the same name—though *that* Mansion closed in 2015, but this is Izzy's dream and he can reopen any South Beach club he likes for the purposes of serendipity or romanticism or any other concept he can't specifically name but understands intuitively—and he'd ensconce himself in a booth and at the shady dude's side. They're sitting VIP of course, though instead of some 80s song he knows but can't name blasting overhead, it's some trippy house shit, something with no words but enough bass to make his balls tingle. And he'd think it was the music—he'd blame the bass—but he'd know instantly upon seeing her that he'd just sealed his fate, like Tony on that night he sees Michelle Pfeiffer, even as she pretends not to notice a piece of trash like him, even as she turns up that pointy-ass nose and twitches from side to side and calls that dancing. He'd know, and then *she'd* know, and then they'd *both* know, and *you'd* know how it was all going to go down because of all the close-ups and cutaways and whatnot.

But that's not how it happens, not at all, as this girl—this woman—pata-sucias herself his way, crossing the intersection with no regard

for the traffic light overhead and trekking past tile-roofed houses en-
circled by chain-link fences, the front yards of each paved over with
concrete, converting them from grass to parking. Izzy worries he's
already gone too far off script when he meets her here on the side-
walk, weeds pushing up between every crack, her car's hood leaking
thick black smoke behind her, her body made up of the kinds of
curves to which he is genetically and culturally predisposed to love
and want. She is two or even three Michelle Pfeiffers glued together.
And though she is light-skinned like him, she's not white, which definitely makes things tricky, as it's a well-known and established fact
that Michelle Pfeiffer, in *Scarface*, is white. In short, this Cuban girl is
all wrong for the part, but maybe—he hopes—this is for the better.

He rubs the back of his head, relishing the feeling of fade going
from skin to spikes across his palm. It isn't yet long enough on top to
comb back, but at least she'll see he can grow a full head of hair.

—Excuse me, she says, though he is the only person close by not
already involved in the car crash or fire. Can I use your phone?

She holds up her own smashed screen. If another car caused whatever's happening to hers, it's long gone now.

—My name is Julisa, by the way. She puts out a hand for him to
shake and he wonders where she might really be from: a handshake
is not a Miami gesture. Where is his kiss on the cheek? Maybe, he reasons, she has a concussion and has forgotten the proper way to greet
strangers in this city. It makes her seem cold, almost, and white, and
suddenly she is again in contention for the role of his very own Michelle Pfeiffer, brought to him by a very literal accident. This, and the
fact that her name ends in an *a* and has the same number of syllables
and even letters as Michelle Pfeiffer's character Elvira, is enough to
make him toss out all the other disqualifications she'd accumulated
in the ten or so seconds she'd taken to walk up to him. He wipes his
hand on his shorts before reaching out. Her skin is as soft as you
think it is because girls like Julisa are serious about lotion.

—That's a pretty name, Izzy says.

The car crackles behind her.

—You think so, she says and it is not at all a question. My mom named me Julisa because she couldn't pick between Julia and Melisa and so she sorta went with both but also neither? She says she made it up. Like that she invented it.

Her hands shake and she hasn't yet blinked. Izzy knew two other Julisas in high school but is, thank god, smart enough to not mention that now. Behind her, little orange flames lick their way around the car's hood.

—Are you – okay? Like nothing's broken on you?

He grabs her hands and turns them palms up, and she lets the already busted phone slip out and down to the sidewalk, lets him run his thumbs across the palms she's had her tía read half a dozen times, always wanting a better future than the one their lines foretell—lines that she can't right then remember if they predicted this moment. She thinks to call her tía to ask and to her dead phone she says, Fuck.

—Call me Ismael, Izzy says. Actually, my friends call me Izzy.

She still hasn't blinked, so he says, I live right over there.

He points with his thumb down the block toward his Tía Tere's townhouse. Passing cars give her a wide berth, their tires rippling through the oily puddles seeping up from the asphalt before flooring it down his street.

Something snaps behind her, some tube or hose in the bowels of what was once a car, and the fire leaps higher as a result. They both duck instinctively and as she crouches and steps closer toward Izzy, she turns to look at the car, her hair sweeping long and wavy across Izzy's forearms, which he holds over his face. He feels his arm hair tingle in response. They aren't close enough to the fire for this to be possible, but that doesn't matter anymore: Izzy registers the tingling as a singe.

Fire fills the front seat and shoots up and out the windows. Izzy peeks between his elbows and sees that halfway down the next block, another dude is holding up his phone to the blaze just as he had; three other people are watching and filming from across the intersection. So Izzy hadn't been the only one out there. *Of all those options, Julisa picked me,* he thinks. *That has to mean something, right? I mean, what are the odds?*

The odds are one out of five: not exactly the longest shot, but let him sit in that wonder for a brief moment, so as to make the next coincidence less foreboding than it should be.

—My brother is going to kill me, Julisa says.

The screen in Izzy's hand lights up, a text from Rudy.

BRO CAN U DRIVE TO WORK TONITE MY SIS HAS DA CAR

ENTER JULISA

Oh, poor Julisa!—though you'd never say that to her face. She doesn't believe in pity. What does she believe in? Righteousness. Acts of service leading to salvation. Scars as proof of worth. Raised Jehovah's Witness and then Adventist and then nothing by an ever-searching chismosa-as-fuck mother who definitely loves Julisa's older brother more and an old-school cubanazo dad who mostly speaks in dichos and misremembered Bible verses, Julisa is newly single for the first time since her quinces. Why is she single? Because a week ago she finally dumped that asshole who pushed her out of the passenger seat of his car for the last time. Why was *that* the last time, after this woman—Julisa—had been shoved out this way on so many other occasions? *That* time was in broad daylight, in the middle of the freaking afternoon, not even a shadow to hide in. And while Julisa felt—for a variety of depressing reasons including and aside from her upbringing—that she could tolerate a shove or two a week from a guy who otherwise took decent care of her, a guy who—she was quick to say when asked—was good to her mother and his own mother, who had never *really* done much more than punch walls *near* her head and the occasional grab-her-by-the-back-of-the-neck-as-she-tried-to-leave because *Goddamn it do not EVER walk away from me when I'm yelling at you*; while Julisa thought that *decent* was all she deserved, she absolutely refuses to be humiliated right in front of the same bus stop she herself used every day of high school, landing on her ass, that familiar ground with its gravel biting into each of her hands as she tried to break the fall, all of it in full view of different versions of herself, all a year or two younger than her, all of them just home from the school from which she'd graduated a year earlier, all of them not even whispering when they said, Oh shit, is that Julisa? Not even hiding that they knew her. Julisa, pobrecita, might fear being single just as much as she once feared all that Mark of the Beast shit talked about in the Book of Revelation, but public humiliation she would not tolerate.

It isn't her fault that she's now standing shoeless on a Hialeah side-walk, her borrowed car magically bursting into flames—though okay, maybe she should've paid attention to all those dashboard thingies lighting up. Still, Julisa is Julisa, so she can't help thinking this is all happening for a reason: that she's boyfriendless, which hasn't been the case in forever, which means she's open to fate in a way she wasn't just a week ago. She looks at Izzy and is overwhelmed by the signs: the explosion behind her, the fire of it heating her back, pushing her toward him; the fact that his phone, which he's cradling in his hands as he types away, is in a pristine case that's as sturdy and strong as he looks; his immediate physicality and the manifestation in one body of every desirable attribute—the deep dimples, the wide nose, the blessing of his height, the immaculate jawline made of bone and not beard, the holy-spirit space between each of his teeth—checking off the major boxes on her list of the perfect guy. Does he have a job? Hopefully he has his own car. There's a gold chain around his neck, probably a cross at the end of it, and Julisa can work with whatever God he comes with.

She beats back the urge to tell him he is The One. She's been training for marriage since she was nine. It started when her mother had her send dried rose petals in the mail, in an envelope covered in hearts but with no return address, to a thirteen-year-old boy from church. It felt like action, like some way to channel that itchy feeling of a crush, and crush is certainly what the postal service did to those rose petals. That poor church boy probably thought some psycho had mailed him rose-scented dust, which is basically the truth if you take Julisa out of the picture and look at the adult who gave her the rose petals, the envelope, the stamp. How could her mother have encour-aged such an idea—or even come up with it? Because of *her* mother, and her mother before her. That kind of drama and manufactured intensity, that propensity to define yourself by who you're with and therefore constantly *needing* to be with or pursuing someone: it's a kind of inheritance Julisa hasn't yet escaped.

She watches the muscles on his forearms flex as he taps away on his phone. Backlit by the sun and therefore sporting what she decides is a legit halo, Izzy to her looks like the kind of guy to whom someone had once mailed rose petals. In a word: he was superhot.

And so is she, what with that car on fire behind her. Her brother's car, or technically: a car on loan from her brother's friend, Danny, which is the way she thinks of him now—as Rudy's friend, not hers. She is *not* looking forward to calling her brother to inform him that he needs to call Danny like immediately—that unfortunately she's given poor Danny one more thing to handle in this city. Keeping a healthy distance from Danny sometimes meant literal safety, but so did staying in proximity to him; she learned this careful dance years ago, and she doesn't know where being semiresponsible for a car fire will put her. What she does know: it won't help her to get caught here looking all thirsty for Izzy, even if the universe obviously sent him to be the love of her life.

More neighbors exit their homes to watch as whatever fueled the explosion burns out and the fire dies down a little, no one at all calling 911 or the cops. Why bother when the show will be long over—and Julisa long gone—by the time they'd arrive? She already feels removed from the immediacy of the scene. Instead, she's watching this story—the story of how she met her husband—unfold, saving only the good details, altering and improving the less convenient ones. Like: she's not sweating in the version she'll tell; she's straightened her hair instead of having it in the natural waves that she figures look super frizzy given the humidity; her eyeliner is perfect; she's definitely wearing shoes; she will have already lasered off every non-head hair on her body instead of feeling the ones on her arms and the backs of her legs searing a little from their recent exposure to flames. She tugs a waiting liga from her wrist, ties back her hair, and decides to keep looking at Izzy so that he'll be taken by surprise at the intensity of her stare once he's done texting whoever the fuck he's texting right now while there is literally both a car on fire and his future wife in front of him. She is asking God and/or Jesus and Yemayá and Oshun and Beyoncé and the ghost of Celia Cruz to make him look up from the phone and down at her to see his destiny.

Izzy steps back without realizing it: a response to Julisa's energy, the telegraphing of a life she's trying to send his way. It's like the new migraines, but instead of his right temple, this feeling originates at the base of his balls, meaning: this response isn't necessarily Lolita's doing, as it's from his balls that his decisions typically originate. *All I have in this world is my balls and my word, and I don't break 'em for no one.* So it is written in the scripture of *Scarface*, one Julisa knows well despite the stronghold the Jehovah's Witnesses had on her childhood, despite the Adventists—who came later, spanning her adolescence— shunning secular entertainment. In this county, in this zip code, Tony Montana is a Holy Ghost, his words ever-hovering between Izzy's teeth and airing in moderately edited form on cable TV every weekend of their childhood, as omnipotent as the water rising beneath them.

And what had Izzy grown up believing? What Word might he not, like his own balls, break? His Tía Tere has raised him vaguely Catholic, though she often invokes God in a way that makes Izzy think the Lord is always watching, always waiting for him to fuck up: more like a cop than any kind of Father he would want. The Orishas she keeps altars to in her part of the townhouse always seemed more approachable to him, more willing to accept him as he was. His Tía Tere has kept this aspect of her faith mostly to herself, but he's always felt those altars winking his way, tugging at him, reminding him of where he came from. Izzy feels a similar tug now at the sound of the last of the car's glass shattering and looks up from his phone (YEA BRO MY WHIP IS GOOD, he's texted back to Rudy). The fire behind Julisa, the smoke: she looks like an offering not yet singed, and just as he did the first and only time he took Communion exactly one year after his arrival in the United States, he opens his mouth to receive it.

AUTOFICTION

You never told me you had a sister, meng, Manolo says to Tony after seeing Gina for the first time, and Al Pacino cuts him off before he can finish the sentence, lashing out with all the spittle he can muster some defensive nonsense, some possessive pronouncement of how very off-limits his little sister is. Manolo, in a subplot kept secret from both Tony and the audience, pursues Gina anyway, and moments after Tony shoots Manolo dead, Gina reveals that she and Manolo got married the day before, unbeknownst to Tony/the audience. Tony shoots Manolo when the latter opens the tremendous door to a Coconut Grove mansion—one that Tony learns Gina has been disappearing to night after night, bringing up yet another subplot kept from Tony and the audience: that of how said house was acquired. Did Manolo buy it for Gina? Did they buy it together? If so, was it *jointly and severally* (because they were not yet married) or did the closing come on the same day as their wedding (so much paperwork!) and thus they purchased it as a married couple—which means ownership of the house automatically transfers solely to Gina the second Manolo dies in the foyer? Was it new construction, and if so, did they still opt for a home inspection? Did Manolo pay cash so as to avoid the hassle of an appraisal and/or a bank loan? What did he tell the home insurance people about his line of work? Were they required to carry flood insurance and hurricane insurance and sinkhole insurance and all the other insurances required of most homes in Miami nowadays? Is there a trampoline on the property—insurance agents always want to know about trampolines. If Gina, as the property's sole owner post-shooting, were to sell it, would she have to disclose Manolo's death, since technically it occurred just inside the house's entrance? Because we remain mostly in Tony's point of view, these questions and many others—particularly regarding early 1980s Miami real es-

tate acquisition—are left unanswered. Which is a shame, because all
the movie's writers had to do to get them talking about this or really
anything complicated was put them in a car together and have them
get stuck in Miami's spectacular and ubiquitous traffic.

What can you say about Miami traffic that hasn't already been
said before? Maybe this: it is a missed opportunity. All that time to
think and reflect! All those hours to practice just accepting what
is rather than trying to fight it with those ultimately useless lane
changes and the opportunistic cutting off of the guy who took a
second too long to look up from his phone! All those chances to
practice connecting with your breath! Imagine how centered you'd
feel if you could reimagine Miami's expressways as infinite-seeming
asphalt yoga mats and your front seat as a sanctuary in which to
practice mindfulness!

This figurative veering is an example of Miami's particular brand
of autofiction: fiction about or involving cars. *Vroom vroom* and *beep
beep*, swerve and crash: a story where you're constantly changing lanes
and you never, ever use your turn signal.

Engine

As they walk to his Tía Tere's townhouse so he can grab his keys and
drive Julisa home (should he give her his shoes? He ignores the impulse to offer them to her), neither has figured out that Rudy already
connects them. The question is: as *Manolo's* sister—a character that
doesn't exist in the movie—what role will Julisa ultimately come to
inhabit? Is she a Gina or a Michelle Pfeiffer? These are the movie's
only two notable options, with neither getting much of a backstory
or much of a story at all: Michelle Pfeiffer, who's introduced first and
eventually gets to tell you she's from Baltimore, conveniently disappears after the *her womb is so polluted* dinner scene; Gina almost makes
it to the end of the movie before being gunned down in its final
scenes while wearing a very silky but blood-smirched robe. Neither
option feels right, and so Julisa's destiny remains as hazy as the smoke
lingering over the intersection as they drive through it and then away
from it, the powerful A/C of Izzy's car blasting them both.

Dashboard

Once Izzy has successfully merged onto the Palmetto, Julisa asks again to borrow his phone. He fishes it out of his pocket and unlocks it—no weird tingling feeling this time, for now, thank god—and hands it to her. She starts dialing.

As she holds it up to her ear, she says, Okay *weird*. You have my brother's number in here.

On his end, Rudy yells, Izzy, bro, dímelo, loud enough that his voice reaches the driver's seat, and that's when Izzy realizes exactly who this is at his side.

—No dumbass, it's me, Julisa says. Bro, I don't care, explain it later. Listen, you have to call Danny.

Izzy leans forward and turns the A/C nob to quiet the fan. It's not that the car is already all the way cool inside; it's that now that Danny's been mentioned, he's trying to listen.

—No, like *now*, Julisa says. Yeah, the car. It's – I don't know what happened but he probably does. I guess tell him I'm okay.

She gives Rudy the intersection so Danny can head over and do whatever he does and says she's heading straight home. She doesn't mention how she's getting there or who's driving before hanging up on him.

She keeps the phone in her hand before remembering it isn't hers, then passes it back to Izzy without saying thank you. Has her brother mentioned anything about this guy? The answer is: nope. She doesn't know, for instance, that both men plan to quit their dishwashing jobs that night. She doesn't know that her brother has already reached out to the professor she found online for him when he'd asked, that he already plans to drop by his office. She only knows her brother's been home less the last couple weeks, seems more serious than usual. Dressing better too. Their mother had asked Julisa if she knew whether Rudy had started seeing anyone, and she'd answered: If he is, she's making him pretty miserable.

Izzy places his phone in the cup holder, knowing the case will protect it from all the dust and crap in there. Each of them is quietly processing the coincidence of the connection, and each sees it as a monumentally good sign. They each choose to ignore the more flagrant and ominous sign from earlier of the car being obliterated by inexplicable flames.

—So you're Rudy's sister, Izzy finally says. Older or younger?

—Younger but barely. I'm almost nineteen. How do you know my brother?

He considers how much to confess given that she's not supposed to appear in his plan until way later—currently she's Step Ten—and he doesn't know if explaining the Scarface thing is a wise move when there's still so much to cross out between now and her. He waits to see if some smart thought comes to him, but all he gets is silence. So he asks himself what Tony would do here and—because he mistakenly thinks it will impress her—decides to say, You know Danny, huh? Me and your brother start working with him Sunday.

She stares straight out the windshield and says, Nobody works *with* Daniel.

Izzy doesn't know what to say to that, except that it's the kind of snippy little comment he remembers Michelle Pfeiffer making, usually right to Tony's face: *Don't get confused, Tony, I don't fuck around with the help.* It should be another awkward silence, but Izzy is thrilled at the perfection of the moment, how gracefully (albeit unwittingly) she's walked into her role. He doesn't even think to ask her what she means—the impulse blocked before the question can materialize. Instead he says, I'm twenty, by the way. So what happened to your shoes?

She sucks her teeth and says, Oh my god I was wearing chanks but I can barely drive in them so you know I always take them off. Shut up, I know it's illegal to drive with no shoes.

—It is? he says but she doesn't stop to clarify or confirm.

—Anyway they're back on the floor of the car.

—Sorry to tell you but those shits are melted.

He winks at her, and she twists in her seat and smacks him on the arm with her purse—which she did manage to grab from the car before running out—just like Michelle Pfeiffer would do if and when she's stuck in a car with Tony.

Like Tony, Izzy smiles inappropriately to himself, though he stops short of saying aloud, *I like you, I liked you the first time I laid eyes on you. I said, She's a tiger, she belong to me.* Like Tony, he feels a watery certainty wash through him, again mostly in his balls, which he adjusts through his shorts when she refocuses on the crawl of cars ahead of them. It would be a perfect moment if not for the traffic.

This afternoon's immense traffic jam—no different from any other day on the Palmetto—seals Julisa to Izzy, the two of them unable to escape the forced proximity of the front seat and its accompanying silence, because even though Izzy has music for days on his phone and even though they have Miami's beloved stations broadcasting their traffic jamz, Izzy thinks his speakers have started to emit this subtle buzz that he cannot tolerate. He flicks the radio on and off so she can see what he means, but Julisa doesn't hear it, because it's not really there: this is another Lolita artifact newly wedged in his water-logged senses. Julisa thinks the speakers sound fine but has been trained to agree with anything critical a man says. So, yes, oh my god she hears it too! The sizzling! And yes, she agrees, it's so annoying as to be borderline painful! No way they can listen to that! He better get it checked out. She knows a guy who'll fix it cheap, maybe even for free depending on what Izzy can do for him in return—Izzy did say he's working for Daniel, right?—but she keeps that knowledge to herself for now.

And then she offers: I guess we could just, you know, talk?

Izzy laughs. He says, I thought that's what we were doing. Talking.

He intends it in the flirty way, meaning: *talking* as a precursor to *dating*, to *going out*. As in: *Me and this guy, we've been talking a couple weeks now and I think it's getting serious.* She feels the seat of the car warming beneath her and wonders if he has heated seats.

—Okay, so we're *talking* talking? What do you want to know?

—I think, he says, that I want to know everything about you.

He says this without looking at her, more to the road than to her—he barely registers what it means. It's not what he would consider a smart thought like the ones he's having lately, but it's an honest one that, if he were fully aware of its escape, he would've rather kept from coming out of his mouth.

Julisa catches him swallowing hard, and in the bounce of his throat, a flash of him as a little boy passes between them, fills her.

She's sure she senses it: some innocence or loss, something she knows never to ask about. She has to wait to hear it. She has to earn it. She believes she is worthy, and this is why she can instantly give him everything: her life's history; a monologue about her job he only grunts at in response; her whole heart.

Backseat

Julisa works part-time as a dispatcher at El Dorado Furniture. It's fine, it's easy, except these days the job has become borderline unbearable because her boss—a genuine born-in-Switzerland Swiss guy named Klaus—started dating another dispatcher, Martha. Martha has plans to kill Klaus and take over his job while wearing his skin like a mask, Julisa is sure of it. She's dreamt it enough times to be bored by the image of Martha's eyes peering through his face's eyeholes, Martha's lips where his mouth used to hang. The other dispatchers all talk in the break room, or out back with the warehouse guys, about how gross they are together. Klaus is new enough to Miami to think Martha is really from here but she isn't: she's from Ohio, or Oregon, or some other *O* place she has no problem dumping for her new adopted identity. And adopted is what she is—she's told each of her coworkers this at one point or another as an excuse as to why she doesn't speak Spanish despite having a Spanish last name. It's not really mine, she says, though she used it to get the job in the first place. Tells people her adoptive parents were *Latins.* Julisa cracks jokes about her parents wearing togas. The real joke's on Klaus for assuming she was bilingual based on nothing but a last name. Joke's also on him because everyone knows Martha is the kind of psycho who considers being a dispatch manager at El Dorado Furniture a thing to strive for. She's fifteen years older than every other dispatcher—all of them still in high school or college—because the others see the job for what it is: a way to pay your bills. *We're meant to move on—that's why the raises are shit.* Klaus was installed by some faceless person at corporate, shuffled and brought over from some en-route-to-being-shuttered warehouse. Why they thought a white Swiss guy would be a good fit for the Miami Gardens warehouse was beyond every employee's thinking but Martha's, the only white americana (last name notwithstanding) working in dispatch, and so she was quick to align herself with him under the pretense of being *a bridge* between him and his staff. She never smoked weed on break like the rest of them; she'd suggested Klaus aim the security cameras at the places she knew they gathered to do it. Klaus rewarded her for doing his bidding: a new headset; a desk with a better view of the rest of the warehouse; sad shit the job trained people to want. The other dispatchers and warehouse crew learned the hard way not to trust her, though honestly, no one ever did, because if there's one thing that will get you hated fast in Miami, it's being a phony in the heart beating behind the fake tits (tits that are, paradoxically, celebrated and deeply coveted by many, as fake tits are not considered indicative of the more offensive variety of fakeness being discussed here). Julisa has an ancestral gift for sniffing out a fake, and from the beginning she kept her distance from Martha. She'd marked the day in her journal—a full month before it happened—when she'd woken from a dream that predicted Klaus and Martha's inevitable alliance, the dream coming the night after witnessing Martha refuse sugar for a bitter cafecito brewed in the break room, saying she preferred her espresso unsweetened. *The actual fuck is wrong with her,* whispered a coworker into his own tacita. Another: *Expresso? Bitch, this is café.*

Julisa had predicted this too: Klaus would move on—transferred elsewhere maybe, or more likely, an aneurysm or heart attack given his addictions to steak and stress—but Martha would be there forever, queen of that tiny, nothing kingdom. Martha might've stood for everything Julisa worked to avoid, but Julisa knows enough to keep that feeling bottled up inside her—that is, until it all comes pouring out in the silence of Izzy's car as the traffic drags on. Why is she telling him this? She wants him to know she has ambitions as big as his, even if she doesn't know what they are just yet. She'd planned to quit El Dorado after graduation, but the job paid better than the work-study FIU had offered her and then rescinded anyway when she decided to enroll half-time. Sitting there in Izzy's car, she wonders what would happen if she just stopped showing up to work—how long it would take Martha or Klaus to admit that what they'd come to see as their whole lives was little more than a thing to get through and past for someone like her. Someone who knows that she wants and can take on much more. Someone who is sitting next to a cute-as-hell guy she hopes is listening, *really listening*, a guy she hopes won't make some dig at her for talking too much about stupid, irrelevant shit—the stuff of her life, which she's been trained by everyone from her mother to her god to discount. And now she's let it out.

The car growls beneath her as its bumper slides up toward the one in front of it.

—It's cute though, Izzy says. How that Martha bitch and her Swiss Santa think they're some kind of power couple. Sad for sure, but also cute.

He'd just read her mind.

More autofiction: Izzy's gaze is still on the bumper ahead of them, riding it daringly close. If he looks away, he'll hit it—they both know that. His hand rests on the stick shift, and Julisa slides her hand over his for just long enough to feel the car's engine rumble up through their fingers, begging for more from the gas pedal. They inch forward. The traffic goes on for miles.

—Fucking Palmetto, she says when she pulls her hand away.

—I know, right? Tell me about it.

Windshield

When talking about expressways, you call them by their names: the Dolphin, the Palmetto, the Don Shula. More specifically, the east-west expressways have names, though the Palmetto runs north-south until it hits Miami Lakes and makes a wide turn east, also given a name—the Big Bend—curving and carving out neighborhoods on each side with drastically different property values. Where I-95 meets the Palmetto and the Florida Turnpike also has a name: the Golden Glades Interchange. Even I-75 has a name for a good stretch of it: Alligator Alley, named for the gators easily spotted on either side as you speed by, because that eighty-mile stretch cuts straight across the Everglades, from the city of Sunrise to Naples.

The Julia Tuttle. The Rickenbacker. The Gratigny. You call them by their names because it's rude to not know the name of something you spend so much time riding. In this way and many others often ignored by cousins along the coast out west—like the Los Angeles set mostly sticking to their numbers—Miami is arguably a very classy place if you're looking for the upside to this city being the birthplace of Pitbull. In this way and others, Miami teaches you to at least acknowledge the bodies you use, to name and respect your enemies and charges. Here, you know your particular stretch of the Palmetto as well as—or maybe even better than—you know your own self. And like your best self, the Palmetto is also and always a work in progress.

In *Scarface*, the overpasses under which are built the tent cities housing Cuban refugees are all located in Los Angeles, another city ripe for autofiction, though their expressways are called *freeways*, whatever that means. It's Miami's own fault that the vast majority of *Scarface* wasn't shot here: the city commissioner at the time, a Cuban exile himself, did all he could to block the permits needed to start production, and when his attempts eventually failed, the Cuban community picked up the protest and purportedly made a lot of noise. The filmmakers got about two weeks' worth of filming done before deciding that most viewers—meaning: viewers not from or familiar with Miami, meaning: their true intended audience—wouldn't care enough to notice the differences between South Florida and Southern California anyway, so they packed up and left, sneaking back into Miami months later for some additional exterior shots to splice in and give it that authentic artificial Miami flavor.

Fat raindrops splatter across Izzy's windshield. The rain comes out of nowhere and will be gone just as fast. He has his wipers on at their highest setting but he can still barely see through the water—not that he really needs to, given the traffic's crawl, and given the strange comfort the water brings him, like he's finally safe to speak without second-guessing himself. He glances up to watch the rain smear and slide across the glass of his moonroof. He feels submerged, wonders if this is how Lolita experiences rain. The answer: yes and no. He nods, glad that he opted for the moonroof package back in 2015 when he leased this car, understanding only now this upgrade's true value.

Brake Lights and Hazards

Izzy no longer has to ask Julisa where they are headed: he already knows where Rudy—and thus Julisa—lives. As they inch through

the rain toward the exit that will spill them back into side-street traffic, talk turns, as it naturally must between young people late every
spring, to the Miami-Dade County Youth Fair. Have you been yet?
They each ask the other, and they both answer: *No, I never go the first
two weeks, too many field trips with too many fucking little kids*; blah blah
blah; excuses, excuses. Neither of them admits it, but both are surprised that the other hasn't gone yet. For Julisa, the real reason is
her recent breakup, as the Fair has always been, for her, a place she's
gone as part of a couple. Izzy's real reason is that he's been a little
broke since the end of his Pitbull days and also he's had absolutely no
fucking desire to go until right now.

   The Dade County Youth Fair: It Just Keeps on Getting Better! This slogan, used by the Fair in the 1990s, contains an essential semihidden
truth: that the Youth Fair needed improvement. Julisa's parents for-
bade her from going at night after they witnessed a stabbing at the
Fair back when they were teenagers, a story they may have fabricated
as a way to justify their generally overprotective approach to parent-
ing. But anyone who's attended in the last few years might rightfully
ask: how could it possibly be any better?! The 2017 version of the Fair
already has arepas, funnel cakes, candy apples and caramel ones, jerk
chicken, empanadas, pinchos, chicharrones, a *beer haven*, a *Zen wine
garden*, banana Nutella spring rolls, pork chops on sticks, pig races (to
avoid becoming pork chops on sticks), a cafecito station sponsored by
Café Bustelo, and fried alligator. Okay, maybe it would be nice if management could somehow stop people from spitting off the Sky Ride
that traverses the fairgrounds. Maybe the petting zoo could smell less
like shit. Maybe no (or at least fewer) stabbings. Maybe there could
be some acknowledgment somewhere of how the Tamiami Park's fairgrounds, where the Fair has sprung up like Brigadoon for over six
decades now, were used as an impromptu processing center during
the Mariel boatlift, staffed almost exclusively by Cuban volunteers,
much like at the Orange Bowl—both sites missing from *Scarface*, as
is the fact that INS and the federal government initially failed to mo-
bilize any ground-level response whatsoever to the boatlift and so let
these makeshift centers stand and then had FEMA (FEMA: because
a human disaster is also a natural disaster) take them over only once

they were firmly in place and functioning smoothly. Imagine that the ground under the Tilt-A-Whirl or the Gravitron is where your best friend's tío got processed as a potential new U.S. citizen. Imagine Tony Montana's interview happening not in a nondescript interrogation room with a portrait of Jimmy Carter ominously hanging in the background—where's the visual interest in *that?*—but instead in front of the vomit-inducing and extra-rusty-looking Zipper ride, puddles of puke dotting the hard-packed land. Land that long before that moment was home to the Miccosukee, the Seminole, the Tequesta, the Okeechobee. Maybe some acknowledgment of that too, a plaque you pass while you're strolling around gnawing on a turkey leg and wearing a just-purchased cap or bandana, your name freshly airbrushed in black and glitter in a cursive font made possible only by a deft hand adorned with pink-and-white acrylics. *Marisol,* the cap says, or maybe *Carlos* or *Lazaro,* or maybe just your nickname: *Mari, Los, Laz.*

A cap like that already sits smashed at the bottom of Rudy's closet. Same goes for Izzy, his reading *Izzy,* not *Ismael.* There's a sample one in the booth where you get them made, perpetually on display: it says *Lolita,* the city's inside joke.

Trunk

At a stoplight, Izzy marvels at the sprays of water arching out from the puddles hugging the curb, wet wings that shoot up from the asphalt whenever a car rolls through them full speed. He's never before noticed their beauty. He's not the poetic type, though he did win a creative writing award through his school when he was eleven, just four years in the U.S. He'd written a poem about Cuba in English that, truth be told, was a rip-off of that old song calling Cuba a pearl lost in the sea. It was supposed to be a haiku but he'd been off by one syllable in each line. Still, he'd won a Youth Fair–branded pen-and-pencil set, which he'd never used but still has in the box it came in. The pen, he has no idea, has long since dried out.

Junior year of high school, classmates of Izzy's who'd won those same pens back in the day started working together to write TV shows and movies, their daydreams filling notebooks as creativity exploded out of them. As a senior project, those classmates wrote a book of limericks making fun of—or maybe honoring: maybe there isn't much difference when the object of scorn/admiration is the 305—their hometown. Izzy kept hovering around them, suggesting lines and topics, wanting to make these guys his friends, wanting them to think he was as smart and clever as they were. But because he was not, he didn't notice that they never wrote down a single thing he said. They'd nod and laugh, pens hovering over their notebooks. This wasn't a mean crew of guys—honestly a rarity in Miami's public schools—but they needed to signal somehow that his contributions were mediocre at best. They could smell on him that he was soon to be the kind of Miami guy who'd try to make his living impersonating Pitbull, chase after *Scarface*. He was not the kind of guy who could invent or imagine anything of his own, as much as he wanted the admiration that came with creation.

His lack of depth (which has nothing to do with the trauma he's endured), his basic-ness, his willingness to be so much of a type: it's exactly what makes him open to Lolita. Exactly why she knows he needs her. Like Tony Montana, Izzy has no creativity, and so he becomes who he's around, a mirror, and this weakness compels her to help him.

Behind him there's honking—the light's turned green.

Transmission

Izzy parks in the driveway. They wait with the car still running for the rain to lighten up enough that Julisa can sprint to her front door without getting soaked. Once it does, she thanks him for the ride, puts her hand on the door latch, and says, Don't worry, my brother's not home.

—I wasn't worried about that, he says.

And it's the truth; he'll be back at this house in a few hours to pick up Rudy, then they'll drive to work and they'll quit pretty much right away so as not to potentially forfeit any additional pay should their boss keep their last (and Izzy's only) paycheck. The thrill of that night's planned exit has evaporated from Izzy during this drive; he knows exactly how it's going to go, and now it's just a thing to be got through, barely worth the line on his list. What he's now daydreaming

about—the new and much more abstract source of his excitement—
is the Fair's White Water ride, how there's not much to it aside from
dropping you down and getting you drenched. Would Julisa ride it
with him? How many times before it seemed weird?

—Good to know, she says. She tells him her phone's insured, she'll
have a new one in no time. She gives him her number, double-checks
for him that he's correctly typed it into his phone.

As he takes it from her and pushes it back in his pocket—the tingling there again but now oddly comforting—he finally, finally asks
Julisa what Lolita's been leading him to express ever since the onset
of the downpour, when the knowledge of the place—a possibility—
reached her: So can I take you to the Fair Saturday?

—You promise to buy me one of those hats with my name airbrushed on it?

—Yeah no, he says. Then he thinks better of it—remembers the
glitter and the elegant wet spray of letters—and says, No yeah, yeah,
of course.

MONSTROUS PICTURES

In Izzy's defense, Rudy never declares his little sister off-limits, as Rudy wasn't raised to conflate possessiveness with protection and has never subscribed to that particular brand of machismo. Lest you mistake Rudy for some kind of feminist though, know that his reasons come from his respect not for Julisa and her autonomy but for Izzy and his ambitions: Izzy is his brand-new business partner, goes his thinking, so why would Izzy make everything weird right from the beginning by going after Julisa? Plus, it doesn't enter Rudy's mind that anyone might find Julisa attractive because that's his sister and therefore that's super gross. Plus, he thinks his sister is a crazy bitch— though of course only Rudy can call her this, and even though they aren't really close anymore, if anyone else were to call her a crazy bitch, he would of course have to fuck them up bigtime, enlisting the strategic assistance of Danny and possibly others to help him in said fucking up; *nobody* talks shit about his little sister but him. Plus, as far as Rudy knows, Julisa still has a boyfriend—a guy Rudy considers a total piece of shit and whom he severely dislikes and so avoids at all costs—and Julisa's not a cheater; you can thank her religious upbringing and her tendency toward unquestioned devotion to her partners for that characteristic. So until Rudy learns that that guy is out of the picture—a status change he'd more likely hear about from their mother than from Julisa herself—Rudy has no reason to think that Julisa is on the hunt for her next soulmate. The possibility of a Julisa-Izzy mash-up is so far from Rudy's mind that when he brings up the previous day's phone call, he blames the fact that Izzy's name came up on his caller ID when it was really his sister calling on some quirk of his phone.

—Weird, right? he says, genuine—as if the weirdness of a caller ID mix-up supersedes the weirdness of a car fire and the reliance on

94

Danny to handle it. Rudy hasn't mentioned Danny or the fire at all this morning as they drive to the University of Miami, and he very obviously avoided the topic during last night's drive, both to and from work, both before and after they quit, which makes Izzy think that asking about Danny would make him look weak and put Rudy in a position of authority over him. So Izzy lets the phone confusion stand, saying, Yeah, bro, that's super weird. My phone's been acting strange too.

The second half of this response isn't really a lie, not for Izzy. He decides the half-truth erases what is otherwise his first instance of keeping something crucial from his Manolo, something that never happens in the movie (until it's too late) and so it's something Izzy wants to undo as soon as it makes sense to do so.

Now isn't that time: they've just arrived at the University of Miami and are driving around, trying to figure out the parking situation. The plan is to meet with the expert Julisa had tracked down for Rudy in exchange for letting her borrow the car: Herbert *Hibertico* Colón, the newly minted Goya/Café Bustelo/Navarro Pharmacy Chair and Professor of Cuban American and General Hispanic Studies. Izzy and Rudy would feel more at home on FIU's campus, the public university only thirty minutes from Hialeah and right off the turnpike (not to mention they'd have the benefit of Julisa's parking pass), but UM's private palm trees and the aura of its most esteemed alumnus, Mr. Dwayne *The Rock* Johnson, lure a different kind of scholar there, and it's the shady conservative-sympathizing ones Izzy and Rudy need.

Talking with a professor type is not, they think, a bad idea. In theory, it's a good one—or at least, it's a better/safer idea than Rudy's original suggestion that they talk with some tío of a guy who works with his dad (and also, that guy never responded to their calls). It's not an idea either of them would've thought of on their own, which is why it's Julisa who suggests it as a trade—information she knows how to find in exchange for the keys to Danny's loaner for the day. Julisa doesn't, however, tell them about office hours, about how you normally have to make appointments with these professor types. They think they are that kind of important, and for some reason, their job doesn't require them to be in their offices from nine to five like most people who actually work for a living. But fortune is on Izzy's side today, and after sucking it up and paying way too much to park in a campus garage, he and Rudy find Hibertico in his office, just visible through his barely open office door, a gold plaque with his name and the names of all the companies sponsoring his salary etched into it.

Colón sits behind a massive metal desk from another era. He's wearing a white collared shirt sans tie underneath a blazer that's the same gray as the strands of hair reaching across his scalp. Izzy feels sorry for the guy, that he doesn't have something more exciting to wear despite the fancy work title. He'd considered wearing his graduation suit jacket in an attempt to look professional but decided that in this case it would make him look kind of desperate, and now that he sees the professor's attire, he knows he was totally right to leave it hanging in his closet, protected from the smell of frying oil by the dry cleaner's plastic bag. Colón is typing on his laptop so hard that Izzy figures he's angry about something, but no, that's just the way these people type, as if trying to convince themselves and anyone in earshot that whatever they're writing is urgent and very much worth responding to immediately.

—Mr. Colón? Izzy says as he knocks on the door. Hey, can we like, ask you some questions?

He shuts his laptop and says, Please, call me Professor Colón. And yes, of course. Do you have an appointment?

Rudy says, With you? Why?

—No one's here, Izzy says.

—Not a problem, not a problem, Colón says, I can always make time for my students. Please, come in, mi gente.

He half-stands and then gestures with both hands to two wooden chairs on the other side of his desk. Izzy and Rudy step inside as he says, Please, leave the door open – new policies in place, ha! I was just composing an email about important departmental matters, but if you don't mind waiting a moment, you may have a seat.

Professor Colón opens his laptop again, the back of its screen adorned with stickers proclaiming THE MASTER'S TOOLS WILL NEVER DISMANTLE THE MASTER'S HOUSE and IF IT'S GOYA, IT HAS TO BE GOOD! On the wall behind him are two framed diplomas—an undergraduate one from Princeton and a doctorate from also Princeton—as well as two framed photos: one of him standing in front of a statue of José Martí, him in a sort of bow-salute combo; and one of him in a Santa suit and standing next to former congressman Lincoln Diaz-Balart, who is also in a Santa suit, with a not-yet-deported Elián González perched between them. In both photos, Colón still has all of his hair, all of it still black. What's left of it clings across his tight scalp in wisps, in full view now as his head stays bowed, as if praying to his keyboard. The building's air conditioner kicks on and the hairs sway; his chair is directly under its vent. He types a final sentence, and there's the digitized sound of an airplane flying, and the laptop is shut once more. Izzy and Rudy both sit up, the chairs already making their backs ache, which of course is by design. As he fans his fingers and slides papers across his desk, looking for nothing, Colón says, Remind me, caballeros, in which of my courses are you enrolled?

—None? We don't go to school here.

—Or at all anymore, Izzy adds, proud of this fact.

—Yeah, we're just like, two people. But my sister goes to FIU.

—Ah! Community members! Yes, even better! Welcome! Welcome to *your* campus, my friends. I have a vested interest in the community – our community – ¡nuestra comunidad! In fact, communities, and in particular *this community*, is what I study. It's my life's work, now generously sponsored by Goya, Café Bustelo, and Navarro Pharmacy, my wonderful benefactors. That was not always the case, of course, but such is the nature of academia in our neoliberal context, yes? Ha! But what a pleasure to serve you! Please, call me Hibertico then.

—My sister found you online and said you study balseros and stuff?

—*Study* is not a strong enough word for what I do, m'ijo. My work is at the intersection of political science, psychology, history, sociology, anthropology, linguistics, communications, radical poetics, and various diasporas both liminal and subliminal, and occasionally sublingual. I have spent my career immersing myself in the ways in which migration, and thus *im*-migration, impact the ways in which communities come to define themselves. I am interested – perhaps some would say obsessed, yes? – in the *living* archive, in the ways in which migration-slash-immigration come to shape concepts of identity and the performance of said identity or, in some cases, such as that of many hispanoamericanos in our community at large, iden-ti-*ties*, plural.

—This dude just say titties?

—Rudy, he can hear you.

But Izzy is incorrect: Professor Colón doesn't hear him. He talks right through the question of titties. Eventually he says, I never – I mean always! – I always have time for members of this community, whether they pay tuition or not. My door is literally always open, thanks in part to the new campus sexual relations policy. I can respect it though I don't agree – the classroom always has been and always will be an erotic space, how can it not, correct? The administration can't bylaw-away that reality, try as they do. ¿Ustedes son cubanos?

They nod, and Professor Colón claps his hands once. Ha! I knew it. I can always tell a fellow Cuban! Tell me, what year did your parents arrive?

That question: shorthand for *Let me make some assumptions about your politics, about where you rank in the social order of this city, and more specifically, in my crusty old mind.*

Rudy leans forward in his chair, the wood creaking, and answers first because he's been raised to be proud of his version of cubanidad.

—Bueno, señor, mis abuelos vinieron de niños.

—Ah sí, Pedro Pan then? I myself came via the Pedro Pan flights. The subject of my most recent anthropological study, actually.

—Uh, no, Rudy says. I mean, that's cool, but they came like, just on a regular flight on a plane? I guess technically they were teenagers.

—I see, he says. I am now a Miami man through and through but would you believe I spent my first year here in Chicago? The misery of that city! Even now I still call it, She-*cago*. Ha!

Rudy laughs despite having heard the joke many times before and Izzy glares at him for encouraging this guy.

—Anyway my dad's side ended up in Puerto Rico for a little while, then –

—¡Borinkén! Colón yells. Izzy jumps a little out of his seat and covers his mouth with his hand, saying into it, Is this guy for real?

—Uh yeah, exactly, Rudy says.

Rudy who can't help but be polite. Rudy who sees his father in this man, sees his abuelo. Izzy has none of that baggage to contend with. He doesn't even know if what Rudy is saying is true, or if it's just some story he's memorized and repeats when prompted, or both.

Over the next few minutes, Rudy tries again and again to share the requested family history—the impulse fueled by the same desire that keeps Colón interrupting with his own. Even Izzy starts to feel it, wants to blurt out, *I was raised by my tía,* just to see if the guy takes the bait, just to toss something unexpected into the typical narratives he's seemingly built his career around. But Izzy knows better, seeing the stop-start of Rudy's offerings, and so keeps his history to himself. The ninth time that Colón stops Rudy mid-sentence, it's to direct Rudy to an article Colón published twenty years ago in a journal that Rudy— or anyone—has never heard of.

—Journal like a diary? Rudy says.

The question gets lost under Colón's insistence that the piece would illuminate for Rudy the ways in which his parents had commodified, compartmentalized, synchronized, and ultimately re-colonized for him his own sense of cubanidad.

Izzy knows from both this rant and the Elián picture not to give this guy anything of himself or his life's story. In *Scarface,* when Tony is interrogated about his family in the first act, he answers without much explanation: *Everybody's dead.* So there's no way that Izzy will reveal that he's basically a balsero who was raised by his aunt, lest he end up framed and on the wall himself. No way he's letting this guy tell him about some book, or worse, put him in a book, his story dissected and evaluated by a bunch of know-it-all strangers. Fuck that shit, he's ready to get out of there, and he's grateful that his Manolo has done his job, has warmed this guy up for him, has shown Izzy exactly how to approach the conversation, which Colón keeps calling a *dialogue.* His phone buzzes in his pocket and on it he sees a text from Julisa—EXCITED FOR FAIR TOMORROW! MEET THERE? OR MAYBE PICK ME UP? WHAT TIME?

He looks up to find Colón's hands crossed over his laptop, his hair still again as the A/C cycles off, the new silence coinciding with the end of his lecture telling Rudy who Rudy is. Apparently Izzy has just been asked a question. It doesn't matter what it was. He already knows what to say in response, no matter the question, because he believes it's what Tony Montana would say in a moment like this. He checks the time—they are still within the zone of the first thirty minutes being free in the parking garage—and slides his phone back in his pocket. He slouches low, splaying his knees wide, and says, What I want to know, Mr. Professor, is how you know everything you think you know about people.

This isn't the question he'd come hoping to ask. He'd planned on asking about rafters, about smugglers, how people communicated about and planned such activities, about the legalities, the risks. He was willing to pay a lot for parking to get those answers. But like Julisa, Izzy knows a fraud when he sees one, and, especially now, when he hears one. This guy is talking about problems no one has—certainly not problems Izzy had ever had or that he'd ever heard his Tía Tere talk about. This guy thinks that going out on a boat once, maybe twice, and that holding a recording device up to someone's face qualifies him to take all the time in the world to write a book no sane person will ever read. This guy doesn't know the answers to anything Izzy wants to ask; this professor isn't connected to real life in a way that lets him realize he should be afraid of the world Izzy's trying to learn about; if this professor were doing his research right, he'd warn Izzy not to ask those questions outside of that office, which admittedly might be the safest place in this city to ask them, because in that office, the questions and their answers are all theoretical in nature; all the professor can do is churn out those theories and write emails to justify his existence. Someone is already paying him a lot of money to sit around and spew a fancy kind of bullshit to people paying even more money to listen. Given his benefactors, they might even be paying him to push one version of the truth over the more sinister and dangerous realities of certain operations. Izzy's never been prouder of himself for not even considering going to college. He can't think of anything more useless.

Colón leans back in his chair and places his folded hands across the top of his hard belly—the same tight drum of a gut every Cuban man in Miami seems to acquire after age fifty-five.

—That's a simple question. Oral histories, firsthand accounts, time in the archive. As a scholar I value fieldwork, of course. But I wonder at the *aggression* beneath your question. I know what I know because people – because *our* people – tell me their stories, and I am, as you must see by now, an excellent listener. I know what I know because I ask the right people the right questions.

Colón says all of this to his office ceiling, perhaps an offering to the air conditioning gods, so he doesn't notice Izzy standing, then motioning for Rudy to do the same. He doesn't realize that the two of them have left until he hears, from his doorway, Izzy throw back a *Thanks anyway, bro.* And Izzy, without even turning around, knowing his face would soon be forgotten by the professor, shouts down the hallway of half-open office doors as he leaves the building, You didn't even ask us our names. And yeah, Rudy, that fool did say titties.

THE RIGHT PEOPLE, THE RIGHT QUESTIONS

Is it strange that he hasn't thought to ask his Tía Tere what she knows about his own crossing, at least before talking to some supposed expert on people like her, people like him? Don't be surprised. Izzy is only twenty after all and, despite what he'd say if interviewed by a professor like that, he doesn't value his tía for the historical resource she might well be. Teresa and Izzy have long struggled to fully trust each other, and they have Izzy's mother to thank for that.

The day Teresa went to claim him at Krome was the first time she ever saw him, though she knew from Alina's sporadic correspondence that he existed—was even conceived in service to the Revolution, according to the letter informing Teresa that she was now an aunt. Alina had said in those letters that she would rather die than come to the United States, and that's essentially what she did, at the very last possible moment, leaving her son's fate up to the waves and to the others on the raft. Teresa knew nothing at all about Alina's plan to leave. She hadn't seen Alina or their mother Ocila since 1973, Alina not yet seven years old and hiding behind Ocila as Teresa said her goodbyes from the yard, no longer welcome in Ocila's house. She barely remembered what Alina looked like, and so the sunburned child she brought into her home and raised as if he were hers didn't remind her of anyone, which she counted as a blessing.

What does Izzy think of Teresa's sacrifice? Does he even think of it as such? She'd relished avoiding motherhood, knowing she would never make the same mistakes Ocila had made. She would never be a disappointment to some ungrateful kid, and she'd thanked God for that freedom.

She'd planned to go on a Mediterranean cruise for her fiftieth birthday, taking two of her best friends with her, her treat, and then almost overnight she'd become responsible for a newly orphaned seven-year-old and she suddenly had to figure out things like what time to put him to bed, what he ate, if he could go to her same dentist, how to register him for school. Which school was he even supposed to attend? There were several she regularly passed on her way to work—some public, some charter, some religious—but she'd bought her house knowing that school districts were irrelevant to her life, and now she cursed herself for her shortsightedness. Except: how could you predict that your extremely Communist half sister who randomly sent you one, maybe two angry letters a year would try to escape? A sister you know for a fact was raised to despise you and Cubans like you, who said as much in those letters? She would've spent every cent of her cruise savings in a bet against that possibility.

Teresa: forty-nine and single and dependent-free when Izzy arrives; older than Alina by thirteen years. Despite sharing a biological mother, the Revolution and Ocila's politically inspired infidelity, which resulted in Alina's existence, made the girls strangers to each other long before Teresa decided to leave Cuba almost three decades before Alina would make the same choice—that is: assuming Alina hadn't been forced onto the raft, which Teresa has entertained as an unlikely possibility. Teresa: sent to live with her father permanently when Alina was born, and so she spent her teenage years in the care of a skeptic to the Revolution's half-truths. Teresa: her father an accountant who found himself an enemy of the state when he refused to join the Communist Party; Alina's sporting the beard and the fatigues and the swagger that comes with a rifle—the timeworn look of a Revolutionary that you've come to associate with the Cuban stories already told.

And Teresa's story, too, is one you already know or think you know, a story some of you want more than the story already underway. The loss, the trauma. That story is easier to tell and—like the salmon Lolita is meant to eat—so much easier to digest; it wafts up from the canals and gutters, a story super-saturated, hanging in the humidity. You want to hear it? You want that tragic exile story regurgitated for you once more? Look for it elsewhere, in the words of those claiming or wishing they were raised hearing it. Or better yet (but granted, far less comfortable for some of you): go for a walk in Hialeah, or the not-yet-gentrified parts of Little Havana. Or just keep it easy on yourself and stick to the touristy sections of Calle Ocho; pose for your photos at Versailles or La Carreta (granted, you've already been to the latter here, though it's the one on Bird Road and that makes a legit difference)—doesn't matter which ventanita you roll up to, because joke's on you, Versailles and La Carreta are both owned by the same company. Order a croqueta and give yourself twenty minutes to find that alcoholic father or that magical abuela type, the ones who'll be dead by story's end because admittedly it's just easier to go that route, to rewarm and rehash some previously perpetuated idea of *authentic*, over and over and over again. Fish out those narratives from the croqueta frying oil for yourself. Because if you're asking, here's the answer: *Everybody's dead.*

Teresa is guilty only of letting this one easy narrative stand: Your mother died trying to bring you to freedom. She deployed it when Izzy was a child because it was the easiest story to tell, and it let Teresa live with his reluctance to talk about the event of his crossing. *Everybody's dead.* But even with the passing of years, she can't bring herself to believe it. She's lost count of how many times she's had an imaginary conversation with him about it, her words spilling over only when she's alone in the shower or washing dishes. If Izzy were to ask her about Alina now that he's more or less a grown man, she wishes she could tell him:

Ay, Ismael, I don't know that Alina was ever really interested in being a mother to you. Some of the stories you would hint at that first year when you arrived, the little you would reveal without meaning to about your time with her and with the random men she left you with, men you barely knew who you couldn't help but think of as potential fathers—it made sense that your first weeks with me, you woke up screaming and crying for anyone but her. She saw you more as some concept, some idea she was proving to people about herself or the Revolution or qué sé yo. Coño, she was probably at the same time trying to prove something by not *taking care of you.*

We had very different fathers. Hers was an assassin, plain and simple, a man who used his commitment to the Revolution as an excuse to not raise her. Our mother—your Abuela Ocila—fell again and again for his bullshit, and I was lucky enough to escape her house when I did, and then Cuba altogether. I was lucky to have a father—may he rest in peace—who loved me as a mother should, who became my mother when Ocila refused me. The more distance I put between her and my idea of home, the safer I was. It's the same for you, is what I felt when you became mine—or at least, my responsibility. When I left Cuba, Alina was still a little girl. A year before you were born, Ocila killed herself. Or maybe she didn't: maybe she really did accidentally fry her eggs in rat poison. Really did mistake that can for the one holding the lard. But who the fuck knows? I've told you this story already, when you asked about your abuela, what she was like, and you were smart, you asked: Who keeps rat poison right next to the lard? I remember it because your question made me think I could raise you. It was the same question I'd asked the primo who'd called from Cuba to tell me the news.

I already had decades of grief under my skin, so your abuela's passing came to me as a relief. But Alina had you in response to that loss, and in that way she put a burden on you that I cannot forgive her for.

You never asked me in those early years about Alina. You seemed set on forgetting her once you were enrolled in school, learning English faster than I had, and I took your desire to forget as you knowing how to take good care of yourself. I didn't know Alina enough to re-create her for you anyway. I always destroyed her letters—in whatever way I felt called to do so, be it burying or burning, even flushing—immediately after reading them, and when you showed up, I was glad I'd done that—a small mercy to myself, that I didn't have to make the decision about whether or not to show them to you.

I have always believed that you were destined to escape her. You and I share that genetic programming. I felt it when I read her letters, how she seemed already to be anticipating your betrayal, blaming everyone but herself with all her excuses for all the ways she was ready to fail you in service to herself. My mother Ocila was a communist y Alina también era comunista, and so why either of you were on that raft will always be a mystery to me. But I'm glad she's gone. I'm sorry, but I'm glad. The way she talked about you in those letters, the things only you knew that you worked hard to forget—it would only bring you harm to know about them now. No child is a mother's concept once you've dropped out of them. You were to her some thing that proved she was capable of love, except that once you were born, you proved to her the opposite. She could no longer deny that she'd been broken by all she'd chosen, by her angry inheritance, and that's why she couldn't stand the sight of you even as she made you call her Mamá.

When Izzy finally gets home from his disappointing and infuriating visit to UM's campus, he finds his Tía Tere in her bedroom, sitting in front of her vanity mirror and putting rollers in her hair. He asks her versions of the questions he'd planned to ask the professor earlier that day, but with her he gets to ask them more honestly, with his own self as part of the questions: How did we get over? How did Alina arrange for us to even get on a raft? Who was on the raft with me besides Alina?

—Ismael, she says. Your mother never told me any of that. Neither did you.

And although she doesn't pull much from the imaginary conversation she's practiced so many times before, she does give him what he insists on knowing: every name, the few details she learned from the people at Krome when he was released to her care, the reluctant facts she'd gathered in her own careful search to answer those exact same questions before accepting that knowing the answers—even just the act of searching them out—was for her a form of self-harm. And a search like that carried other dangers, depending on who in the community found out about the asking, how much or how little they wanted to be known. What if Teresa, looking to clear up some innocent doubt about the duration of Izzy's crossing, asked the wrong question of someone who knew someone—someone with the power to act on their own concerns, who might decide in time that she's too much like her drowned sister? Better to have let her doubts dissolve. Better with all these years to be only grateful for the gift of his arrival.

The names Teresa reluctantly gives him aren't a lot, but they're so much more than any professor could ever provide. And because, unlike the professor, Teresa loves Izzy and wants to keep him from harm, and because she believes his questions are coming from a new place of longing rather than from his *Scarface* hopes, she gives him this warning too: Leave that wound alone, Ismael. That scab is protection.

But he doesn't hear it—the throbbing in his head begins almost immediately after he hears the names. And he's learned by now that the pain will only subside if he chugs as much water as he can and closes his eyes.

A BLESSING, A CURSE

In high school, Izzy dated a girl who'd been instructed by her mother to keep an elaborate journal detailing everything about her migraines to discover if there was some pattern to them that offered a chance at intervention—avoiding certain foods, for instance. The journal revealed instead that the headaches corresponded with the onset of her period, and the girl's mother considered her doomed until menopause. *Nothing you can do about that,* she'd said, not knowing about acupuncture or the various herbs—black cohosh, borage, wild yam—that could help. Her mother wouldn't have trusted those remedies anyway even if she'd known about them, would've associated them with brujería, as is typical for the kind of white Catholic Cuban woman who sees pain as deserved for one reason or another, the kind who feels sanctified by suffering. *Now you know how Jesucristo felt on the cross*, she'd said to her daughter, and her daughter repeated this to Izzy, her then-boyfriend, looking to him for some clue as to how she should feel about her mother's pronouncement. But Izzy was newly eighteen then, two months from starting senior year, and he interpreted this potential mother-in-law's comments to mean that his girlfriend's family was more fucked up than he was willing to take on, his Tía Tere having drilled into him that particularly Caribbean adage: when you marry someone, you're marrying that whole family, you're taking on that whole lineage. She'd meant *taking on* as in *choosing to make it yours*, taking on the pleasures and burdens of it, but Izzy had heard *take on* as in: to fight.

Either way, he did not want to *take on* a mother-in-law who thought her own kid should have to know how it felt to have a crown of thorns smashed into your head, who thought there was anything to be gained from experiencing a debilitating level of pain in one's brain every twenty-eight or so days. That girl's mom was coocoo in other ways too: she'd once told Izzy that, if he ever hurt her daughter, she would hunt him down like the dog she was sure he was and kill him. He'd been too afraid to break up with her after that, certain that breaking up with her would count as hurting her, so he'd waited for an opportunity to say something that prompted *her* to dump him. The Jesucristo comment was it: when she repeated her mother's pronouncement about the migraines to him, Izzy said in all honesty and with an absence of creativity, Your mother is a crazy bitch.

Just to guarantee his fate he added, And even Jesus only got crucified once. Shit, one time is easy. Imagine he had to go through that shit once a month. You really think he'd be down for that? Yeah right, no thanks.

And the girl—because she was not even seventeen and so still at an age where she made the mistake of believing that her mother was her best friend—raised her hand to slap Izzy's face at what she'll forever think of as blasphemy times two, but then she remembered some lesson about turning the other cheek and couldn't recall if Jesucristo ever slapped anybody in the Bible, and so she lowered her hand and delivered instead what Izzy was aiming for but what she believed to be a more devastating blow, ending their five-months-long relationship right then and there, after school in the parking lot of Hialeah Lakes High.

—I can't be with someone that would disrespect my mom so disrespectfully, she told her mother that afternoon when she explained why Izzy wouldn't be coming over for dinner that night, or ever again. She left out the blasphemy part because she worried she sort of agreed with Izzy about Jesucristo saying thanks but no thanks to a monthly crucifixion. And her mother embraced her, and this cycle of perverse loyalty will rinse and repeat until this mother dies, her daughter by her side, their hands holding tight, fingers snarled together like the teeth of a crocodile's snapped-shut bite.

Does Izzy see his new migraines as a punishment from that mother? Perhaps she's ventured away from Jesucristo and toward the Orishas she'd previously feared and thus dismissed, performing some trabajo on him for calling her a crazy bitch and it's only just now kicking in. Is that what his idea of revenge looks like? Does he think to take his cues from that girlfriend, how she'd note everything she ate, how many hours she slept, how much water she drank—how it all made her feel? What would his migraine journal, were he to keep one, reveal about the pattern of his pain?

He doesn't drink wine or eat fancy cheeses or dark chocolate, but if he did, he wouldn't find any correlation there, or with any foods at all. He wouldn't see a clear connection to dehydration or a poor night's sleep, to physical exertion or bright lights or specific scents. There'd be no pattern to his suffering because there is no pattern to Lolita's. There is no pattern to the pain caused by the infection in her eyes—the tearing and itching, the sensation that there's some foreign body scratching her that she can't for the life of her blink away. Better to keep that eye closed. Better still to close them both, to imagine herself elsewhere. No pattern to the pain in her teeth. The only pattern she can rely on: the sun and the moon and the tides, her holy trinity, her signals that another day has come or gone and she is still alive enough to witness it. And each morning she greets the sunrise at the edge of her tank where the light first crests the roof above the bleachers, and she spits water onto the spot, an offering to another day arriving. And ever since the afternoon when Izzy paid his visit, this is the exact moment when Izzy—never an early riser—turns in his sleep and wakes from the pain at his temple, the surge of it disappearing just as suddenly as it comes on. But she knows he's awake now; she'd sent him to bed with pain the night before. She's trained him to do this and he's finally learned: do not fight the pain. Do not attempt to power through. She needs him asleep, to get him out of his own way. Lucky him that he sleeps at all: it's something her mind doesn't do—no orca does it—the two hemispheres of her brain trading off awareness as one half rests and the other does the waking work of sending her to the surface to breathe.

Lucky him that he can escape his own consciousness.

Lucky her that she can sway his dreams.

She never had a baby, has not even been near a baby since her capture. She has been both spared from and denied that experience, and she knows from her body that the chance for one of her own has passed for good. She felt that shift—half a decade ago now and several years in the making—one so rare in nature that only humans with ovaries are known to share it: this move from latent life-giver to sustainer, to elder. Had she never been taken, she would be a hunter again now, an expert, a teacher. She would've maybe had the chance to mother, to grandmother, but in this tank, it's a fate she avoided, a miracle given their plans for her, given the fates of so many like her. She mourns and celebrates the absence, those feelings swaying like waves, like the currents she creates with her own turning in the tank. What a blessing, to have avoided the pain and heartache of the inevitable separation from the only family close to her in years—as the Seaquarium owners would've almost certainly sold the calf off to another park or kept the calf and instead moved her to another jointly owned facility. What a curse, to still feel that longing, to wonder always at what was denied: the chance to love in some new-to-her way. How good a mother would she have been, considering how brief her own time being mothered was? Had she even learned enough? She cannot imagine subjecting a new life to the life she's endured—is still enduring. And because she cannot imagine this, she knows herself capable of maternal love—the love of wanting better for your own, of protecting your own from what you were made to endure.

She wonders if her own mother regrets having her and knows instantly that she does not, because all her mother knows is that her child is gone but still alive—not of the suffering, the loneliness, the fear, the madness. Her own mother has no idea, and she is grateful for that. She thanks and curses her body for what it never did, for all it refused her, from all it spared her.

What keeps her from total madness? An awareness of her own body, its complex inner workings. She scans the ventricles of her heart almost hourly, tracking her blood's flow around and through each of her wet organs. She knows her lungs so well they have become her own children. Her twin calves, safe inside her. She can see the infections that plague them and pushes those masses off, down, back. She sends her vibrations into herself, knowing her tank never changes anyway—the concrete sending back everything in distorted echoes. Her own body is where she's made her home in her most desperate moments. She's not sure if other orca can do this, if her mother can do this: turn this power, which she'd learned from her family to use to scan prey, back on herself, to see using only sound and buzz in the darkest water—to turn this inward to linger on the landscape of her own viscera. She had mastered searching for prey this way by the time of her capture but had never hunted alone—would never do so as a member of her family—and so she suspects this self-hunting ability might be unnatural despite being possible. How did she even discover it? She remembers, each time she does it, that it began when she accidentally landed on a trainer during a performance, back when trainers still got in the water. She'd missed a cue—which rarely happened—and feared she'd broken every bone in that woman's body. And without deciding to do so, she found her awareness sweeping over the woman's limbs, her hips, her torso and the organs within it. The discovery that her trainer was pregnant—something the trainer didn't yet know—the trainer's heart, beating wildly—the trainer's hands then moving through the water to her heart—and Lolita understanding that her trainer could feel this awareness, this invasion, like a frantic ticking within the body, strong enough that it rocked every cell. The trainer could feel the looking—and so just as automatically and without decision Lolita stopped, not wanting to share this gift. And when she pulled it back, when it snapped back toward her, it entered her own body and she saw her own heart, its valves and ventricles pumping just as frantically—felt the same vibration her trainer felt, somehow emitting and receiving it at the same time. A whistle from above meant the moment was over. Her trainer had been dragged out of the tank but Lolita already knew the extent of the damage—bruises on bones and new fear—but otherwise the trainer was intact. The embryo too, which the trainer would learn of later that day while being examined for injuries at Jackson Memorial Hospital. The whistle called Lolita out of the self-inflicted trance she'd inadvertently ricocheted back into her own body, but not before she'd followed the blood from her heart to her lungs, lingering for an instant in the thousands and thousands of vessels there, seeing and hearing them from within herself for the first time and thinking, There is a lifetime's worth to watch.

And so it is here that she returns in her worst waking moments, which is every moment she is not eating or performing or calling for her mother or now, for Izzy. She imagines herself his mother. She senses—in the tank's filtered and too-warm salt water that was once in the very nearby sea—his mother's bones, her cells, the atoms of her memories and thoughts. She absorbs each particle, and with each comes the promise and the threat: she'll tell him exactly what he wants to know.

I KNOW YOU WANT ME; YOU KNOW I WANT YOU

THE FIRST DATE

Izzy meets Julisa at the Youth Fair instead of picking her up and driving her there. Why? Because he kind of wants to punish her for wasting his time yesterday with the professor. Also he doesn't want to be the one to explain this date to Rudy; also, if they meet there, he can deny that this outing even *is* a date, which might be necessary depending on how the date goes. He woke that morning from a night full of dreams he can't remember but can still feel, and as he and Julisa stand in line at the Fair's entrance gates, the heat feeling lethal this early afternoon hour, he debates warning her that he doesn't feel like himself, though that's not exactly true: what he feels is actually *more* himself—like he has access to a sense of himself he's never known or noticed, like a neighbor you haven't met who's suddenly at your front door, knocking.

Izzy offers to buy Julisa's entrada because he mistakenly thinks that her being enrolled at FIU means she gets a discount and because he doesn't remember that admission is more expensive on the weekends. When the gate attendant tells them the total cost for two unlimited ride tickets, Julisa says, You sure? And he says, Okay okay we can split it.

How does he make up for this disappointing start? Does he even sense Julisa's disappointment—how she's rationalizing it away by blaming herself for offering to cover her half—or is he still distracted by what he learned from his Tía Tere yesterday: the names of the other people who'd been on the raft, seven people besides him and his mother; that no, she's never spoken directly with any of them, and no, she had no idea if any of them would be willing to talk to him, especially once they figured out who he was.

Izzy tells Julisa this and what little else his Tía Tere told him—but not the reasons why he'd asked—an hour into their adventure

117

as they traverse the fairgrounds overhead on the Sky Ride, th
feet dangling from a glider on a cable suspended high above th
pavement, the rides far below them looking like tossed-out Lego
blocks. From up there they can see the acres of parking, the air
conditioning units squatting on the flat roofs of any and every
enclosed space, the seemingly dozens of kiddie rides and carni-
val game booths they'd walked past to get to the real rides and
then eventually the Sky Ride. The new blisters on Julisa's heels are
getting a needed break: she'd picked out a pair of strappy platform wedges to wear to make up for the bare feet she'd sported the
day they met. She wants him to know she is a serious person who
he could and should get serious about. Also they made her look
taller and therefore skinnier, which seemed important for reasons
she can't articulate. Her legs soak in the sun to the point that she
thinks she can see them darkening in real time; the C-shaped swing
carrying them over and across the fairgrounds offers them little in
the way of shade.

—Look at this shit, Izzy says.

He pulls a folded-up piece of paper from his wallet and hands it to
her. On it are the names his Tía Tere had given him, which he'd written down in his notebook before taking two aspirin and passing out.
He'd torn the page from the notebook that morning and tucked the
folded square into his wallet as a way of signaling—to whom?—that
he understood the information was valuable.

—Don't drop it, he says.

It's not a joke but she thinks it is. Still, she holds the paper with
both hands.

—Yamileisis y Mikael Gutierrez. Dayesi Rivera. Odlanier Vasquez.
Odlanier? Oh my god is that just Reinaldo backwards? Damn these
are some reffy names. Oh shit, no offense, Izzy. I forgot. Please don't
hate me.

She's only known since they stumbled off the Gravitron, when
she'd used the word *seasick* instead of *dizzy*, that he came on a raft
himself.

Izzy laughs it off. She's not wrong; he's often felt surprised that

whoever named him—he isn't sure it was his mother—stuck with an *I* instead of tossing a *Y* up front. Given where he was born and the year—1997—his name is practically old-school.

There are three other names on the sheet but they don't rise to Julisa's level of perceived reffiness to compel her to read them aloud: Rafael, Manuela y Olivia C——.

Still, she pauses over them, presses her thumbnail into the paper, underlines the surname with a fresh dent. Their Sky Ride glider humps over a chunky part of the cable and sends them swaying. Eventually she says the last name aloud and asks, You think they're related to like, *the* C—— family?

Izzy has no idea what she's talking about. He knows very little about the hierarchies of Miami's Cuban American communities, only that, as a balsero, he's near the bottom of them, though granted, some of that is canceled out by the fact that he was so young, that he had no say in deciding how he got here. He's only ever lived in his corner of Miami, relatively safe in his Tía Tere's townhouse, so he knows nothing about the storied families that claim to have built this city and/or the ones whose patriarchs have senators on speed dial and/or the ones the local universities can count on as donors—families so powerful and connected that they can't be named outright here: families just like the C—— family.

All he knows for now is what his Tía Tere is willing to tell him about his own story and her version of life in Miami. And so Izzy doesn't think to ask Julisa what she means, to find out what she's come to understand about this city's social history by virtue of her Miami birth or her parents' warnings couched as stories: the names their strata of Miami Cubans recognize and respect almost as royalty, as the ones who made good and first proved that all Cubans deserved a chance here. Izzy simply assumes the C—— family are just random rich people, which, in a way, he's not wrong.

Julisa sucks her teeth and answers the question for herself: Nah, can't be. The C—— people are old-school, been here since the beginning, like the fifties and sixties, when Miami was barely Miami.

She lets her shoe slip from her heel and dangle from her toes before remembering how high up she is, the damage a shoe falling from that high could cause.

—Besides, she says, I'm pretty sure if they had any of their people left over there, I doubt they'd have to resort to floating for days on a raft, no offense.

He doesn't want to admit she knows something he doesn't when he's supposed to be the budding mastermind here, so he says, No offense taken.

—Have you showed this to my brother yet? Do you need help? Like, finding these people? Is *that* what you guys are doing? Why?

—I'm seeing your brother tomorrow. I wanted to show you first.

—Okay but *why*?

—I don't *know* why. I just did.

Julisa takes his answering the wrong question as yet another sign of their inevitable marriage, but Izzy isn't even trying to flirt. He's telling her exactly what he thinks. He seems incapable of fully guarding himself around her and he's definitely not aware of this development—which he'd consider a weakness, if he understood that it was happening.

Below them—they are nearing the Sky Ride's endpoint, where you have to dismount and make the line all over again if you want to go back to where you came from—a siren blast erupts from the Polar Express ride, signaling that it's about to spin riders backward at varying speeds (based on crowd screams) for roughly three minutes. Before the siren drops out, the house music starts up, the ride starts moving, and the sudden rise of screams and bass reminds both Izzy and Julisa of a nightclub dance floor. The ride operator's voice pounces over both the music and the siren: You're riding the best, why ride the rest?!

—Maybe you should go back to that professor? Show him this list?

—¡Ese tipo es un comemierda!

He says it again and with more force—Un comemierda—rolling the *R* in an unnecessary, exaggerated way.

Then he says it one more time, yelling it to the sky, so loudly that the people in the swing ahead of them, who are seconds away from dismounting, hear it over the Polar Express's ruckus. They turn around to see who's doing all that cursing and the motion sends their swing swaying.

Julisa laughs more than she means and says, He can't be *that* full of shit if his job is sponsored by Goya or Bacardi Limón or whatever. Plus he's written all those books.

She says this while still staring at the paper, willing herself to re-member these names. Izzy snatches it from between her fingers and says, Please, Julisa. People who write books are the biggest comemier-das of all.

Back on the ground, Julisa's full weight once again in those punish-ing shoes, they take an obligatory air-conditioned walk past a bunch of crap no one buys and through the massive exhibition hall that warehouses the student projects from schools around the county: dioramas of obscure revolutionary war battles; shitty poems backed by construction paper and tacked up to temporary walls; national and state and county seals re-created with tiny beads glued to slabs of wood; stretched canvases with abstract representations of middle and high school pain painted on them, in both oil and watercolor; wobbly kiln-fired vases proving that their makers had access to every single color of glaze; handmade ornaments and decorations for any holidays listed in the exhibitor guidelines, including Christ-mas, Hanukkah, Martin Luther King Junior Day, New Year's Day, Father's Day, Grandparent's Day (Izzy: That's a thing?), Fourth of July, Mother's Day, St. Patrick's Day, Thanksgiving, Valentine's Day (Julisa: My favorite!), Halloween, Easter, President's Day, Birthdays (Izzy: But like, whose?), Passover, Columbus Day (Julisa: Pretty sure this one's supposably canceled?), and Earth Day; all kinds of shit made with popsicle sticks—bird houses, mobiles, magic wands, peo-ple; scarecrows no taller than two feet; shit sewn by hand; shit sewn using a sewing machine; functional items—lamps, purses, jewelry boxes, toys—constructed solely out of recyclable materials; aisles and aisles and aisles of effort, all of it on display. Every single entry sports a sticker denoting the ribbon it's earned: first, second, third, or fourth, with some bearing both a blue first-place sticker and a purple rosette sticker, the later indicating a best-in-category sort of thing.

—Somebody actually has to judge all this crap, Izzy says.

—I think it's a few somebodies, Julisa says, and he says, No yeah, obviously.

They look up and down the aisles for entries from the middle schools they'd attended, laugh at how much those projects seem to suck compared to the ones from private schools. They find the entries from schools rated worse than theirs and laugh harder.

When they reach the section dedicated to projects celebrating and/or commemorating American Heritage and World History, Julisa says, You know actually I got a purple rosette in eighth grade for a project I did.

—For real?

—Yeah, for this paper-mache shit I did. My social studies teacher was this americana, so I did a model of this Civil War thing, The Battle Above the Clouds, which happened on Lookout Mountain in Tennessee. I used like a thousand cotton balls to make it like, clouds all around the paper-mache mountain, and I made like a hundred super tiny soldiers out of clay and put beads on them for eyes, used red paint for blood and twisted up pieces of pipe cleaners for their little guns. It was a mission. But the teacher freaking loved it and I won best project in eighth grade and then a purple rosette here. That model for real came out good though. You couldn't even tell from it who won that fight, the North or South.

Izzy stops his slow stroll. He is impressed by her attention to detail. Her care, her enthusiasm—her lack of embarrassment about either. He catches himself wishing that she were his Manolo instead of Rudy. But what would that make Rudy? No way Rudy could be his Michelle Pfeiffer, no offense to Rudy. Izzy shakes his head at the thought and Julisa smiles, punches his arm and says, What? What is it?

He's not going to tell her any of this, and so instead he reminds her about the haiku, his one Youth Fair contribution: the poem his teacher entered into the Fair when he was eleven; how he'd won second place (along with dozens of other students); about the pen and pencil set he still has. The haiku with a few too many syllables in it that his teacher had assumed was about Cuba—he didn't tell Julisa this part—and he'd let that teacher believe that assumption. The truth was, the poem was about his Tía Tere: it was her he was thinking about when he wrote it, though that made little sense; his tía wasn't a pearl he'd lost in the ocean, but even by eleven, he sensed something like a longing to her way with him, some protection that was also a pulling away.

—That is so cute, Julisa says. What was your poem about?

—Losing a pearl to the ocean, he says. But really it was about my mom.

He doesn't recognize the lie or where it came from, not before Julisa slides her hand in his, stumbling in her wedges just enough that he has to press his body against hers to keep her from toppling over.

They blast through the exhibition hall with even more crap you can buy (hermit crabs, water filtration systems, amulets to ward off the evil eye) and through the tents with the animals—as anyone who doesn't enjoy the smell of shit should—and emerge on the other side of the midway, still holding hands. At the edge of the tent just as they are stepping back into the sun, Julisa spots a girl maybe nine or ten years old, sucking on an ear of corn that she's clearly already finished eating—no kernels left. She keeps putting the whole thing in her mouth as far back as it can go, then pulling it out, back and forth over and over again. Julisa stops herself from tapping Izzy's shoulder to point it out and laugh, realizing that the girl is of course too little to know what she's miming, which then leads Julisa to think that what she's witnessing is a sign from the universe that she should, very soon, suck Izzy's dick in a sacred and very spiritual way. The Sacred Blowjob, after which its recipient can never again deny her power. Her mouth literally waters at the idea—not the blowjob part, but the part about someone seeing everything she's truly capable of doing, the part about her power. She squeezes Izzy's hand tighter and he says, Okay fine you win.

Can he read her mind? No. He thinks she's squeezed in response to the booth now right in front of them, the one housing the hats, where you pay to have your name spray-painted in the most perfect cursive onto them, then sealed with a clear spray tinged with glitter. Bucket hats, trucker caps, bandanas—the booth has it all.

If he buys her a hat without making her beg, she'll take it as the ultimate sign to treat him like that corn cob as soon as they are somewhere private enough—maybe even the backseat of his car; she can't remember if his window tints are dark enough. Yes, it's fast, especially for her, but she will not deny the universe's command that she suck his dick right away.

But alas, Izzy can't help himself and he plays at cruelty, pretends once they are in line that he doesn't want to buy it for her, that he thinks they're cheesy. He says, Okay okay what if I split it with you? She is angry—not so much at his game, but at how often the signs never sync up with what she wants. They move up in line and he keeps at it: doesn't she want to buy it herself, independent college-going woman that she is, ha ha ha? Then he reminds her that technically he's unemployed as of two days ago, that he hasn't yet gotten the details about how much Danny plans on paying him.

She finally responds by crossing her arms and saying, Sounds like Daniel.

She glows with the knowledge of what Izzy's missed out on for now, of what he will have to wait to experience. She smiles in a mean way, waiting for him to ask why she calls him Daniel when everyone else calls him Danny, but instead he says, Fine fine, a promise is a promise.

When it's their turn, she picks out a white mesh-back trucker hat, not thinking at all of Raúl Castro, because it has the widest surface area for the name to be airbrushed. Every decision Julisa makes is a practical one unless the universe tells her otherwise.

—What should it say, the designer asks her, and Izzy blurts out, Lolita!

He's pointing to a sample hat, one perched on a foam mannequin's head, the name in an arc over a not-exactly-proportional depiction of an orca.

—No joke, that's like, my favorite whale, he says.

—You have a favorite whale, Julisa says. Okay.

—I'm telling you, she'll be mine someday.

—That's the dumbest shit I've ever heard.

Then she asks: Wait, are you *really* talking about Lolita?

He winks and says, Of course.

So that's the name she asks for on the hat: *Lolita,* not realizing that again, he wasn't flirting, just being honest. She insists on purple for the accent color, because that's *her* favorite. And she insists on extra glitter. And he pays for it all. A promise is a promise and a sign is a sign.

Once it's on her head, he stands in front of her and tugs the brim down over her eyes and says, I love it, I fucking love it.

—In the future though, she says, I see you getting my name tattooed on your body, somewhere everyone can see.

—No fucking way. That's some insecure nonsense right there. That's the last thing you want.

She takes a step back, and before she can feel too crestfallen at what she's taking as a rejection (she should've gotten her own freaking name on the hat!), he explains: People only do that shit when they're guilty of something. Everybody I know with like, their kid's name somewhere, where people can see it? They aren't raising that kid. That, or that kid is dead. One of those two without fail. That's a fact.

He slides his hands to her hips and grips them, says, Never trust anyone who does that shit.

He's thinking more like a dad than a boyfriend and she loves this, loves how forcefully he expresses a strong opinion about something so unimportant to her. She takes it as another good sign, so she grabs his face and kisses his mouth, and after a solid five seconds, when he pulls away, he says: I was supposed to kiss you first.

She gives him an insincere *Oh poor baby, I'm so sorry* and as a joke, she offers to buy him some fried alligator bites to make up for it.

—You think I won't eat that? I eat literally anything. Especially if someone else is paying for it.

The fried gator bites taste like fish and chicken at the same time. Neither Julisa nor Izzy have ever eaten gator before, and neither would have any idea where to buy alligator for eating outside of the Fair—it's a novelty food to them, like the candy apples and funnel cakes. They sit at a cluster of bench tables to eat it, side by side instead of across from each other so they can both be in the shade. The tables are in a spot where, thirty-seven years earlier, a volunteer was puzzling over a form as he tried to help a Mariel boatlift refugee locate the others in her family—she'd made it on to one boat but her husband and son were on another. The volunteer wondered if he and the woman should just start shouting her husband's name while wandering through the crowds. They eventually learned from doing exactly that that the husband and son were on a school bus belonging to another volunteer, already on their way up from Key West to Tamiami Park for processing. They were reunited just before sunset, and they slept that night under these same trees; back then, their branches didn't give nearly as much protection as they do now.

Izzy gets up to ask for more dipping sauce and also some ketchup, and as he returns, he asks: So tell me what I need to know about Danny.

He hopes she can't tell that he's been planning on asking this all afternoon, waiting for the right moment when it would seem the most natural. This moment is not it.

—You'll see for yourself. What does he have you guys doing?

—Rudy hasn't told you anything?

—My brother doesn't talk to me about his life. Plus he doesn't know I'm here with you.

So they're a secret still, for now. Izzy needs to change this as soon as possible, because in the movie, Manolo knows that Tony's making moves to win Michelle Pfeiffer away from whatever that old Cuban guy's name is. Frank? Frank—Michelle Pfeiffer's original man and the one Tony ends up killing once he figures out that Frank set him up. The secret relationship in the film—between Manolo and Gina—leads to Manolo's death. Izzy does not want to end up dead like Manolo; he wants to end up dead like Tony. Also, he likes both Rudy and Julisa enough to not want either of them hurt and/or shot in the guts.

—Danny has us meeting him at this park in Palm Springs North

on Monday. Says we got a job there. Your brother said Danny's trying to get into wildlife management or some shit. Probably he needs
some strong guys to help with traps.

He curls his arms to flex his biceps but gives up when it's clear
Julisa is distracted, playing with her food.

—Whatever it is, it sounds nuts, he says. But he's paying us cash
and says there's bigger jobs coming if things work out.

She nudges a piece of fried gator away from her with her finger.

—That sounds like a good idea to you?

—It's just temporary. I have bigger plans than whatever Danny's
got going on, remember?

He takes out his wallet, flashes at her the square of paper with
the names again. There's absolutely no cash in the space where cash
should be, just a dozen or so slips of paper—credit card receipts.

—Plus Rudy says we'll probably make tomorrow what it would've
taken me two weeks to earn washing dishes.

—Can't argue with my brother's math, I guess.

He puts his wallet away and says, Is there something you wanna
tell me?

Julisa lifts the piece she pushed away and takes another bite of alligator. It's too hot out for fried food. Even in the shade she's sweating.
Her blisters are past aching and are now straight up sizzling. Has Izzy
asked her a single question today about herself? Does Julisa know she
should be hoping for more from a guy she's planning on giving The
Sacred Blowjob?

—Have you ever eaten iguana? she asks him.

—Iguanas like, the lizards? This is alligator, he says. Wait, is this
about what's happening tomorrow? Please tell me he's not cooking
lizards.

She puts her lips around the rest of the fried nugget and holds
it there, tonguing the flakes of meat inside. She doesn't want to say
much more but she also doesn't want to lie. She nibbles, swallows.

—You should probably know me and Daniel have a history. He
looks out for me, is what I mean. He's basically another brother to
me. Or more like a cousin.

He puts down his gator (but possibly iguana now? he's confused) bite and says, If there's anything I've heard about history, it's that it repeats itself.

—Me and him never had sex, she says. I was like super young. It wasn't like that, not really. I was just like, there for him. He was messed up for a long time because his mom died.

—Fuck, his mom's dead too? Izzy blurts, and the sun dips below the branch that's been shielding them and hits his eyes and instantly he feels the start of a throb just at his right temple. It always starts there, the migraines seemingly out of nowhere. He knows this pain well enough already. He has maybe an hour to take something for it, otherwise he's out until tomorrow. He wishes he could snatch Julisa's hat from her, to shield himself from any more brightness, the way Tony does with Michelle Pfeiffer's hat in that scene in his car, the one where Tony gets her to start liking him by intentionally making himself look like an idiot. He sits on his hands to avoid the temptation; it's time for him to go.

—So you got a thing for guys with dead moms?

Julisa wipes her hands with a paper napkin, throws the ball of it on the table, then uses her ring fingers to wipe under her eyes before any tears fall out and smudge the eyeliner rimming her lower lids.

—What the fuck is wrong with you? she says.

Izzy rubs at his temple. Maybe it's good if she hates him a little bit. Makes it more like the movie.

THE CROTCH

Early on in *Scarface*, an immigration officer—one of three interrogating the film's protagonist—shoves Tony's face to the side and asks, *How'd you get that scar? Eating pussy?*

The scar is long, running down his left brow, skipping over his eye, picking back up on his cheek. It will change size, location, and intensity as the film progresses. It is the protagonist of its own, separate story.

Tony responds with a (much more reasonable) question of his own: *How am I gonna get a scar like that eating pussy, meng?*

It's a question that merits speculation.

The pussy is perhaps unusually sharp.

If occurring in a bed: the bed is made of razor blades and/or covered in broken glass.

A jealous (and knife-wielding) lover you did or did not know existed (current or former, doesn't really matter) caught you in the act, and they sliced your face just as you were about to stop eating a pussy.

The pussy's owner is a secret agent of some sort and was therefore concealing a sharp weapon near or around the pussy in question.

A shard of glass falls from a light fixture overhead (feasibility depends on position).

The pussy itself is home to razor blades and/or a switch blade, or perhaps knives (magical realism).

The pussy is possessed by a seventeenth-century fencing champion (magical realism, appropriated by a white person).

The pussy's owner throws a vase at your face in confusion and/or passion (Miami realism).

The pussy is a cat (realism realism).

Or most likely, and the most relevant to the typical heterosexual relationship in Miami involving people under the age of thirty: the scar is metaphorical, but even so, that pussy tried to kill you.

INVASIVE SPECIES

Danny is again shirtless but vest-clad, and for this meetup he wears a gold grill over his teeth, but not for long: he sucks out the spit as he removes it and flings it onto his Escalade's dashboard. He pours out of the driver's seat and says, I got that at the flea market.

Although he means the gold grill—and who doesn't have a years-old gold or silver flea market grill lurking at the back of a drawer in their parents' house?—Rudy incorrectly assumes Danny means the cigar in his hand, which is already lit and is the width of a baby's arm. Rudy whispers to Izzy, They sell cigars at the flea market? And Izzy hits him in the chest with the back of his hand after rubbing the sleep from his own eyes. It's too early for a Sunday, just past sunrise.

Dawn is a slow hour for the city's iguanas, though technically they don't belong to the city at all, even as it now belongs to them, making them the reptile most like Miami's Cuban population: an accident of history and poor planning, invasive and everywhere these days. But unlike Miami's Cubans, all iguanas are literally and figuratively cold-blooded. Along the edge of the canal, just past the parking lot in which they stand, are dozens and dozens of these giant lizards, all waiting for the sun to hit them, charge them up, propel them back into their long-term plan of taking over the city—the same vague goal that these days motivates Izzy to get out of bed. He thinks of the bits of gator still clogging his system. He can feel the last of it prowling its way out, looking for the exit. They had to be up so early to meet Danny for this job that he hasn't yet had the chance to take his morning dump.

Despite it being out of character for the character Izzy's trying to embody, he can't help that he was raised by a kind tía—another accident of history—and so he doesn't stop himself from saying, Bro, sorry about your car catching fire last week. That's some crazy shit. I mean like, obviously I had nothing to do with that, but I saw it happening so, yeah, that sucks.

Danny looks like he has no idea what Izzy is referencing, but then his face softens and he says, Oh yeah! Shit! Bro, don't even worry about it. That's already ancient history. He laughs and says, You don't know this but you actually did me a *huge* favor.

—No seriously, I had nothing to do with it. I was just there recording it with my phone.

—Okay, then I guess thank Julisa for me.

Danny winks and holds the cigar to his mouth and Izzy asks nothing more—no *How'd you know I talked to Julisa?* Or *You got something in your eye, bro?*—because by then he's caught himself and remembered he's supposed to have some ill-fated sense of pride. He just shakes his head no and rubs the last of the sleep from his face, hoping Danny takes the gesture as some kind of dismissal, but Danny is still just standing there, actually inhaling.

Danny points the lit cigar at Rudy and through a cloud of new smoke says, Have you ever eaten iguana?

It's the same question Julisa asked Izzy at the Fair, and he looks around now, between Rudy and Danny and then into Danny's truck, wondering if someone is truly fucking with him.

Danny doesn't wait for them to answer: It's disgusting, he says. I mean yeah, you can find some old-school Florida cracker that'll say they eat these shits up and swear it tastes decent but lemme tell you, denial is not just a river in Africa.

An almost-neon-green iguana scurries off the side of the road and darts across the parking lot, and Danny says to its swishing tail, Tastes like you're eating something dead but not like in a regular way like how hamburger is dead. Dead like rotting.

—So, number one, you can't even eat them, he says facing Izzy again. Number two, they're fucking up the sides of the canals, climbing with their claws. It's called erosion and it's a real thing, look it up. Number three, they aren't afraid of shit and they fuck with people's dogs and they eat baby ducks and sometimes the parent ducks, and they fucking *destroy* people's landscaping. My point is, it's basically a completely useless fish, and you can't just drive over the grown ones without possibly damaging your tires. Assuming they don't run away first like our friend just did.

He aims the cigar in the direction of the just-departed iguana.

—I don't think iguanas are fish, Rudy says, and Izzy says, I have *not* had enough café for this Animal Planet bullshit.

Danny raises his arms out to his sides and the vest spreads open, revealing his menagerie of tattoos. Does Julisa have any, in places Izzy hasn't yet seen? Is that something Danny would know?

—That's why *we* are here, he says. To round up these babies and get rid of them so that the nice people living in the townhouses across from this canal don't have to waste any more of their time harassing these guys.

Izzy says, They hired you to do this?

Danny heads to the trunk of his Escalade, the cigar in his mouth as he pulls out a pole and a heavy sack. Three huge coolers wait inside.

—No, *I* hired us to do this. Or you guys. I hired you guys.

There's a curled-up length of fishing wire on the pole, a tiny noose dangling at its end. He takes another pull from the cigar—how he doesn't cough from inhaling, Izzy cannot figure out—and says, I'm basically just supervising. And I, you know, take care of them, after you guys round them up, hence the need for me to conserve my energy so to speak.

Both Izzy and Rudy stand with their legs spread apart and their arms crossed over their chests. The boots Danny had asked them to bring are still in Izzy's trunk, along with a change of clothes; the requested bathing suits already cinched around their waists, though their phones and wallets are still in their pockets. They now understand what it is they've been brought here to do. They just have no idea how they're supposed to go about doing it, and from the way Danny drops the pole and the sack on the ground and tells them to get to it, the words crawling out around the branch of the cigar, they know Danny has no clear idea either.

—Have you done this before? Izzy says.

—You just sort of lasso them, like a cowboy but not fast and without spinning it over your head first, Danny says. You actually have to go super slow and kinda sneak up on them.

Izzy picks up the pole and says, How the fuck is that like a cowboy?

—Once you slip it over their heads, you pull it back and they're gonna death roll. Be ready for that, my friends. Think alligator but like way way faster. Because they're smaller.

Rudy asks, Which ones do we have to catch?

Some are black, some are green, others brown or rust-colored. Rudy thinks some are supposed to be there while others aren't but he's wrong: none of them should be there, so they are to corral and remove every iguana they can manage to catch and store in either of the three coolers, no need to sort them.

—There's ice in the coolers, Danny says. To literally chill them out. Keeps them from fighting in there. We don't want anyone getting hurt.

They have been standing there long enough that some iguanas have started to edge closer, raising themselves up higher off the ground by extending their front legs. One gets within a few feet of Izzy and appears to do a series of push-ups. Another—yellow-eyed and so orange he looks sunburned, gigantic enough that they're surprised by his speed as they each take a reflexive step back—passes within lunging distance of Rudy and tears all the way across the street. Danny is correct that they are afraid of nothing.

—There goes Gordo, Danny says. He turns fully toward the iguana, cups his hands around his mouth and yells, Get that money, kid!

He explains to no one in particular, except maybe to the iguana trudging away from them: Gordo fights other iguanas for rights to that sidewalk almost daily. Dude continues to win. I think he's getting stronger and gaining the skills to challenge the people that live in the complex someday.

Izzy says, Hold up, you *named* that one? Like just now?

—My guess is, another year of this unchecked, and the other iguanas will rise above their current status as neighborhood Instagram content and eventually join Gordo's army. My guess is, the people living there will someday have to break into their own apartments to steal back what was once theirs while Gordo the Iguana King is across the way, taking his daily swim.

Izzy had no idea what he was manifesting when he wrote *Get hooked up with shady dudes* on his list of action items, but this wasn't at all what he had in mind. He drops the pole on the asphalt and whispers to Rudy, Bro, I don't know about this guy.

—He's not wrong, Izzy. These things are swimming up through the sewers into people's toilets. People leaving their toilet seats up keep finding wet iguanas laying themselves out to dry on their nice bath mats and shit. We're doing a service, bro. We're helping the community.

Before Izzy can explain that that's not what he meant, Danny says through a cloud of smoke, You guys gotta work together. One of you uses the pole and catches them with the noose, the other one grabs them and puts them in the bag. You sneak up on them slow but then gotta be super fast getting them in the bag.

Of course Rudy is nodding throughout all this, as if he's Danny's Manolo instead of Izzy's.

—You can take turns and switch jobs but for real, one of you will be better at one part than the other. Whichever one of you has longer arms should probably do the grabbing and bagging.

Rudy sticks out his arms, looks them over, motions with his chin to Izzy to hold out his own for comparison. Izzy sucks his teeth and swats Rudy's arm away. He tries to conjure what Tony Montana would say in a moment like this, to signal to Danny that Izzy will ultimately be the one in charge. Something like: *Nobody ever made me catch no fucking iguanas in Cuba, meng. I want my jew-meng rights!*

—The minute we get close to those things they're gonna jump in the water, he says.

—Nah, Danny says almost laughing at him. They don't wanna get back in the water because right now they're getting nice and warm. Once you got one in your hands it's easy. Flip them over and they go into a trance. You can rub their bellies and everything, it's super cute.

Izzy wants to ask how much they are getting paid for this nonsense but thinks it would make him look weak to do so. Rudy had said only, when he'd first brought up the job, *A lot, and in cash.* But how much was *a lot*? Two hundred bucks? Three? Very un-Scarface of him to not ask for an exact figure from Rudy, to not make his Manolo bring him complete information. Think of that scene where Tony threatens to make everyone count the laundered money again—after having spent all night counting bills and cooking books—at just the mere threat of there being a small discrepancy. Izzy's Scarface game is already slipping, and there's no explanation in his mind other than Julisa, her sudden appearance in his life, out of order, him getting too excited and showing her that list of names his Tía Tere gave him, him already telling Julisa too much even when he's barely told her anything.

Danny half-correctly reads Izzy's grimace and says, Don't worry, bro. You aren't getting paid by the piece, so no pressure, though I would love to get those coolers full. We only got a couple hours before they get warm enough to go back in the water as it is. A deal is a deal. Don't worry, I got you.

He walks back to his Escalade, hauls out the coolers. Izzy motions for Rudy to follow him to the trunk of his car, presumably for their boots.

—What deal's he talking about, Izzy hisses. How much we getting paid for this?

He's mad at himself for asking his Manolo Manolo-like questions, but no way he's getting shredded by a bunch of fucking iguanas for less than two hundred dollars, even if it is only a couple hours of work. Izzy pops the trunk and they grab their boots, turning to sit on the trunk's lip to lace them up.

—Danny's been hooking people up since forever. You gotta trust me on this, bro.

I trust nobody, he hears Al Pacino say in a fake Cuban accent. But Tony did trust people, didn't he? He trusted Manolo, at least for a while, and look how that turned out: he ended up having to kill him. Izzy thrusts his hands in his pockets, pulls out his wallet and his phone, sees on his screen a text from Julisa. More distractions—Julisa texting this early in the morning really is bad news—but he can't help himself: he wants to read it, but he can't risk Rudy asking any questions such as, *Who the fuck is texting you before the sun is even up?* He tosses the phone in his trunk and tells himself that reading her message later will be his reward for surviving whatever iguana encounters await him. It's a romantic thought, a sweet one, but he doesn't register it as such.

When he turns around, Danny is there, his arm extended and pressing a pair of canvas work gloves into Izzy's chest. He recognizes them as the kind hanging near the registers at Home Depot, the ones you grab as an afterthought on your way out. Merry Christmas, Danny says. He tosses Rudy a matching pair.

Another iguana trudges closer; perhaps he's interested in the very early holiday gift into which Rudy is shoving his hands. Rudy squats down to take a hard look and says, Bro, these are fucking miniature dinosaurs.

He lunges for the base of the animal's tail and of course he misses, falling onto his hands and knees and yelling, These shits have legit claws!

—That's why I gave you the gloves, my friend!

As Danny walks back to his Escalade, hands in his pockets, they overhear him humming a tune and can make out only two words from the chorus:

—Ca-Ri-Bee-Inn / Am-Phi-Bee-Inn

—Isn't that song from *Sesame Street*? Rudy says only to Izzy.

Izzy wouldn't know if it was; he'd never watched the show, didn't have access to it as a child. He didn't have a television in Cuba—or at least, he doesn't remember ever watching it—and even though he had one once he was living with his Tía Tere, his childhood had ended the moment he'd stepped onto that raft: he spent Saturday mornings of those first years in the United States on his Tía Tere's couch, watching cooking shows with her. So he had no idea what Rudy was talking about, and Rudy should know that by now, so Izzy doesn't even bother to tell Rudy to shut the fuck up.

Instead, Izzy swings his leg over the guardrail meant to keep them away from the water, and when his foot lands, every iguana dashes away from him. Despite what Danny said, one flies into the canal with a leg-sprawled leap, landing far enough from them that they don't get splashed. The iguanas have caught on faster than Rudy, definitely faster than Danny; they already know that when it comes to Izzy and what he's capable of, they should be a little afraid.

It's undeniable now that the sun is coming up. There's the magenta light it brings, of course, but bigger than even that are the sudden birds: thousands of squawks and flaps coming off the canal's water from miles around, a reminder of just how close to the Everglades this metropolis is perched. Danny stands above him—he and Rudy are down near the water's edge. How hard would Izzy have to throw to hit Danny from there with a caught iguana?

As the sky brightens and the birds thunder, Danny yells from the top of the canal: You hear all them birds? That's every one of them saying, *Hey you other birds out there, here I am! Come fuck me!*

He slips his fingers inside his vest and opens it wide to the air, throwing his head back as if looking to swallow bird shit, and Izzy pictures the near-end of *Scarface.* Danny as a version of Tony's sister Gina, wearing that thin shiny bathrobe, yelling *Come fuck me, Tony* to her brother as he sits at his desk behind a pile of cocaine in what's arguably one of the strangest and most disturbing scenes in the movie. Seconds later, the shock of hundreds of bullets tear that robe open, giving you a good peek at Gina's breasts before she dies. Izzy too now gets a healthy glimpse of Danny's pepperoni nipples, but instead of gunfire, this version of that bizarre scene gets interrupted by the blast of birds, flocks of them materializing overhead as if Danny has single-handedly summoned them, the crack of their wings and their calls drowning out Danny's pleas: You hear them? That's what they're saying! *Here I am, I'm a bird! Tweet tweet, motherfuckers! Let's fuck!*

BIRDS OF MIAMI-DADE COUNTY

There are probably hundreds of different species, many of which are flying high above that canal and Danny's outstretched arms, but truth be told, there are likely only four types that will stick around in the long run because they are resilient enough to withstand the rising waters and extreme heat, and so only these four species are relevant to the version of urban Miami being depicted here.

The Seagull

There's no need to waste time on seagulls because they are obvious and basic, dumb and desperate enough to land repeatedly in Lolita's tank, albeit lured there by strategically deployed orca vomit and/or the coolers of fish on stage during her shows. Seagulls are everywhere and not at all unique to Miami and you already know them from how they steal your chips at the beach. The seagull doesn't count as one of the four.

The Pelican

Briefly mentioned earlier, in the description of various internet videos featuring these feathered pterodactyls being utterly destroyed by very bored captive orca, many a pelican has fallen for the same vomit trick as the seagull. But pelicans are less often consumed and more just fucked with, being delicately plucked from below the water's surface just seconds after landing, then dragged down to almost-drown, then brought back up for a quick thrash and a flap or two, then back down, the whole cycle repeating again and again until the whale gets bored with how little the pelican responds—too tired to thrash and flap anymore, and where's the fun in that?—and leaves it for a trainer to scoop up with a net and put out of its misery.

Two types of pelicans live in Miami, according to the laminated

Birds of South Florida field guide you can purchase at any Books &
Books, the city's best loved and best-for-a-date-night independent
bookstore (sadly, Izzy's never been there, doesn't even know it exists).
These are the creatively named Brown Pelican and White Pelican.
Both are on the page of the guide under the heading COMMON BIRDS.

The White Pelican isn't a full-time South Florida resident. The
White Pelican calls Miami home from November to March, so more
or less the inverse of hurricane season. The field guide says that they
are the second-largest flying bird in North America, which seems
like it can't be true, but as previously mentioned, this field guide is
laminated—it says WATERPROOF right on the front at the very top—
and that lends it an air of certainty that feels hard to dispute. The
White Pelican's length is listed at 62 inches, its wingspan 108 inches,
which are admittedly the two biggest numbers for each of those char-
acteristics of any other bird in the field guide (by comparison, the
Bald Eagle, which is listed on the guide's two-page BIRDS OF PREY
spread despite maybe never being spotted in Miami by anyone ever,
has a wingspan of a puny 80 inches). The White Pelican is the pelican
most featured in advertisements featuring pelicans; probably because
it's so white, it's considered a universal pelican by marketing people,
who are also largely white.

The Brown Pelican, by literal and figurative contrast, is a *full-time
coastal Florida resident*, again according to this field guide. This is the
pelican you're going to watch from the beach as it pulls in its wings
and plummets to the ocean's surface after a fish. Why does it not
die when it does this? Why doesn't the drop—sometimes from as
high as fifty feet—snap every hollow bone in its not-as-large-as-the-
White-Pelican's body upon impact? Because air sacs in its shoulders
and neck area cushion the blow, again according to this field guide,
which is most certainly making this shit up to sell copies (granted,
lying about real things is a purportedly effective strategy for selling
books). The Brown Pelican is 51 inches long and has a 79-inch wingspan, which presumably makes it faster than the white one, though
this is noted nowhere in the field guide. In the drawing provided,
the Brown Pelican appears to actually be pretty gray looking, with
light gray wing feathers and dark gray-to-black feathers at each wing's

outer edges. Only the back of its neck looks brown, and the top of its head looks kind of yellow. One cannot be sure if this discrepancy is an artifact of the field guide's printing or its aforementioned lamination, or if the Brown Pelican just got an inaccurate name out of the gate—bad branding, done haphazardly based on a set of incorrect assumptions made by the aforementioned white marketing folks who no doubt had a say in the naming of all things at some point in time.

Overall, it cannot be debated that the pelican is a majestic bird. So majestic, in fact, that in one of the later scenes in *Scarface*, Tony Montana—while smoking a cigar, soaking up to his nipples in bubbles in an equally majestic tub the size of the stingray petting tank at the Seaquarium, as he studiously ignores Manolo, who is perched awkwardly in a solid gold chair, leaning down to offer Tony advice he won't take—watches on his tub's television set a nature program, where on the screen, a flock of flamingos takes flight, and Tony removes the cigar from his mouth to laugh and say with abject glee, *Fly, pelican, fly!*

The Rooster

Before discussing those misidentified flamingos, however, attention must first be paid to the rooster, that dutiful and technically illegal alarm clock of the city, which in Miami (specifically Hialeah) is far more prevalent than the flamingo but less evocative of South Florida with regard to the region's various branding initiatives. The rooster isn't listed in the field guide at all, which only adds to the suspicion of its deep inaccuracies. Were the rooster to be included, it would likely appear on the COMMON BIRDS page, or perhaps on the page titled WADING BIRDS, as they are often found pecking near the edges of Hialeah's puddles.

These are not the beautiful roosters you see on social media being raised by people in Berkeley and Vermont. These guys are typically quite scraggly through no fault of their own: blame the humidity, the water migrating from the air to their feathers, giving most of them a perpetually bedraggled look, hence one possible reason why they're not included in the field guide, which is beautifully illustrated—there is no way to make a wet rooster look good. They'll survive sea level rise, but they won't be cute while doing it. Sometimes found among a harem of chickens, sometimes just alone, their natural habitat is on or near a chain-link fence in reasonably close proximity to someone's abuelo or old tío, who when asked claims that the rooster does not live there or belong to him, he's *just feeding it.* Why the disavowal? Because roosters (not chickens) are, as previously mentioned, illegal to own in the City of Miami, with the statute only being enforced when you piss off a neighbor with some unrelated slight and they call animal control on you in an act of vengeance.

The Flamingo

The all-powerful and awe-inspiring flamingo is, unbelievably, not included in this field guide either, and so here's where it can be abandoned as a guide of any sort, as it's revealed itself to be full of falsehoods. These pink birds, made so by their consumption of shrimp, embody Miami's festive and colorful atmosphere: you can instantly make any body of water more Miami by placing a flamingo in it. You can find them everywhere: on billboards, painted on the sides of buildings, on lottery tickets. They're regularly spotted—albeit in plastic form—in the residential areas of Miami-Dade, faded by the sun and dotting people's lawns. Flamingos are also extremely stylish when illustrated wearing a pair of sunglasses, which—as is the case for Pitbull when he throws on those aviators—only increases their ridiculous yet emblematic nature.

Arguably, South Florida's most famous flamingos are those that call the Hialeah Park Racetrack home. This specific flock was brought from Cuba in 1934—so they're *those* kind of Cubans: immigrant birds, not birds in exile—and hatched right there at the racetrack. Descendants of that flock were featured in the opening credits of *Miami Vice,* but you can't hold that against them, as it's not like they signed off on being part of that nonsense. Because the Hialeah racetrack is, inexplicably, *the only place the species has been successfully reproduced outside its wild state* (this according to the Hialeah Park Casino's website), the racetrack's infield, where the birds live hashtag-305FullTime, is a legitimate National Audubon Sanctuary, the various horse races happening around them notwithstanding.

The laminated field guide features two birds that look like distant cousins of the flamingo: both potential primos are listed on the WAD-ING BIRDS spread, which is where the flamingo would be listed if this field guide were more accurate. There's the Roseate Spoonbill, which on its body has pink feathers like a flamingo; and something called the Reddish Egret, which is, unsurprisingly, reddish enough to pass for pink. If the flamingo were on here, maybe the guide would note that, like other wading birds, the flamingo prefers shallow marsh-lands, or that it's part of the heron family. Based on the basic nature of the facts listed for the other birds (i.e., the Greater Yellowlegs, the following written right next to its image: *Slender, with long, distinctly yel-low legs.*), it's doubtful the guide would've noted some of the flamin-go's more intriguing facts, like that their nests are made of clay and shaped like volcanos, or that when a baby flamingo hatches, it imme-diately devours the shell from which it just emerged. Or that up until recently, Zoo Miami a.k.a. Metro Zoo stored their flock of fifty or so flamingos in the park's men's restroom whenever a hurricane threat-ened. A staff member spent their afternoon covering that bathroom's floor in a foot of straw as if that would keep the delicate yet mighty flamingo from absolutely losing its shit, when what really kept each of them calm were the mirrors: as storms hit, they gazed at themselves for hours on end, huddling up against the sinks en masse, vying to get closer to the glass, like chongas in a club's bathroom wrestling for the vantage point from which they could best reapply their lip liner.

The Ibis

Hurricanes bring about the fourth and final relevant Miami-Dade bird: the ibis. Not the ibis in the field guide, not exactly, though that ibis—the White Ibis, also a wading bird—is noted by the guide to be *gregarious.* (The only other fact about it given: *Probes for crustaceans in shallow ponds and edges.* Illuminating!) No, this listing is specifically about one ibis: Sebastian the Ibis, mascot for the Miami Hurricanes, the city's OG college football team.

This bird is technically a human in a bird costume, but the cos-tume is likely covered in hundreds of thousands of actual ibis feath-ers, each feather handstitched by lifetime members of the Audubon

Society, making it more like an ibis than any actual ibis could ever be. He is SuperIbis, Ibis Über Alles. He is the Tony Montana of Ibises.

These days, Sebastian wears a University of Miami jersey with the number zero on it, which is uncommon for ibises in the wild. He used to wear a green sweater, presumably for camouflage, though rising temperatures caused by the upcoming/ongoing climate catastrophe have made the cold-weather-wear inhospitable. He still sports a little white sailor hat though, which is both a reminder that the campus is close to the beach and also that Sebastian is a member of the Merchant Marine. Sebastian does not, however, wear pants, as is common with birds of this nature (Donald Duck of Orlando, et cetera).

Sebastian the Ibis was once arrested for trying to extinguish, with a literal fire extinguisher, the flaming spear thrown on the field by a white guy dressed up as Chief Osceola (a.k.a. the blatantly racist mascot for UM's main rival, the Florida State Seminoles a.k.a. the Criminoles a.k.a. Football School University). Sebastian didn't make it past the sidelines before Tallahassee police tackled him to the ground and slapped handcuffs on his wing-wrists (this happened years before those same police would somehow misplace and then destroy evidence—a cell phone with a video recording of their star quarterback raping an unconscious woman—in the days leading up to the quarterback's indictment, the timing of which, should the indictment have occurred based on the now-nonexistent evidence, would've made him ineligible to play in the upcoming championship Rose Bowl game). Sebastian the Ibis was ultimately not arrested because he did nothing illegal, and because FSU beat the Hurricanes that day, hence swiftly rendering Tallahassee's police force intoxicated by benevolence/beer.

Sebastian the Ibis can appear at your private Miami-Dade County event for $321 for a maximum of two hours, $318 for the same amount of time if you're in Broward County. These rates are more than twice the amount Izzy charged when he worked as a Pitbull impersonator, which perhaps explains why he got so many gigs before the real Pitbull shut him down: Izzy was a bargain compared to Sebastian. And Sebastian, being a delicate person in a delicate bird costume, requires lots of special handling: you need to give Sebastian at least three weeks' notice before the requested appearance, and he also requires a private and secure changing room where he can lock his valuables. You must provide him with drinking water, preferably bottled. You must also provide an on-site contact to escort Sebastian into and out of his vehicle—Sebastian can drive!—which is why he'll survive the flooding; he'll just take the turnpike north. Basically, you have to be Sebastian's bodyguard whenever he's on or near your habitat. Sebastian also gets a break after an hour, and he reserves the right to walk away at any point and for any reason with no expectation of even a partial refund. Unlike a non-university-affiliated ibis, Sebastian is unable to appear in inclement or severe weather and will therefore become much harder to spot before he leaves the city altogether.

None of this is in the field guide. Like the missing flamingos, Sebastian's absence is a lie by omission. And like the missing flamingos and the lonely roosters, Sebastian typically cannot reproduce in captivity, no matter how wild or desperate the sound of his calls.

FOR SHADOWING

Julisa gets up super early the morning after the Fair to study for her communications class while listening to Power96, the radio station that's all but ruined a generation of Miami residents for serious, sane partnerships, what with the Power Love Hour's focus on songs conveying desperation, volatility, infidelity; inspiring the keying of cars as a perfectly acceptable response to a broken heart; normalizing both emotional and physical violences great and small again and again; ending it all with Jagged Edge's proclamation, *Girl, let's just get married*, reminding his bride-to-be that, despite the ups and downs of their relationship, *We ain't getting no younger, girl, we might as well do it.*

And so despite their only dayslong courtship, and despite Izzy not fully participating in said courtship, and despite the abrupt end to their first date because he claimed he had a headache, these are the scenarios that Julisa imagines as to how Izzy will propose marriage:

1. On the Sky Ride at the Fair next year, obviously.
2. At Santa's Enchanted Forest, right as they pose for a photo with a super tall inflatable snowman—she'll look over at him (Izzy, not the snowman), and see that he's down on one knee, and she'll cover her mouth and scream.
3. At the beach, right as the sun is coming up after a night spent dancing at clubs she's technically not yet old enough to enter, on the deck of one of those cute lifeguard stands the city painted for the tourists.
4. At the Venetian Pool, which she's never been to but has heard is super nice. She imagines him coming up out of the water in front of her, a fake but waterproof clam in his hand, which he opens and *bam!* There's the ring, a Tiffany diamond solitaire at least a carat big that he bought from a jewelry store at The Falls

down in Pinecrest, which she feels strongly is Miami's classiest mall—fuck Aventura Mall and the clusterfuck that is the Ives Dairy Road exit off I-95, fuck that shit straight to hell—the ring classy and elegant, just like her and just like The Falls.

5. At Vizcaya, the museum and gardens where she did *not* take her quinces pictures because her parents didn't want to pay the extra hundred dollars the photographer charged if you picked that location for your photoshoot setting over the ruins of Coral Gables, which was free but you ran the risk of having parked cars in the background of all your pictures.

6. At a Marc Anthony concert—because Julisa loves old-school romantic songs like his and she likes that one track about the rain that he did with Pitbull, and her parents *really* love Marc Anthony, especially once he divorced that J-Lo puta—with Izzy somehow having enlisted Marc Anthony himself in orchestrating the proposal. She acknowledges to herself that this one is unlikely. She knows that. She's not an idiot. These are her *dreams*, remember? And as a good semireligious girl who listens to her parents ninety-nine percent of the time, she deserves a proposal this grand. She's allowed to dream big—Marc Anthony pulling her up on stage in front of thousands of screaming fans big—because it's *her* engagement, something she's waited so long for: her parents had already been married a year by the time they were her age.

7. Disney.

8. At the Miami Seaquarium, just as Lolita splashes down into the tank after some final, majestic cartwheeling aerial flip, a maneuver possible only in Julisa's imagination not because Lolita is incapable of executing it, but because, were Lolita to attempt it, she would—given the tank's illegally small size—land somewhere in the audience.

This last daydream takes Julisa by surprise. She hasn't been to the Seaquarium since going with a church group when she was nine or ten. But of course it makes sense: Izzy had told her just the day before that Lolita was his favorite whale, that she'd belong to him someday, and Julisa took the comment for what it absolutely wasn't—a coded message about their future as a couple. But it's with this proposal version in mind that she decides to push her textbook off her lap, pull her phone into bed with her, and text Izzy the address to one of the names she'd remembered from the list he'd shown her on the Sky Ride. She wants him to understand that she'd be that kind of girlfriend, that kind of wife—the helping kind. The kind who gladly works behind the scenes to make her man look good, so long as her man acknowledges that debt by taking care of her in every way taking care of someone can be construed, minus the violent ones.

It hadn't been hard to find Odlanier Vasquez. She'd used her mom's Facebook the night before, after getting back from the Fair, and found they were already connected, though her mother claimed to have no idea who he was when she'd asked (*I just add people it says I know, I don't know them!*). Then she sent Mr. Vasquez an extremely polite message saying she was his Facebook friend Caridad's daughter doing a school project on vintage cars, specifically Volkswagen Beetles—she'd seen enough pictures on his Facebook to know exactly which kind of lie would get him to respond—and could she por favor have his home address to mail him a questionnaire, and Odlanier is old enough and not-good-at-being-safe-at-computers enough to have written back almost right away with his address: a house in P.S.N. Julisa doesn't know that Izzy is already in that neighborhood, about to be chest-deep in a canal chasing after iguanas. She imagines, when she sends him the texts, him coming to her house after his job with Daniel to thank her. He'll pick her up and spin her around and kiss her and say, How did I get so lucky to find you? And she will say, It's not luck, and he will put his finger over her lips to stop her from saying the next thing, which he already knows: it's destiny.

Julisa is a virgin in both her vagina and her butthole and she is extremely proud of this fact, at how she's avoided close calls by diverting men with The Sacred Blowjob. She took a purity pledge at one youth group or another when she was fifteen, a few months after

en all three coolers are full of iguanas, Izzy and Rudy hoist each
 back into Danny's Escalade, then head to Izzy's car to clean them-
es up. The job didn't take long, as it turns out Izzy is a natural with
 noose; he is also better at bagging, and so the system became Izzy
gging and then handing the pole over to Rudy to hold still while
then dealt with the flailing and rolling at the other end. The guys
 el off more sweat than canal water as Danny takes out a roll of bills
m the glove compartment, walks it over to them at Izzy's trunk.
 e cigar is long gone but the smell lingers, mixing with the iron
ell of blood from their scrapes—both from iguana claws and from
pping over rocks and asphalt edges. They are done just in time too:
 e sun is high enough that the iguanas seem supercharged, able to
trun cars as they bolt across the street. Izzy picks up his phone to
ke a picture of one, to text to Julisa later.

The bills Danny breaks off into Izzy's free hand aren't twenties,
 it hundreds. He almost stops the guy to point out that there must
 some mistake when Danny keeps going after the fourth bill. Izzy
ently breathes in *Tony* and exhales *Montana* to keep his face from
traying his surprise at the amount accumulating in his palm. He
akes a show of looking at his phone to prove how not a big deal
is is, sees Julisa's name, pretends to be reading her texts: he's too
istracted to actually read them. The counting out stops and Izzy
ances up, nods a thanks, then tries hard not to watch Rudy's turn.
fter the same amount lands in his hand, there's a sense of awe at the
ickness left over in Danny's fist—a substantial wad still there, and
his is after he's paid them each a grand out if it. A fucking thousand
ollars, just like that, and somehow the dude still has thousands more
n a tight roll held together by a fucking rubber band.

A thousand bucks in one hand, his phone in the other, Izzy slides

her quinces photos were taken and exactly a w
her then-boyfriend—who she really did think she
though he was so, so fucked up—rub the tip of h
vagina's opening. She took the youth group leader
to stop this rubbing behavior immediately, before
was the purity pledge, she has thought ever since,
whoever) to give her the gift of The Sacred Blowjol

Is it a gift or is it a calling? It had proven most
kind of power—her newfound ability felt divine, mir
scendent for all involved. She wished she could tell l
it: she felt that sort of pride in the way she simultan
and resurrected the men on which she's chosen to k

The then-boyfriend was the first one, the one w
had a gift. Even without knowledge of The Sacred E
ents had prayed for that relationship to end becaus
ents were, the company they were known to keep—th
and prominence—the easy money they always seem
prayers had worked, and even better, Julisa and the
ended things on friendly terms, the circumstance
about the breakup—Julisa's growing commitment to
with her wanting to focus on doing well in high scho
just started—allowed her to remain blameless and safe

The then-boyfriend did not go to any church or
pledge-providing youth group, but he believed in sp
ences and knew one when he got one, was not abou
more when getting head from Julisa already felt so clea
ral. Also, his being five years older than her made him fe
to respect her pledge or face possible jail time, and h
enough to fear in the maybe-getting-arrested departme
related pursuits unrelated to sex with a minor. The th
had been raised with at least that much sense, instilled
dead mother. The then-boyfriend was Daniel.

his thumb for real this time and sees Julisa's text: LOOK WHO I FOUND, it says, followed by an address for Odlanier Vasquez. An address that shares a zip code with these iguanas.

He is too amped up to register the rest of her other messages and so disregards Julisa saying she hopes that he'll call her when he can, so she can explain how she found it, to talk through next steps and what his plans might be, the best way to arrange a meeting, et cetera. But who the fuck cares how she got it or what the fuck she thinks about his plans! He doesn't have time to call her! He is a man on a mission! First you get the money—done!—and it turns out the saying is true: then you get the power. Izzy feels it, finally, like an electric pulse: the power he's been waiting for. He didn't need a suit jacket to give him an aura of authority—all he really needed was a fistful of hundreds! Tony Montana was nothing if not a man of action, and Izzy—thanks to the money-then-the-power he now feels surging through him, making his hands and the tip of his dick tingle—is ready for big moves, for action.

—So what do we do now? Rudy says.

Izzy almost answers before seeing that Rudy's asking Danny about the coolers of iguanas. A trickle of blood runs from Rudy's elbow down his forearm: turns out Izzy's arms are the longer ones.

—*We* do nothing. You guys are good. Me, I take these babies to the canal behind my house for processing.

—Which involves what?

—Letting them warm back up on my dad's boat ramp, then pushing them with a broom into the canal behind my house.

Rudy says, Are you fucking serious, and laughs like an idiot—that's what the money does to him.

Izzy's thinking is more like: Whatever. This Danny guy is soft. Fucking freak can't even finish the job. Izzy folds his bills in half, slides them in his pocket for now. He'll have his own roll and rubber band in no time.

Danny winks at him, something Izzy almost warns him to never do again, and says, Gables by the Sea could use some extra erosion. We'll be in touch.

DOES THE WHALE DIMINISH?

In captivity, orca regularly find the exact place on a trainer's wetsuit with enough slack in it to pinch with their teeth without nipping the skin underneath, and from this place they pull said trainer into the water, sometimes as a joke to entertain themselves, sometimes out of frustration, sometimes both. It could be said they also use the objects tossed into their tanks for the same purpose—Lolita is regularly given a diving suit and a beach ball, for example—but mostly, they flip these objects into the stands surrounding their tanks, then watch as their trainers retrieve them. What's more entertaining: pushing a beach ball around a tank, or training someone to repeatedly climb over bleacher steps to fetch said beach ball and bring it back?

In captivity, orca regularly stick their heads out of the water to communicate with their trainers, using a pared-down version of the language they use when communicating with other orca. Such above-water vocalizations are rare among themselves and almost unheard of in the wild. It's the orca who've adapted to compensate for the inability of the trainers.

In captivity, orca regularly show preferences for certain trainers over others. This is likely based on touch, which is another way of saying: an exchange of energy between themselves and the trainer.

In captivity, orca regularly train the humans assigned to work with them to be unafraid of their teeth. When they catch their assigned human sitting at the tank's edge, feet dangling in the water, they will approach slowly, then very quickly open their mouths and drag their teeth across the tops of the trainer's feet—enough to elicit fear but not blood. The human unfailingly pulls their feet out of the water as a primal reflex. The orca will practice this over and over again, sometimes a dozen times in a row, until the human learns to trust the orca and leave their feet in the water as the whale drags their teeth across the tops of them. When the human consistently stops pulling their feet and legs up to safety, the orca ends the training. They usually then resume their listless swimming around the tank.

In captivity, orca regularly demand that a trainer's hand brush against their teeth and tongue during feedings as a way of proving the trainer's trust in them. Through repetition and insistence and even protests, orca have successfully forced humans to integrate this practice into standard orca husbandry procedures.

In captivity, nothing can be said to be regular for the orca given how little their environment replicates the one inhabited by their wild counterparts. In captivity, the mark of a good trainer is measured by how long that trainer can maintain an orca's sanity given their confinement. In captivity, given the frequency of trainings and performances, orca know for exactly how long each of their trainers can hold their breath.

THE FIRST RAFTER

According to the map on Izzy's phone, Odlanier Vasquez's house is just on the other side of Palm Springs North, an unincorporated part of Miami-Dade County that's cut off from getting to count itself as Miami Lakes by canals: the same canals Izzy and Rudy have been in and out of all morning while trapping iguanas under Danny's supervision. Izzy knows Palm Springs North—P.S.N.—as Pot Smoking Neighborhood, had once eaten the best ceviche of his life so far at a little storefront in one of the neighborhood's strip malls, a restaurant whose name he doesn't remember until they pass it now—Te Amo Perú. Next to it is one of P.S.N.'s last remaining local pizza places, Tony's House of Pizza. Izzy's never eaten there but takes the restaurant's name as a sign that going straight from the job with Danny to the address Julisa texted him is the right move, totally in line with his Tony Montana plan, despite Rudy's protests that they go back home and shower first. Izzy still needs to tell Rudy about the day before—the Fair with Julisa—and decides to maybe mention it after they make this house call: Rudy still seems pissed that Izzy made him change out of his bathing suit and into his pants in the backseat. Izzy keeps one hand on the steering wheel as the other finds his front pocket, his palm cupping the mound made by the folded hundred-dollar bills there.

The zip code of this neighborhood, 33015, is Hialeah according to the U.S. Postal Service (and unincorporated Miami-Dade County according to everything else), but the canals also work with I-75 and the Palmetto to rope this community off from the Hialeah of Mylander Park and Westland Mall fame. It's northwest Hialeah, closer to Miami Gardens, a city only as old as Izzy and the county's largest majority Black municipality, and so this area is less Cuban/more diverse than the Hialeah of the racetrack, of Ñooo Qué Barato fame.

No flamingos or drawings of flamingos here. But still, there's a vendor at every exit off the Palmetto, selling gladiolas or maní or limones or mamoncillos or bottled water or already-blooming roses. The kids who live up here go to American High, named that because the school was founded in 1976, the bicentennial, to relieve overcrowding at Carol City High and Hialeah-Miami Lakes High. Izzy sees all these schools as rivals.

Izzy also knows P.S.N. as the neighborhood responsible for a certain caliber of clientele at his pre-dishwashing part-time job, the one at Don Shula's in nearby Miami Lakes. He'd learned how to tell the P.S.N. women from the Miami Lakes ones on days when his shifts involved checking in ladies for the resort's Zumba classes. The P.S.N. women never came alone—always in pairs or groups of three, often wearing faded, oversized Disney-themed T-shirts rather than the dedicated workout attire favored by the Miami Lakes set, oftentimes sporting patterned one-size-fits-all leggings they'd bought from a mall kiosk as a substitute for actual activity-friendly-and-sweat-wicking yoga pants. They tended to gather at the back of the class and talk loud about how tired they were or hungover they were or how ridiculous the premise of a Zumba class was: *People pay to just copy somebody's dancing? And no drinks?* Hungover or not, these women always killed it in class, keeping in perfect step with the backup Miami Heat dancers Don Shula's tended to hire to lead Zumba—women Izzy's age who he let in the building an hour before class time, who, when he'd greet them, would ignore his hello, barely acknowledging that the two of them could've been in the same homeroom just a couple years earlier. Not so for the P.S.N. ladies, who always greeted him by his name even on the days he'd forgotten to wear his name tag. Their acrylic nails clicked soothingly against the keys of whatever device Izzy presented them with at check-in to verify their payment. And they always paid by the class, never had memberships like the Miami Lakes set. They were there for a laugh or to cash in some gift card some well-meaning but oblivious boss had given them last Christmas. *It might be expired,* they'd say, and Izzy would always assure them that such a thing was impossible, as if Don Shula himself—or more accurately, Don Shula's ghost—had declared expiration dates on gift cards a sin against humankind.

The follow-up question accompanying the handing over of said gift card, *But does this have like, money on it? Like to get back?*, was always a dead giveaway he was dealing with a P.S.N. lady.

It's one of the P.S.N. women—Izzy can tell immediately from the oversized Minnie Mouse shirt hanging almost to her knees over black tights—who answers Odlanier's front door. A band of gray roots frames her forehead, her hair limp and stick-straight from years of bootleg keratin treatments administered in a Hialeah Gardens garage, one converted into a salon space years ago by a distant but chivalrous husband for his then-wife after she left her receptionist position at a Miami Lakes salon to work for herself sans-cosmetology license. The keratin treatments were extremely well priced but were definitely diluted with ammonia or paint thinner or maybe even Nair, because the cream made your eyes water and your scalp burn and your hair break and/or fall out. Though to be fair, the broken hair you'd find in clumps in your brush was super straight—nothing would ever resuscitate its natural curl. A long honey-brown ponytail of this dead sleekness hangs over this woman's shoulder.

This isn't a neighborhood where people open their front doors to knocks from strangers. Izzy had been prepared to explain who he was and how he was connected to Odlanier through both the rails of their front door and the front door itself. But now that Izzy is weeks out from his dedication to impersonating Pitbull, now that he has Lolita ingrained in his mind, people can see he has a niño bueno face, a face women like this can't resist because he appears to them like the son they never had or the son they wish their actual sons still were before this Miami locura turned them into a joke or a loser or both. Izzy with his light skin and his healthy complexion, his smooth cheeks, his dimples flashing whenever he in any way moved his mouth, his face emanating an involuntary halo of respect toward any woman over forty. Izzy with his naturally tidy eyebrows, his thick lashes, his sad Cuban eyes. The gold cross hanging from a chain around his neck—the thinness of the chain making the cross seem more sincere, not for show; the pronounced absence of earrings—so common in the lobes of Miami men his age and even older; no visible tattoos (a miracle), no ridiculous swirls or false parts shaved into his hair: this was one of the few remaining good boys in this city. He has nothing to sell and no favor to ask; he asks only if this is the home of the Odlanier Vasquez who came from Cuba on a raft in 2004; she says it is, and he's her husband and yes, her husband is home. God has brought this boy to her door for a reason, she can feel this in her chest; her husband has told her next to nothing about his days on the balsa, and she lets this young man into her home before even registering the friend lurking in his shadow.

Odlanier dislikes his wife much of the time but especially now, when she makes demands on his weekend time for socializing. Yes, he knows he is lucky to have found her, for the ways she's rescued him from his brutal family here in the U.S., the older brothers who came long before he did only to squander their better fortunes, becoming instead the same drains on society that they would've been had they remained in Communist Cuba, well on their way to drinking themselves to early deaths despite all the privileges granted that generation of exiles—privileges denied to him, not that he's bitter of course.

His wife invites them all to sit at the dinette set tucked up behind their couch, an area she calls the dining room despite not being a room or the place they typically eat their meals. She knows it's her job to immediately offer the men café and to make it even if they say no thank you, but this would require her to go to the kitchen—which, because this is one of the as-yet-unremodeled homes in P.S.N., is closed off from the living room they're sitting in—and she's not leaving that table until she hears for herself what business this niño bueno, sweet soul that he is, has with her husband.

Odlanier greets them with a perfunctory Buenas and sighs dramatically as he lowers himself into the chair, waiting for his wife to explain how she knows them. One of them is staring at him in a way Odlanier doesn't like at all. It's the other one who speaks first though, thanking them in English for being willing to talk to them, thus setting the terms for which language would dominate the conversation. He introduces himself as Rudy and his friend as Izzy.

Odlanier sits back in his chair and glares at his wife. She avoids his stare, already knowing the question inside it—*You don't know these people? Why did you let them in?*—and tries to draw attention away from it by asking a question of her own.

—You mentioned Odlanier's coming from Cuba. That was before I knew him. How did you know about that?

—So, I was the kid on the raft – or, I *am*, I guess? The one whose mom drowned.

Odlanier sits up and puts both hands flat on the table. The wife crosses herself then drags a finger under each eye, already heading off the mess of her tears. She knows if she looks at Odlanier, he'll ask for the café she should've already offered to make, but she can't make herself move out of earshot. She wants to hear everything Odlanier might say, how much he must've suffered, how close to death he was for who knows how many days. He's always difficult with her about important, hard things. She knows God brought her into his life to help him with this stubbornness, even if he still refuses her help. She makes the mistake of looking at him—she can't help it! ¡Ay, cómo ha sufrido este pobre hombre! ¡Qué lástima tiene ella por él!—and Odlanier pounces on the eye contact.

—Mima, please, un cafecito, he says.

—And a glass of water for me please, Rudy says. I appreciate it.

Rudy raises his hands and puts his palms together as if praying and bows to her. She saves her grunt for the kitchen where no one will hear it. Instead, she sighs, smiles, slaps her hands on her thighs and pushes off of her chair.

—Of course, she says. I was just about to ask.

Odlanier wants all these people, his wife included, not just out of his house—it's technically her house; he knows he should be grateful for that too—but out of his neighborhood. How could his wife put him in this position, to have to talk to this kid? Except, how could she know when he's never told her any details about his time on the raft: this was for her own safety, given how much worse it could've gone and the people he suspects were ultimately involved. In fact, how does he even know that this Izzy guy is the kid he's claiming to be? What if this ghost is here on behalf of someone else—someone looking for answers about a long-ago mistake come back to haunt him? How does Odlanier know this isn't a trap? So what if this guy looks exactly like a grown version of the boy from the raft, someone he's insisted he's forgotten; so what if he knew exactly who this was the moment he entered: what if he's a fake? Everyone should be skeptical of their own memories, especially when they come back to haunt you in the flesh. He is extra suspicious of the second guy, how he has his phone out, typing on it, clearly ready to take notes on whatever Odlanier says, the way the guy's thumbs hover over his screen. He can tell this one is U.S. born, but he still reminds Odlanier of people in the CDR: his spy neighbors in Cuba, coming over to his house whenever they pleased, watching him, inventorying his things, threatening always to report him. People like this boy's mother. He could barely hide his disgust when she and this boy showed up at the date and time he'd been given by his contact at the beach from where their raft would launch. He'd thought she was there to catch him in the act, not join him. He remembers wishing with all his heart that those CDR people would die horrible deaths, and then he watched as one of them did.

—You were not the only kid on the raft.

Odlanier looks over his shoulder, hears water coming out of the tap.

—There was another, a girl with both her parents, older than you, though I didn't actually know your ages and thought it better not to ask. There weren't supposed to be any children on the raft. But the girl, she wasn't an age we needed to worry about. She was thirteen or fourteen, I believe. She's maybe twenty-six now? My guess anyway.

Rudy leans forward, ready for Izzy to ask why there weren't supposed to be any kids. It's the natural question, the one that leads to the answers they're looking for. Even he sees this and he's just the Manolo.

—I'm here to ask about my mother, Izzy says. About if you knew her, what she was like. About what happened to her.

The approach surprises Rudy but he tries not to show it. Izzy hasn't filled him in on this part of their plan, this playing upon people's sympathy, but Rudy gets it right away, thinks that Izzy might be brilliant. He cannot wait to tell Izzy just that, once they're back in the car, all the info they need typed into a note on his phone: *Bro, you are fucking brilliant.*

—We didn't know anything about anyone. That was on purpose. In the end it was better that way. Less likely to get caught. Less temptation to talk to others about what you were about to do. Which meant less to overhear.

Another glance behind him.

—Your mother was in the CDR, do you know that? I knew her only as a spy for Castro. She wasn't assigned to my home but everyone knew about her. She got a lot of people in trouble, do you know that? That's how she gained so much prominence with the Party. She destroyed a lot of lives.

Odlanier catches himself, leans back in his chair, feels the reassuring sturdiness of his Rooms-To-Go dinette set seat against his shoulders, its cushion under his butt. He is sitting here and he is fine.

—Señor, Izzy starts. Then: No, sir, I didn't know any of that. I don't remember much about Cuba. I was barely seven.

Odlanier hisses, Well clearly there'd been a mistake. We were guaranteed a safe passage, and a child your age was a problem.

Again Rudy readies himself to type, because clearly Izzy will now ask who did the guaranteeing. Or at least he'd ask what exactly Odlanier meant by *a problem*. He puts down his phone for a second and wipes the palms of his hands against the front of his shorts before picking it back up again.

—Was my mother the only one that drowned?

A question Rudy is not sure is relevant to their needs, but he knows he's not in charge here. He's not sure what's going on, to be honest. From the stories he's heard, he knows that having a relative in the CDR isn't a legacy you want in Miami, that this revelation is something he and Izzy won't ever talk about if they can avoid it. They'll write this viejo off as batshit crazy, but maybe also not talk to any more people from Izzy's crossing because obviously, if they did get help at sea, whoever coordinated that trip had done a lot of work to make sure no one would talk about it afterward, as evidenced by this old guy still seeming pretty paranoid and definitely angry at Izzy for just existing. In profile, Izzy isn't looking like himself: his eyes are more watery, his chin weaker. Maybe one of his iguana scratches is already infected and starting to do weird things to his brain. Maybe Rudy should offer to drive when they leave. He bows his head, the only thing that makes sense to do when someone brings up their drowned mother.

—Yes, she was the only one who drowned. A miracle.

Is this ambiguity going too far? Odlanier does not like thinking of this time in his life, not at all. He thanks god that the boy doesn't seem to remember him from the raft; he thanks his wife, silently and without her knowing, for the pounds her cooking and her love have put on his bones, rendering him unrecognizable even to himself. Look at this life he has. Look at his cars, the vintage Volkswagen Beetle he owns just to show it off and which he's practically famous for according to people on Facebook, the plaques for its car show wins on the wall of his garage, the little pickup truck he drives regularly, sparkling in the driveway. Look at the driveway itself, the painted concrete holding up to the rain and flooding better than anyone else's for blocks. He should be more grateful, he knows. He knows he should spend better time with his wife instead of on the computer talking to strangers about cars. He has his wife to thank for all he's managed to forget since leaving Cuba. It finds him only in dreams, and even those she's helped to replace with the mundane things of life: the latest hurricane warning, the iguanas threatening their plumbing. He knew a wife like her would replace this and everything else he never wanted to think about again. He hears a spoon clacking against the batidora: the frantic beating of sugar with the first drops of café. He has another minute, maybe two, before she returns. He doesn't know what this boy wants him to admit, if this boy actually understands what it is he's asking Odlanier to tell him.

And so Odlanier changes his approach. He asks, What *do* you remember?

—From Cuba? I remember standing in lines a lot and being mad at my mom about it.

—No. From the time on the water.

What does Izzy remember? This is the question he's hoping Odlanier can help him answer. He remembers nothing except sensations, a physicality his body won't let him forget. The way the seawater dried on his skin and made the sunburn itch even more. Hunger, thirst. Someone encircling each of his forearms in a viselike clench, squeezing, then almost ripping his arms out of his body, swinging him through the air in an arc. And now he's allowed to remember more: the smell of gasoline where before there was only salt and wind and sweat. His hands over his ears, protecting them from noise, from roaring.

—A boat, Izzy says. I think I remember a boat finding us and helping us.

Finally, we're back on track, getting what we came here to get! thinks
Rudy. He picks up his phone again, ready to type, relieved of the
worry that Izzy had fallen into some sad trance or something. He
mentally rehearses the breezy tone he'll take in the car, bringing this
moment up later. *Whew, bro, you good? Seemed sorta like, like you were
losing it there for a second.*

—I thought you might say that, Odlanier says, a new snarl on his
face. What you think you remember is very much against the law, you
know that?

His wife is still in the kitchen; he hears her opening and shutting
a cabinet door.

He says, There was no boat, not for you or for your mother. I know
for a fact she knew that. But the others believed her, even though
we *knew* everyone was supposed to be old enough to not risk saying
something to INS. The interviews once we made it to land, turned
ourselves in – no one could say *anything* that might jeopardize us
being able to stay here. She took advantage of our position, us literally climbing onto the raft, no time for anyone to ask any questions.
I knew the whole time she was lying. I don't know what her plan was,
but here you are.

Behind him: the tinkling sound of cafecito cups being placed on
a tray, the cups and the single glass of water all rattling a little as the
tray is lifted. He hears the slaps of chancletas hitting the bottoms of
feet, moving faster than usual.

He leans across the table and hisses, No one can blame me for
being worried we'd be sent back. Forget for a second who she was,
that wasn't important in the end. Seven was too young. Everybody
knew that.

He leans back in his chair, rolls his shoulders and his neck.

—I am now an American citizen, he says. And I am grateful to this
country. Especially for my wife, even though she's crazy and gets on
my nerves. That we are all here right now is a miracle.

She slaps him on his shoulder, knowing she's missed something she'd rushed the café to hear. He takes his café from the tray and downs it in a single gulp.

Rudy mumbles gracias—this Odlanier guy is proving to be worse than useless—and, eager to get away from the burnt smell of coffee and this bitter old dude and the ghost of Izzy's mom, drinks his café like a shot, chasing it with the requested water, which Odlanier's wife has made sure is grossly warm from the tap.

Izzy leaves his café untouched. The wife had to place it in front of him, which she's happy to do considering his stunned state. She asks him if everything is all right and tells him that he'll have to forgive her husband, he can be a bit antisocial.

—He's been through a lot, she says. And so have you.

Odlanier takes his café cup and replaces it on the tray too roughly. His wife senses his short patience and puts her hand on his, something he hates. He pulls his hand out from underneath hers and grabs at the various cups on the table, putting them all back on her tray. He downs Izzy's untouched café. He's not one to waste something he's at some point paid for, and he's not going to let the café sit there, accusing him of anything. His wife turns now with the tray of collected café cups and the water glass, the latter having left a wet ring on the table. She'll bring back a rag to dry it up, heads to the kitchen with the tray to find one that doesn't already smell of mildew.

—Look, your mother should've never put you in that position. No one blames you for anything, okay? There's nothing worth discovering about that time. You were very young.

Odlanier says this as soon as he knows his wife won't hear it. He's answering a question no one has asked.

It takes his wife just long enough to find a clean-smelling rag that Odlanier can dart over to a desk, open a middle drawer, and fish out an old-school address book, little and leather and spiral bound. He pulls out a folded receipt lodged in his back pocket, clicks open a pen. On the blank side of the receipt he writes the phone number of the girl from the raft, a woman now. He has her address too, to what he believes is her new house in the Miami Shores area, but he doesn't dare share it out of fear this boy will drive straight there. He never wrote this woman's name in the book, afraid his wife might see it and wonder what it was doing there, but he knows it by heart: Olivia C——, daughter of Rafael y Manuela. As far as he knows, Olivia didn't change her last name when she married, and given who her family is, he doubts that she would want to, but it's possible she did: he has no idea what kind of woman she's turned out to be. The only contact he'd had directly from her was a thank-you card for a wedding gift he'd sent her just over a year ago. He'd been shocked and confused and even ashamed that her parents had sent him an invitation: did they really want him there, on their daughter's wedding day, a reminder of all they'd had to do to guarantee that a celebration like that would occur here, in this country, or was the invitation meant to send a different message—that after all this time, they still knew where he lived? He'd thrown the invitation in the garbage after tearing it up, then squirted Hershey's chocolate sauce all over it to keep his wife from discovering it in the trash and asking him how he could possibly know that family, but not before he'd copied down the phone number to which he would RSVP a very gracious no, along with where and under what names they were registered for gifts. He'd sent her the first available thing he saw on the registry website: a salad spinner, whatever that was.

—I don't really talk about that time. But she will, he whispers. That's all I can do for you. Put that away. Now.

He gestures with his chin at the folded scrap of paper he's just passed to Izzy between two fingers.

Izzy asks no other questions, just nods, silent, does as he's told. As if they're passing between them a memory they're agreeing to forget.

SHOWTIME

And where is Lolita? The answer to that question is always the same: in her tank.

How often does she consider escape, even though it means death? What is it that she remembers about Hugo's suicide that keeps her from doing the same thing? Is it the lingering, centuries-old feeling that she herself is divine? Considering the monotony of her daily existence, it's enough to provide, here, the relevant details of a single typical performance as an accurate reflection of how she spends the portion of her life that can be easily witnessed—that is, the segments consumed by a paying audience.

The show begins not in the tank but on a screen: images of waves crashing over rock stacks and against cliffs—a terrain nothing like the flat, edifice-clogged Miami coastline. A man's voice provides some history that's impossible to hear over the children in the crowd and the voices of adults trying to make them sit down. The giant screen, perched above the tank's back edge, has some busted panels in it, and those flicker a faker, more pixelated blue.

At the center of the tank itself, dividing it into front and back zones, is an island of stage—platforms low enough to let waves wash over them—connected to the tank's outer edge on only one side by the kind of wooden bridge more typically seen on mini-golf courses.

On each end of the stage is a cooler of fish hidden inside a stationary crate with the Miami Seaquarium logo on it, and it's behind one of these crates that Lolita waits—in full view of the crowd, the sun flashing off her slick black head—for the three trainers. The three trainers are always women. They are always wearing matching black-and-white wetsuits and ponytails, always the same foam-tipped microphones hugging their jawlines. One trainer controls Lolita's cooler, another controls the cooler out of which are fed the two dolphins who share Lolita's tank, and the third does nothing but talk in an attempt to distract the audience from noticing that fourteen of the show's seventeen minutes are spent feeding Lolita fish, one by one.

The entire show is an acoustic hellscape, as all sound bounces off the concrete steps doubling as bleachers and collides with the fizzling, guitar-heavy background music at the show's opening or the amped-up pulsing techno remix that closes it out. It seems this way by design, to encourage people to ignore the trainer's robotically cheery voice and the potential for disaster, like in the minutes before an airplane takes off when you're told to keep in mind that the closest exit may be behind you and to secure your mask before securing the masks of others.

Aiding in the efforts to obscure all comprehension are the various seagulls who flock to the Killer Whale and Dolphin Stadium for the perceived all-you-can-eat lunch special, like old people to a Golden Corral. They appear to be cued not by the opening video but by the sight of Lolita's tongue, the dive-bombing and squawking starting as soon as she opens her mouth to receive the first of the dozens of fish she'll be fed during any moment she's not jumping, flapping, flopping, screaming, or splashing. There's also an egret or a heron or maybe it's a real-life ibis—whatever it is, it's a big fucking white bird as tall as the shortest trainer, and it lands on the railing behind the stage and pivots its gaze between the coolers, biding its time.

The trainers have probably been instructed by someone official to keep their hands off the birds, that it looks bad to smack them away, and besides, their squawks provide an act-of-nature excuse should anyone complain that they couldn't understand a single complete sentence from the performance.

Lolita's first maneuver is a slow-motion backflip out of the water. As she executes it, she turns a little in the air and lands on her side, sending gallons and gallons of water over all the little kids who materialize out of nowhere by the tank wall. The kids run for their lives as soon as the water touches them—the chill of it a surprise every time—and the tank roils with Lolita-made waves. She bobs her way to the front of the stage, just a few feet from where she landed, and sticks her head out of the water and opens her mouth, ready for the fish payment she's due for that jump.

Her second maneuver is the same as the first, but on the other side of the tank. In fact, most of the behaviors that constitute her performance are slightly altered versions of this first one, repeated for both sides of the crowd. No matter what part of her body first emerges from the murk, no matter the movement she's made before she lands: the point is to get as much water out of the tank and onto the paying public as possible.

There are a handful of exceptions, of course. There's the behavior where Lolita dunks beneath the surface then rises while rolling her whole body—pushing her white belly out of the water—then lifts her pectoral fins above the surface and flaps them for a few seconds while her trainer waves hello to the crowd from the stage (the egret-ibis spontaneously doing the same, to the crowd's delight). And there's the part where Lolita's trainer raises one arm, like she has the answer to a question, and in response Lolita rolls to her side and lifts her pectoral fin straight up into the air. The trainer then slaps the shit out of her own thigh, and then Lolita slams her pectoral fin against the water, the sound of it sudden and surprisingly deep, like a big balloon popping. They each slap-slap two more times before the trainer blows her whistle and kneels to toss fish in Lolita's mouth.

A favorite moment for the audience—one that, given the abundance of background noise up to this point, sounds surprisingly and suspiciously clear when it comes—involves Lolita screaming in a display of the power of orca communication. The scream is accompanied by a little puff of mist from her blowhole, and then, as the trainer waves her hand back and forth slowly at her waist in a we-are-the-world kind of way, it melts into a completely different sound: a police siren coming through a kazoo, something out of a cartoon, vaguely unnerving or maybe hilarious. The trainer stops waving and the weird sound ends, replaced almost instantly with the sound of a foghorn, or maybe it's Lolita doing an impression of a fart.

There's also the moment when Lolita moves in close to the stage and dunks her head, aiming her blowhole toward the trainer, then rises just as the trainer leans over the water. A plume of mist shoots out and the trainer turns her face to the right, away from it, grimacing at the stench. Whether this last act counts as a true trained behavior or not depends on what you think constitutes *training*.

The two dolphins are used to fill in the moments between Lolita's behaviors, meaning: they are the bulk of the show's action despite not getting first billing. Their behaviors include: jumping together as high as they can; jumping one by one as high as they can; swimming together as fast as they can; wiggling their flukes while floating on their backs; water cartwheels; hugs, kisses, whistles. One dolphin slides up on the back of the stage, completely out of the water, and the crowd gives an *Awwwww* because compared to Lolita, size-wise, it is pretty cute. But then the cuteness evaporates as the dolphin pumps its body and gets back in the pool by doing the worm in reverse.

Interspersed between both Lolita's maneuvers and the dolphins' antics are overly long video segments purporting to be educational, though the information they provide, when audible, asks patrons to believe that Lolita has it much better at the Seaquarium than her wild counterparts in the Pacific Northwest because in captivity there's no pollution like in real nature. Also something something something because chinook salmon aren't even a thing anymore, nothing is sustainable, et cetera. Also did you know that in real nature, you legally have to stay two hundred feet away from any whales if you go whale watching, otherwise there's penalties and stiff fines and blah blah blah? Probably you won't see any whales because of how endangered they are. Also remember, when you're out in real nature, please be whale-wise and for more information about conservation efforts, please go to whatever-whatever website dot com.

The other point of the videos, from a visual perspective, seems to be that there is absolutely nothing Miami about the Pacific Northwest.

The show's unsung hero is the big white bird, the egret-ibis that waits for the tank waves to die down a little before gliding the ten or so feet from the railing to center stage. It comes and goes, the residue of Lolita's infrequent jumps sometimes forcing the egret-ibis to flap its wings and levitate for a moment to avoid getting splashed. During the performance's final video segment, this egret-ibis grows bold. It hops back to the railing, turns and opens its wings as if wanting to collectively embrace the sweating audience. It points its beak to the sky, thinking, *This is my time to shine!* And it bolts into the air, disappearing into the sun. Then suddenly it drops from the sky onto the middle of the stage out of nowhere like Lady Gaga at the Super Bowl. The egret-ibis struts to center stage and stands between the trainers, looks down at the dolphins, shakes its head. It has learned over the years that the videos sync up with the parts of the show when the trainers are the most distracted by their charges and the coolers are the most unprotected and open to the sky. It has learned that the last video is the longest. The egret-ibis laughs with this knowledge, cawing into the sky, summoning its seagull brethren to the feast, and then it high-steps between the coolers, guzzling fish left and right, pausing each time it passes through the middle, face always to the crowd, as if knowing it's being photographed. The trainers give it a wide birth.

The show tries, as best as it can, to build to something momentous, something poignant. The egret retires to the railing, belly full, and from its vantage point the show is over. It flies off, missing the various sequences that pass for the grand finale. These begin with a trainer repeatedly claiming that at the Miami Seaquarium, all the animals are part of one big happy family, which for killer whales is also known as a pod, and that Lolita's pod includes these trainers and these two random dolphins. The trainer puts a hand to her mouth and makes a kissing sound, sends the kiss out to the crowd. Lolita nods her head until she hears the high whistle. The trainer turns to the cooler: Lolita already has her mouth open for more fish.

As Lolita eats, the dolphins finish out the show by doing a frenetic motion around the tank where they are basically humping the water while standing up in it. It makes everyone crack up. The dolphins themselves also seem to be laughing.

Then Lolita closes her mouth and swiftly backs away from the stage—this, of course, is the show's real ending. There's just something that shifts and everyone knows it, though they don't know how or why they know it. Of course it couldn't end with dolphins humping water. Of course it ends with her.

Lolita pushes herself out of the water while still facing her trainer, then flings herself backward, sending massive splays of water into the crowd. She comes so close to the tank wall that people in the stands instinctively flinch, imagining shattered glass, blood.

She disappears into the murk. The trainers raise their arms and faces to the sun, palms open to the sky. They hold the pose, like they are summoning a god.

What emerges is Lolita's bottom half, her powerful flukes, the white undersides newly ominous and facing the crowd.

She stills them there for all to behold, and then, with what seems like only inches to spare, she starts thrusting underwater while upside-down, the motion sending her flukes smacking against the surface in the direction of the crowd, over and over and over again.

Everyone in the audience—every time, without realizing it—screams.

Screaming is the only way to release what you feel at the sight of her true power. This is why the egret left: out of respect for all she can induce.

The screaming keeps going through each and every slam, like the crowd is shocked she's still going, that she still has so much strength near the show's end. Like she was holding herself back until this very moment.

Like the screams themselves are the real reward.

FEEL THIS MOMENT

GLOBAL WARMING

He'd texted Julisa from her own driveway just as Rudy slid inside their house, asking her to have dinner with him that coming Friday. Rudy had disappeared behind their front door without so much as a goodbye wave. Maybe Izzy should've fessed up during the drive there from Odlanier's house about the situation between him and Julisa, but he'd instead used that drive to convince himself there wasn't a situation with her at all. He told himself dinner was just a thank you for Odlanier's address and nothing more. In the week leading up to the dinner, he's officially decided that Julisa has appeared a little too soon in his plan; at best she was a distraction; at worst maybe a wedge between him and Rudy; or even more at worst, someone with plans for him of her own. And also: she *had a history*, whatever that meant, with someone like Danny, a guy who'd spent a Sunday morning communing with a canal by narrating soap operas starring neighborhood iguanas—a guy who thought he could talk to birds. Not the best judgment on Julisa's part, though okay, who even knows what they're doing at fifteen? At least she'd been smart enough not to have sex with him, right? But also she'd kissed Izzy first at the Fair and then been weird about it the rest of the afternoon. The truth was he barely knew her. Better to relax a little, keep talking but leave it at that for now: talking. After confirming the dinner details, he hadn't sent her a single text all week.

Except he now stands in the bathroom on that Friday night, dousing himself in Brut cologne like a real OG, ensuring he smells like someone's dad, which in his experience makes women fall in love faster than anything else he could do. The cologne's cloud brings even his Tía Tere out from the living room, away from her shows, and into the hallway to talk to him. Izzy stands with a towel wrapped around his waist, fresh from a shower, inspecting his face as he turns it side to side in the mirror. The sink is dappled with hair. She recognizes the ritual: the preening, the just-trimmed chest, the rinse before he fumigates the bathroom. She blocks the doorway with her body and says, This smells serious.

He keeps his eyes on his jawline in the mirror as he explains why he feels he owes Julisa a meal, a nice night out: how she'd hooked him up with Odlanier's address, how he'd actually paid him a visit last Sunday. He prepares himself for her speech about treating girls with respect, about remembering that this girl is someone's daughter, someone's sister—as if Izzy hasn't been thinking about that complication since inviting her to the Fair.

But instead his Tía Tere says in a deep voice she reserves for only his most serious transgressions, Ismael, please tell me you're joking.

Izzy turns on the water in the sink, rinsing the hairs down the drain rather than wiping them up with a piece of toilet paper and throwing them away in the bathroom garbage can like she's asked. She put the garbage can in there for only that reason.

—Knowing their names is one thing, she says. But showing up where they live is – I thought you knew better than to do something so reckless. You don't know who these people are.

She puts a hand on the doorjamb to steady herself. There is water all over the countertop now.

—I can't believe this from you, Ismael. What could you even want from any of them?

—I was on that raft too, Tía.

—And? Don't make me regret being honest with you.

He finally looks at her in the mirror's reflection and says, You think you've been honest?

She takes a small step backward into the hallway, lowers her hand from the doorframe.

—If this is really about your mother, you can ask me anything you want. I've never said otherwise. You've just never cared to know, not until now all of a sudden.

Is this about Alina? He'd said so to Odlanier, thinking it would get the guy to talk more openly about the crossing, about Izzy's memory of the speedboat, its veracity. But he'd lost his hold on himself, asking questions about the wrong things. He was almost certain now they'd been assisted at sea, that what Odlanier had insisted was a miracle was in reality due to intricate planning and illegal transactions Alina had to have known about, possibly even participated in. Before zoning out on the drive back from Odlanier's house, Izzy had told Rudy, when he asked why Izzy had taken the approach he had, that these people would be loyal to him because they'd all almost died together, hadn't they? Never mind what other loyalties they might still hold, and never mind what Odlanier had claimed about Alina's allegiances; Izzy still thought that resurrecting her and their crossing would be the most direct way into the heart of the world they were trying to infiltrate. And he really believed this as he'd knocked on that door: he'd walked into Odlanier's house thinking the dude would hand him a business card, *Fulano's Speedboat for Hire, Serving All Your Balsero-Rescuing Needs!* And then what? Fulano would hire Izzy and Rudy even though he didn't know them from shit to help him bring rafters closer to shore? Then somehow they'd take over Fulano's boat and run their own operation and make millions? Was the Wet Foot/Dry Foot rule still even in place with this new president? He'd seen the memes online of the guy signing all those news laws or whatever in his first five minutes on the job, getting shit done. What had Izzy accomplished off his notebook's main list? He'd quit a dishwashing job, wasted an afternoon at UM talking to a comemierda asshole, and gotten an address from a viejo who'd made Izzy want to know the wrong things. He'd found himself asking questions that followed up on the wrong parts of Odlanier's answers, making him feel confused and like he maybe cared about what people thought about his mother, which was not in the plan at all.

The feeling floating just above these questions had washed in and out of him all week—sensations he kept to himself and doesn't share now with his Tía Tere, a new-to-him longing that Izzy feels but cannot articulate. It would be impossible for him no matter what, the usual hurdles largely irrelevant to his current circumstances, but still, had he gone to college; had he gone to a better high school; had he read more as a child; had he landed in a better neighborhood; had he not had his life interrupted by the fleeing; had he not been born into a dictatorship; had his mother not been born into a dictatorship; had

his grandmother chosen instead to flee in the face of the rising dictatorship: maybe then Izzy could find some way to articulate to his
Tía Tere at least some aspect of these sensations rising just beneath
the threshold of awareness—feelings that have flooded his dreams all
week and that keep his mind swimming in circles.

And what else had Izzy accomplished since his pivot from Pitbull
to Scarface? There was Julisa—though she couldn't count as an ac-
complishment, not yet. He'd made a thousand bucks, a real thing
he could count, most of the money tucked safely in a pair of still-
boxed Jordans he'd only worn once. Though his gut says Danny is
the brand of lunatic he'll need to keep at arm's length, the money
from the job had made Izzy feel powerful, on his way to greatness;
that was before Odlanier had given him next to nothing in response
to questions he'd heard himself ask and a phone number he'd
called and called, going to voicemail every time, him never leaving
a message.

No, he decides this is not about Alina. Tony Montana never let any
woman distract him, not even his mother. For almost half the movie
you think she's dead exactly because Tony said so—*Everybody's dead*—
while being interrogated by immigration officers in an early scene; it's
a surprise, later, when he and Manolo pull up to her house, which is
on a dusty patch of land in what is obviously Los Angeles (technically
it's Torrance) that fails in every way to look like a run-down Miami. No,
he refuses to admit he lost his focus: there must have been something
strange lacing the café that guy's wife made him, in the steam coming
off of it, wafting up to his face.

—Tía, he says, Who paid for me and Alina to come over?

—What are you talking about? What do you mean *paid?*

—I know there was a boat, like maybe a speedboat.

—Did someone tell you that? I doubt ese hombre said anything
like that to you.

—It picked us up, brought us closer to shore.

—No digas eso, you don't know that for sure.

But he does, and not because anyone told him anything, not yet.
The knowledge of it soaked into him during his shower, through the
water spraying him from above, rinsing away the last of his trimmed

chest hair—water that's been all over the city in a cycle Lolita knows as well as the ancient pulsing of her own dark blood.

—You shouldn't talk about this with anyone, she says. But have I suspected that maybe your raft had help in arriving? Absolutely, yes. It was either that or you had some powerful protective spell put on you before you left. So many people die—the sun, dehydration, the sharks, the shit rafts I've seen on the news. Y pa' mí era tan extraño que every person on that raft was a stranger to you. I know the INS people suspected something for that same reason. You refused to speak a word to me about what happened, and the people handling your case at Krome told me the same thing – that they'd even thought you were mute at first. So can I know anything for sure? No. But your mother – ultimately, there is no way that I can see that she would've found the money for both of you, for the kind of arrangement you're asking about. I sent her money almost every month once I knew about you being born, but that was nowhere near enough for un pasaje like that.

—So it wasn't you that paid for us?

—Ismael, no one *paid* for you. You surviving that trip was a miracle.

Because he still won't look at her, she decides to say this too: That you were even on that raft in the first place is a miracle, given your mother.

Teresa leaves him there, turns away with her hands shaking to walk back to the living room before she's tempted to say anything else. Did Teresa love Alina, this half sister she'd barely known through letters she assumes their mother had no clue Alina was sending, letters that came only after Alina was an adult herself? Her sister hadn't even been the one to call when their mother passed, and Teresa hasn't yet forgiven her for that. For making her learn about it from some cousin who didn't even know Teresa's name, had referred to her only as la otra hija de Ocila. Otra, as if she hadn't come first. Could Teresa love someone who for so many years the very thought of caused instantaneous intestinal distress, an ailment she'd wasted so much money on special doctors and tests and scans trying to figure out and had even, for a miserable three months when Izzy was nine, given up café to see if that was the cause? Those were the years she hated Alina even as she was growing to love Ismael more and more. In fact, it was an inverse relationship, her hate for one and her love for the other. She remembers the letter where Alina informed her of Ismael's birth—no word of her pregnancy in any letter before that—where the sentence ended not with the details of his arrival—his weight, his length, the exact time—but with the fact that having a baby had not increased her ration allotments as much as she'd planned, what a disappointment it was, blaming the catastrophic miscalculation on the embargo, and so Teresa owed it to her, as a traitor to their homeland living in the very country hellbent on killing her and her newborn son, to send the maximum amount of money allowed by U.S. law. Alina had to know by then that tourists had no trouble buying milk, soap, toilet paper—that just as Batista had done, Alina's noble Fidel had no problem exploiting the island in service to the Revolution rather than in service to those living under it. Teresa had never sent money before, believing that most of those dollars went instead toward keeping the regime functioning during those most destitute years. But she couldn't help imagining the nephew she was certain she'd never meet sick and starving. She imagined him in a bassinet next to a bed, napping as her sister whored herself out to a Canadian or a Spaniard in exchange for a trip to the tourist-only grocery store. So she sent what she could. Tried not to think about how Alina had somehow still managed to get the extra money she'd planned on by exploiting her son's existence.

She steadies her hands by reminding herself that she settled these things in her heart and gut long ago. She sits down on her couch in front of the TV, takes a sip of water from a teal plastic tumbler she always refers to as her *water glass*. She likes the color, how to her it makes the water taste cleaner, the blueish tint more natural-looking to her than plain clear. On the TV is a commercial for Olive Garden. The screen says *We're All Family Here*, and she raises her glass to toast the words, trying to believe them, taking a near-freezing sip to make the slogan sink in, not knowing—despite all her other careful beliefs—that it's bad luck to toast with water. She holds it in her mouth before swallowing, letting it chill her teeth for long enough to make them ache. She feels the cold move through her, all the way down.

THE SECOND DATE

They are heading east on Coral Way when Izzy pulls into a gas station—does he actually need to get gas? Julisa isn't super high maintenance but even so, this is not a good sign: that he didn't think to fill his tank *before* picking her up. Probably means he's inconsiderate, inattentive. Does he expect her to just sit in the car and *wait*? Without the radio on, with no A/C, no company aside from her phone? Except actually, he's passed the pumps and is rolling into an adjacent dirt lot, stopping beneath one of those gross floodlights that'll reveal the extent of her makeup, the intensity of her foundation and concealer application obvious in the fluorescence no matter how good the free color match session at Sephora turned out.

He has for real turned off his car. Has removed the keys from the ignition. Is he about to make a move? Before they even eat? Before he even pumps the gas? Does he think she's the kind of girl who would give him The Sacred Blowjob on an empty stomach? Is this really the same guy who'd seemed too shy to kiss her first at the Fair a week ago?

She refuses to acknowledge that they've stopped by making no motion to unbuckle her seatbelt even after he clicks his off.

—We're here, Izzy says.

—Here where?

—This is the place. Let's go.

He has to see the disgust on her face as she steps into that garish light, the fakeness of her smooth face exposed, her cute sandals sinking into the lot's dirt and getting mud on her deep red toenails. She is horrified. A gas station. Their second date—which she's decided is actually their first one because this one's at night—is about to happen at *a gas station*. She's ready for him to admit this is some bad joke; at this point, she'll still give him permission to start over.

He doesn't take her hand. Another bad sign. He walks ahead of her across the paved part of the lot. Also bad. She is trying to stay calm but he is ruining the story of this date for their future children. There will be so much she'll need to revise or even leave out. Because yes, he's invited her to dinner, made it for a Friday night, which means he's serious, but he'd asked over text instead of calling like a proper caballero. He'd typed—instead of said—that dinner was his thank you for Odlanier's address, which seemed weird to her but it felt even weirder over text to ask what he meant. He'd typed in the same message that they'd be celebrating, then ignored her for a week. Celebrating what, she didn't know, but the only thing that made sense to her despite the days of silence was that they were celebrating themselves—their imminent coupledom. Crazier shit has happened, and she certainly deserves to be wifed up by a guy who is obviously her soulmate. She has so much to offer; finding and then giving him Odlanier's address is just a fraction of what she's capable of, of how much being with her would help him, of what an asset she'll prove to be. But now, the space between them in the parking lot is growing— maybe he's rushing ahead to open the door for her? The back of his shirt is already dark with sweat near the middle by the waistband. At least it's a real shirt with a collar and long sleeves. Julisa likes to think that being brought up in various Christian faiths has taught her to always look on the bright side, and her spirit gets a much-needed boost when he does, in fact, hold open the door.

The freezing air of the gas station whooshes over her as she steps inside, and Izzy says, Don't worry, I'm not feeding you Doritos.

Another line she'll probably leave out when their yet-to-be-conceived daughter someday asks about this night.

At least it's a clean, bright gas station—aisles of chips and candy and other junk, a back wall lined with energy drinks and sodas and bottled water displayed behind freezer doors. There are random people buying cigarettes and ten bucks' worth of gas lined up at the bulletproof-glass-encased register area. It looks like almost every other gas station she's ever been inside of except for two things: one, there's a cluster of well-dressed people huddling around an opening in the wall directly across from the store's entrance; and two, the rest of that wall has a wine section eight shelves high, lined with hundreds of varietals, the likes of which—in its vastness and quality—she's never seen at all but especially not in a gas station on Coral Way.

Izzy puts his hand on the middle of her back and presses her deeper inside. He mumbles *excuse me* and *permiso* as they cut the line at the register in half to get to the other side of it. Behind the well-dressed crowd is a pass-through marked off by dark faux columns wrapped in plastic grapevines, the short hallway behind it painted red. They get closer and she sees that the back wall, in addition to all those fancy wine bottles, has a square cut out of it for where a big pane of glass must've once been; through it she glimpses a bustling low-lit restaurant crammed with white-cloth-covered tables, a little cavern of elegance, windowless and almost romantic.

Reservations

In truth, Julisa's hometown is overflowing with places like this; she just doesn't know it and wouldn't appreciate it even if she did. But some of the city's best restaurants are hidden this way, a spell of protection against being found by tourists and travel guide writers and people like Julisa's parents. They have raised their daughter to believe that the nicest dinners to be had are at Olive Garden and Cheesecake Factory. It's the latter Julisa was hoping for tonight; she's been craving their strawberry lemonade. At least Izzy knew not to take her to La Carreta. At least he knew to get her out of Hialeah—no Rey's Pizza, no Rey de la Frita, no Spanish-Word-for-King of Any Crap Food the Likes of Which She Ate on Dates in High School. None of that. She's grateful too that he didn't take her to Melrose Cafe, the closest nice place to her house and a favorite of her mom's (Caridad's go-to when she guilts her husband into taking her out for a date night and the wait at Cheesecake is too long), home of bread even better than Olive Garden's. Melrose Cafe meant great bread, yes, but also burgers and salads and wraps and other feels-more-like-lunch-to-her foods, but worse than that it meant running the risk of bumping into people they vaguely knew from high school; Hialeah Lakes grads make up the revolving cast of servers and line cooks there, and she isn't interested in anyone spitting in her food.

—Reservation for two, Izzy Reyes, he says to a woman dressed in all black who is very officially cradling an iPad.

Izzy has made a reservation. An actual reservation. It's a sign: that he's thoughtful, that he knows how to plan ahead, that he is definitely boyfriend/fiancé/husband material. She will be sure to tell their future daughter to write off anyone who doesn't make a reservation for dinner on a first date the way her papi did for theirs.

—What kind of restaurant is this? she says.

—Spanish, he says. Tapas.

Oh my god, she fucking *loves* tapas—or at least, the one time she's had them she loved them. Or at least, loved the *concept* of them. Little plates! How did he know? Of course it's a sign. Yes, they are technically inside a gas station (a *nice* gas station, at least), but at least this weird tapas place is an attempt at leveling up. At least it shows creativity, maybe. And as the hostess takes them to a table where she sits with her back to the gas station section in an attempt to erase it, Izzy sitting across from her, the large oversized sheet of the menu now blocking his face and giving her a chance to use her phone's camera to check her lipstick, she's grateful for the same reason that he'd decided on tapas in the first place: if dinner takes a bad turn, they can just stop ordering stuff, pay, and cut the story short.

There's no drink menu on the table, and even though they aren't legally old enough to drink, she was looking forward to ordering a mango margarita (her Cheesecake Factory hope was tied with the hope of going to Bahama Breeze up in Broward, out by Pembroke Lakes Mall) and betting that she didn't get carded. This works half the time. When it fails and a server asks to see her ID, she just pretends to change her mind and instead orders a ginger ale, telling the server with a laugh, *My bad, I keep forgetting I'm pregnant.*

—So have you been here before? she says.

Izzy lowers the menu for only a second and says, No way. Never.

Still Water

Izzy's choice of this place reflects his own ambivalence about what this night should mean. He wanted to take her somewhere fancy to impress her, but not so fancy that he inadvertently propels them toward an actual relationship. She's part of his plan, but only as a marker of progress, and he's decided he needs to first talk with the Miami

Shores woman Odlanier directed him toward before suggesting to Julisa anything more about the Hot and Mostly Passive Girlfriend Role he hopes she'll take on. He doesn't need another Manolo, and the only way to put her in her place is to tap the brakes, but not so hard that he fast-forwards to the scene of the final dinner with Michelle Pfeiffer, Manolo joining them for no reason whatsoever: the one where she walks out of Tony's life forever/just in time to avoid getting killed in the final surprise raid scene. And thank god too—good for Michelle Pfeiffer not having to pretend to writhe with gunfire like the woman who played Gina had to do, though did you really ever doubt that out of every possibility, the screenwriters would choose to save the only white woman character from the gruesome deaths that befall every non-white character in the movie?

In his idealized version of tonight, Izzy would've taken Julisa to a place like the Babylon Club, and sadly, he'd actually wondered if it was still around, if he just didn't know about it, had even tried Googling it before stumbling on this tapas place, not understanding that the Babylon Club was *never* around, that the exterior shots were of a now-gone establishment way up north in Davie, and that the scenes taking place inside—with its many-mirrored walls, its purple carpeting, its way-too-shiny-to-be-safe onyx dance floor—were in fact filmed on one of Hollywood's largest soundstages. Poor Izzy, trying to live a Miami Scarface life when all the movie has given him in terms of location possibilities is a made-up map of places long since dismantled.

After the server introduces herself, she asks them if they'd like any water, and when they both say yes, she asks, Still or sparkling?

—Still? Izzy ventures, and a minute later, there's a cold liter bottle of Evian on their table, fresh from the wall-fridges next door, the sticker with the gas station's price still on it.

The server asks if they have any questions about the menu, and Julisa waits until it's just her and Izzy before asking, Is *everything* gonna come from over there?

Menu

Julisa does not want to admit that much on the menu grosses her out. Who actually expects her to eat gas station octopus? It doesn't matter that they're just on the other side of a wall of fancy wine in the nice part of said gas station. Rice made with squid ink? No thank you. Luckily the menu is as big as the paper it's printed on and there are some recognizable things, once you read the little descriptions. Patatas bravas are basically french fries in spicy tomato sauce which is basically ketchup. Albóndigas is meatballs in Spanish, so that's doable. She likes olives and almonds and cheese, and this place puts all those things together on one plate along with some ham, cool cool. There's camarones in garlic but—better to avoid everything from the sea in general because: gas station. Garbanzo beans but fancy, that sounds fine. There's even croquetas, which, you can't go wrong in Miami. All that plus bread, which it looks from a quick glance at the tables around them that they'll have to order and pay for—this obviously *isn't* Olive Garden—and they'll definitely be okay. She giggles to herself thinking of how hilarious this will all sound to Julisa Junior someday.

—What's so funny? Izzy says.

—Nothing, she says. This place is weird, right?

—Doesn't sound like nothing, he says. You were definitely laughing.

—I was thinking about how I'd tell someone about this place, how it's nice but also in a gas station which is crazy to me.

He lets his menu float back to the table and says, Obviously this is on me, since I invited, so order whatever you want. I'm down to try whatever, especially the fish stuff.

Drinks

Their server takes their order—and since he's let Julisa do the choosing, there is sadly no fish stuff—and promises to bring it out in a staggered enough way that it'll feel like a real meal. She also informs them of how the wine list works: there is no wine list; if they would like wine with dinner, they should feel free to browse one of South Dade's best wine selections, the hundreds of bottles lining the wall just outside the seating area, and pick one out. They are to pay for it in the gas station and then bring it back to their table in the paper bag in which it will be placed, then she—their server—can open it for them. She tells them there is a five-dollar corkage charge, and neither asks the server what that means because they pretty quickly figure it out. Izzy stops himself from calling the fee a jack: this side of the gas station is a fancy place and he's not trying to start trouble. Also he remembers that he has three hundred in cash in his wallet right now—bring on your ridiculous whatever corkage fee, lady! His budget for the night is basically unlimited.

When the server steps away, Julisa's face is glowing. She hunches closer to the table and whispers, She thinks we're twenty-one.

He sweeps an arm out to the side of their table, almost brushing against the people beside them, and says, After you.

—To the wine wall! she says, but he doesn't laugh.

Varietals

She of course has no idea what to look for in a wine. But she figures neither does Izzy, so she pretends to know things, have certain preferences.

—What are your thoughts on the pink wines? she says, and Izzy says, I don't know, I've never tried one.

—It's just white wine and red wine mixed together, she says. Super tasty, super good with Sprite, but I'm not really feeling that tonight. That's more for when you're drinking outside. Tonight I think I'm in the mood for something more *serious*.

She tosses her hair over her shoulder to watch him take in that word—serious—and sees that he's got his phone out, scanning the label of some bottle featuring some old-timey criminal that, when scanned, makes it look on your phone's screen like the label is talking to you.

—Check this shit out, he says.

But she ignores him. A wine that needs your phone just to show you a commercial built into the label isn't the kind of fancy she's aiming for, and she doesn't want to encourage him looking at distractions when he should be following her down the aisle. At least he's looking at the wines. At least he's not in another aisle looking to buy a bag of Combos, saying he's too hungry to wait, promising to share them with her as an appetizer.

The signs jutting out from the shelves of wine all name different places in the world—Germany, Chile, Washington—rather than one of the three colors she knows wine to have. She recognizes the faint music piping in overhead from a speaker near one of the signs as a love song, but she can't make out the specific one, only—from the way the singer sounds super in pain—that it's supposed to be romantic. Izzy is trailing behind her, laughing at something on his phone's screen, so she says, Should we go for France or keep it authentic and get something from Spain?

—Whatever you want is good, he says, his face lit up from below.

Maybe he's actually not that cute? No, maybe it's just the angle of the screen's glow, not super flattering. She is standing now in front of Portugal, raises her hand to a bottle's label.

—Oh damn. This one has way more alcohol than the other ones.

She pulls the bottle off the shelf, runs her thumb against the label's embossed lettering. It is a bottle of port.

—Lemme see that, Izzy says, suddenly right next to her. He takes the bottle from her hands.

—I think we should do this one, he says. It's red, right? You said that's what you wanted? Red is supposed to be the fanciest of the wines.

—The most serious, yeah. That's what I was saying before.

He holds it up above his head, inspecting the bottom of the bottle, checking for who knows what.

—This one looks good, he says.

She waits for a wink that doesn't come, walking away only when he says, I'll meet you back at the table.

Port

Oh shit, this is when they're going to card him, at the register. Why didn't he think of that before? Of course the waitress didn't give a shit, recommending the wine wall—it isn't her job to shut him down. It's about to be this guy's, this americano dude at the register. He pulls out his wallet anyway, goes through the motions to save as much face as possible.

But Izzy is lucky in his unluckiness here: the gas station attendant is an older white man. He does not see a niño bueno face the way Odlanier's wife did. No, he reads Izzy as someone to be mildly afraid of; he's seen this type before, this cocky Hispanic troublemaker. He could be twenty or he could be forty—the white man honestly can't tell from their faces, they all look alike to him anyway. These types are everywhere and have been for years now. Why hadn't he headed north to Tallahassee or Jacksonville like so many others when the first waves of them showed up? Because leaving meant letting them win, and yet here he is, three decades into this protest, more of them washing up every day, and so they'd won thanks to sheer numbers, which made him the loser. He didn't want trouble from this hoodlum, didn't need to make an example out of him at the risk of his own safety. These types always had a firearm on them. Let this spic have his port, goes his thinking. We've got the president on our side now, after eight years of insults and disgrace, so enjoy your last sips, chico. You loud lazy fuckers will be gone faster than you took over, you just wait.

Bread

The server opens the port at their request without a word. Doesn't even ask if they know it's a dessert wine. She knows for sure they aren't old enough, she just doesn't care. Not her job, that's Gringo Gary's job, and obviously Gringo Gary doesn't give a fuck, so why should she? Her job is to bring food to whoever is at her tables until they close at eleven p.m., and then she's out—half of her tips in her purse and ready to be spent at whatever club her girls are planning to hit up tonight. She won't catch these two kids down there, not the places she goes: twenty-one and over as a rule now, ever since her twenty-fourth birthday, when she accidentally made out with that sixteen-year-old dude with the fake ID at a place that was eighteen and over. Super embarrassing. That was two years ago now, and her girls still sometimes call her CM, short for child molester, on any night she looks, to them, especially slutty. CM's coming out to play, they'll cackle before reaching out and squeezing her maybe-too-out-there tits. God she loves those bitches—her friends, not her tits. Her tits she wishes were bigger, but her boyfriend has promised to buy her one tit for Christmas this year. She's saving for the other titty—that's what the other half of her tip money goes toward. Which is why she's pissed at the hostess for seating basically two toddlers at one of her tables. She's never getting those double Ds at this rate, not with the type of customers who consider rounding up the bill to the next highest tens a fair tipping strategy populating her section. And these kids in particular, ordering all the cheapest, most basic menu items. She might as well bring them each a bag of pizza-flavored Combos from next door. God forbid either one of them ask her for a recommendation, as if she hasn't tried everything on the menu at some point in the ten months she's worked here. Who orders the croquetas when there's a bakery making better ones literally on every corner for miles around? She would've low-key told them that if they'd asked, but the guy keeps his phone right on the table and so he's obviously a chump, and the girl is so desperate for his attention that her face is basically doing an impression of a pit bull on death row at a shelter trying to get herself adopted. Pobrecita too, because she's super pretty, even shellacked in all that old lady makeup. The way her voice shook when she asked for *some bread for the table, please,* her little *thank you* while the guy sat there chugging half of his just-poured Fisher-Price wine without even waiting to cheers with her first? Super freaking sad, the whole thing is a tragedy and who even knows why.

Patatas Bravas

Julisa takes a sip as the server walks away.

—This is the best wine I've ever had. It's super sweet. Not that I drink like, a lot of red wine all the time, but still. This is tasty.

—Yeah it's good, right? Izzy says.

As if he'd picked it out. As if she wasn't the one who noticed the high alcohol content and thus the good deal this bottle is. But that's her point: mira qué amazing she makes him!

He shifts forward, clears his throat a few times as he sits up in his chair.

—I shouldn't say this, but you look really beautiful tonight.

—Oh god no, I'm hideous. Wait, why shouldn't you say that?

—Okay fine, you're hideous then.

—Why do you think you shouldn't tell me I look good?

—I hate when girls do that thing where they say they're ugly just to make you say something nice back.

—But you said I looked beautiful first though. I didn't ask you for that compliment.

He leans back in his chair and picks up his wine glass, takes another too-big swallow.

—I shouldn't tell you that you look beautiful because I don't want to give you the wrong idea about all this.

He waves the glass over the table like he's casting a spell, the whole bowl resting in his palm, wine sloshing around inside of it, the stem hanging down between his fingers.

—And what's *all this*, Izzy?

—This dinner, this night. I like you but I don't want you thinking this is a date or anything.

Is this their first fight? She definitely doesn't count the weirdness while eating alligator at the Fair as their first fight. More of a disagreement, she'd decided. More like just awkward. She'd kissed him and he'd kissed her back, right? But then later, he'd gotten short with her, then quiet, then he'd claimed to have a headache, which okay, that happens: they'd done a lot of round-and-round rides, eaten that alligator plus way too much sugar. A headache made sense. They couldn't have been fighting then. But maybe they are right now? Because if this isn't a date, what the fuck are they doing there?

—I *know* it's not a date, she decides to say.

He must be teasing her, trying to get her to relax. That has to be it, right? Because he opened the door for her and this is a Friday night and he's paying and he's wearing a long-sleeve shirt on a ninety-degree night and they have a bottle of very thick-tasting wine sitting between them—and also *he just said I like you*, didn't he?—and here's the plate with the olives and cheese and hams and stuff on it and also the potatoes with fancy ketchup, thank god, because this wine must be getting to him if he thinks this kind of flirting is her thing, but she's trying, oh man is she trying.

—Good, he says, I'm glad we have an understanding.

And then he does it: he winks.

Albóndigas

He has maybe drunk his first glass too quickly. Not that he feels intoxicated—his tolerance is better built up than that—but somewhere above and behind his right temple, he feels a pulsing. He can ignore it for now, still talk, still tolerate the tiny vibrations that the sound of his own voice sends through the bones in his face and jaw and skull. He tries to pretend he doesn't even feel it, this inevitable end to their night. But the port—maybe it's the sulfites, or the high alcohol content, or the varietal of grape; he has no idea because he isn't tracking anything about these migraines—has wiggled its way into his brain's chemistry and started a chain reaction. There is no turning back from it, and deep down he understands what's coming—*I'm glad we have an understanding*—and so he takes another sip, because he might as well enjoy the taste of the poison.

He really didn't mean to wink. It's a try-hard thing to do, and it snuck out without warning, borderline involuntary, like something was trapped there that he needed to blink away. Even if he'd wanted to signal to her that he was just playing about the not-a-date line, a wink wouldn't have been his way of showing it. Izzy likes to think he's slicker than that, more romantic, more like that scene in *Scarface* where Tony drags Michelle Pfeiffer to a car dealership to watch him buy a new Porsche after she's complained that his current car, a yellow Cadillac convertible with tiger print interior, *looks like somebody's nightmare.* As Tony lists off all the extras he wants added to the Porsche, she sarcastically suggests he get fog lights, and he tells her that's a good idea, and you start to think, maybe she really will fall for this asshole. But a scene like that between Izzy and Julisa is a long way off, especially from a financial perspective. Izzy hopes his words were clear enough. Wink or no wink, he said what he said: he does not consider this a date. He shouldn't have to say anything else.

But he does, because of the port, and because he knows he doesn't have all night before the pain really starts. Because he wants to show off about the iguanas and the money, about taking her text and running with it by talking to Odlanier right away, about the woman in Miami Shores, his next move. Because he doesn't understand that telling her a story about how he's left her out will hurt her. That understanding lies elsewhere.

Garbanzos

The children at her table are wasted—or at least, the girl is. She's gathered that from having observed the girl's posture over the last twenty minutes, which she'd described to her fellow server as *melting*. As in, *Bro, my girl over there is melting*, and she'd indicated the couple with her chin on her way back from bringing them free bread because she was not about to have that girl puke at the table. She wanted to slap the guy, because obviously this was his fault. She'd brought over the garbanzos just in time to hear the girl say, *I just feel super rejectable right now*, and so she'd asked loudly if she could bring them some more water, on the house. The guy had said no thanks without even really hearing the question—he was in the middle of some story, trying to make himself the hero—and she'd brought the water anyway, two glasses filled from the kitchen sink—a move her manager hates because it gave the other customers ideas about getting free water. No ice for them, though. She isn't trying to get fired.

Croquetas

Julisa has her head on her arms, resting on the table, when she feels a glass of water press against the back of her bicep, the server walking away before Julisa can remember to say thank you.

—Can you please sit up already? Izzy says.

—But what I don't understand is how you could go without me, she says into her elbow.

—What did you think I was gonna do with that address?

She bolts up and says, I don't know! At least talk with me about it first before just *driving* over there? I thought it would make you call me! Did you tell my brother?

—He was already with me, he went with me. Coño, Julisa, he's my right-hand man.

—So you told him. Him you talk to but not me?

She pounds both fists on the table and says, I can't believe this shit!

He sits up and puts his hand over one of her fists, tells her to calm down.

—Have you even told him about us?

—What is there to tell? That we hung out at the Fair? That I'm thanking you for hooking me up with some dude's address?

But his hand is still on hers.

—Izzy, we *kissed* at the Fair. I am not some little hoochie that just kisses people at the Fair like that.

—I don't think that about you.

—Then what *do* you think? Because I don't like how you're playing with me.

His free hand goes to his temple, rubbing at the mounting pain there.

—Look, okay? I'm just not ready for you, he says.

—But you *do* feel it too though, right? The connection?

The server pops up and says, All done? but she doesn't wait for an answer. She begins stacking their dishes—*clank, rattle, clank-clank*—making as much noise as possible. She lunges across the table to take away their knives and forks, then uses Izzy's to scrape all remaining food into one super gross pile. The sauces of everything pool together and anyone watching would say it looks like vomit.

Mercifully for all three of them, that's it: no other plates are coming to the table.

Fish Stuff

What connection is Julisa inadvertently asking about here? Think for a second how Izzy trying to tell her might sound, assuming he's even aware of the connection, the full extent of it: Lolita from the Miami Seaquarium is—what exactly? Infiltrating his thoughts? Afflicting him with migraines as a means of influencing his behavior? To what end—her freedom? Really? *This* guy?

In theory, you could put it as simply as this: he saw an orca in a wretched tank and she has not left his mind since. That having been in such close proximity to her magnificence, which radiates from her despite the abysmal circumstances of her environment, opened up something in him—about who he is and where he came from—that he isn't sure he should trust.

He could let himself say it that way, if only he could summon the wisdom and the words. He could then see how Julisa might respond to such an admission. There's a chance she might be the one person in Izzy's life right now who could access a reverential enough place to really hear him. She might even take what he'd say as a sign.

But his hands are rubbing circles at both his temples now. The pain—definitive and sharp—is solely on the right side, but there's no denying it. It's the only thing he understands. He needs to get her home before it gets much worse.

—Look, Julisa. It's complicated.

—Me and you having a crazy connection *or not* is not complicated. It's yes or no, Izzy.

She stifles a hiccup and says, Is this because you're friends with my brother?

—What? No! I mean, we're friends but it's more of a business arrangement right now.

—Oh my god, she says.

She leans away from the table, bows her head, cups her hands over her nose and mouth, as if trying to smell her own breath.

She lowers her hands and places them flat on the table and says, a little too loud and almost laughing, Is this about Daniel?

The Check

She'd promised herself that tonight she'd warn him about Daniel. She didn't do that at the Fair when Izzy asked her outright if there was anything he should know because she didn't want the warning getting all mixed up with the news that she and Daniel had a history—which was probably totally irrelevant, but you know how jealous guys can get—and she's felt shitty about it in the days since. But that was the tricky thing about the world Daniel moved in and out of: what was there really to warn Izzy about if he'd gone looking to be part of it? How could she explain the danger in a way that captured how she felt about it, which is: it sounds bad when you just like, *say* it, but really Daniel would never like, *do* anything. At least, she doesn't totally think so.

How about: it's not so much Daniel but the company he keeps, friends of friends, the grown children of people his parents have had no choice but to associate with, this being Miami and them being real estate developers and construction people and whatnot, people who necessarily have to have their hands in everything. Daniel's just doing what he has to do, proving his loyalty only when he has to, but at the end of the day he really does want to help people and animals. He really does have a good heart—a heart of gold to go along with access to lots of actual gold for some reason.

How about: it's not really Daniel you need to be afraid of, but Daniel has a lot of acquaintances who want to make sure that Daniel stays the helpful, generous, loving soul that he is—un niño inocente after all, just a boy still reeling from his mom's illness and death and his father's way-too-quick remarriage, the success and wealth that soon followed. His father's business dealings mean Daniel has close and useful ties to people who are widely understood to be deeply invested in Miami's Cuban American community, people with honorable reputations to uphold, so those people necessarily tend to outsource any unfortunate dirty work that might be needed to maintain their standing. And at least as far as Daniel's involvement, is that work truly *dirty* if—by protecting those who continue to do so much for their people—it's ultimately in service to the community they all claim and love?

How about: on paper, it sort of looks like Daniel has a lot of guns? At least like, access to them? Because most of them aren't really his. But then Izzy would obviously ask what the guns are for, and Julisa didn't know the answer to that. Even Daniel couldn't always answer that one. Her guess: They weren't *guns* so much as *arms*, meaning they had some greater purpose, and if Daniel had access to them, that meant those arms were destined to help something noble and important happen—keeping something in check or furthering some agenda. Only occasionally would you find Daniel shooting them off into the perceived nothingness of the Everglades or holding them for friends who were waiting for something or other to cool off. She didn't like thinking about it, and besides, the gun stuff was something that started after they'd broken up anyway.

She'd thought through these explanations and others all week leading up to this date that was apparently no longer a real date but hadn't decided on any. She'd wanted to wait to see how the night went. If Izzy proved to be The One, she'd make sure to tell him what she knew in the interest of keeping him safe—not that she was clear about what he needed to be kept safe from, other than the fact that being at Daniel's side could sometimes turn into a dangerous place to be, depending on whomever reached out to him and what they felt was needed. Either way, she wasn't going to take any chances with her fucking heaven-sent soulmate. But now she has her answer. This isn't a date. He said so himself. She owes him nothing.

—People have pasts, Izzy.

She pulls her napkin off her lap, drops it on the table. The server materializes by her side with yet another glass of tap water and the check. They haven't asked for either.

Gratuity

The children end up leaving her barely ten percent. She'd thought maybe the girl would throw some cash on the table on her way out to make up for her chump date's cheapness despite the hundred-dollar bills she glimpsed in his wallet as she hovered by the table while he paid, but no. No thanks for helping to end homegirl's misery. No thanks for keeping her from embarrassing herself more than she already had. No thanks for the extra bread and free water when she could've kept bringing them marked up bottles from the gas station like her manager insists she do even when people are clearly drunk and clearly not interested in paying for more water. Her manager always says, *This is a restaurant, not a bar, we have no obligation here, make them pay for it.* She always wants to say back, *But this is also a gas station! And it's just water from the sink! People sometimes go overboard and people could literally die!* But no, just like Gringo Gary over at the register, her manager doesn't care. Sometimes she worries that this whole city—the place she was born and the place she'll always think of as home no matter how deep underwater it ends up—is full of people learning not to care. Because look, look what caring got her: not even ten percent. Nowhere close to enough to keep her on track for her half of a new set of tits.

Nightcap

In the car, after immediately killing the radio and as soon as he's successfully maneuvered out of the not-a-parking lot, thus ending their not-a-date, Izzy says, By the way no, it's not about Danny. It's much bigger than that.

She does not say, *Everything involving Daniel is much bigger than Daniel.*

She says nothing at all.

Into her silence, he talks as little as possible to avoid the crescendo of pain those sound waves send over his brain: It's hard to explain, he says.

—Then don't try, she says.

He's grateful that she's whispered it. He's grateful that he's at least delayed their inevitableness. He's grateful that she's looking hard out her window, her whole body turned away from him, so that she cannot make the mistake of thinking he's crying over her, over anything. It's the lights from oncoming cars, the pain each beam brings him, making his eyes water and water and water.

MORE JULISA, PLEASE

It's just not possible, given the constraints—and despite all the other constraints so obviously and brazenly strained against. There's already been so much more Julisa than there ever was of Michelle Pfeiffer or Gina in *Scarface*, but maybe not so much that it surpasses the screen time of both those women combined. Lumping together the *Scarface* women is perhaps a loophole, granted, but her introduction did warn that her ultimate role—a Gina or a Michelle Pfeiffer—was uncertain given her status as the sidekick's sister. Even that fact is more than we get about Michelle Pfeiffer: does her character Elvira even *have* siblings? Does she even have *parents*? Are they all waiting for her back in Baltimore? Has she told any of them about her cocaine-induced infertility issues vis-à-vis her womb being so polluted?

Tony lamenting her supposed reproductive troubles offers up the last potential fact we get about her before she storms from the dinner table and exits the movie entirely. In the end, knowing so little about her: maybe it can be attributed to something else, in addition to a lack of imagination on the part of the men who wrote the movie. Maybe hovering at the edges of someone else's story turns into a kind of inadvertent protection. No one cared enough to know her well, to even ask the most natural of questions—how'd she get from Baltimore to Miami?—and so when the guns come out, no one thinks to track her down.

As Julisa largely makes her narrative exit toward a similar safety, it's time to mourn the necessary omission of a recollection of her quinceañera—because *Scarface* never mentioned if Gina or Michelle Pfeiffer ever had one—an event that left Julisa's parents with a credit card debt of twenty grand that they're still paying off; and of the scene from a day the summer before third grade, when her mother, angry at Julisa's dad over some perceived slight, tricked Julisa into sitting for an unflattering layered haircut, enticing her by calling it a mami-daughter bonding experience and convincing her she'd look like an older cousin she admired (for already menstruating) and without taking into account that the texture and thickness of Julisa's hair (an intentional miscalculation, as she'd inherited both from her dad) made that style a physical impossibility—Julisa looking in the mirror at the puff-ball result of the stylist's misguided exertions and at her mother's smug reflection as she stood behind her, Julisa suddenly knowing, bone-deep and early enough to protect her from much else, that her mother was largely incapable of loving anyone but herself; and of the scene of Julisa in class at FIU the Wednesday before her gas-station-tapas date with Izzy, her sitting in the second row of a lecture hall because she thinks the first row is for try-hards, and even though she does indeed try hard, she doesn't want anyone to notice this about her. Anyway, zoom in on her notebook, where she's supposedly writing down the important things her professor says: she's scrawled the words *Izzy* and *Ismael* and *Julisa Reyes* all over the place, in her most calculated dumb-girl bubble script.

Izzy where her lecture notes are supposed to be. This man as distraction. This man hogging the stage, the page. This man as a container the shape and size of the tank that holds Lolita. Twenty feet deep at its deepest point, most of it only twelve feet deep. How far can she really go given the constraints?

Think of Tony Montana in that ridiculous bathtub—*Fly, pelican, fly!*—bubbles covering the water's surface. But imagine the tub absolutely inescapable. Imagine that he can never leave it. Replace Tony with Julisa, and imagine her whole story having to unfold inside this tub. Only any leaps out of the water—those brief moments suspended outside the constraints of the world she's trapped in—would be worth watching. Only the scenes where you could pretend the tub wasn't there just beneath her, waiting for her to splash back down into those bubbles.

Julisa jumped out of a burning car and into the tank of Izzy's life, a space in which she'd been trained to exist, her performance watched and rewarded from every direction from an early age. Except once she was there, she did a better, more efficient job at moving through the tasks on Izzy's main list—without even knowing about said document—and for that he decides she must go, for now, and from this story for good.

When she exits his car for the last time and enters her home without once looking back at him, Izzy feels a melancholic relief and a momentary respite from the agony of his migraine. He believes he's done the right thing, feels that knowledge seep into him through the pain-induced tears that have not yet ceased. He doesn't understand this, but sure, you could say he's set her free. You could say she's left anyone watching to wonder—even marvel—at all that she could be, if given the space. Or better still: if the tank didn't exist to begin with.

THE SECOND RAFTER

One woman exits just as another enters: Monday morning at exactly nine a.m.—as if it's the very first thing listed in someone's planner—the number Izzy's been calling twice a day for a week with no answer other than the voicemail repeating the number back to him shows up on his phone's screen. The buzzing wakes him, and he's still half asleep when he recognizes whose number it is: Olivia C——, or at least it's the one Odlanier had given him, claiming that's who it belonged to. She doesn't confirm her name during the call: she only checks that he's in fact the Ismael Reyes who'd visited Odlanier Vasquez a little over a week ago at his home, and when he says yeah, she gives him an address in Miami Shores and the instruction to come alone and right away, immediately. He's about to ask if she's Olivia C—— when she says without prompting: I was the girl on the raft.

The chance at this meeting is so random and rushed that Izzy doesn't initially feel terrible about leaving Rudy out of it. On the drive over, he's actually kind of relieved it's happening this way; he isn't sure what, if anything, Julisa might've told Rudy about Friday's dinner. His guess is nothing, at least not yet, but he'll clear everything up with Rudy later and explain how actually, he'd strategically let things with Julisa crash and burn in order to preserve his working relationship with Rudy, not tank it. And as he nears the address Olivia gave him, he admits something else about the circumstances of choosing to do this solo, another benefit he can blame on the urgency that made him leave Rudy behind: now Izzy can ask whatever questions come to him and not feel Rudy's confusion or pity or judgment when those questions lingered on Alina longer than they did on the logistics of their crossing or how to get in touch with bona fide smugglers. Without Rudy, Izzy doesn't have to pretend that business is his only motivation.

These are the excuses he makes for himself while speeding to Olivia's house to justify abandoning his Manolo, something he can't remember Tony Montana doing at this stage without it having serious repercussions, i.e.: that scene where that random guy named Omar gets hanged from a helicopter flying overhead while a Bolivian drug lord named Sosa has Tony watch through binoculars. As Izzy parks in her paver-covered driveway and shoves his phone in his front pocket, he tries not to think of how that guy's body jerked and swung so realistically, not knowing that the filmmakers used an actual human for that scene—a stuntman instead of a dummy.

Though most of the C—— family calls Coral Gables or Pinecrest home, Olivia C—— came of age in Hialeah: her parents held her quinceañera at My Dreams Banquet Hall II in the strip mall on West 16th Avenue and the party was spectacular (she came out of a clam shell; she was the pearl); the venue also hosted her college graduation party (she went to UCF and came home almost every weekend), though for her wedding a year ago, they'd of course rented a salón on the beach—beach-adjacent, really, as they'd gone with a ballroom and wedding package at Jungle Island, the theme park formerly known as Parrot Jungle Island (and as Parrot Jungle before that) right off the MacArthur Causeway, on the *way* to Miami Beach. Beach or beach-adjacent, Jungle Island was a big step up from My Dreams II in terms of vistas and price point, and the Hialeah C——s got to say that they'd spared no expense. They were a family that liked to celebrate their only daughter's life milestones with parties that required formal invitations; it was a way of keeping them relevant to the siblings and cousins and tíos to whom they owed so much.

Olivia graduated from Hialeah Lakes High just like Izzy, half a decade before he'd step foot on that campus. Her husband went there as well, but they hadn't known each other then despite both being in marching band: he was on the drumline, she'd played the clarinet, and in the world of big public schools with big marching bands, that separation—coupled with her being a year ahead of him grade-wise—was enough for them to only know the other by sight but not by name. They married seven years after her graduation following a brief courtship conducted mostly online. Despite the wedding photos showing evidence to the contrary, her parents weren't thrilled by the match; all members of the C—— lineage rightly consider themselves a prominent Miami family, having built an empire out of building the city itself, though Olivia's particular branch left Cuba too late and in the wrong way—by raft, not by plane—to really count as the type of people who need to be worried about how their daughter's choice of husband impacts their standing in Miami's Cuban exile community. Still, when any of the C—— family are asked, they say Olivia and her husband (who is not important enough to be mentioned by name) were high school sweethearts.

For the wedding's signature Cockatiel Cocktail Hour, they'd opted for the Premium Parrot Photo Package, which came with two full hours for them and their guests to pose with a selection of Jungle Island's friendliest birds, and the parrot-laden photos now adorn the living room wall in her new house, which sits five blocks east of I-95, in an area she describes as *Wynwood Adjacent* but that is really just the edge of Miami Shores, a good twenty-minute drive from the restaurants and bars to which she's claiming proximity. It's been only a few months since she and her husband signed a thirty-year mortgage to finance the half-a-million-dollar two-bedroom, one-bathroom house that's expected to be underwater in twenty to twenty-five years. No one told them about those projections outright, and as first-time home buyers using the money their extended family generously gifted them when they married, they didn't see the cost of the flood insurance they're required to carry as a red flag. Everyone in this area has to have that coverage, that's just how it is these days. That's the most they would've been told, had they known to ask. They'd barely asked anything; on the day they closed on the house, they were still glowing from the thrill of having won the bidding war and of getting to live in a neighborhood they thought of as eclectic and grown-up and not Hialeah.

Olivia C—— answers the door without Izzy having to knock first; she's been watching for him from between the blinds of her house's biggest front window. She tells Izzy this—I was watching for you from right there, she says, laughing and pointing to a white couch under that window—and then invites him in to sit on said couch, across from the wall adorned with the mosaic of photos, each framed in silver.

She locks the door behind him and says, The doorbell freaks this little guy out.

Trapped in the crook of Olivia's elbow is an ancient, tiny dog with a dick big enough to count as another leg. Both its legs and its dick dangle below her forearm, the legs paddling the air, searching for something solid to stand on. Its bark is so quiet and scratchy it sounds like it's lost its voice, or like the sound is actually coming from somewhere far away. The dog's eyes bulge from its apple-shaped head, and when it stops its pathetic yipping, its tongue slips out and hangs from the side of its toothless mouth like the extra slack on a belt.

—This is my fur-baby Braulio Sebastian. We call him BS for short. Can you believe we found him right in front of the house eating our garbage?

—Yeah I can. It's a dog?

—And he almost drowned! It was a big rain day plus there was king tide, so we had water up to the front steps out there.

She tilts her head back toward the door behind her.

—We got water in the garage but the rest of the house was fine. Ruined all my maticas out front though. Half my new landscaping floated away. Gotta love home ownership!

—Felicidades on that, he says. On the house, he clarifies.

The dog is not worth any sort of congratulations.

—It needs some love, for sure. Definitely needs another bathroom. But you can't beat the area. Panther Coffee is like fifteen minutes away.

She sits down across from him on a matching loveseat. According to Panther Coffee's website, their founders, a married couple from Oregon, visited Miami on vacation in 2008, and soon after decided to relocate to the city to build their coffee empire after they *quickly realized that although there was an abundance of Cuban style coffee shops, the specialty coffee scene was nonexistent,* to quote their site's About Us page. Izzy has never heard of it and assumes it's basically a glorified Starbucks but with way worse parking, which: maybe he's not wrong.

Olivia doesn't offer him café or water or anything, which makes Izzy wonder why she insisted that he meet her at her house instead of somewhere public like Panther Coffee. He raises an arm to lay it across the back cushions, and his hand falls on three wallet-sized pieces of cardboard dangling off the couch's corner. Similar tags hang from the edges of her throw pillows. He flips them around in his fingers but stops short of reading them, thinking it might be rude.

—New couch? he says.

—Not really, she says. Got it pretty much right after we closed. I just like leaving the tags on. That way they stay feeling new.

Tags wave at him from the loveseat, from the TV cabinet, from the seats of her dining chairs. The house is small and open, the living room and dining room really all just one space, almost everything in it white or gray, the only color coming from the backyard, visible through a sliding glass door—the terra-cotta tiles of the back patio, the lush greens and yellows of the palms fanning up from the ground, hiding a wooden privacy fence. Olivia reaches over from the loveseat and tugs a baby blanket off a nearby dining chair and wraps it around the dog, who immediately tries to wiggle out of it. She sits the poorly swaddled dog in her lap facing Izzy. Its dick pushes out from the blanket and points at him, bobbing in sync with the animal's labored breaths.

—Can I ask, what kind of dog is that?

—Oh my god I know, right? He's an alien. Like he's literally from outer space.

She holds the dog up in front of her and turns it her way so that its dick is at eye level.

—Mira este macho, huh? Have you ever seen a dog this small with a pipi so big?

She turns the dog back toward Izzy and holds it out for inspection.

—It's, yeah, it's *a lot*, Izzy says. He laughs and says, I thought maybe you didn't notice it was like, *out* there like that.

—Are you kidding me? Do I look like an idiot? This dog's pipi saved his life, it's always like this. It's the reason we kept him, because it's so freaking hilarious. He makes me so happy.

She turns the dog back toward her and rubs her cheek against the top of its head before returning it in her lap, where it flops over in half at the waist so that its dick is just under its chin.

—Honestly, after we found him, I took him to a vet and made the mistake of saying I'd picked him up on the street, because then they scanned him and saw he was microchipped. His owner's address was right there in the system. I was like, Oh! Okay! Just give me the address and I'll take him back, no problem. Mind you, they aren't supposed to do that but you know how people are and here I was offering to give them one less thing to worry about, so—*boop!*—I put him in my little doggie BabyBjörn and brought him back here.

She bends down to kiss the dog's head.

—If people are irresponsible enough to lose their dogs in the first place, they probably shouldn't get them back, right? I mean, look at his dick! This dog cracks me up and I deserve a little happiness in my life. That's what I told my husband when I said I was keeping him. He was all like, Let's put up flyers or whatever blah blah blah. No thanks.

—Wait, so your husband doesn't know about the real owners?

—Of course not. Also, excuse me but, *real* owners? It was *their* job not to lose him, not *my* job to return a possibly abused and neglected animal eating *my* garbage and almost drowning on *my* flooded street in front of *my* property. As far as I'm concerned this dog was destined to be mine.

Izzy adjusts his seat on the couch, moving a throw pillow, careful not to bend the tags as he tosses it to the couch's other side. He's here because he needs information from Olivia and so he doesn't give his honest opinion about what he would argue constitutes kidnapping. The pillow lands and bounces a little, and he thinks of Danny freeing all those iguanas they'd spent the day catching, the way their legs must've stretched out as Danny swept them one by one into the canal behind his house, as if they would hit the water and run instead of swim. Could those iguanas do it though, make it all the way back to the waterway they'd come from?

—No yeah, he says, hands in the air, surrendering. You can't stop what's meant to be.

—Exactly, she says.

He cannot wait to tell Julisa about this woman and this dog and this story until he remembers that Julisa is over him in a way he's orchestrated, a way he hopes he can eventually undo. The photos behind Olivia are of her in a wedding dress and her husband in a tux, their arms lifted like they are being crucified, a dozen parrots perched across them. Olivia and her husband are both laugh-screaming in one photo, their faces perfectly composed and smiling in another, with exaggerated frowns in another still. The birds look to Izzy like cartoon drawings of parrots, they are that perfect. The wall is full of photos only from the wedding, as if nothing else in their lives had ever happened to them.

—I can guess why you're here if Odlanier Vasquez sent you. What did he say about me?

—Only that you'd talk to me. About stuff *he* didn't want to talk about.

She says, That figures.

She says, He didn't come to my wedding but my parents told me that would happen, I think we've seen him maybe once since Krome, at an Easter Mass, and even that was just random. They sent him an invitation out of loyalty—my family is all about loyalty but you probably know that already—but also to like, remind him that they still knew where he lived, you know? Anyway, it was sweet of him to send a present. We still haven't used that salad spinner, we registered for so much mierda we never use, it's ridiculous.

She hugs the dog to her chest as if about to breastfeed and says, But honestly, my parents are just like him, they don't like thinking about that time either. They definitely don't talk about it. Obviously I don't either, but I don't care so much because honestly, people do what they have to do, you can't blame people for taking advantage of the resources available to them. Your mother certainly took advantage in her own ways, no offense.

—None taken, he says, an automatic response he doesn't mean or understand.

—That's why you're here, right? Because of that woman? I mean, of course literally but also more like, that's what I've heard you've been asking around about.

—I've only – other than you I've only talked to Mr. Vasquez.

She jiggles the dog up and down the way you would a crying baby and says, That's good to know.

Then he says something he couldn't have said if Rudy were there: Look, I'm gonna be real with you, I don't totally get what you're talking about, especially when it comes to my mother, but I'm guessing it has to do with how we got here. Whether we were assisted at sea or not.

—Lemme see your phone, she says.

He wants to ask why, but then she says, Actually, stand up.

He does so and she does too, putting the dog and his blanket on the seat cushion where her butt just was. The dog starts to dig around, dragging his dick over the blanket while pawing the fabric into a little nest for himself as Olivia puts her hands flat against Izzy's chest. She presses hard across his pecs, around and under them, she's close to his face now, her forehead just under his chin, and she starts smoothing her palms downward, feeling over his belly, then stroking up and down his sides, around what's left of his love handles and then around his back, pulling him into her, hugging him almost, and Izzy is laughing a little—because it tickles in spots and also it feels good and he doesn't really want to ask any questions because he doesn't want the touching to stop—until she drops her hands to his back pockets and he realizes she is frisking him, checking him for a wire or some other recording device. She takes his phone from his front pocket and runs a palm across his crotch as an afterthought while looking at his screen. Then she tosses the phone onto the spot next to her on the loveseat, the thud of its landing causing the dog to jerk up and begin his frantic round-and-round pawing again. She picks up the dog before sitting back down, leaves Izzy standing in front of her with just the slightest boner.

—What the fuck was that? he says.

—It doesn't matter how long ago it happened. You never know who you're dealing with, my parents tell me all the time you can't be too careful. Especially with this new president looking to deport people for any reason, though honestly my parents probably voted for him. I have no idea, we don't talk about politics.

Izzy decides he better sit, to hide the boner.

—You just felt me up for a wire? Who do you think I am?

She flips the dog over on its back and starts scratching its belly in long passes with the tips of her fingernails.

—Oh, I know you're the kid from the raft. That I believe. I just needed to be sure you haven't changed. Why are you really here?

He wants to ask her what she means. Changed from what to what? Instead he says, I just wanna know what happened. I wanna know what you remember.

—And what do *you* remember?

—Honestly? That the trip was shorter than it probably should've been.

—That's for sure accurate. Do you remember what happened to your mother?

He tells her the truth: I know she died, she drowned. I remember us being sunburned. Mostly I remember seeing my tía at Krome and thinking she looked like my mother. But I barely remember Alina, even from before the raft. I remember her waking me up and making me walk to the beach and that I didn't want to go. What I want to know now though is about the trip, about who helped us.

—Okay, she says. But everything I tell you I will deny if it ever leaves this room.

Izzy nods at this in accidental rhythm with the rise and fall of the dog's dick.

—What I remember is that we were on the raft for like a day or two, and then one night, we heard it before we saw it, and at first of course we were scared, well I know I was and my mom was because what if it was the Coast Guard, if they intercepted us we'd be sent back, and then we'd basically be dead. But then we saw it was the speedboat from Miami, the one we'd been waiting for because everyone on that raft had paid for that exact thing to happen. Everyone except your mother, and you.

She looks down at the dog and says, Your mother must've known when and from where our raft was leaving because of her position in the CDR, that's just my guess. I don't know why she picked us and not someone else, so many people left all the time, except maybe she knew about the smuggling arrangement, but that seems impossible. I don't know why she didn't just turn us in before we even had the chance to leave. But when she showed up there, we all knew there was no way she'd bought herself and you a way over. *You* were why we knew your mother was lying, you were what, five? Six? Whatever you were, you were too little to be trusted once we made it to land and turned ourselves in and asked for asylum. But everyone was afraid to ask anything. No one was supposed to ask anyone anything personal. My dad was the only one brave enough to say something. The boat that met us at sea was a family hookup, so we had more at stake. We didn't want our Miami people getting in trouble because of some stupid kid. So he said something to her about your age.

She stops scratching the dog and says, Are you sure you want to know this shit? Because you can't unknow it, you know.

—I'm here, aren't I?

—Fine. She takes a deep, practiced breath in through her nose and says, My dad said something to her about you compromising us on the other side. Everyone knew for a fact that the people who were helping us out were strict about no one under twelve being allowed. I was twelve turning thirteen and even that had been a mission to get them to agree to. It's funny because my parents were ready to say I was mentally retarded if I started talking about the speedboat to anyone at Krome. That's how desperate they were. They told me so later, after my quinces party. Not like in a speech or anything – they would never say anything in public about it, and like I said, they still don't talk about that time unless they have to, which, hello, they need mental help big time. They are totally in denial about their trauma.

She goes back to tickling the dog's chest.

—What did she say though? My mother, when your dad confronted her?

—Oh, that's when she probably figured out that his question meant we'd be getting help at sea, though who knows, maybe she knew that already, though I have no idea how. Either way, that's when she threatened everyone the first time. She said if we didn't let both of you on the raft, she'd go back and alert authorities that we'd left and they'd intercept us before we made it out of Cuban waters and we'd all go to jail or worse. Which, I mean, she'd done it to other people, so we all knew she had it in her, to even say something like that to us at that moment.

—Fucking shit.

—I know, right? Odlanier, he was so mad at her. He worried the boat wouldn't take any of us because of you two. Or if they did, some of us worried that if your mom *did* know about the boat beforehand – and that's why she picked us and not some other raft – that she'd coached you to snitch about us getting help at sea, which guaranteed we'd all be sent back or at least detained for way longer. Plus also it would get the whole smuggling operation on the radar, which she probably wanted to happen because then people on *this* side who helped would be in trouble. Nobody as little as you was supposed to be on the raft for that reason. You can't trust little kid brains. They always tell the truth exactly when you don't want them to.

Izzy puts his elbows on his knees, then his face in his hands.

—I'd joke that afterward Odlanier was trying to convince people to throw you to the sharks, but honestly it wouldn't be a joke. He doesn't know that I know this but I heard him suggest it while it was getting dark, when you were sleeping and he thought I was too. Your mother had already drowned by then.

—Are you fucking serious?

—You have to see it from his perspective. The only reason I can talk about it easily is because I don't feel anything about it anymore. Like, nothing at all. What happened, happened, and that's it. I feel totally fine. It's honestly no big deal.

She reaches a hand between the dog's legs and gives its dick the gentlest of strokes.

—Anyway, the Miami people found us, we all climbed onto their boat, and the person driving it, who nobody knew personally because that was how it was gonna work, tugged our shitty little raft to within a doable amount of miles of Miami, we got back on that horrible raft and launched out again from there so when we reached land it would look like we'd arrived unassisted and all get our papers and get to stay.

He couldn't believe it: his mother had compromised everyone's passage by bringing Izzy. He couldn't blame them for doing what they felt they had to do.

—So they threw my mother off the raft?

—No! Oh god no, holy fuck. No, bro, she jumped off all on her own. Also while you were asleep. She told us to do whatever we wanted with you but that it would be on our conscience forever, whatever we did. Super fucking dramatic, no offense. That was her second threat – and after, that's when the idea came up that she'd coached you. Her banking that with her gone, we'd let you stay but we'd all be forced back once you talked. Literally dying for Castro. She told us all about your tía already over here.

He is so grateful that he's alone, that Rudy is not there to hear any of this.

—Why would Alina . . . jump off the raft like that? Leave me behind with – no offense, but with strangers? With no guarantee that you guys or the Miami boat or even my tía would – look out for me?

—You think I haven't wondered the same thing? Communism is a mindfuck. Patria o muerte, bro. She made her choice. You're just lucky we weren't savages.

—Why'd you let me stay?

—You were too cute. Also, you'd stopped talking. Like, completely you were frozen. My guess is I think the older men might've put the fear of God in you. I don't really think about it. My parents told me not to look at you and not to talk to you, not to acknowledge you at all, in case something else needed to happen. Mostly I did what they said. They didn't want me to remember you.

She is looking behind him now, out her window.

—I never doubted that one day you'd be here asking me about all this, to be honest.

—Why's that?

—Look, she says. You don't know this, but I owe you this conversation, because for everyone's safety it needs to be the last one you have about this shit.

—Why the last one?

—Honestly, because it's gonna lead to major problems, definitely for you and maybe for other people.

—My tía told me the same thing. Does she know about all this?

—Oh I doubt it. She sounds like a smart lady. You should listen to her. You owe her at least that much for raising you.

—How do you know that? That she raised me?

She lets out a snort and says, What did I just say about the questions? You gotta stop. These people – they don't fuck around. You're lucky I barely leave my house anymore and this can end here.

She moves her hand away from the dog's dick, sighs, and says, Besides, who else but your tía could've paid them for the extra passenger, which was you? Someone must've paid, otherwise it's not fair to everyone else. That's not important now though. What's important *now* is that after you leave this house, you stop asking people about what they do or don't remember. Just be grateful your tía was here to claim you and that all of this is in your past.

He doesn't know what to say because there is nothing he wants to say that isn't a question. And besides, what he wanted to ask wasn't a question for her. It was one he'd already posed to his Tía Tere.

—But she told me she didn't pay for me.

Olivia has her palm pressed against the dog's chest, smashing its dick into its own body.

—Well then, Ismael, I guess one of us is remembering it wrong or just lying.

He says, There's no way though, and she says, Honestly, I used to think about your mother a lot. About how fucked up she was, no offense. Those thoughts made me kind of messed up for a while. It's what made me read all these self-help articles and books about positivity and living your best life, to get over the whole thing. To this day I don't know what was going through her head when she jumped off the raft. Did she want us to stop her? Did she think we would? Was she gonna try and swim back to Cuba? I mean, hello, sharks? Someone looks around the house and says, What do *you* fucking do?

could ask you the same questions. But I don't want trouble in

. I'm past all that. I still know better.

e unlocks the front door with her free hand and smiles so that all

eth are visible—the same forced grin from the wedding photos.

Thank you for the visit, she says. Don't forget your phone.

on the raft said she had her period. That she was bl
never to think about it.

—Who else might've known her, on the raft I m

—Nobody. Nobody who you want knowing yc
that's why I'm telling you this is your last conversati

He looks up at the wedding photos, at the sm
her nameless husband, at the guests who in their j
familiar and generic. When Manolo warns Tony to
boss's lady as they head home from the Babylon Cl
spends an evening ill-advisedly trying to dance witl
he tells Tony, *Be happy with what you got.* Tony spits
Me, I want what's coming to me. Izzy ignores the sou
bored breathing and says, I need to know who were
with the boat.

She stands up, shifting the dog to her elbow ag
gle, its legs paddling more frantically than befor
from Izzy toward the door, the underside of the
red in Izzy's direction.

He stands but stays put, his calves barely brushi
ric, and asks, Are they still . . . helping people? Do

She spins on her heel and says, Even if I knew
you really think I would just *tell* you? Are you fuck

—So you don't know, he says. Or you do and
you with the real owners of that thing there?

He thrusts his chin at the dog. Anger, he th
nize. Anger, he knows how to engage, manipulate
thinks he sees flash over her face, but he's wrong.

The dog starts its pathetic barking again—a scr
it's nonstop.

She says, You of all people should already knc
to stay quiet. You understood the importance of t
don't act like you don't know it now.

—Know what? Silent about what?

Her eyes watering, she says, My husband will b

—It's like ten in the morning. What does he e

A SQUEEZE OF THE HAND

On the drive home, Izzy imagines different scenarios of what happened to his mother to contradict what Olivia told him.

She slipped off the raft and they refused to pull her back on. He imagines their fingers prying her own off the raft's edges.

She rolled off the edge while sleeping and everyone else was also sleeping and no one realized it until it was too late.

She dove into the water in a state of delirium to escape the sun's heat, became disoriented, and couldn't find her way back despite everyone's panicked calls and outstretched arms. Or she dove in to catch a fish that wasn't there, also in a state of delirium. Or she dove in to escape the guilt of having forced her way onto a raft. Or the guilt of bringing her son with her. Or the guilt of having jeopardized the passage of the others. Or the guilt of having been such a terrifying part of the lives they'd been driven to flee in the first place.

The others covered her mouth so he wouldn't awaken when she screamed, stabbed her, and threw her to the sharks.

He remembers, at a red light, the crazy story from a few years after he'd arrived about how an actual fucking shark showed up on the Metromover downtown. And in Miami Beach last fall, the king tide left an octopus stranded in a parking garage. All sorts of creatures showing up where they're not supposed to be, having to be dealt with, the only explanations for how they got there to begin with being the stuff of worst-case scenarios.

Where the street meets his Tía Tere's driveway, a recurring puddle grows and shrinks with the rains, the tides. His car glides through it now and the thought finds him: only the water knows the truth of what happened.

He laughs, pulls the key from the ignition, shakes his head as he says aloud to no one, Maybe I should ask Lolita.

*   *   *

Back at the Seaquarium, Lolita circles her tank. She is mildly dehy-
drated as her show begins because the protocol requires that she be
hungry for the shows to guarantee her cooperation, and all the water
in her body comes solely from the fish she consumes. And with each
fish comes, along with the water and in the form of the nutrition they
offer, a realm of memories and sensations generations old, each bone
and scale bringing her some stored aspect of the world into which she
was born. And although she was never meant to eat the type of fish
she's fed here, and although these fish are already dead when they're
tossed into her mouth, she is grateful to each of them for what they
tell her as she swallows.

She waits at the edge of the tank's stage for the trainer to get on
her knees, for the hands that will reach across the water to feed her
more.

That night, Izzy again asks his Tía Tere if she's who paid the smugglers.
He doesn't give her the chance to debate with him about whether or
not a boat assisted their raft to shore. He wants to know how much it
cost, how long they waited before finding her, and whatever else she
remembers about them when they came to collect.

She again denies that she ever paid anything: Ismael, please, it
never happened. Why would I lie to you? Why would I deny something that would make me look good?

She tells him he can inspect her bank statements himself if he
wants. She's kept paper copies of each of them dating back to when
she bought this house. When he asks if anyone at all ever tried to
get her to pay, she says no, absolutely not, that whoever helped them
at sea—something for which they have no proof, she reminds him,
so this is all hypothetical—wouldn't have tried to collect from her
because she could rightfully claim that she never agreed to any deal.
Noble or not, given the illegality of what they'd done, it's not like they
could sue her, and she didn't fear for her life either, because if they
were the kinds of smugglers who'd kill her for nonpayment, they'd

have to kill Izzy too, which made no sense considering they'd already risked so much to save his life. The people she knew of through various exile organizations who volunteered for this kind of work thought of themselves as in the business of saving lives, not destroying them.

—If they were the type to charge, you think they'd risk their whole operation and out themselves for a few thousand bucks? she says. They just took the loss. How much space did you really take up? You were like this, she says, holding up her pinky finger.

She owns no photos of Izzy from before the age of seven, has no idea what he looked like as a baby, if he was born with a full head of hair like her or bald like his mother. Pictures from his first few months in the U.S. are sparse because she didn't want to remember him like that. So he has nothing of himself that young to look back at, no image to interrogate.

He asks her why the smugglers would've let him on their boat in the first place. She guesses: Because it happened so fast? Because they'd all have to live with themselves knowing they'd sent a child to his death if they didn't? Because what if they'd left you to die and by some miracle you still made it to shore, or the Coast Guard or someone else found you, and you told them what happened? Because they were ultimately good people? Because they felt sorry for you?

Then he tells her what Olivia C—— said about his mother, how Alina jumped off the raft, though he credits the information to Odlanier to keep his Tía Tere from worrying.

—No way in hell, she says. I don't believe that for a second.

—How do you know?

—I didn't know Alina well, that's true. But what I do know from her own words and from people who knew her in Cuba was how much – how much she prided herself on having a Revolutionary for a father, a man who executed people – people like me and my father, people who were trying to leave. She was proud to be the daughter of a murderer. Proud of things she should've been ashamed of, even embracing them, using that violent legacy for her own gain. I'm not surprised that she grew into someone who informed on people, that she got so high up in the CDR. You know, she barely knew her father – he came and went with his orders – but you wouldn't know that from how she flaunted the connection, used it to scare people. In truth he was nobody – he killed people but in the end he wasn't any more important than any of Castro's degenerates – but can you imagine being *proud* of what he'd done? She thought it made her someone worth listening to.

She says, She never thought about who he'd hurt, who she was hurting. She never thought about anyone but herself. She would've never thrown herself off that raft, never. She would've tried to kill everyone else on it first.

His Tía Tere doesn't say it—would never say it—but he knows her next thought: *She would've thrown you off first.*

MONTAGE

Tony Montana's meteoric rise to the top of Miami's drug game is delivered in a montage set to a power ballad titled (Scarface) Push It to the Limit, a song no one has ever heard outside of the movie itself. The montage covers an indeterminate amount of time and flashes through the following images:

A lot of money in the form of physical bills getting fanned through a money counting machine;

Tony laughing maniacally into various phones, an equally maniacally laughing Sosa, the Bolivian drug czar (played by a white guy in brownface), on the other end of the calls;

A lot of money in the form of physical bills being brought into a bank via huge sacks, Rich Uncle Pennybags–style;

Tony and Manolo and some other dudes wearing white or light gray suits, walking in front of a couple different marble-column-adorned buildings with the words MONTANA MANAGEMENT on one and MONTANA TRAVEL CO. on the other, thus subtly signaling how all this drug money is being laundered through tourism deals and real estate development and construction contracts, thus subtly being the most realistic element of the film as it pertains to Miami, thus subtly foreshadowing the fact that when you poke around at one end of an operation, you will inevitably disturb its other side;

Tony's sister Gina finally getting her own salon, which Tony has bought for her with all that money in the sacks. Hooray for her! Tony and Manolo are there for the grand opening—orchestrated as a ribbon cutting—and Tony doesn't notice Manolo making sexy eyes at Gina, hence his shock later when he finds out they got married, which leads to Tony shooting him (not part of the montage);

A lot of money in the form of physical bills yet again going through that money counting machine and then again being brought into a bank via huge sacks, with the banker who's watching making a stunned face that suggests that all this cash is getting much harder to hide;

Tony and Michelle Pfeiffer getting married. Hooray for them! Look at them standing at the altar, eye to eye—only after multiple screenings do you realize that Tony Montana is kind of short—Michelle Pfeiffer's thin shoulders barely holding up those poufy sleeves, Tony in an off-white tux with a blood-colored bowtie, Manolo as his best man by his side, Gina there too, presumably the maid of honor. They are pronounced husband and wife and Tony makes out with his bride in front of the priest for a long time, so the camara floats away to focus on some even more very pointed, very sexy looks being exchanged between Gina and Manolo, which of course Tony can't see because of the aforementioned making out, so he can't be blamed for missing this exchange, especially once he and his bride start running down some steps and across the lawn toward—

A lot of money in the form of a pet tiger and its way-too-small back-yard habitat, the latter of which is apparently part of Tony's man-sion's landscaping, very safely behind a moat or a stream or some water-based protection. The tiger is snarling and straining at the end of its chain and looks ready to kill whoever stuck him down there. Poor, poor tiger, but hooray for Tony fulfilling his lifelong dream of owning an animal evolutionarily designed to consume him;

A giant sheet falling away to reveal a life-size portrait of Tony and Mi-chelle Pfeiffer, Tony in a black tux, standing behind a seated Michelle Pfeiffer in a flowy-looking red halter gown. Tony has his hand on her arm as if trying to keep her in the chair, with what looks like the hint of a sunset behind them. Neither of them is smiling. Omitted from the movie and the montage are the hiring of the portrait's artist and the many hours they must have spent sitting for said portrait;

Gina admiring herself and twirling in front of a wall of mirrors at a designer clothing store while Tony watches her, half-smiling and slumped in a chair. She's wearing a beige dress that resembles a stunning bathrobe—as apparently was the style—and it goes by fast enough that you don't really wonder where Manolo is, or why Tony's the one taking her clothes shopping instead of using this outing as a bonding opportunity with her new sister-in-law;

A freshly bathed Michelle Pfeiffer sitting at a vanity, an ashtray full of cigarettes perched on its corner and a plate-sized mirror piled with cocaine right in front of her. As the camera zooms in, she uses a super-tiny silver spoon—rather than any of her magnificently long fingernails—to scoop the cutest amount of coke into one nostril, then into the other, then a third scoop into her mouth. She moves her lips and jaw in a way that suggests she's using her tongue to push the coke around and into her gums, leading you to think Michelle Pfeiffer has definitely done her research as to how the typical drug lord's wife takes her yeyo. The camera stays on her as she takes a drag of her cigarette and sips some liquor from an elegant heavy-bottomed glass, then looks off into nothing, presumably feeling some regret at her marital situation and/or forlorn at being left out of the previously glimpsed shopping trip.

The montage signals the beginning of the end, a.k.a. the beginning of the Final Act.

PUSH IT TO THE LIMIT

Izzy's rise is less meteoric but still warrants documenting despite not having a power-ballad backing. As is the case in the movie, the montage covers an indeterminate amount of time but is arranged in such a way as to convey its passage. It includes:

A lot of money in the form of physical bills moving from Danny's hands to Izzy's and Rudy's wallets after an afternoon in the Everglades spent trying to catch Burmese pythons, where they catch zero pythons;

Izzy finding multiple phone numbers corresponding to every name left on his list and, despite Olivia's warnings, trying them all, over and over and over again;

A lot of money in the form of physical bills that Danny pays out to multiple guys, Izzy and Rudy included, none of whom get introduced by name, all of whom have joined him on a somewhat illegal midnight hunt, again in the Everglades, for wild boar and black bear—before, during, and after which Izzy catches multiple glimpses of all those guns Julisa never mentioned;

The few times people do pick up when Izzy calls, the conversation ending as soon as Izzy explains how they might know each other. All four Dayesi Riveras he tries hang up on him. A couple sounded young (and even cute) over the phone, so he at least knows (or thinks he knows) that neither of them are the right Dayesi Rivera, but still: he is certain one of the other two is the Dayesi Rivera from the raft, and so he keeps trying those two until one of the numbers stops working, newly disconnected. The other stops leading to a voicemail and just rings and rings and rings so he thinks she must have him blocked. He gets desperate enough that for all the other numbers, he starts leaving messages where he states his full name, that he's looking for the people who came with him on a balsa from Cuba in 2004, that he wants to know what happened to his mother. He tells them her name. No one calls him back;

Everyone Izzy calls who understands what he's asking being terrified enough about what his persistence might lead to that several of them reach out to people who know people, people *they* don't know, people they never knew but to whom they owe everything, and so they remain loyal. Olivia C——, phone wedged between shoulder and ear, scratching her fingernails along the back of her tiny big-dicked dog;

A lot of money in the form of physical bills being handed over from Danny to a bartender—a gray-haired guy who'll show up again briefly near the start of the Final Act—who works, among other places, on a yacht, serving drinks on sunset wedding cruises, the men slapping backs and hugging, suggesting they've known each other a long time and that whatever arrangement they've just come to is one they've made before;

Izzy and Rudy fighting at the park near Rudy's house after Rudy finds out that, according to Julisa, Izzy broke his sister's heart. Izzy is confused because he thought breaking her heart was the best way to keep things with Rudy good. When he tells Rudy this, Rudy says, Bro, what the fuck is wrong with you? And then he says, I'm not mad that you took her out and maybe liked her, I'm mad you lied to me about it. I thought we were partners, bro. Izzy says: We aren't partners, you're supposed to be my Manolo. Then Izzy goes full Tony on him, yelling to Rudy that his sister is crazy, that she's thirsty and sad, that she was trying to force her way into his plan. Rudy says: What fucking plan, bro? He doesn't tell Izzy that he thinks they should abandon the plan, or that Izzy is the one who seems crazy lately given all the fucked-up mom stuff. Rudy sees Izzy's outburst as the final sign he needs to back away slowly. Rudy does exactly that: literally backing away slowly from

Izzy, who is still busy deploying many *fuck you*s and a couple *you don't tell me what to do*s to Rudy, then to Rudy's back as Rudy walks away, jogs down the block, runs home toward—

A lot of money in the form of pounds and pounds of frozen unidentified meat that Rudy asks absolutely no questions about, that Danny has asked for help in picking up from a ranch down in Homestead but that he's been asked to deliver on his own to a private residence out on Key Biscayne. On the drive to drop off Rudy, Danny asks him what the deal is with his friend Izzy, why didn't he show up to help with the job as usual, that he's been thinking maybe this Izzy guy is trouble. Rudy explains calmly that Izzy isn't his friend, never was, really, but especially not now, not after how he messed with Julisa— something Danny didn't even know about until exactly that moment. He keeps his eyes on the road and lets Rudy talk, remembering to breathe and laugh at the right spots and to agree that yeah, that fool sounds fucking nuts. Better to keep your distance, they agree. Poor, poor Julisa, again with the broken heart, but hooray for Danny getting whatever sign he needed to feel at peace with the small ways he's agreed to help;

Izzy in front of a sink rinsing his dinner dishes as he stares at a line of tiny ants strolling across his Tía Tere's kitchen counter from the window above the sink, around the sink itself, down a corner of the cabinets, disappearing somewhere along the baseboards. The ants appear fuzzy to him. They are so small they look gray. These ants are everywhere, all over this city, a line of them in every home despite the chemicals sprayed into the earth to keep them out. He's thinking: they know something. He has the strong urge to press them gently with a dripping-wet pointer finger, then raise the finger to his mouth and swallow them, to know what they know by making them part of him. He stands staring at them, his hands fully under the waterfall of the tap's stream, until his Tía Tere yells, Izzy please you're wasting water;

Izzy calling Julisa one Saturday afternoon despite not having contacted her in way too long and despite Rudy's silence since the park blowout, Julisa initially refusing to pick up, but he calls a second time, then a third. She thinks his sudden persistence could be a sign that he really is The One—why would the universe bring him back to her this way if not?—so she finally gives in on his third attempt and answers. When he asks if he can see her, that he's struggling, that he needs her help tracking down people like she did with Odlanier, she says: No, Izzy, as much as I want that, you need to get your karma right. Fix that shit and see what comes back to you. We both need a sign;

Izzy, thinking hard about his karma and signs after hanging up, getting the idea to return that night to Olivia C——'s house under the cover of darkness and kidnap her dog, to undo *her* original kidnapping of *it*. Or him, as that dog was definitely a him. The universe sent Izzy that dog as a test. He wants to right a wrong, and if he can do that, Julisa will see him again, Rudy will show him some respect, the people he needs to talk to will call him back, his migraines will stop, et cetera, et cetera, it is all perfectly clear to him now. The dog was the beginning of the end. He just needs to get his hands on it/him and reunite it/him with its/his real family. And for that mission, he knows who he needs to convince to help him, and because it involves an animal—an animal needing rescuing; that's going to be his pitch—it might not even be hard to get the help he's hoping for.

He sends the text BRO U AROUND? U FREE TONITE? to the number he's saved in his phone as Gator Whisperer, a.k.a. Danny.

GIVE ME EVERYTHING (TONIGHT)

THE RESCUE

Danny stresses it multiple times during the brief call: don't be late and come dressed nice. I need you looking sharp, he says, And if you're late by even a minute, I won't be there.

Danny doesn't want any details over the phone even as Izzy keeps forcing them out. He doesn't appreciate how Danny's been testing him like this, giving orders and watching to see if he follows them. Tony Montana put it succinctly and poetically: *The only thing in this world that gives orders is balls.* He wants Danny to know that this time, Izzy's balls are going to be the ones in charge.

—This crazy bitch, Izzy says. She has this dog held captive. It's fucking sick. I thought the idea of rescuing the dog might appeal to you.

When Danny says nothing in response, Izzy looks at his phone and realizes the call's been over—since when, he can't tell.

Danny has given Izzy just under three hours to change into better clothes and get to the address he'd recited over the phone, refusing to text it. And so Izzy is again wearing his black graduation suit pants and a slick belt that matches his black shoes and a white dress shirt he found hanging in his closet, still in the plastic from the dry cleaners. The shirt's tucked in, the shoes almost shine, and he has his suit jacket in the car just in case Danny meant even fancier. He looks good and he smells good, like a fancy restaurant's waiter or someone going to the funeral of a teacher they really admired.

It's a funeral Izzy's afraid he's heading to: when he puts the address Danny gave him into his phone, the directions it spits back take him to Broward County, to Fort Lauderdale, to a building along the Intracoastal. A hotel, or more accurately, something next to or behind a hotel. A place near a drawbridge.

He drives north along I-95—an expressway he rarely takes past the Aventura exits, having always thought of Aventura as *the last stop* before Florida got weird to him—and eventually pulls into the parking garage of some megachain hotel named after a rich white guy, one fancy enough that he's never stepped inside any of their lobbies but not fancy enough in elegance or prestige to have hosted his high school's annual prom, prom being the only thing Hialeah Lakes did that involved elegance or prestige. Finding an open spot in the garage is a mission and he's surprised by this because he incorrectly thinks of Broward County as empty compared to Miami. He finally finds a spot with enough time that he doesn't have to run to the water's edge and risk sweating up his clothes. Danny said sharp, not soaked.

Danny greets him with a tremendous and sincere hug, and from it, Izzy's convinced he'll be able to get Danny on board with this kidnapping rescue. Look at him, his hair parted down the middle and just long enough to tuck behind his ears, full-on Jesus beard in the works, his slim but sturdy build sporting a trim Hawaiian shirt over white tuxedo pants, a too-big blue blazer hanging over the whole ensemble. Is he actually wearing white sneakers? Yes, he is—a pair of rare Jordans that cost several hundred dollars, so clean they look fresh out of the box. The laces are as loose as his blazer, as the hair floating around his face at the sudden relief of the Intracoastal's breeze tousling it. He lifts Izzy in the circle of his arms off the ground, puts him down, lifts him up again with a growl. He's just so fucking sweet, this guy, weird animal stuff and gun collection aside. Of course, Izzy doesn't plan on mentioning his true reasons behind the rescue—his own karma or Julisa—and like all the other people who have called on Danny for dubious and/or expensive favors, Izzy thinks he can bank on Danny's supposed goodness and silliness and sense of loyalty and adventure, along with his borderline psychotic appreciation for non-human beings.

—You're right on time, Danny says. How fucking beautiful is this?

He raises his arms to indicate the boat behind him, a three-level party yacht, disco ball visible through the large windows encasing its main deck. On the uncovered upper deck, a crowd is milling around, people leaning over the railing, taking pictures of themselves. The air is filled with the din of voices and laughter layered over music being played on a piano.

—Is this . . . yours?

—Fuck no, Danny says. Are you serious?

And then he laughs for a solid minute, doubling over and then coughing and then the laugh coming back after the cough, the whole outburst ending when he puts his hands on his waist and says, Bro, I'm telling you, you crack me up. He sniffs and rubs his nose and says, This thing is basically a floating banquet hall. There's about to be a wedding on it.

—Oh, nice, okay.

Izzy hasn't been on a boat since arriving in Miami as a child. He realizes this instantly, wondering if it's something he was subconsciously avoiding. In middle school, after his eighth grade graduation dance, a group of his friends accompanied by their still-young parents all kept the celebration going by driving to Bayside and boarding an all-ages party boat—in that case, a floating dance floor where your ticket got you two hours on board with a lazy DJ and some swirling lights—but he hadn't gone, and now he can't remember what had been his excuse. Maybe his Tía Tere's reluctance at being the oldest parent there? But she would've danced harder and longer than anyone; they would've had to drag her off that boat, he knew that. And then there was the girlfriend who'd had the migraines, how she'd once gone with some girlfriends and their boyfriends on a celebrity homes cruise around Star Island and Fisher Island, claiming it was ironic but then being genuinely impressed by Gloria Estefan's compound and the mansion owned by the guy who invented Viagra, and Izzy can't remember why he didn't go with her—he didn't think they were an official couple yet and it felt like too much pressure? Was that it? He knows for sure he has never been to a wedding on a boat before and is about to say so when Danny says, Let's go before they push off.

—Go where?

—On board. Surprise, you're my plus one.

—You're invited to this shit?

—Yeah. This is my second one today.

—Your second wedding? Where was the first one?

—On this same fucking boat, bro. Let's go, they don't play around, they *will* leave our asses behind.

As they cross over a plank from dock to boat, seemingly the last two people to join the voyage—the plank gets pulled up after them and then there's cheering from overhead—Izzy asks, You were invited to *both* weddings on this boat?

—Technically just the second one, but I know the people who own the company. It's a family business. They knew my mom. The food is excellent, though I get why people are skeptical. They make it right on the boat – hey, hello, how are you, bro, yes, good to see you!

Inside they immediately hit a wall of greetings and chatting people, some with drinks already in their hands. Danny hugs and slaps the backs of man after man, the act punctuating what feels like a sales pitch for the boat's all-inclusive wedding vendor services. He introduces Izzy to no one, and no one seems at all curious about his presence. He feels the boat sway under him—can he really feel that on a boat this big?—and wonders for a quick second if he's somehow turned invisible. The ceiling feels lower than it should; he resists the urge to raise his hand and see if he can reach it. The space feels crowded despite the big windows encasing the reception space: a dozen white-clothed tables on the periphery of a smallish dance floor, the tables themselves ringed with gold-painted cane chairs and topped with centerpieces—clots of sunset-hued roses and white hydrangeas. Izzy can barely see it all through the people blocking his view, seemingly all of them waiting to give Danny a kiss on the cheek in greeting. He's got his suit jacket draped across his arm and wishes he could use it to blot the sweat he feels sprouting from his forehead. On his date that was not a date weeks ago with Julisa, he'd had the same wish but no jacket, so he'd walked way ahead of her, rushing to the A/C of the gas station in the hopes he'd cool off before she'd notice. Danny's back is moving through the crowd and away from him now, toward a tunnel of a staircase located near the middle of the room. Izzy pushes after him: he wants to propose the dog rescue to him before the ceremony, before there's a chance for any more distractions. He thinks of the dog's legs and dick dangling and looking for a place to land, how they paddled the air but would've made the same motion in water. He has no idea what he's doing on this fucking boat.

On his way up the narrow stairs to the upper deck, he yells to Danny's back, Who's getting married?

—I don't know.

He can't have heard him right. He says, Why were you even invited then?

Danny turns around with a finger over his lips and says, Shhhh.

The sun is about to set but they can't see it for all the buildings around. The boat is moving now, Izzy knows for sure, he can see the buildings glide past, can hear the engine better from up there. No one else seems to be swaying, but he has to stay close to the metal walls surrounding the staircase to keep from feeling like he's about to fall over. At the center of the upper deck's stern side is a flower-laden arch and a couple rows of white chairs. There is also a lady dressed in all black sitting behind a harp.

—There's not enough seats for everyone, Izzy says.

—Most of us stand. The seats are for the viejos and stuff. This part's usually over pretty quick anyway. The standard package is three hours unless you pay for more.

—Is this a standard package?

—Don't tell me you're getting seasick. I can find you something to help with that.

Izzy worries he might throw up. He can't believe he'll be on this boat for three hours, maybe longer. He needs to spit out the plan about the dog before he starts feeling any worse. It's not like with the migraines, not exactly, but the urgency feels similar, more like panic. He leans his back fully against the wall and says, Actually, bro, I got something else I need help with. I was trying to tell you over the phone.

—Relax, bro, we got time. We got so much time. Let's get a drink. Ginger ale will settle your stomach.

He lets Danny slap him on the back and then put an arm around him, lead him away from the wall's protective stability. It's not his stomach he feels roiling. It's somewhere higher up, in his chest. Is he having a heart attack? He laughs at himself. He is twenty years old. He can't have a heart attack. Maybe he had too much café and not enough food, though it's been hours since his last cafecito. Maybe he's nervous. Nervous about asking Danny—who from his mass appeal at this wedding so far is obviously a more influential dude than Izzy had initially suspected—for what could be seen as a favor. He'd practiced what to say on the drive over, talking to himself from his balls, but he'd visualized the exchange happening on dry land. How to get back to that head-and-ballspace. This boat is barely a boat. What had Danny called it? A floating banquet hall. The capacity to hold over four hundred guests. Some kind of industrial carpet smelling faintly of mold and Lysol under his feet. There's a fucking baby grand piano somewhere beneath him. There's that lady getting ready to play the harp, and behind her, buildings crawling by as if he were just jogging alongside them, the Intracoastal narrow enough here that it could feel like nothing more than a rich person's canal. No waves. No bumps. Just the barest humming of an engine. He couldn't be on a boat. He was not on a real boat.

At the bar, Danny skips the line and slides his body behind it, a gray-haired bartender greeting him in Spanish while pouring yet another rum and coke for someone into a full glass of ice. Danny slaps the man on the back and grabs a can of ginger ale, then crams a bill of a denomination large enough that Izzy doesn't recognize it into the man's tip jar.

—Eugenio is my favorite bartender here, Danny says. If you need anything, he'll take care of you.

Danny shoves the soda into Izzy's hand. The can hisses as he opens it. He takes a couple sips.

—You seem to know where everything is without him, Izzy says. Did you used to work here?

Danny sucks his teeth and shakes his head, dismissing Izzy's question.

He says, You're feeling better. And Izzy says, Yeah yeah, thanks.

—Not a question though, was it? Danny says.

He slaps Izzy's back again—harder this time, the soda swishing heavy inside the can as Izzy's forced to take a balance-keeping step forward. Izzy hears a sudden cascade of ethereal notes, and he jerks his head up to the sky, mistaking the sound for something celestial: entrance music for an angel about to land.

Danny laughs at this jolt and says, Ceremony's starting. Let's go find a place to stand. Near the railing, so I can keep an eye on you.

EVENT SPACE

As the ceremony begins, Izzy finds himself wishing it were happening on the beach, with the ocean in the background rather than directly beneath him. It just seems like overkill: isn't it enough to get married *in front* of the ocean? Is it really necessary to be all the way *on* it? Is it worth the inevitability of leaving some guests behind on shore if they don't make it on time because of trouble finding parking? Is it worth having to hand out Dramamine as a wedding favor? These worries reveal that Izzy doesn't fully appreciate the blessing of water, of how marrying on the sea invites generations of ancestors to witness your union: that's what the wedding planner that comes with the yacht says to potential clients when they tour the yacht and raise the same concerns. With so much access to water and coastline, there's a lot of competition in South Florida for wedding business. Even the Miami Seaquarium gets a piece of this action: Lolita's been within listening range of her fair share of weddings thanks to the Seaquarium's Sunset Cove, an event space inside the park that, just like with these floating banquet halls, comes with its own wedding planner.

What would that wedding planner list as essential to the typical Miami Cuban wedding—what would this person insist your event needs to feel *authentic*?

You must have a real-live cigar roller in a yellowing guayabera, preferably the same one who rolled the cigars at your great-grandmother's one-hundredth birthday party, but this time your family pays to upgrade to the personalized cigar labels because hello, you only get married once, twice if you're lucky.

The cigar roller should spend half the reception trapped behind the little wooden table he uses for all these gigs, its surface piled high with tobacco leaves that stink of feet.

The steel drum band that plays as your wedding party saunters down the aisle must continue playing through your cocktail hour and should help instigate and maintain the conga line that parades most of your guests straight into the reception space.

No fewer than seven bridesmaids or the ceremony is not legit. At least half of them must be the daughters of your mother's cousins whose lives you know nothing about. Groomsmen should all be either cousins or guys you know from CrossFit or both.

What else?

There must be some exquisite family drama all set to play out before or even during the ceremony. Possible options include: your hoochiest cousin texts last minute that she is bringing a date she met on the dance floor at a club the night before the wedding, mentioning also that he drives a Lamborghini; the bride's aunt kicked her husband out of their house two weeks prior, but as the biologically related relative, he insists he'll still be there, mistress in tow; the DJ is no longer on speaking terms with the cousin who hooked you up with his services and he's now threatening to not show up; your cousin with the four-year-old daughter is boycotting the ceremony because you asked your cousin with the six-year-old daughter if her kid would be the flower girl, and why couldn't you just have two fucking flower girls; an estranged uncle who everyone was very careful not to invite or even let on that there was a wedding at all has RSVPed yes and written *plus four* on the reply card that no one has any idea how he got ahold of, and people are taking bets on whether or not he'll show up; at the last minute, the mother of the groom invited an ex-girlfriend of his who she wishes he were marrying instead, insisting she is still a close family friend and insisting she sit at their family table; no one has any idea what the mother of the groom has decided to wear and calling her fashion tastes questionable is a tremendous generosity.

The wedding planner reminds you often that you can plan all you want, but you can't control other people, especially when they have plans of their own.

What else?

Jordan almonds wrapped in tulle at every seat or else everyone will complain.

At least one of the food options you select must be recognizable as a version of arroz con pollo or else none of the viejos at the reception afterward will eat anything.

Before the food is even served, the women at the various tables must argue over who will take home the centerpieces. You should ask your DJ to make an announcement to please not move them until the photographer can get a picture of every table. That photographer should be the same one who took the pictures at your quinces and thus be the same person who photographed your parents' wedding. That was the case for Olivia C——'s wedding, and you've already seen how great those pictures came out. All those parrots! At the Seaquarium, if you get married at Sunset Cove, the built-in wedding planner can book you a photo session with a couple of dolphins and a trainer to direct them, but it's up to your photographer to time the pictures with the dolphins' jumps.

At this wedding, the photographer knows to keep Danny and his guest out of the photos. Told so by Danny himself: Consider us part of the staff as usual, he'd said. The photographer knows well not to ask any questions about such a request, that there's always a good reason behind it—one it's best they not know. That's partly why they've been in business for so long, why the same families keep using this photographer year after year, event after event. In this city, that's how you build a legacy.

THE DECK

The ceremony is as brief as Danny claimed it would be, the whole thing rushed just enough that the photos coincide with the edge of sunset, apparently part of this particular package's guarantee. The captain officiates and Izzy wants to ask who, then, is steering the boat, but the sting of Danny's hand from the slap earlier still lingers on his back, and he's confused about what that slap meant. He wants to ask again who invited Danny if he really doesn't know this couple getting married. The groom is clearly stoned out of his mind, barely containing his laughs, eyes so red and glassy Izzy notices them from his spot way across the deck. He hopes for the bride's sake that the photographer can fix that later when they touch up the photos. Her face— the bride's—he can't see except in the moments she turns to give her maid of honor her flowers, when the ring exchange happens, and then again when she takes the bouquet back. She looks pissed, like getting stoned was something she'd explicitly asked him not to do on this of all days and he'd promised he wouldn't, and then he'd forgotten all about that promise when a groomsman sparked a joint and passed it around as they waited for the boat to launch. The groom sways back and forth on the balls of his feet, his hands clasped together in a fist over his crotch. Izzy focuses on the gigantic harp behind the swaying groom so as to stave off a dizziness he's refusing to feel. He had no idea harps were so big. He had no idea they were so gold.

When it's over, the harpist floats her hands across the strings and Izzy changes his mind: it no longer sounds like the sky to him, but like water, like theme music for a mermaid, like an anthem for a whale's arched breach.

Danny takes him by the elbow, keeps him there by the railing.

—Let's let everyone head down to the reception first, he says. Give me and you a chance to talk.

*   *   *

But Danny is a one-man receiving line. Izzy counts only a handful of people—the bride and groom and wedding party among them—who don't give him a quick hug or a handshake or a perfunctory kiss on the cheek. Old women grab his hand as they walk past him, squeeze it in both of theirs, tug it along with them as they shuffle past Danny's spot along the railing, dropping it only after giving Danny a demure smile and getting a head bow back from him. Danny seems to be expecting the attention in that he's not at all surprised by it, but it's enough that Izzy wants very badly to ask what the fuck is going on—the one question he has the sense not to ask. If Izzy hadn't been the one to reach out to Danny that afternoon to talk, he would've suspected the whole evening so far was some extremely elaborate setup, some prank of Danny's or one of Danny's mysterious acquaintances meant to impress and intimidate but also entertain Izzy. But there's no way Danny orchestrated all this is in less than three hours. Gators in an Escalade is one thing, but this has way too many people involved to be a trap. And there's no way Izzy can imagine being worth all that effort.

Finally the flow of greetings slows, and then stops. And then it is just Danny and Izzy and Eugenio the bartender and the harpist and a crew of people breaking down the chairs and the flower arch, all the men doing that work dressed exactly and unfortunately like Izzy.

He hears a crowd's roar from the deck beneath them—the bride and groom appearing again to their guests, this time as husband and wife.

—So if you don't know the people getting married, how do you know basically every fucking person here?

—Why you asking questions, Danny says. Them knowing me is not the same as me knowing them.

He opens and then sips from a can of sparkling lemonade and Izzy has no idea where it came from. Did he have it tucked inside a pocket of his giant blazer this whole time?

—I'm glad you texted me actually. I've been wanting to talk to you. Without Rudy around. Been waiting for you to reach out first though. For reasons.

This is what Izzy's been waiting for. His chance to level up. So what if he's lost his way, if he has no idea who Danny's *Scarface* equivalent is. So what if Danny is grooming him to be Manolo—couldn't one argue that's what that Bolivian drug lord Sosa does with Tony Montana? Granted, Tony's days as an assassin come back to haunt him when Sosa asks him to help kill an ambassador who Sosa and his associates want to keep from giving a speech at the United Nations. Of course, that far into the movie, Tony's reached a level where he doesn't have to do that dirty work himself, like he did at the film's beginning—this time, he just has to work as a translator for the guy planting and detonating the car bomb. It's the only time in the movie where Al Pacino has to speak Spanish, and man is it hilarious. But in exchange for his assassin-sitting, Sosa promises to make Tony's tax woes disappear, keeping him from the jail time Tony's lawyer is certain he'll have to do. Sosa gives Tony a path forward. Sosa is Tony's potential savior. Maybe Izzy hasn't lost his way at all. Maybe Danny is Izzy's Sosa. Except it's Sosa and his extremely international team of extremely dangerous and extremely well-connected people—crooked ambassadors, corrupt generals, a veritable Who's Who of Bad Guys Secretly Running the Whole World, each getting a few seconds of screen time—who all work together to later send several hundred assassins to Tony's mansion to eliminate him from this planet in a torrent of bullets. Danny stands on his toes—he's a solid three inches shorter than his plus one—and puts his arm around Izzy's shoulders, almost wrapping Izzy in that way-too-big blazer. Izzy catches a whiff of weed, or maybe it's a lack of deodorant. Danny slips a foot out of his sneaker, scratches the arch of the foot with his middle finger, then returns the foot to the shoe, all while still holding tight to Izzy. No, Izzy thinks as Danny wiggles his foot back into hiding. Danny couldn't possibly be his Sosa.

—I'm glad too, Izzy says. I appreciate you – inviting? – me to all this, but like okay, all these people know you, but why though? Are you fucking royalty or something?

—There you go with the questions, he laughs. Bro, you really do have a big mouth.

Izzy laughs back a *fuck you*, and from across the deck, Eugenio the bartender yells, Daniel! and thankfully Danny nods and holds up a finger to him, asking for a minute. But Eugenio either doesn't get the message or doesn't care; he comes over with a tray on his hand, a single drink on it. A scotch, no ice or water in it.

—Got your Johnnie Walker Black for you, sir. Just how you like it.

Danny takes the drink and says, You know better than that *sir* shit. Thank you, thank you.

Now is when he'll introduce Izzy; it would be awkward *not* to, for Eugenio not to ask *And what can I get you?* and then hustle back to the bar to fetch it. In fact, it's almost weird that he didn't yell out asking for Izzy's drink request, to save himself the trip. But no, Eugenio takes the tray, smacks Danny on the thigh with it, then tucks it under his arm and jogs back to his bar.

Danny turns away from Eugenio, has Izzy do the same before handing him the drink, not bothering to take a sip of his own first.

—Here, for you, Danny says. I don't actually drink this shit but no matter how many times it happens, I can't bear to tell him that. He's such a fucking sweetheart.

—Cheers, bro. Izzy takes a sip and says, How do you know even the *bartenders?*

—Still with the questions, Izzy. You're not doing yourself any favors, lemme tell you. He looks out at the city crawling by and says, That guy used to work for my mom. Before she died.

Izzy sips and swallows more scotch. I'm sorry. How'd she die?

—I don't know. I don't remember, Danny says.

He flicks a finger against the glass in Izzy's fist and says, See? It's easy to say, even when it's not true. A lot easier to say than all the shit you keep talking to people in those messages you left.

—What? How do you know about that?

—I get it now why people are worrying, Danny says. About you, asking too many questions. The problems that could cause for the folks who run the little operations that helped you get here.

Izzy swallows to push down the sudden burn in his chest. The lights in and outside the buildings along the Intracoastal start to flip on, now that the sun is really gone.

—People like Olivia and the C—— family for one. But not just them, Danny says over the railing. There's lots of concerned people saying you're trying to bring up stuff no one's interested in remembering. I was under the impression Olivia advised you to stop but you kept at it. She tried to do you a favor by telling you to shut the fuck up. I kept hoping you'd listen. I was even rooting for you for a while. Know that.

Does Izzy feel scared? Maybe he should, except there is nothing at all menacing in Danny's tone, nothing of the kind of aggression he sees and himself exhibits on any given day as a man living in Miami. Danny even seems kinder, softer around the edges than just moments before, like he's trying to keep Izzy from embarrassing himself. Izzy takes another slug of scotch to keep from having to say anything. More searing as he swallows it, so he chases the searing with a second smaller sip. His legs feeling weak underneath him suddenly, he wants to ask if they can sit down somewhere but is now hyperconscious of how many questions he's asked and how many more are jumping to the front of his mind. If only he could send them to Danny telepathically, forehead to forehead or like some kind of sonar. He tries to concentrate to see if he can make the impossible happen.

—You know, I was at Olivia's C——'s wedding too. Of course I was, Danny laughs. Our families are friends from way way back. Not super close though. More like business associates. Really I only went because she had it on Jungle Island. I fucking love that place. I left after the birds, the cocktail hour thing. Paid my respects, fell in love with some parrots, then bounced. You didn't notice me in the pictures when you were over there?

The only word Izzy manages is: No.

But had Danny been in the pictures though? Izzy hadn't registered anyone in them but the newlyweds and the birds, all the other faces a generic, smiling blur—he remembers thinking that was on purpose, like no one else but the happy couple mattered that day. He feels a relaxed kind of sleepy, remembering that day, how her house would soon be underwater. He adds: I wasn't paying too good attention though. I was distracted by her dog's gigantic dick.

Danny laughs and says, Do you know the story of how she rescued him? She fished that poor thing out from a canal. He was fighting an iguana and got dragged in.

—Brave little guy, Izzy says. He laughs into his glass; he's sniffing the scotch, nose almost touching the little left in there, wondering if he's ever really like, *smelled* scotch before. This one smells to him like smoke and dirty ocean water, and then he remembers the king tide flooding on Olivia's block, the story she told him about finding the dog eating garbage, and says, That's not the version I got though, about how she supposably rescued that dog I mean.

—I bet it's not. The point is, the universe sent her that dog to give her something to distract her. The universe wanted her to have him. Does it really matter how it happened if the end is the same?

Danny is looking right at him again. He thinks the answer is yes, it matters. It matters how what we might love is lost or found. How could it not matter? It's the difference between a blessing and a curse. If it didn't matter what happened, if it didn't matter which version of events was true, then what is Izzy even doing there? Not just on this boat, but here in this city, in this country instead of the one where he was born? His tongue feels thick in his mouth in an extremely pleasant way that he doesn't want to interrupt with talking. Music vibrates the deck—he feels the bass pulsing up through his shoes, permeating his toe bones and ankles—and he is surprised to find that he really wants to get down there and join the party, see what's going on. He feels heavy and he wants to move.

—How's that drink tasting? Danny says.

Izzy holds it up to Danny's chest in a faux toast and says, Good, *thank* you, but yeah, where's yours?

Danny gives a quick shake of the head no, says, That's not for me. Not much of a spirits guy, to be honest. Don't get high on your own supply, right?

He slugs Danny in the shoulder and says, Fuck you, bro, did Rudy tell you about my shit?

—What shit?

—Why would you say that if he didn't tell you?

—Say what? Tell me what?

—That's lesson number two from the movie, bro! My *Scarface* shit, my stupid plan.

—I don't talk to Rudy, not like that. We're close but we're not *close*.

Danny sniffs hard and says out to the water, We could've been brothers though.

How could Izzy not see it before? He and Danny are two men hurt by the same woman, aren't they? *They* could be brothers. The wedding of Julisa's dreams—one version of it, anyway—churning right below them, Izzy confesses: Julisa's part of my plan too, I think. It's weird.

He leans forward to squeeze Danny's shoulder but Danny deflects it, grabbing Izzy by the collar of his shirt and propping him up against the railing.

—Let's keep her name out of your mouth, shall we?

Eugenio yells, ¿Todo bien, Daniel?

Danny lifts the same finger as before, and Eugenio glides over wordlessly with an unopened bottle of water. Some kind of code between these two, okay. Izzy is proud he's figured that out, thinks it means he's smarter than he really is. He leans fully against the railing, letting it hold all his weight. So what if he falls overboard? The Intracoastal is narrow enough he could easily swim across it, and he wouldn't even have to do that, because the boat is splitting the waterway in half. In fact the idea of swimming suddenly feels like a very, very good one. He's not scared of the idea at all, even though it's getting dark. He kind of wants to take off his pants? He's being a little ridiculous, isn't he. The cold bottle of water thrills his hand. Is it a sign to get wet? Is that what Julisa would think? Is she thinking of him right that second and he's heard it, intercepting the thought somehow?

—Drink some water, Danny says. We'll go downstairs in a second. I just wanna make sure you and I have an understanding about this whole situation.

He stands squarely before Izzy, close enough that their toes almost touch.

Danny says in a whisper, At the end of the day, the C—— family is good people, done a lotta good for the community – you included, when they really didn't have to. Now you show up like a ghost, got them worrying about their reputation, trying to blow up their shit all these years later? Me personally, I don't believe you meant the harm they think you meant, but that's not my call to make. Point is, you got mixed up, made a lotta noise. You offended the wrong people. It happens. It's a real shame. You should've listened to Olivia's good advice. Your tía's good advice, if anything. You know a lotta men's suffering would be avoided if they just listened to the women around them. And this part *is* personal, but you *really* should've never even looked twice at Julisa.

—Julisa though, Izzy says. She gave me the old dude's address.

—You think I don't know what Julisa gets up to? You think I don't look out for her? That if I asked her she wouldn't talk to me about the scheme you put her on to, having her track people down? *That* shit sealed your fate.

—I didn't ask anything. He swallows, says, Didn't ask her to do anything. She just did it.

—Got people asking me how I know you and why, telling me you've got people upset, worrying about why you asking all these questions.

—One guy's address, like weeks ago.

—Asking about your mother all of a sudden too, like you want *that* association haunting you *at all*. As if knowing how she died would do you any good.

—She drowned. Everybody says she drowned. I just wanna know how – like did she really *jump*? Someone throw her off or what?

Danny shakes his head slowly at Izzy having failed some test. He says, Trust me, you'd rather *not* know. You really shouldn't have asked so many questions, Izzy. I'm sorry you didn't figure that out sooner.

Danny squeezes Izzy's bicep and the sensation jolts him upright, buzzing through him like he suddenly needs to take a piss. He drops the bottle of water and smacks Danny's hand off of him. Danny takes a step in and drops his voice, saying, Yo, *relax*.

—All I was asking was the people who knew because I had this idea, me thinking that coming on a balsa meant I knew some shit but really, I don't.

Danny nods at all this and picks up the water bottle, unscrews its cap, takes a sip from it, then hands it to Izzy to drink. He reaches out and takes the scotch from Izzy's other hand, then throws the drink, glass and all, overboard.

—I'm not trying to fuck with nobody, I swear, Izzy says. It's all gone to shit now anyway.

—You can let all that go, bro. Just release that plan into the universe and see what comes back to you.

Julisa's words about his karma—that's what comes back. Izzy leans forward, too close to Danny's face, and says, Exactly. I was gonna ask if you'd help me kidnap that bitch's dog. I need to fix my karma.

—I can see that. Not sure how kidnapping someone's dog is gonna help. Or that referring to someone who tried to keep you out of trouble as a bitch is gonna help either. Keep digging that grave for yourself.

—First you get the money, then you get the power. Never underestimate the other guy's greed, lesson number one. That's from *Scarface*. No one remembers lesson number one because lesson number two is catchier.

—Lesson number two.

—You said it before. Don't get high on your own supply.

—That's from *Scarface*? Danny says.

—You know it's from fucking *Scarface*, bro.

—I've actually never seen that movie. Not all the way through.

—You're lying.

—Why would I lie about that?

—Do you know how it ends?

—Not really. *The world is yours* or something?

—Nah, bro, not at all.

—It's gotta have a happy ending though, right? If you picked him as a role model.

—Actually I started out as Pitbull but ran into some legal troubles.

—Wipe your face, bro, this ain't a funeral.

Danny holds out a paper napkin. Other people are drifting up the staircase now, looking for a shorter bar line and some fresh air. Mostly the air smells like low tide, the salt in the breeze doing almost enough to mask the smell of wet trash. But it's better than downstairs, where the cold mildew tinge to the air subconsciously reminds almost every guest of the tío's house they least enjoy visiting. The napkin feels extra rough on Izzy's cheeks—it's Danny, wiping at the tears on Izzy's face.

—Look, bro, Danny says. It sounds like your problem was that you kept looking at other people instead of looking at yourself. Let me take it from here.

Danny is so wise and his blazer looks so warm inside and Izzy sees how he and Julisa probably made a beautiful couple, two people following their hearts and listening to the universe and fixing their karma left and right all day long. Fuck, bro, he wanted something that perfect for himself just once. Danny had lost his mother too, and look how great he's doing. Everyone at this wedding is his best friend! But Izzy—even his own Manolo was ignoring his texts. The whole fucking city of Miami was ignoring him.

—I'm in a bad place, he tells Danny.

—Oh I know, bro.

—You're fucking lying, Izzy says. About never seeing *Scarface*.

—Okay yeah, Danny says. Yeah, I am.

The music from beneath makes Izzy's knees tingle—he feels it like white light spilling through each joint. He feels the same light prickling just above his right temple and raises his hand to the spot, rubbing it away to keep it from congealing into pain. Danny pulls him off the railing, shakes him a little, walks with him toward the stairwell.

—Let me make a couple phone calls. Figure out what's next for you. By the time this wedding docks, I'll have something amazing set up.

—You serious?

—Yeah, bro. You know I make moves. We'll take my car – don't worry about driving. You head down, have a few drinks, enjoy yourself. Make sure you eat something. Seriously, the food is amazing.

—I believe you, he says.

Danny is right: Izzy won't be driving, not for a while. Is he thinking about how much parking is going to cost him in that garage? Nope. He barely remembers his car exists. And even though he's already in a state he vaguely recognizes as drunk—he's never done any drug more substantial than weed, and so he's mistaken his sedation for intoxication—when he sits at a random table—the centerpiece already pulled off-center, claimed by some tía or prima as hers—with his plate piled high with buffet-line prime rib and salmon and chicken cordon blue that's really just a glorified arroz con pollo, he tells himself he needs the food to stave off the migraine whose aura is bathing his right eye's vision in a kind of static. He flags down the server gripping a napkin-swathed bottle of wine.

The server's outfit matches his own perfectly, and he takes that as a sign he's finally in the right place. The wine poured into his glass is red, and he takes *that* as a sign about Julisa—no idea what it means, just that it's about her. The wine doesn't immediately hurt his head, that's good, and it isn't at all sweet like the one they drank together at that tapas place—this one makes his mouth dry, the sides of his tongue hurt; it tastes metallic like blood, or like he's sucking on a rock from the ocean—and he takes that as a sign too.

STEREOTYPIES

What else.

What else?

Yes, what else.

Well, during the reception, the wedding boat's DJ knows from experience to play the song Suavemente by Elvis Crespo because if not, the event will be deemed a complete failure of a celebration.

The DJ also knows to play the song La Negra Tiene Tumbao by Celia Cruz because if not, see above.

Yes, good, but what else.

What else? Okay, once the cake's been cut, no woman on the dance floor should be wearing shoes. Ultimately the reception should feel more like a club than a wedding. Strobe lights, lasers, fog machines if possible, et cetera.

But what about maybe including an actual club, like on South Beach, the Miami people already know. More mentions of palm trees and neon lights. Some Art Deco stuff. Oh, dominoes! Those old Cuban guys at that park playing them! Have them smoking cigars. Bring the cigars back that way.

Dominoes? Art Deco stuff? Is this still just about weddings?

What about more direct nostalgia-laced talk of Cuba. Maybe a nod to the Buena Vista Social Club, since people like seeing things they recognize.

What about a splash or two more of Santeria. People have come to expect that.

Seriously: Cigars! Maybe make it so a cigar lector is telling the whole thing to a bunch of poor cigar rollers in a really hot factory a long time ago in Cuba. Make the telling work like smoke.

But it's Miami. The telling works like water.

Yes! About that: what about Lolita, where did she go.

She never left. She's trapped in this city. She's everywhere and nowhere, like a wave crashing.

A scene at the beach! Thongs! More thongs and more butts, excessive and superfluous descriptions of tanned butt-cheeks for sure. Make it sexy!

Speaking of skin: descriptions of a grandmother's hands and what they smell like (cigar smoke, the sea, etc.). Include some letters from her, have her call everyone m'ijo. *Kill her off but have her come back as a ghost and add a whole thread of that ancestor stuff. Set that stuff in Cuba. Sorry, Coo-ba. Make it come down from the mountains (in the form of cigar smoke!). Make it spooky but keep it approachable. Again, think smoke. Lean into the magical realism. Again, ancestor stuff.*

Ancestors are not magical realism.

Think too about making it quirkier. Maybe some mermaids. Swamp stuff, you know. This is Florida, after all.

Miami is not Florida.

And actually, what happened to that early promise of baseball players. Actually, Fidel Castro was a pitcher; it's a pretty well-known fact, actually. Consider actually having a struggling baseball player named Fidel sacrifice a goat or a chicken during some Santeria ritual in the first thirty pages, if possible. Also and actually, consider providing the cultural and historical significance of baseball to all Cubans, just so that's clear to everyone.

Who counts as *everyone?*

Just regular old everyone, ha ha! Make it LOUDER. More music, more food smells. More colors—Miami is colorful, describe the colors more. The flooding stuff is depressing. Also, Wynwood! That place is all over everyone's Miami vacations on social media. Get the Wynwood Walls in here.

Hardly any of those murals are by Miami artists anymore.

Have you read Joan Didion's book about Miami. She spent several months or weeks down there at some point. Evoke more of Didion's seedy Miami underbelly.

The preference here has been for Lolita's underbelly.

People want to see real, devastating pain and experience empathy but while also smelling the ocean, feeling its breeze, hearing its waves crash, etc. They want to escape, but also to really feel like they know the people and the place by the time they finish.

But how can anyone claim to know a place or a community from a single work of art? And when you say *people*, who exactly do you mean?

That's a hard question to answer!

Is it? Doesn't seem hard to answer from here.

One possible solution is to add more flavor! Really spice it up!

Think: fiery! Think: Pitbull's Miami, or maybe the Miami from Miami Vice*!*

Think: Lolita's performance, the familiarity of it, how well it works. Think about making a splash by doing the same thing you've seen done already, over and over again.

But it's boring and it's killing her.

So what if she's obsessively peeling the paint off the walls between shows. So what if her literal brain is being rewired to have less agency and imagination with every repetitive turn in her tank. Stereotypes exist for a reason!

It's stereotypies. That's what those behaviors are called. The word is *stereotypy.*

Yes! The Spanish so far is great, really lends an authentic taste. Definitely add even more Spanish, but maybe consider italicizing it, for clarity.

Clarity for who? What if it's already perfectly clear?

It's whom. *And one last note: give people even more. More terror, more violence, more trauma. Open those veins!*

What the actual fuck.

Yes! Give even more fucks!

Shut the fuck up because that's literally impossible right now.

Well then just more fucks in general. More fucks, more palm trees, more Pitbull, more Scarface. *Much, much more* Scarface.

MIAMI VICES

Okay fine, but only because at this point it's inevitable: the mansion is in Miami Beach; the mansion is in Coral Gables; the mansion is in Pinecrest; the mansion is in Coconut Grove; the mansion is in Bal Harbour; the mansion is in Key Biscayne; the mansion is possibly in any of these neighborhoods because one thing they have in common—aside from being neighborhoods that have an abundance of genuine, authentic mansions in them—is that Izzy has never had any reason whatsoever to venture into them, and so he has no idea where he is; he slept through most of the car ride there and thus he has no way of identifying where in the county this mansion is located. The fact that he senses he's near the water doesn't help; so much of the city is near water of some sort; all of it is basically on top of water. Izzy knows areas with houses this massive exist, has seen comparable imitations of them behind overblown gates in Miami Lakes. These areas are all an easy enough drive from his Tía Tere's townhouse, but ask yourself this: what aspect of Izzy's life up to now would ever bring him to these zip codes as anything other than someone here to work for someone else or as a kind of tourist? How could he be here as anything other than Danny's oblivious charge?

Beginning again, *for clarity*: The fucking mansion is in fucking Key Biscayne. Izzy slept through the fucking toll you pay to get on (but not off) the fucking island; through the stunning fucking view of the technicolored backside of downtown from the Rickenbacker Causeway; through the sky lit so fucking neon by the city's glow; through the glint of the gold half-dome housing the Miami Seaquarium's sea lion show—in fact, through all of Virginia Key, that fucking pit stop of an island, home to the marine theme park some of South Florida's fucking wealthiest residents pass each fucking day on their way to or from home; through Crandon Park, a place his Tía Tere had

253

once taken Izzy as a newly arrived kid for a picnic with some of her friends from her then-job as a receptionist at an accounting firm (in that park's sand, he'd found and played with a fucking used condom, carrying it over to his aunt on the end of a stick); through the palm-flanked-and-lined entrance to the Grand Bay Residences and the Ritz-Fucking-Carlton; through the gauntlet of glitzy condos, Izzy coming to only as Danny turned off the fucking causeway and into what passes for a fucking neighborhood. Fuck.

Izzy didn't mean to fall fully asleep. He'd closed his eyes against the headlights of oncoming cars to stave off the migraine that began blooming while he was swaying alone on the wedding boat's dance floor, during the reggaetón breakdown in the song La Negra Tiene Tumbao. Five songs later and the wedding was docked, and when he told Danny his head didn't feel so good and maybe they should call it a night, Danny handed him a pair of aviator sunglasses and told him, *You got this*, which is what people say when they want you to do something but they think you might get hurt so they want you believing it's your own idea should the worst transpire. The extra darkness from the shades had helped for a time, but only closing his eyes—aided by the tranquilizers still tingling through his bloodstream—took the pain away completely.

As they pull into an exquisitely paved U-shaped driveway, Izzy asks, Where are we, and Danny answers, This is my cousin's house.

Izzy flips the visor down and checks himself for drool in the mirror. In the dim light, he sees his reflection twice, in the mirror and in the sunglasses, and he turns to Danny and says, See, don't I look like him?

—Like who?

—Like fucking Pitbull, bro!

Hands still on the steering wheel, Danny leans back, taking him all in, another pair of aviator sunglasses on his own face—was he wearing them in solidarity?—and yet another pair on his head doing the job of a headband. How many pairs does he own and where is he stashing them all?

—Nah, I don't see it, Danny says. Like not at all.

He turns off the car and slides the single key into his blazer pocket.

Before them looms a massive house, one dropped on this block straight from the version of Miami that Izzy has up to now only seen on TV and in movies, a version that he didn't believe really existed. There is no need to even describe this house: whatever you're imagining is likely correct and enough; but yes, it is bright white and looks like boxes stacked on other boxes, walls made of glass and stuccoed cinderblocks, the kind of house designed to telegraph *Modern* but that now only signals that it was built in the 1980s.

Izzy hates the look of it instantly. He hates that he's so often wrong about this city, that this too is a realistic version of Miami. It's not the real Miami to him, but there it is, real and in Miami nonetheless. He feels very confused and a little irritable. It hits him also that he very much needs to pee.

Down from the car, doors slamming—*bam, bam*—and Izzy finds his legs a little wobbly but they come back to him thanks to the energy in his bladder. He jogs into the landscaping, a huddle of palm trees working as a fence along the property's edge, and has his dick out before he's fully hidden in them. Mid-piss and Danny's next to him, nodding.

—A-plus hydration, he says.

The piss puddles on top of the dirt at the base of a palm, a tail of froth curling into itself, the ground too sodden with water to absorb anything else.

—Thanks, Izzy says. He shakes and zips and turns and starts up toward the house, but Danny stops him.

—We go this way, he says, nodding in the direction of even more palm trees, a long row of them squeezed in alongside the house, growing unchecked and cluttering a service path to the backyard. He bows to Izzy and says, After you.

From what Izzy can see as he pushes palm fronds out of his face, every single light on the first floor of the house is on, glaring in a way that feels interrogative—he's grateful, again, for the sunglasses—but there's no one at all inside. There's also no furniture anywhere, and there's nothing on the walls. Everything is painted white; the floors are some shiny slabs that are also white. It looks like the inside of a freezer. It's as blank as his memory of the drive over.

The second floor and the balcony surrounding it are completely dark. Izzy stops his trek through the dense landscaping and around the boulders of various A/C compressors to look up at it, willing himself to see if it's as barren as the first floor. Danny is suddenly right next to him, his hand pushing on Izzy's back.

—He rents it out a lot, my cousin.

—So more of an investment property? Izzy says.

Danny laughs and says, Our party's out back.

A pool, no water in it, in the process of being retiled or de-tiled. Dusty bags of some powder—concrete or grout—stacked on pallets where lounge chairs should be. Some party this shit is. Did Izzy just say that out loud?

—Yeah, the pool situation is a mess, Danny says. My cousin keeps changing his mind about the tile. You should meet him, he's an interesting character. People say he looks a lot like Enrique Iglesias. You guys could go on tour together.

Izzy nods, knowing on a visceral level that meeting this cousin will never, ever happen. Despite the heat, he shivers like he has to pee again.

Across the dry pool and behind a cluster of tarp-covered lounge furniture is a pool house with its own patio, a barbecue grill and a bar built into its side. Two men sit on stools at this bar, silent as Izzy and Danny pass, seemingly trying to escape detection.

—Other cousins, Danny says with no further explanation.

Danny waves at them far on the other side, their faces masked by the dark, and each man slowly waves back. One says something to the other in a low voice. The bright orange flare of a lit cigar hovers in front of each face as they suck smoke into their mouths. Izzy sniffs the air but gets no whiff of it, the yard is that wide.

They pass the pool and the pool house and the palms lining it all, each frond swaying a warning away from the water. Before them is the expanse of Biscayne Bay. Along the inky horizon, the clouds touch the ocean, the city's skyline a milky blur. Izzy says nothing about the spectacular view because he's learning he's not supposed to sound impressed, that the long whistle he holds back would give something away about his own life, and he's with Danny now, Danny who apparently sees this kind of view all the time because he doesn't stop for even one second to take it in, seems almost angry at the beauty of it. A woman's laugh floats up toward them, backed by the sudden *boom* of a just-dropped bass.

—Down there, Danny says. That's my cousin's boat. Different cousin.

—You got a lot of fucking cousins, Izzy says.

A metal platform runs over the first few feet of the bay, spanning almost the entire length of the backyard. The lights along it are off, but docked next to it is a black cigarette speedboat with too many outboard engines (there are five) attached to what Izzy thinks of as the butt of the boat. The lights lining the seating of the front hull are enough to illuminate the scene: three guys and four women, the latter all wearing intricately woven straps meant to serve as either bathing suits or sexy tops. The men are shirtless and wearing loose trunks tied at their waists, except for one of them, who wears an unzipped wetsuit he's pulled half off, freeing his arms and chest. They are close enough now that Izzy can see they are all wearing sunglasses, all of them aviators like his own, like Pitbull's—the ones on loan from Danny. Izzy lifts a hand in greeting as he reaches the dock, sidestepping some very strange art that doubles as outdoor furniture and raising his glasses to his head so everyone on the boat can see his eyes. No one returns the gesture, not even Danny. Izzy lowers his frames back to his nose in case the light from the skyline proves painful. Also, it seems expected of him somehow. It's just past midnight.

On the platform, the sea breeze feels good on his head, helping a little with the pain. The salt in the air also feels good as it goes in and out of his nose, heavy and hot thanks to the humidity, the smallest trace of rotting fish smell coming only at the end of an inhalation. It feels familiar, easy to breathe. Despite the breeze, the bay water is still and makes no sound beneath or against the boat or the dock, like it's waiting to be disturbed. Izzy wants to ask what these people are doing out there, but he can guess based on the cooler in the boat, the electronic dance music coming up from its cabin speakers: pre-partying. Something he does himself, though usually in his car after finding a spot in a South Beach parking garage, chugging half a can of Sprite and then filling the can with Bacardi Limón, swirling it a little to mix it, then chugging again. Not the most fun activity but it definitely saved him a good amount of money at whatever club whatever girl he'd met online suggested they meet up at; he'd only done this a handful of times before realizing the girl would either never materialize or would show up with three to five friends who all expected him to pay for their drinks. The guy on the boat wearing the half-a-wetsuit opens a bottle of champagne or something champagne-adjacent—lots of foam spills out, the guy holding the bottle over the water to keep the fizz off the boat's deck—and then hands the bottle to one of the women. She proceeds to chug straight from its mouth. Maybe Izzy is witnessing the Key Biscayne version of his pre-partying drinking strategy, subbing bubbles for Bacardi, docked boat for parked car, except: if you can afford a boat and a house on the water, you could probably afford to drink all you want at the club, so why the need to pre-party? Maybe Izzy is witnessing the party itself. He looks down into the boat and feels very tall and also a little dizzy.

—This your friend? one of the guys in shorts says.

Danny laughs and says, Yeah, this is him. See anyone else with me?

One of the women sucks her teeth and lets out a long *Great.*

She puts her giant phone in her tiny jean shorts—the pockets exposed and hanging down out of the shorts like flippers against her thighs—plants a foot on the boat's padded seat, and lifts herself up with just one leg, no hands. Her other leg swings up from the boat's deck and reaches all the way to the dock. She never skips leg day at the gym and wants everyone to know this: again without using her hands to push off of anything, she raises her whole self out of the boat. By her own estimate she has done over like one million squats and she's only twenty-five. Her ass is super tan; her butt-cheeks are so strong she could crush a man's fingers between them; she's wearing a thong under her shorts. Her hair is perfectly straight, dark as the water, and it reaches her waist—she has to swing it behind her with her hands as she turns around to face the boat she's just exited. She bends over and puts out both her arms, signaling to the one white woman in the boat—plain enough in her face and with the kind of short, shorn haircut that betrays her hope that the style would make her look edgy—that it's time to go and that she better keep her sun-glasses on. As one woman hoists the other out—the white one stumbling once back on land and turning away from them, a huge tattoo of what Izzy guesses is a cabbage on the slab of her back—Izzy thinks this white woman can't possibly be friends with these people, must be some kind of journalist or dog-sitter (except there's no dog) or person assigned to take photos of the other woman, who must be a model of some sort. Same goes for the two women still on the boat, who are now also exiting the same way the first woman did: with the same grace and show of strength, one holding the bottle of champagne by its neck as she steps up and out; who are both equally stunning, legs and butt-cheeks equally chiseled. Even the men in the boat are gorgeous, their facial hair precise, their fingernails manicured and cuticle-free, their arms and legs lasered hairless and their skin stretched tight over their muscles in a way that reminds Izzy of dolphins. He suddenly wants to rip at their slick biceps with his teeth: these beautiful people are Miami too, the version of it that gets Miami listed as one of the fittest cities in the U.S. year after year. Fit beyond belief, sculpted and enhanced surgically and/or steroidally and/or by sheer force of will. Physical perfection so ubiquitous in parts of this county that Izzy might not have even registered it if not for the white girl—now wrapping herself in a towel and scurrying after them across the dock—being there for comparison (maybe that's why they keep her around?).

The white girl trails the three beautiful women, who fall in step with each other and link arms, looking nothing alike and yet looking like a set. All three of them remind Izzy of Julisa. All three of them walk up toward the empty house without turning their heads, without so much as a goodbye.

In the boat it's now just the three men. If this is a party, it feels very suddenly over, even with the music still pulsing from the boat's speakers. Izzy wants to say something clever about the girls leaving but he takes too long and the moment passes. He is swaying a little on the balls of his feet.

Danny points to the wet-suited guy and says, That's my cousin Miguelito.

The sunglasses hide the sideways glances the other two men give each other at the mention of a name. The one who's now going by Miguelito reaches a hand up from the boat to the dock, and Izzy squats down to shake it. Miguelito maybe looks a little like Enrique Iglesias but then Izzy remembers this is supposed to be a different cousin altogether. This is the cousin with the boat, the one foretold to Izzy by the guy who sold him the waterproof phone case back when he was still searching for his Manolo—the First Rudy, the loser with the sweaty back trapped inside that mall kiosk. Izzy sees his own face in Miguelito's sunglasses, distorted and bloated, and decides it's not himself being reflected back. It's some asshole who's crashed a party. It's some other sweaty, sad loser. It's Pitbull, probably. He braces himself to get tugged into the boat by this guy, preparing for the macho posturing the moment feels ripe with, but Miguelito shakes his hand without a word, staying silent even after Izzy says, Nice to meet you, bro, call me Izzy. He pops back up from the squat, trying to prove to himself that the vertigo he's feeling isn't real. The two other men sit down on the padded benches where the women have just been sitting, spreading their arms out across the seat backs, waiting for something to begin.

—Miguelito was thinking maybe you'd want to go for a little midnight cruise, Danny says. You know, for your plan, your research. Way more promising than the boat we just came from.

—For real? Izzy says. That sounds like a good time. The girls coming back?

—Hop in, Danny says, a hand on Izzy's shoulder now. I'll run up and see if anyone's interested.

The boat thunks against the dock and glides a little away as Izzy stares down into it, then into the ocean visible between it and the dock. His throat starts to—not hurt, exactly. There's something high and tight—yes, something tightening—at the top of his larynx. Not pain, not an itch either—something in between, almost a clenching, a sudden roughness, a collapsing. Is he going to cry? He can't. He can't: tears won't come out even if he were to let them. The pinky and ring fingers on his left hand feel tingly, then cold, then numb. He clears his throat twice to loosen the sensation and the sound of that gesture makes everyone look at him, which is worse than the throat feeling—which only makes the feeling itself stronger, scarier. He has no memory of this sensation but it's happened before. His body remembers it and so his mouth floods with saliva and he swallows and swallows, a reflex, trying to relax his throat. He rubs at the depression between his collarbones. His body lets out a cough that makes his eyes water, and then it remembers to breathe.

—Nah, bro, we can both go up to the house, Izzy says. Still getting my legs anyways.

—You know what? Danny says. You're right, fuck the girls.

He steps closer to the dock's edge and Izzy does too, because Danny hasn't released his grip on his shoulder.

—They'll be here when you get back, Miguelito says to the boat's helm. The control panel looks like it's floating beneath his fingers. Only five of this particular cigarette speedboat exist in the world at this exact moment, but that's a fact Miguelito wants to hold on to in case Izzy needs some additional convincing. He can't get a solid read on this guy, Danny's latest, but most of the time, facts like this don't even have to be true to work. Let's do this, he says, swiping his fingers across the controls.

Danny jumps down into the bow and says, Izzy, close your mouth, bro. Since when are you a mouth breather?

But Izzy is again not breathing, not really. He isn't sure his breath is making it all the way into his lungs. It's stuck at the base of his tongue, he's sure of it. His feet are moving, walking him closer, and now he's leaning over, his fist pressing against the metal dock, helping his body keep balance—despite his own muscles, he is nowhere near as strong as any of the probably-models—as his right leg and then his left leg step down, the boat's deck swaying up to meet each foot. He is watching his body do these things, watching it stand close to Danny on the deck, but he cannot feel it. He is behind himself, then above himself. He cannot be on this boat. Only his body is doing this, not the him inside, watching from a safer place. Danny's hand clamps onto his shoulder again and Izzy jumps, confused at how Danny's touch has brought him back. He whips his face toward him and feels the ache rise at his temple, awakening.

Miguelito smacks Izzy full force on the back and Izzy folds in half at the impact.

—What, you scared, bro?

—I'm not scared, Izzy says.

He stands up straight, sucks in a real breath best he can, making this proclamation look true to anyone watching (which is still everyone) and maybe even to himself, at least for a few more minutes. Because the fastest way to make any Miami man run head-on into real danger is to accuse him—especially in front of other men—of being afraid. This reaction predates Tony Montana and Pitbull, who are themselves victims of it: Izzy spent his whole adolescence being *Never Scared*; being not sad after an accusation of oncoming tears; being not soft when recognized and ridiculed for showing kindness or weakness of any sort. The thing he's most allowed to be is what he suddenly feels now, the emotion that always rushes in to protect him in these instances: angry.

—Wait 'til we open this shit up, Miguelito says. Hold on or you'll fly the fuck out. This shit's been clocked at ninety miles per hour.

Another fact he likes to use to entice the people Danny and his associates bring his way.

—Fuck you, man, you don't know who you're talking to, Izzy says. This boat ain't shit. Ninety miles an hour ain't shit.

Ninety miles an hour is definitely some shit, but Izzy doesn't know anything about speedboats. Just because he'd once been saved by one doesn't make him an expert, but he's pretending to be one now to calm his nerves. He walks over to the controls and says, How long you had this?

—Not mine, Miguelito says.

—Danny, I thought you said –

—I said a different cousin. I also said stop asking questions, right?

Izzy takes off the sunglasses. They aren't helping with the pain anymore, and he figures they're about to fly off his face anyway.

—Hey, you can see why this is an opportunity, Danny says. Access to a boat like this? To other boats like it? For what we talked about earlier? Miguelito here is happy to fill you in, right, bro?

Miguelito depresses a button, summoning a tremendous rumble

that drowns out anything he might be saying in response to Danny's question. The two shirtless men stand and move toward the dock, messing with ropes at either end. Izzy looks at the five outboards: he doesn't remember the boat he'd come on having those.

That boat—the memory of it surfacing now that his body is back in a similar place—had a little roof on it, a little perch with room for one or two people—a place to stand with your fishing poles, a girl's voice had told him when he asked what it was he'd seen. That question: the first words out of Izzy's mouth in hours, and the last ones for days; Odlanier had smacked the girl, then Izzy, had told them both it was just a dream, to not speak of it, and no other adult—not even the girl's parents—had stepped in to defend their innocent talking. They were on the raft again, had never left the raft, and that was the only truth from then on, and they'd make it to shore very soon. But Izzy feels it now, on a boat again waiting in water: how he and the others were fished out of the ocean and pulled up by someone standing at the stern. He'd climbed up into the boat before they'd lashed the raft to it, slipped a little, a new voice yelling for him to wait but he was scrambling instead, and then a grown man's callused hands on his forearms, yanking him aboard. How each of the man's hands left a white hyper-color imprint on him, something he could see in the moonlight.

He touches his arm now as a reaction to this sudden memory. It was the moon, not a spotlight. The boat that had helped them had found their raft at night.

He is trying not to panic, not to cry, and he is grateful that the speedboat's noise covers the crack he hears in his own voice as he yells Danny's name. The thundering outboards make his temples pound. He's still grasping his own forearm, now holding it against his chest, the sunglasses clasped in his fingers. Danny plucks them from his hand and yells, Thanks, bro, you're welcome.

One of the shirtless guys throws his rope up onto the dock and steps over to Danny, makes a show of gesturing toward the house, both men making sure Izzy catches enough of the conversation to understand that, yes, Danny is getting out of the speedboat, *needs* to get out of the speedboat for some reason, nothing that should alarm

Izzy at all of course. He's just running up real quick to check some-thing, the shirtless man explains while he blocks Izzy from getting closer to the dock, the other shirtless man coming up behind Izzy and obstructing an unlikely dive, the space between the boat and the dock widening as Miguelito gets them underway—or is it just Izzy's vision that's tunneling now that he feels the fullness of the water under him, the slight rocking in the wake their boarding and Danny's disembark-ing created?

He is on a boat for the second time today but this is the first time since his crossing when he was seven that he's stood on the sea in a vessel this size. Maybe this is just one of Danny's schemes. Maybe Rudy put him up to this, the two of them collaborating to keep him away from Julisa. Thoughts—or are they hopes?—that Izzy can barely register now. Maybe he should call somebody. Who would he even call—what would he even say? He feels his phone through his front pocket, the waterproof case that once felt like a kind of promise now seeming like a real bad omen. Did the First Rudy sense Izzy's judg-ment about his back sweat and thus put a curse on him through the phone case? Do curses work that way? Maybe his Tía Tere would know the answer to that—could he call her now and ask her without seem-ing like a giant baby for stopping to do what would look to these guys like him calling for his mami?

The boat is maybe thirty feet from the dock when Izzy starts to truly feel afraid—not because he's on a boat with three strangers, watching Danny and his still-hidden eyes get smaller and smaller, but because Izzy's body is back in a space it still fears, remembering more than he wants to let it, the layers and years of his *Never Scared* mantra evaporating off of him, and he's powerless to stop it.

And so no, Danny is not a stand-in for Sosa, not in this version of Izzy's plan. Izzy sees it clearly and finally, his last coherent thought before his memories override his present: Danny has delivered him to these men, these strangers who, still in their shades, now look every bit as menacing as those cast to play the International Bad Guys sit-ting around in Sosa's mansion, each patiently waiting for Tony Mon-tana to agree to do their dirty work. Yes, Danny is their Tony, and more than that, he hasn't fucked up the job by sparing anyone's life.

Their Tony has done exactly what he was asked to do, and if Izzy's no longer the Tony in this story, then he has only the vaguest idea about which role he's actually playing and how this part might end.

Danny waves goodbye from the dock, his other hand on his hip, apparently dropping the guise of having to run up to the house for something. His part is over. He's done a good job. He can (but won't) guess at what they've got planned for Izzy, but as is always the case when he works with these guys, sweethearts all of them, he can honestly say he has no idea—good or bad—what Izzy's got coming to him.

POINT OF VIEW

The infection present for years now in Lolita's eyes—the one that makes her feel like she constantly has something scratching her eyeball, something she can't blink away—has become so severe that she sometimes performs entire shows with her right eye shut. It helps the performance go by quickly. Sometimes she shuts both eyes. Vision isn't crucial for her in the way it is for Izzy, though the pain is a constant and triggering distraction. Like Izzy with the migraines, she has learned to surrender to it. But unlike Izzy, she has no reason to fear what might find her when she lets the pain rise.

The muscles surrounding an orca's eye allow them to see in all directions, even behind them as they swim forward. That circle of muscle contracts as a precursor to aggression, meaning their eyes literally bulge out when angry or upset. But this is the point to remember: they can look wherever they want, no matter where they are headed. They can move forward while looking backward. They can turn their gaze anywhere, even toward whatever they've left in their wake.

This boat out there, bringing him back again. Returning him to her.

MIDNIGHT, ALOFT

Sunlight

They aren't going very fast at all when Izzy leans over the starboard side of the speedboat to vomit. He's not seasick. It's the migraine, which—thanks to the speedboat's outboard engines and the wedding alcohol and the tranquilizer wearing off and his being closer to Lolita than he's been in weeks—has reached a new and brutal intensity out there on Biscayne Bay. His cheekbones and jaw buzz just as Lolita's would with the boat's noise, his eyes vibrate with a searing he's never before experienced, his body unable to perform any additional functions other than surviving the anguish in the hopes it will somehow pass. It takes every ounce of bodily energy, nothing left over for the chore of digestion, and so now every drink and all the prime rib and salmon from the first boat go overboard on this one.

Facing down into the water over the speedboat's edge, the food a trail floating away and away, Izzy watches the ocean and its depths for something he recognizes.

Twilight

One of the two guys in swim trunks grabs Izzy by the back of his shirt—did he think Izzy was trying to jump?—and yells, No no no! The opposite of pushing him over, which: that's what he's been worrying these guys have planned for him. So they *don't* want him dead? Pulling him back from possibly going overboard is a good sign, unless Izzy is already dying and that's what this pain is trying to tell him.

His eyes are closed, the input from his burning vision too much to bear. The pain is mostly on the right side of his head, behind his right eye, so he squeezes that one shut while peeking through the left one, so he can see which of the two guys he needs to thank for not shoving him into the ocean, the thought of his imminent death being at the front of his throbbing mind since watching and now remembering that hand as beckoning him while waving goodbye.

Midnight

Except he doesn't recognize the face of the man who's pulled him back from the boat's edge. Not even as Miguelito or one of the two shirtless men near him just moments ago. This man is older and is yelling down at him—No no no!—and is so much taller than Izzy, who is a boy again. The man is backlit by the spotlight of the moon. Thick dark hair cut close to his head and brushed back from his forehead, the black smear of a mustache. White shirt unbuttoned almost to the navel, wind ballooning it open.

Izzy can't make out what the man is saying now, if he's yelling at Izzy or at someone else. Izzy tries to say something but no sound comes out, not even any air. This man still has Izzy by the forearm, whipping it left and right as he speaks to someone close behind Izzy, pressing up behind him. And then a younger version of Odlanier appears, circling around him and now standing next to this man, nodding.

Odlanier's hand reaching down and clamping onto Izzy's shoulder. The broad fingernails with dirt lining them underneath, the skin of his hands spotted like an overripe mango.

The numbers don't match, this man says.

Odlanier says he understands. He tells this man that there's an aunt in Miami. That this aunt must know people, Odlanier has no idea, maybe she's who sent for him, who knows.

That the mother drowned hours earlier. That yes, he thinks she was telling the truth about the aunt.

That the decision whether or not to let the boy stay rests with him—with this man—and isn't Odlanier's to make even if he'd thought so at first.

That to leave him behind might evoke Yemayá's wrath and they still had miles to float on the other side once they relaunched.

But also that perhaps the boy's mother wasn't enough of an offering, given what Odlanier knew of her soul. He tells the man about her threats, her promise to turn them in. Maybe the fates wanted the boy too. His mother's actions seemed to suggest as much.

Odlanier tells this man: She called him to her but he didn't go. She wanted him to drown with her.

None of the others look at Izzy except for the girl, who thinks Izzy looks so tiny, like a doll she'd like to play with once they are in Miami. Except she's too big to play with dolls now, that time is over. Girls who still played with dolls couldn't be on the raft. Her parents had trained her to know that well before leaving. She looks away like the other grown-ups.

The boy will not talk: Odlanier is assuring the man that Izzy will not talk. He is swearing on his own life that the boy won't talk and the man laughs weary and says he's heard enough.

Fate took that woman away to protect him, this man says.

He moves his grip from Izzy's forearm to the back of Izzy's neck and squeezes, not thinking of his sunburned skin.

Izzy looks down, hiding from the man the shame of his face, his tears.

Abyss

Hours earlier, and the tops of Izzy's feet are burnt and blistered, the sun over them unrelenting. They are waiting for night, for the dark to bring the boat that will take them closer to shore: everyone but Izzy knows this.

The raft below them is rope and inner tube and corrugated metal. Surrounding all this are parts of what was once a boat, its bottom expanded to create a wider vessel. Izzy is standing at the edge, the lip of their raft digging into his knees, looking out at his mother.

She is calling to him from the ocean, choking on seawater, trying to swim with one arm raised out of the water as she waves him to her, saying she'll catch him.

She has jumped off, they have pushed her off—no, he saw her a moment before: she thought he was sleeping but he wasn't, they all thought he was sleeping through the hottest part of the day, but his eyes were little slits against the sunlight, he was only pretending. And so he saw her: her feet leaping off, launching herself into the ocean.

Then he closed his eyes for real and imagined her turning back to face them, treading water, claiming her son from them—these people he heard calling her loca and selfish and monster, telling her to stop.

Ismael, despiértate, she said. And he stood up, because he was already despierto. He rubbed the pretend-sleep from his eyes to keep up the lie that he didn't see her jump. Already he is lying to himself, rewriting the memory.

Brinca, she orders from the water. Ismael, brinca, ven, no tengas miedo. But he is afraid, so afraid of what she's done, what she's asking. She is insisting he come with her. That he drown with her, that they die Cuban together. He doesn't move. They are just going to throw you overboard, she spits. Like they did to me.

Except that's not what he saw moments ago, is he wrong? The memory of this threat from his mother's mouth coming in English, which she didn't speak: can he trust this?

The others on the raft silent behind him, him having to decide by himself which gamble to take, because either way to them, he is a risk. They don't know that he was pretending to sleep. They worry he believes his mother's lie, that if he stays—if they let him stay—he will be a problem once they reach land. But he doesn't understand that a boat is coming to help. To him the boat will be a miracle.

He's so thirsty, his tongue searches his gums for anything wet.

Trenches

With every struggling breath, his mother calls them traitors.

He is frozen on the raft for eternity and so she calls *him* a traitor.

Then she changes her mind, tries to swim back to the raft. They've continued to float away and away. Time slows and it takes another eternity for her hand to reach up, for her fingers to curl around the torn metal railing that constitutes the raft's starboard side.

He raises his blistered foot and screams *No.*

He stomps her fingers hard enough that she cuts them on the raft's edge, slicing them open, and the adults grab him and lift him away because the raft can't be subjected to any impact that they can otherwise avoid. A girl's voice muffled by someone's body, yelling, What's he doing? What did he do?

But it was him. He'd been the one to do it, to keep her from coming back. And it was this act that had made the others trust him not to talk about the coming boat, about any of it. Because to tell the story would mean to speak of his choice, of his loyalties, of her blood in the water.

Midnight

Hours passing. His own silence as Odlanier and the others whisper their options.

The sun setting fast, the first time he remembers feeling—really understanding this—that it's not the sun that sets, it's the earth that spins.

Twilight

The speedboat's engines roaring, rushing over Biscayne Bay.

From outside, laughing.

A voice from above: The fuck is wrong with him? Another voice: This fucker is freaking the fuck out.

—Don't touch him yet, says a third voice—Miguelito's. He's making it easy for us.

The speedboat slows.

A sign now as they approach an otherwise abandoned concrete-lined pull-in just deep enough for speedboats like this one, tucked amidst the water-processing bowels of the Seaquarium. It reads: MAKE No WAKE.

From where he's balled up on the speedboat's deck, hugging his knees to his chest, Izzy lifts his head and sees through his open left eye the blur of this sign pass. He looks as tormented as Tony Montana at his desk near the film's end, head bowing to a mountain of cocaine, except Izzy's lowering his head instead to the cradle of his arms.

Midnight

Izzy settles back down into the darkness made by the walls of his chest and thighs, looking again for his mother. Instead he finds his Tía Tere there with him. They are in a car, and she is driving them through a flood, the kind that comes almost weekly, but this flood is his first here, the water after a rain rising to her bumper, nowhere else to go. Slowing down, slower, to keep the water from rippling any higher. We'd be better off in a boat, she says in English, knowing he won't really understand although they've been practicing. She's driving him to his new school for the first time. He puts his hand flat against the window. She asks him what he's thinking about, and he asks if there are sharks in the water, and she says no and asks him nothing else. She wants him to forget whatever he needs to forget. He hears himself ask why they are going so slow and if he will be late for school, and she says, I hope not, and then, Because we don't want to make a wake for the other cars, and he asks, What is a wake, and she answers: It's like a trail through the water, made by some disturbance.

They keep driving, so slow Izzy thinks maybe they've stopped.

She keeps trying.

A wake can also mean the aftermath of something.

A wake is also what americanos call a funeral.

He lets these other definitions wash over him, then pushes them away. He is happy because she let him ride in the front seat. His breath fogs up the spot on the window in front of his mouth, and he presses his lips to it, pulls back to see the imprint of them in the condensation. He kisses the waves outside the window goodbye. The water is lapping at the car door, the water coming for him again. He erases the kiss with his fist and forever turns away from the close-by ocean, away from all it remembers, reaching with his other hand for his Tía Tere, her own hands steady on the wheel.

Twilight

The speedboat's engines are silent. The deck sways only up and down now, no wind. Miguelito's voice is there, and then the hands of the other two men wrestling Izzy's legs out from under him, tying them together. He knows now he should fight, use his arms as something other than a shield for his face, but he can't. He feels the memory of his mother's knuckles under his heel.

The men grab him from behind, make him stand, put something over his head. Darkness and his own breath close in on his face.

They lift him high and away. He hopes they are taking him somewhere safe. He hopes his mother will be there somehow to answer his questions, even though he's afraid of what she'll say. He hopes they don't drop him into the water. He knows well what sharks can do.

Solid ground under his feet now. He is so grateful he is off that boat, safe.

To the back of his head, a blast of pain: a sudden, almost welcome relief.

Sunlight

Why couldn't I jump in the water after her? Why didn't I go when she called for me?

Because you already knew how to save yourself.

But she was my mother. What if this time I make a different choice?

A DIFFERENT CHOICE

Whether an oversight or by design, there is no one at the Seaquarium at night solely dedicated to watching Lolita. Soon after the park closes, metal security doors roll down over each entrance to her stadium—the same doors that close off access to the stadium between shows; the guy known tonight as Miguelito has once again obtained a copy of the keys—and are dead-bolted shut, and that's it. Not just nights: they seal her in and abandon her regularly, any time there's the threat of a hurricane, for instance. No plan to feed her or regulate the water temperature, no plan for the guaranteed flooding or potential electrocution via a downed powerline. People learn about this on the news during the onslaught of pre-storm coverage that accompanies every hurricane watch and warning. People are reminded that her tank is only as deep as she is long. People get angry, promise themselves that after the storm they will call someone, they will write something, they will Do Their Part to change this situation. They'll give money to the rehoming project, what the news is calling Lolita's Retirement Plan. But then the storm hits and there's so much other devastation to deal with, or the storm doesn't hit and you have to deal with these fucking shutters—maybe just suck it up and install those high-impact windows already. And now you're online looking at the price of those fucking windows and thinking, Shit, for that you'll just buy a new house. Or wait to cash in the insurance when the next storm wipes the house off the planet. Because this is Miami and so another storm is always on the way. And this is Miami: iguanas coming up drain pipes and alligators in an Escalade and a captive orca capable of infiltrating a young man's mind with memories and the promise of more and more—and now you don't believe this incredible city could've brought Izzy here, to her tank, when it has already bombarded you with all its glorious power—power it's been flexing all along? Do you even read, bro?

This time, Izzy has jumped in the water, or they have thrown him in, or he has fallen in: all Lolita knows is he's finally come back to her, and all he knows for certain is the feeling of relief as he regains awareness—his migraine immediately lifting in the freezing, sudden water all around him.

He can taste it, salt water, but too cold and too bright as the darkness slips from his face, tugged away, so gently and without snagging a single hair, from the top of his head.

They are so close now.

THE SYMPHONY

Lolita has found the slack in the black fabric hood covering his head and lovingly pulls him free. She knows to swallow it before he can fully open his eyes. She feels him savor the migraine's release, the sensation radiating between them, coming from the center of his brow.

Izzy opens his eyes.

She turns her head to see him and as always there is flailing, fear, the turn to leave the tank. The reluctance to understand that hiding his thoughts is hopeless. His thoughts are almost irrelevant. She is listening to his body and hears where it's just returned from, memories she's felt flow in and around her before, cries she feels and knows. She puts herself between him and the tank wall. He rises for a breath and comes back under to her.

Can you tell me?

What happened to her.

Do you know?

What you did or didn't do. Of course I know.

But you won't tell me.

It requires too much of you.

What do you need?

Ismael, you already know.

He flails again, splashing water in high arcs as he tries to swim around her. She allows it. Allows him to get all the way to the edge. He turns to lift himself out of the tank, his arms reaching up, fingers curling over the thick glass, and she grabs on to his foot, gently gently, teaching him, no blood, not a scrape, pulling him back in.

I only – I want to know the truth.

You will.

I'm scared. Why this way? Why isn't the water enough?

That is a good question.

Am I supposed to free you now? How?

She closes her eyes. She will not come from beneath him like she does with the ducklings, whose mother brings them herself. Instead, she opens her mouth. The teeth inside in varying states of decay. Pain radiating from so many of them now, these decades in this tank, the scraping, the gnashing, everything tasting like paint and concrete. She lets him take in the damage. How much more profound a presence will he have on this earth as a memory, reunited with all he's sought to know, at peace on a molecular level—a solace she longs for herself. A freedom. What she has longed to offer him.

You wanted to make a different choice.

Now you can try.

He swims closer. She opens her jaw wider.

He rises up, takes a breath, then dives down, in.

His hands graze the roof of her mouth, then her tongue. He rubs it with both hands, slides his palms and wrists along and under it, almost hugging it. This is how she knows there is trust, how she's trained him and others before him to show it. She knows from the touch all his sadness, all he's lost and forgotten, the ultimate nothingness of him and of herself against the vastness of the realms holding them here. Only she can know this, and only she can give it over to him now. She hears his heart rate slowing.

What you're looking for is here. You will find it.

He reaches deeper and fingers the rotting holes in her back teeth, the ones drilled and flushed and medicated into a numbness that for the night has already worn off, like his own.

The pain in these teeth made sharper as she bites him in half and swallows. *You will find it*: her lie, a mercy—in his mother's voice—the last thing he feels.

She bites again and swallows again. Only Teresa missing him, she knows—a pain she releases by absorbing it: what does that pain even add to all that she already holds, all she already knows? Not even another drop. Like everything else, she bears it, and then it thins, dissolves, all but disappears. She bites and swallows.

She circles her tank.

She circles her tank.

She surfaces for her next breath and in the mist of that exhalation, there is no new knowledge. Because above and before all else, there was nothing for Izzy to absorb except this: he was born already knowing that his mother was never a mother to him.

The mist settles and she circles her tank. She was born a predator. Another relation under the waves. An emissary from the realm of the dead. She is millions of years of evolution coming to an end right here, in this too-warm, too-small existence.

The world is yours.

Isn't that the promise? Isn't that how it ends?

She circles her tank.

ARS POETICA

Ismael: I obtained your name and address weeks ago but have only now found the time while on tour to sit and write to you. Forgive the intrusion, but I've been thinking that perhaps your desire to imitate me stems from some larger, more powerful desire to be an artist, specifically an artist from Miami, someone who may claim this city as fiercely and loudly as I have. If that's the case (and forgive this indulgence if it's not, though I sense I'm correct in my assumption), I'd like to offer you some hard-earned consejos from this side of things. Poor compensation maybe, compared to what you might've made with your budding Pitbull impersonating business, but life is long and so: maybe not.

Perhaps I should've opened with this sentiment: I apologize for taking as long as I have to write you. When my legal team first notified me months ago about the need for a cease and desist—news that came to me in a torrent of other information I get via a weekly call with my various attorneys and representatives—I barely registered it. It was presented to me as something already handled, something routine. They were sure you would comply, had dismissed your efforts as juvenile, calling you "some little scrub" or a "jit" or some such slang for someone not to be taken seriously, epithets slapped on me and my work when I was coming up in the rap game. And only later, as I was trying to fall asleep that evening on a flight from Oregon to Arkansas for a concert with Blake Shelton sponsored by Walmart (forgive me, Miami), did I realize how little difference there was between me and someone like you. I took offense at them characterizing you as someone unimaginative and lacking creativity—Lord knows the same has been said about me (though with reason, given the bulk of my oeuvre). What if that lack of imagination and creativity was itself the point? What if that's what you were trying to show me: how easy it is to do what I do. You were

281

holding up a mirror to me and asking me, "Do you like what you see? Are you proud of this?"

I normally sleep well on flights (granted, having your own plane basically guarantees that), but that night I couldn't. I wanted to meet you and not turn it into a social media stunt or a publicity event. I wanted to take you out for that proverbial cafecito that our city has cheapened into its own trademark and ask you questions I needed to ask myself: who were you when you started this journey? What did you love about this city that made you want to make art about it, and when did you start thinking that claiming to represent it—that calling yourself "Mr. 305," the audacity of that—was in fact a wise idea? Does the music I've made even count as art? Is that a question I can answer? I know my music embodies something of Miami's crassness (see: "Culo"), its vibrant, even flagrant sexuality. My career wouldn't have—couldn't have—taken off if there wasn't something accurate at the core of every track. That might be the best verdict I can bestow on my work, in my most generous moments.

British novelist John Fowels once referred to Miami as "the unwiped anus" of the United States, saying, "All that is worst in the country pours through it and stands to be seen." I remember a time, very early in my music career, when I wondered if that cruel (and certainly racist) characterization was something to fight or to exploit. Obviously from my body of work you can tell what angle I chose, having deemed that approach far more profitable. But every day I wake up knowing I've helped to perpetuate a damaging version of our hometown (I'm assuming you were "born and raised in the county of Dade" as well, given your age, but perhaps I'm incorrect?), one that degrades it, one that asserts rather than contradicts Fowels's pronouncement that our city and the people in it are a proverbial shit stain.

Perhaps it was a mistake to identify myself and my music so closely with a place. You can see that worry as the impetus for me to transition from Mr. 305 to Mr. Worldwide (the slant rhyme was lost on most fans, but it's there and that's what matters). But was that shift successful? The 2012 Facebook campaign where I promised to give a concert anywhere in the world based on people's votes sent me to a Walmart in Kodiak, Alaska (population 6,100). Perhaps that's my answer. (In truth that event was wonderful; I had time enough to meet with Alutiiq elders and watched them perform a graceful and moving welcome dance seeped in history and tradition; it made me long for some semblance of connection to the Taino people my ancestors undoubtedly helped murder; I was also given the key to the city of Kodiak and gifted a bottle of excellent bear repellent.) I've gotten to see so much of the world because of my music, and yet the more I saw, the more I realized that despite its catchiness, despite the wildly successful branding that calling myself Mr. 305 created for me and my team, it is at its core a falsity. No one person can "be" a place, for one thing. And for another: what of Miss or Mx 305? How has my branding excluded other genders from their sense of belonging to the look and sound of Miami?

There is no Mr. 305; we are all Mr. 305; etc., etc.

As you may have guessed, the model for my success—up to a point—is arguably the original Mr. 305: Al Pacino as Tony Montana in *Scarface.* Swap the drugs for the music, and you'll understand what I mean. I can't stress enough the film's importance for so many musical artists, especially in the rap and hip-hop genres (though I'd argue even someone as purposefully bland as Taylor Swift has some Tony Montana in her; inside every artist you'll find some level of megalomania). As an homage to the film, I once cast Steven Bauer, the Cuban American actor who played Manolo in the film, as a Tony Montana–esque figure in one of my music videos (though sadly, we had to cut all his lines from the final version due to some complicated copyright issues). Snoop Dogg supposedly watched *Scarface* once a month for the majority of his career, though I'm guessing he's fallen off on his viewings since his *Family Feud* appearance or since co-hosting that cooking show with Martha Stewart, but maybe not: we are each still hustling in our own ways, some of us in ways that acknowledge how we've aged, changed, grown. (Though certainly not all of us: I can't say that's the case for Chris Brown, for example, an artist with whom I continue to collaborate despite his well-documented abuse of the women he purports to love. I've repeatedly stated that I've never put my hands on a woman in anger, and that this is why I keep working with him—in the hopes that my influence will rub off on him. That, and of course it's extremely profitable for us both, which is admittedly shameful, yes, but is that my fault? As I say in interviews when asked about this, "My daughter taught me that inside the word *impossible* is *possible*, inside the word *don't* is *do*, and inside *won't* is *won*." Other dichos I've come to rely on to deflect questions about my various moral and/or artistic choices: "You gotta live your life, you can't let life live you." And: "We all need haters in our life [*sic*], it means we're doing something right." And: "New York is the Big Apple, Miami is the Pineapple." And my personal favorite, if only because it comes closest to my truest self: "My kids can't eat awards.")

Did you know the word "fuck" is said in *Scarface* 207 times? It was the first film in history to use that particular expletive over two hundred times. What a record to hold. I read somewhere that blink-182 picked that number because that's the number of fucks they counted when they watched. Perhaps they all went to the bathroom at the same time? What other explanation is there for missing over twenty fucks? Granted, that level of inattentiveness is reflected in their music as well, though we both know that from a critical standpoint, I'm no one to talk.

Dare I expand on the wisdom already contained in the cinematic masterpiece that is *Scarface*? The answer is obviously yes, especially as it pertains to someone theoretically looking to succeed in the music industry. I really have found the overreliance on inane and borderline-nonsensical sayings as interview responses extremely helpful. My reasoning for adopting this was simple enough: since my lyrics already traffic heavily in repetition and cliché, why not be on-brand in everything I say outside of the music, keep it easy for people? Unsurprisingly, no one has ever pressed me with a follow-up question after hearing me say that Miami is the Pineapple. In fact, they often purse their lips and nod, as if what I've just said makes any kind of sense.

To that end, I can also recommend coming up with a narrative around your life that can't be penetrated and that is mostly completely unverifiable. Case in point: my own story of my parents meeting (stripper mother, drug-dealer father, etc., etc.), how she'd reversed her tubal ligation so that I could be conceived after my father pointed to a star in the sky and proclaimed, "That will be our son." Is this story true? Who can say? I've told and retold it so many times that it's true now, and who's really going to try to dig up a medical record that I could always argue just never survived, as it was in the era before everything went digital? But I always lead with the fact that my mother came from Cuba on the Pedro Pan flights as what we're now calling an unaccompanied minor, because that *is* true, *that* is verifiable, and that ingratiates me to an audience in a way that sells. People always forget the first rule given in *Scarface*: Never underestimate the other guy's greed.

Ultimately, *Scarface* is more cautionary tale than inspiration, isn't it? People forget also that the 1983 film is itself a remake of a 1932 film of the same name, and *that* film is an adaptation of a 1929 novel, also titled *Scarface*—a book that bears little resemblance to any iteration of the finished film. I read somewhere that the screenwriter (or one of them, as several people were cycled on and off the project while it was in development) saw his iteration of the script as his farewell to cocaine, and yet it glorified coke beyond belief. Is that how we say goodbye to something? To pursue it until its ridiculous, improbable end? Am I saying goodbye to Miami every time I appear on the remix of someone else's track yelling the same nonsense I've been yelling for years? Like my own success, the end of *Scarface* similarly abandons all realism; it propels itself into something more like an opera. Perhaps that's the future of my career, the next role to add to the long list—rapper, motivational speaker, entrepreneur, brand ambassador, charter school founder— of things I already call myself: librettist. Maybe an opera under a pen name that would somehow awaken our fellow Miami residents to the climate catastrophe already well underway. Something that speaks to our city's passions without degrading her in the process. Art that would require me to care for her so much more than I care about myself, and so it will likely never happen.

Do you read poetry? Here's another consejo for you: you should. We all should. The world would be a better place if more people did so. There's a poem that appeared a couple years ago in *Poetry* magazine (sadly I've let my subscription lapse—too much travel) by a writer named Patrick Rosal that begins with these words:

> One way to erase an island is to invent
> a second island absolved of all the sounds
> the first one ever made.

The speaker of Rosal's poem isn't talking about Cuba or Miami (the poet himself is the son of Filipino immigrants, so we do share a colonizer), but the lines struck me as an apt description of my work. My work thus far is beyond absolution. I have repeatedly erased the first island by obliterating it through perversion, replacing it with "a second island"—not that of Miami, but that of my own self— Mr. 305. A kind of success, yes, but it's come at the cost of having never created anything that will truly outlive me, and in the face of all the flooding coming with our impending climate catastrophe, that's even come to mean my own children.

The guilt of all this has of late made me understand that I must capitalize on my outward complacency and use it to undermine my own success: I have to invest in Miami, this second island that is in truth my first—I was born in Miami and not Cuba, after all— for however long this city is above water and inhabitable, in a way that creates the kind of citizens who would recognize my music as the pandering nonsense it so often is (one lively exception to my ear being "Rain Over Me" off my album *Global Warming*, a song which, I'd argue, in its evoking of the coming Latinx majority in the United States and its subliminal screed against ageism ["Forty is the new thirty / Baby you a rock star / Dale veterana, que tú sabe' "] threads the needle between [supposed] high and low culture quite spectacularly, in large part due to the appearance of Marc Anthony on the track. I'm assuming of course that you know his work. His marital history and substance abuse issues notwithstanding, he's a joy and such a pleasure to collaborate with. I'd do it again in a heartbeat if only he'd return my calls).

The more I write here, the clearer to me it becomes that sending you this missive, along with the implied risk that you'd release it to the media, would be the quickest way to undermine my empire, assuming anyone would believe you. Would they? Like sea level rise, it's likely already too late: my music has created and shaped a generation of people who don't even recognize the fact that art creates and shapes (and yes, eventually reflects) a culture. It doesn't matter if I confess all this, if I send you this note or not, because people will still listen to the songs I've produced for close to two decades now, and they'll still sing along with the raunchiness, chanting "culo" just as that arrogant novelist claimed they would. My songs will still, with every listen, make them think of home.

I want to believe I've made my peace with the immense failure that my kind of success rests upon.

I say all this to you knowing you are still young and, Lord willing, you have a lot of life left ahead of you to figure out who it is you really want to be, what you want your one precious life, as they say, to amount to. So I'll end by urging you now to not be like me or like Tony Montana. Don't even be the self you see so obviously coming for you in this sinking city, the self my music has helped to shape. I'm urging you to make a different choice even as I have no idea what choices you might right now be facing. What I do know is this: Miami may have made you, and you can love her. You can't help that. But you must keep some real part of yourself separate and safe from her if you hope to turn her into art, which now I suppose is just another way of saying if you hope to outlast her. Whatever you do, don't let her define you. Don't let her consume you.

ABOUT THE TYPE

This book was set in ITC New Baskerville, which was designed by John Quaranda as a late twentieth-century interpretation of John Baskerville's work. Baskerville was known as a writing master and printer in Birmingham, England, and especially popular for the masterpiece folio Bible he produced for Cambridge University.

ABOUT THE AUTHOR

Jennine Capó Crucet is the author of four books, including the novel *Make Your Home Among Strangers*, which won the International Latino Book Award and was named a *New York Times* Editors' Choice book, and the multiple award-winning story collection *How to Leave Hialeah*. Her essay collection, *My Time Among the Whites: Notes from an Unfinished Education*, based on her columns in the *New York Times*, was longlisted for the PEN Open Book Award. A PEN/O. Henry Prize winner, her writing has appeared on *PBS NewsHour*, NPR, and in *The Atlantic*, among other publications. Born and raised in Miami to Cuban parents, she now lives in North Carolina with her family.

www.JCapoCrucet.com